I SN'T THERE ANYWHERE YOU REALLY FIT IN THE WORLD? Are you missing out on the Real? Come to Avalon University. Learning and free-spiritedness romp hand-in-hand here, and the magical delight of education as its own reward is so spell-binding that no one gives a zot about what they're going to be when they graduate.

Of course, Avalon is changing – all the universities are. The Sixties profs who pioneered this educational Camelot are retired now. They're hanging out at the Mall, teaching in their Convocation robes, cap-in-hand, for handouts for their Dental Plan. The Chairman of the Board can't get rid of them. Neither can his new Dean who's been brought in to downsize the university and make it compatible with cyberspace. The corporate jaws are closing – as they are everywhere, but nothing can bring this oral village into line. Ebullient personality, high-spirited intrigue, delirious behaviour, transgressive sexuality, and talk and laughter. It's all still going on here at Avalon.

SEAN KANE

Virtual Freedom

MCARTHUR & COMPANY
Toronto

This edition published in Canada in 2001 by
MCARTHUR & COMPANY
322 King Street West, Suite 402
Toronto, ON M5V 1J2

National Library of Canada Cataloguing in Publication Data

    Kane, Sean
        Virtual freedom

    ISBN 1-55278-242-5

    1. Title

    PS8571.A433V57 2001   C813'.54   C2001-901506-2
    PR9199.3.K35V57 2001

Design and composition by Kelly Liberty at Clóscríobh
Cover design by Mad Dog Design Connection, Inc.
Printed in Canada by Transcontinental Printing, Inc.

Originally published in 1998 by Ordinary Press

The publisher would like to acknowledge the financial support of the Government of Canada through the Book Publishing Industry Development Program
(BPIDP) and the Canada Council for our publishing activities. The publisher further wishes to acknowledge the financial support of the Ontario Arts Council
for our publishing program.

10 9 8 7 6 5 4 3 2 1

This book
is dedicated to
Thomas H. B. Symons
Founding President
Trent University

Part One

SEPTEMBER

I

Do you know Avalon University? I don't suppose you do. Not many people have heard of it. Nothing notable comes out of the place – no ground-breaking research, no great works of authorship, no inventions that have changed the way we live. Nothing, really, comes out of Avalon except its graduates, and rather than rising to the tops of corporations they are scattered to the four winds, so I am not surprised you don't know of the university. In fact, it would just be another of those forgotten liberal arts colleges in the hinterland, were it not for Hugh Sinclair D'Arnay. Owner of Andromeda Networks, he controls the magazine that ranks the nation's best universities. I refer to the *Choosing Your College* special issue that hits the stores in November. There, in the pages of that magazine, Avalon emerges from obscurity once a year to be ranked among the nation's best universities in the small liberal arts category. Avalon shows well because of its reputation for personal teaching. Sound personal teaching – that's what Avalon does best. It is practically a way of life there.

Of course, there are particular reasons why Avalon ranks high in its class, but we will not go into them here. Those reasons are illustrated for magazine readers by graphs and numerical samples that every high-school graduate with a training in Advanced Statistics immediately understands. The categories of excellence have to do with such things as the number of bound volumes in the library and the percentage of staff with a PH.D. These factors may be of little interest to the average magazine reader, but they matter greatly to the high-school graduates who pore over their copies of the special issue, wondering which universities to apply to in the fall. Such factors draw students to our nation's centers of learning. Especially the number of bound volumes in the library. You do not know what this means to an undergraduate until you hear her boast to a former schoolmate at March Break: "Av has five hundred and fifty-eight thousand bound volumes in its library – it says so in the magazine!"

That is how important Hugh D'Arnay's magazine is to the nation's young.

The fact that D'Arnay is Chairman of the Board of Governors at Avalon is of no consequence. It is of no consequence at all. Indeed, if you were to put that fact to him, catching him, say, for a half an hour at the airport while he is getting into his private jet, or talking with him at length at a government reception in Shanghai, he would tell you that he is chairman of many other concerns as well. There are so many of them, he says, that only a moron or a leftist would think that he could possibly control them all. No – D'Arnay will reply that he is seeking in his various media no more than a fair hearing of a range of intelligent views. They range from the intelligent moderate conservative to the intelligent far right. Probably out of respect for that fairness of treatment which D'Arnay displays in the majority of the nation's newspapers, his editors give a fair hearing once a year to Avalon. For that is the only time you hear of the place – in the *Choosing Your College* special issue – if you hear of Avalon at all.

The place is hard to find too. You have to drive north from the Greater Metropolitan area to find it. You drive through mile after mile of degraded industrial beltland held up by service sector wages. Then, if you remember the turnoff, you pass the tumble-down barns on your way to cottage country. Suddenly, the farmland gives way to wilderness; the air becomes fresher; you smell the pine forest. You are in the North and your car is tugging at the leash. There is that sudden dip in the road with the town of Severnville at your feet. Then if you follow the river road north of town you will find it – that maze of modernist buildings running in and out of each other like an Escher puzzle, the complicated bridges and walkways that suggest a castle, with the ancient river flowing right through it all and the primeval forest stretching to the top of the world. The Founding Fathers chose the spot well. Here in the middle of the wilderness they built a university. All that space and light and silence. Nothing could disturb the life of the mind here.

It hasn't changed much over the years. The pine trees have grown to the height of the buildings – Avalon boasts that its campus has more trees than students. There is a gleaming new Ecology Building now. Behind it is the new shopping mall, the University Heights Mall, that was built on university land in order to pay for the Ecology Building. At first there was talk of the university selling its soul for a science building, but the students flock to the mall between classes, and so the mall has become, by a happy accident, the student center of the University. It is where Av's traditional protests and demonstrations are organized.

For, yes, the students haven't changed much over the years either. They are still padding about in Birkenstocks, wearing woolen Tibetan gloves with each finger knitted in a different colour. They still carry Outward Bound knapsacks and water bottles. I said that nothing really comes out of Avalon, but I was wrong. What comes out of Avalon is a style of free-spiritedness in its graduates. You will see those free spirits in every corner of the world. They are saving a mahogany forest in Thailand. They are leading an animal rights demonstration in Peking. They are setting up illegal radio transmitters on the rooftops of Mexico City. They are manning a native land claim blockade in British Columbia. Later in their thirties, they start to pair off, to settle into the anonymity of perpetual studenthood, teaching in an aboriginal school in Alaska, or guiding wilderness tours in the Andes, or making films on UNESCO grants in East Timor. If there is an oasis of idealism left in the world, if there is a pocket of resistance anywhere, you will find cause-besotted Avalonians in the thick of it, contesting a corporate world they have been taught by their professors to despise.

And the professors? They were young idealists themselves when they founded an alternative university in the Sixties. That was a time ago, wasn't it? It was a time when governments smiled on education and dreams were bottomless, like the pockets of voters.

Then, every politician had to have a university in his district. The politicians came and made speeches about the town having an Oxford of the Boreal Forest or a Harvard of the Cottage Country, and they quoted educators like Playdough on how the unexamined life is not worth living. Have you ever heard a politician speak on how the unexamined life is not worth living? They can speak forever on the subject. You couldn't keep a politician away from the universities then. Now, no politician will be caught dead at one.

Do those phrases seem wistful today – community of scholars, a life of the mind, learning as its own reward? Perhaps they do. But that was the Sixties for you. Some say it was an age of ephemeral pipe-dreams, but I have it on good authority – Professor Leland in Philosophy told me this, and he said he heard it from Weisberg in Politics who heard it from someone in Physics – that in the year 1967 there was a sudden burst of sunspot activity and the earth grew warmer. That was when Avalon University was founded. After eighteen months, the sunspots abated and funding for higher education dried up. The only other time anyone was idealistic about education, Leland says, was during the Twelfth Century.

Today, most of the Founding Fathers of Avalon are retired. They gather daily in the Food Court of the University Heights Mall, nattering about how the university is losing its principles, and how, in spite of their obvious seniority, it has deprived them of their offices. They sit beneath the skylight of the Food Court, eating Taco Bells and gazing at the fountain statue that displays the symbol of the Camelot they founded – the Lady of the Lake, her naked body rising out of the water with fairy arm extended, to hold, point downward, the sword of Arthur.

Yes, you have to take a long drive out of Metro, a long drive out of the present, to find this community of aging baby boomers instructing the young in the utter uselessness of education.

On the particular afternoon my story begins, just at the beginning of term, three of the Founding Fathers are sitting in the Food Court. They are Jake Weisberg, Professor Emeritus of Politics and sometime Dean of Avalon. And Tony Leland (Philosophy Emeritus) is there – he was Vice-President once. The third individual is Waasagunackank of the Center for the First Nations. His name means "He-who-Leaves-the-Imprint-of-his-Foot-Shining-in-the-Snow," but he rarely uses it – the people just call him "Joe." He founded the Center for the First Nations here. (Natives, and the issues that concern them, are prominent at Avalon, which is deep in Anishnaabe territory). And there is a fourth person just joining them, holding a tray with enough french fries to feed a labour union. Since he is a focus of this story, let me describe him first.

He is Ruairi MacDonald, historian, the only one of the group who is not retired.

Now, Big Mac, as the students call him, hardly looks like the distinguished authority who wrote the history of the shipping trade in the era of European expansion. Huge of girth and bulk and monumental as a statue, with his long white hair falling out of his ponytail and cigar ashes clinging to his beard, he resembles more a vengeful sea god from maps of that period. Beneath eyebrows of Bulldog steel wool, his eyes roll dreadfully, and an eye will transfix you as if the particular eyeball has a mind and will of its own. The dreadful wild look in his eyes is not the legacy of MacDonald's Highland ancestry. Three divorces and twenty years battling the Avalon Administration have made him look that way. And here he comes to the cafeteria table, wearing a Scottish tweed jacket over a black Harley-Davidson T-shirt.

Ruairi MacDonald, as you have guessed, is a legend at Avalon. How could you not take a course from this figure who blasts up to the lecture hall on his antique 1200 C.C. motorcycle, then proceeds to describe without notes the cargo of every ship trading with the Lowlands between 1642 and 1776? Those facts seem overwhelming in their importance when Professor MacDonald cites them; perhaps they have lost some of their urgency now. But the truth is, you don't take MacDonald's course to remember facts. You take it to learn academic rigour. Is there no Avalon student who can't recite the rhyme of Rudyard Kipling's that MacDonald bellows out at every opportunity?

> *I keep six honest serving men –*
> *They taught me all I knew.*
> *Their names are what and how and when*
> *And why and where and who.*

And yes – the students take Mac's course because MacDonald genuinely likes students. He especially likes helping them shape their essays, which he does in private interviews. That allows the teacher to know the minds of each of his students, to observe their habits of amassing the evidence tidily, of examining it dispassionately, of drawing out conclusions modestly. They say he found two of his wives that way.

Among the faculty at Avalon, MacDonald is a different kind of legend. As permanent head of the Faculty Union, it was MacDonald who brought the Administration to its knees in two strikes, winning exceptional salaries and benefits while being the reason for the resignations of two presidents, a dean, and a vice-president (finance). Administrators came and went, none of them a match for the brooding restless intelligence of Ruairi MacDonald. He could sniff out hidden budgets with the nose of a bloodhound; he carried the entire balance sheet of the university in his memory. One felt a loyalty to MacDonald. Exuding a warm clannishness, he in his turn treated his colleagues as family – they were his *clanna*, his "children." Because of this tribal loyalty, faculty of every persuasion – conservative and radical alike – trusted "the Laird" to articulate the dissent which was the permanent voice of the Avalon professorate. MacDonald, for his part, had no political persuasion. Instead, he had a mission. Fed by the fury of uprooted Highland clans, fanned by the zeal of the Covenanters, fuelled by the conviction of the Scottish Labour Movement, his mission was single-minded. It was to overthrow the Administration of Avalon University.

The appointment of Hugh D'Arnay as Chairman of the Board, and now of a dean hired by D'Arnay from outside the university, presented a new challenge to that mission. And so MacDonald was consulting the tribal memory of Avalon embodied in the three Founding Fathers and former administrators who sat over the remains of their fast-food lunches.

MacDonald sighed wearily and eased his bulk into one of the laminated metal chairs of the Food Court. "Ach! These chairs were designed for teenagers and mothers wi' bairns."

"Sit down, Mac. We were just talking about the Pension Plan Surplus." The speaker was Jake Weisberg. Wisps of hair hung over a perpetually furrowed brow. He was wearing slippers and track pants and a faded jersey with the name "Columbia" on it.

"Och, God – not the bluidy Pension Surplus! What a wheen o blethers!"

"It's about our teeth, you see?" Tony Leland, in his electric wheelchair, opened his mouth and grinned savagely. His voice was sibilant and he spoke with the clipped flattened vowels of English intellectual aristocracy. "Our teeth are rotting away eating this food. There's a hefty Pension Surplus, and we would like to have a Dental Plan."

"So will you in a few years – if you live that long," Weisberg put in.

"Pity ye didn't think of that when ye lot were administrators."

"I wish to advise," said Leland, "that if we don't obtain a Dental Plan, we shall embarrass the University by putting our teeth on the table." Leland extracted his false teeth and placed them beside a half-eaten hamburger. Then he drew the folds of his black academic gown around his gaunt body and resumed his darning. Leland was darning old woolen socks, which he did by stitching up the hole around a light bulb held inside the sock.

"Ye're already an embarrassment to the Univairrsity. Sittin' here all day and helpin' students with their essays – you droolin' auld lechers!"

"We are advancing knowledge," declared Joe. He was wearing jeans held up by red suspenders tangled around a green tartan shirt. Joe was a lean veteran of a thousand histories. Beneath his Blue Jays cap he had a face that had been thoroughly lived in.

Leland replaced his false teeth. "Assisting the youthful enquirer is a consolation of our demanding profession."

"We call ourselves the Interactive Academic Skills Center," said Weisberg.

MacDonald shrugged. He took a mouthful of french-fries and looked around the Mall.

"The Board sure made a right fankle when they let this Mall be built right on our ain doorstep," he said, changing the topic.

"It's a grander Faculty Lounge than any of us ever dreamed of," Weisberg admitted.

The professors admired the Mall. September sunlight fell through the skylight, illuminating the great indoor fig tree and the green Avalon banners hanging over the escalators. The fountain sprayed its tiny jets on the Lady of the Lake. There was a stillness and emptiness to the place. The mothers with babies had gone home.

"They can't kick us out or they'll lose the student business," Leland commented.

"They were counting on a new subdivision out here to support the Mall. But you foxed it good – you gouty old bugger!" Weisberg gave MacDonald a hearty slam on his back, which brought forth a spasm of coughing.

"Aye – well, the *de-vel-o-per* shouldna' ha' bin on the Avalon Board when they made the deal," MacDonald declared, once his coughing had subsided. At the remembered indignity, the dialect of his ancestors grew thicker. One outrage prodded loose another in his memory. "Hae' ye seen all the new wee signs tellin' us where the Administration Building is? Does nobody remember anymore where the Administration Building is?"

"Another futile attempt at bureaucratic centralization," commented Weisberg, lapsing into his own dialect, which was that of

Sixties activism. "Every time we get a new chairman of the board, we get a new display of corporate signage."

"*My thruaighe art a thir, th'an caoirach mhor a' teachd!* Woe to thee, oh land, the Great Sheep is coming! And what in the name of God is this *a-tro-ci-ty*?"

MacDonald pointed a quivering finger of contempt at a computer screen installed under the escalator of the Food Court.

"It's for university e-mail and videophoning," Joe said innocently.

"Och, I know what it is, laddie! It's part of the new *com-pu-ter* system. Everywhere ye turn, ye find one of these now. If ye go into the Library" – MacDonald emphasized the word *library* with dripping scorn – "ye'll find more of these than books."

"We never had such a thing as e-mail at Oxford in my day," Leland said. "Duns Scotus did quite well without e-mail, thank you."

MacDonald ignored the comment. It was Leland who during the planning of the university had protested against the installation of central heating, citing Aristotle to the effect that a cold memory takes a better impression.

"My people never had e-mail neither," said Joe.

"Used to be – the students met in the morning at the college mailboxes to open their mail," Weisberg remembered. "Shrieks of joy at getting a letter from home and sharing it. Now all you hear is silence and the manic tap-tap-tapping of a keyboard."

"Aye, the glens are silenced, except for the bleating of innumerable sheep." MacDonald lit a cigar and blew the smoke over the No Smoking sign in the mall.

"I wonder what it cost," said Leland, remembering his time as an administrator.

There was a snort of cigar smoke, thick and choking like a Clydeside ferry during the Industrial Revolution. This was followed by a fit of emphysemic wheezing. The men waited until the attack was over.

"I'll tell ye what it cost! It cost four hundred thousand dollars.

That's what it costs. The Board hid the item under Academic Support Services, but I found it oot, I did. The rascals! It fair made my heid birl."

"I rather suspect the Board made a deal with Andromeda Networks," Leland offered.

"Andromeda – my aunt Fanny! Ye know as well as I do what it is for." MacDonald, apparently disgusted with his cigar, stubbed it out on the Food Court floor. "It's an attempt to cash out the excess of the Operating Budget when we come up to renegotiate our salaries. That's what it is. Disgraceful!"

"Nonetheless, it's D'Arnay's doing," Weisberg noted. "D'Arnay, functioning through that stooge of a dean he's brought in."

At the mention of D'Arnay, the four men turned in their seats to look at the statue of the Lady of the Lake. Holding Excalibur, she seemed to look through the mall doors to some distant horizon, waiting for a champion to ride in and take the sword. Rivulets ran down her upstretched arm, her shoulders, her heavy breasts.

"Twould be a funny thing if she were here now," MacDonald said, as if referring to the statue.

Leland sighed. "Indeed, she's with us now in a manner of speaking. Forever young in stone."

"She kind of belongs in this place," agreed Joe Waasagunackank.

"Aye – she canna' fade, though thou hast not thy bliss … "

Leland remembered the quotation. Sitting upright in his wheelchair, he declaimed the verse in high style:

> *When old age shall this generation waste*
> *Thou shalt remain, in midst of other woe*
> *Than ours, a friend to man …*

Leland beamed with satisfaction. His memory was still working. Like most academics what he feared most was losing his mind.

The four professors gazed at the statue fondly.

"Jerónimo sure did a good job sculpting her," Joe said. "They say she had to hold that pose for a whole day, with her arm stretched up like that."

"It's the only time she ever stayed still," MacDonald muttered gruffly.

They admired the statue in her timelessness. In that timelessness you could hear the water dripping from her breasts. Dripping into the pool, the water was drained, only to shoot forever in tiny jets onto the goddess.

"He made her boobs too big," said Weisberg suddenly.

Six eyes swung in one movement from the statue to Jake Weisberg. There was a silence during which an eternity went by.

"I didn't know ye taught Jennifer D'Arnay," MacDonald said at last.

Weisberg's eyes fastened on a distant leaf at the top of the fig tree. "Well, she was Jenny Seton then. And it was a time when Academic Freedom meant something."

Weisberg seemed frozen in the memory of that time. Frozen, he too looked like he was going to turn to stone.

"She was a public good," he said eventually.

"Aye, she was unprivatizable," MacDonald agreed. "What about you, Tony? Did ye teach her too?"

Professor Leland's eyes sunk to the floor, pretending to notice a defect in his carpet slipper. Joe Waasagunackank's face lost all expression. As if on a signal, three coffee containers rose to three mouths in unison.

"Weel, ye should'a taught her better – all of ye! Ye should'a taught her so well that she wouldnae' ha' gone off sudden-like and mairrit yon blethering skite D'Arnay." MacDonald glared balefully at the men. "The puir wee gerrl!"

"She thought she could reform him. She thought she could turn him into a champagne socialist," Weisberg offered apologetically.

"Ach! There's no such thing!" MacDonald growled. "Anyways, dinna fash yersel: she's free of that daftie now," he added, as if pardoning Weisberg.

"Nobody's free of Hugh D'Arnay, least of all ourselves," Weisberg replied.

"No, indeed we're not," Leland agreed. "He took the Avalon chairship just so he could settle a score with our Jenny and all she stands for."

"Marriages niver end – they only go on gettin' more and more gruesome," said MacDonald.

Weisberg frowned and scratched his balding head. "I think you've finally met your nemesis in Hugh D'Arnay. He's going to replace you with a CD-ROM."

MacDonald snorted and rose from his chair. He drew himself up to his full height, towering over the professors. "He will – will he?" Then he leaned his great hands on the cafeteria table. His eyes rolled with a flashing joy three inches from Weisberg's face. "But then we'll fight 'im, won't we lads? And his Hanoverian poodle of a dean too! The rascals! We'll bring 'em to their heels!"

Leland was shaking his head sadly. "It's a different world now, Mac. It's changed. The magisterial life of the mind is no more. All the universities are selling themselves to corporations."

"And the corporations are bringing in their management teams to run the universities," added Weisberg. "Communist robots from hell."

These words might just as well have fallen into the fountain – for MacDonald was oblivious to them. He was oblivious to everything. His mind was fixed on a distant struggle, a final battle. "Aye, we'll fight the whole lot of 'em!" he went on triumphantly. "Dunno yet where we'll make our stand. But I'll tell ye this, laddie" – MacDonald glared at Leland who seemed to shrivel up inside his gown – "we won't pick level ground like we did at Culloden Moor in the year seventeen hundred and forty-six, t' be cut doon by bayonets an' grapeshot. No, that we won't!"

MacDonald stood there for a while, taut with purpose. Then, his will resolved, he allowed himself to relax. He strode over to the statue of the Lady of the Lake and gazed at her thoughtfully. There was the whirring of an electric wheelchair behind his back. Leland had come. And Weisberg too. Finally Joe Waasagunackank got up wearily and joined them at the fountain.

MacDonald pulled a coin from his pocket and threw it in the pool at the lady's feet. "Here's somethin' fer luck, gerrl!"

Tony was fumbling with great effort for his coin. Finally he threw it in. "For my memory," he whispered.

"Arteriosclerosis," Waasagunackank confided, throwing in his coin. "They won't let me eat goosefat nomore."

Weisberg seemed to be holding back. There was a pause while the other men looked at him.

"B.P.H.," he confessed finally. "Benign prostatic hypertrophy." He flipped his coin in a long curving arc into the fountain. "It comes from going to too many conferences, sitting on hard chairs listening to unedifying papers by boring colleagues."

"People only go to conferences to smell each other's bums," Joe observed.

Leland led the men back to the table. MacDonald smiled, noticing his lunch as if for the first time.

"The new dean. I hear tell he's a downsizer," Joe said mischievously.

But Mac's mood had changed. "Och, I checked him oot with our brothers and sisters at the Greater Metropolitan University. He's like all the others. He's an *im-pro-ver*. We'll just have to educate him in the traditions of our community, that's all."

"Has he any human weakness we can exploit?" Jake asked.

The group laughed.

"Jake – you're dreadful!" Leland said.

MacDonald chuckled. "He has nary but the weakness that we all have. The weakness of being a puir human being. He will become besotted with this place as we all have. And that will be the end of him."

The professors smiled wanly and looked again at the statue of the water fairy. They considered the prospect of another member added to their company. High overhead, in the September sunlight streaming through the skylight, a leaf detached itself from the top of the fig tree and fell slowly into the fountain.

2

Cameron Galt, Dean-designate of Avalon, remembered the excitement of new beginnings at the three universities he had joined as a student, teacher and administrator. Nothing matched the excitement of this. Here he was, virtually descending on his new institution from above. Beside him, at the controls, Hugh D'Arnay might actually be parachuting his new dean in.

D'Arnay banked the plane so the dean could have a better look. Galt, struggling to regain balance, surveyed the elongated farmers' fields, the ovoid drumlins, the lakes stretching like a giant's fingers over the horizon, the Kenomagaywakon River. Everything pulled north. Aeons ago, the Ice Age glacier had clawed that land into line, an emperor with colonies transfixed in the direction of his departure.

Then Galt saw Avalon University.

It was a toy castle on a family-room floor, an assembly of Lego, a half-created jigsaw puzzle. Galt sensed a playfulness in the design of the university with its ascending terraces, curving stairways, low-angled rainforest roofs, dramatic facades of fieldstone sunk sideways into cement walls, medieval slit windows, little chimneys everywhere. The effect was singular – part Oxford college, part medieval castle, part West-Coast native village, part Aztec temple. The Founding Fathers, with unlimited funds at their disposal, had determined that Avalon should have the dreamy otherworldliness of the King Arthur stories. What couldn't you do with Sixties-style sculpted cement and Sixties-style captial development funds? There was the Library: from its hub, footbridges extended to each of the colleges.

The campus was designed to be a pedestrian's community, with no building farther than a ten-minute walk between classes from another. Even from the air, the parking lots and roadways were hard to see; they were sunk below the walker's eye level, hidden by clumps of cedar or sumac. The design of the university had a certain logic when viewed from above. Once inside it, Galt knew, the place was a baffling labyrinth of terraces and walkways.

D'Arnay tilted the plane again in a wicked slip-slide, taking a bearing on the river bridge. The main pedestrian avenue of the university, the footbridge spanned the river in a single lyrical leap of sculpted cement. Galt made out the Ecology Building at its right end and, blinking through trees, the red neon sign of the University Heights Mall.

"There she is," D'Arnay stated. "All yours."

"Mine!" thought Galt. He had mixed feelings.

"She's all wired up and ready to sing inside herself," D'Arnay said proudly. "We put enough multiplex in there, you can click on a couple of interactive whales having a conversation off Iceland. You can hear the shifting sands of Jupiter. Sweet knowledge! And a P.C. in every residence room – also kindness of Andromeda Networks. There isn't anything on this planet a student can't access."

Galt looked into a pair of fifty-year-old eyes regarding him from deep inside a boyish athletic face. They were the same level eyes that surveyed him years ago from the head prefect's platform at the front of assembly at Colborne College. Eyes since made level by reading so many bottom lines, Galt thought.

"That'll get the faculty off their buttocks," D'Arnay said with a grin. "They'll have to scramble to keep up with their students. Perchance, they'll even make some educational products themselves."

"Oh Dad – it's not a software company," came Jan's voice from the back of the plane. "It's kind of cute. It's, like, playschool."

D'Arnay bellowed his reply over the roar of the engine. "My wonderful daughter – you're perfectly right! That's precisely what it is! It's an ongoing experiment in new forms of social and political

relationship. It's a mating ground for young people who have no intention of mating. It's an interminable dance of denim and tweed."

Galt smiled inwardly and held his peace. D'Arnay's language still
hit like wet towels in the locker room at Colborne College. Then
they had the Napoleonic grandiosity of a head prefect. Now they
sounded the neo-conservative baroque.

It would be a mistake, however, to suggest that Cameron Galt
was intimidated by the media magnate's style, or that he had any
particular loyalty to the man or his ideas. The two of them had
attended the same exclusive school together, it is true, and they had
adjacent summer cottages, north of the university, on Stoney Lake.
But as far as Galt was concerned these class ties had no bearing on
his thinking. For Galt had grown up to be an academic administrator. That meant he had no ties to anything. Perhaps this is not
a kind thing to say about the fastest-rising dean in the Metro University system, but in fact it is testimony to his success. Contrary to
academic custom, deans are no longer leaders of the faculty. They
are its managers. And as a manager Galt was one of the best. He was
one of the best because he never let a single idea or loyalty trouble
him. As a result he functioned smoothly as a sort of gyroscope
shifting the consensus of the university community first this way,
then that way, sponging up dissent − indeed, making dissent un-
thinkable. He embodied an ever-changing equilibrium. Nothing
could be more fatal to that role than entertaining an original idea.
Such fixities trouble the living flow of a community through time.
In fact, to confuse an idea with truth or mistake rhetoric for meaning would be to topple to one side or the other of the ever-evolv-
ing consensus. And even to be self-conscious of this balancing-act
would be to destroy its managerial innocence. Does a tightrope
walker pause to think about what he is doing? No, of course not.
Neither did Galt, who buried self-consciousness, as soon as it arose,
in the anonymity of his soul, matter for some future performance
appraisal. He came from a long line of administrators right back
to colonial times − he allowed himself that pride. Handsome, tall,

bearded ancestors in whom nothing stuck out awkwardly, people with power held in reserve. Unlike D'Arnay who was opinionated to the point of vulgarity and threw his weight around.

Reflecting on his *noblesse oblige*, Galt watched the university loom closer, turning by degrees from a toy fantasy to a reality he must manage.

"Mom wants me to go to Avalon," announced Jan.

At the reference to Jennifer D'Arnay, the plane seemed to hit an air pocket. Galt's Yacht Club lunch hit the roof of his mouth. Suddenly the river left its riverbed and rose up to meet them. Pine trees shot by, each one individual and distinct. Now D'Arnay was trimming the plane. Galt felt forces assailing the machine like demons from three directions. The engine noise increased to a manic roar.

"Precisely what the public can't afford now," D'Arnay yelled in Galt's ear. "Flakey anarchic monuments to a ritualized middle-class bulemia."

"Dad, you're not going to put down here? It's too rough!"

D'Arnay was lining the plane up with the arch of the river bridge.

"Who says I'm going to land, honey?"

Oh god, thought Galt. He's not really going to do it! Motion in three directions was D'Arnay's thrill, but this was pushing it. Galt, at home in the safe world of administration, felt his internal gyroscope wobble.

"I have a message for the congeries of scabby detrimentals down there," D'Arnay announced. "Apocalypse Now! The new corporate order has arrived."

Yes, it was clear D'Arnay was going to dive-bomb the bridge. A group on the bridge thought so too. Galt made out a black-cloaked figure on a motorized wheelchair, and three other men, one of whom, a great bearded giant, was shaking his fist at the plane. White-faced, they dove beneath the cement parapet, leaving the wheelchair person alone and exposed. Suddenly, Galt felt Jan's hands on his shoulders.

"Hmmm. This is going to be a tight squeeze," D'Arnay said.

God – he's going *under* the bridge!

Galt tried to close his eyes, but the spectacle of the bridge rushing toward him at superhuman speed was mesmerizing. Uselessly, he checked the seat-belt release, he checked the door handle, he concentrated on the Andromeda Networks spiral on the underside of the wing. He imagined the possible headline in the student newspaper: "Incoming Dean Goes Splat Against River Bridge." Jan's fingers were tightening on his shoulders.

Whoosh! It was over. The plane bounced, then clawed skyward in a roar.

"*Yee-haw!*" cried D'Arnay exultantly.

Jan released her hands from the Dean's shoulders. "Dad, you're crazy!"

D'Arnay gave a grunt of satisfaction. "I've always wanted to do that."

Galt knew that he would have an image burned in his mind for the rest of his life. It was the image of the bridge rushing at him like an obstacle on a racing-car speedway in an arcade game. Was the world real to Hugh D'Arnay, or was it just a simulation?

"Let them know who's boss," D'Arnay declared.

Maybe the thrill had been intended for him by D'Arnay, Galt reflected. An initiation hazing.

D'Arnay was following the river north to Stoney Lake, their destination. "I'm putting a new dean in there who understands quick-change retooling and just-in-time educational inventory."

Over the roar of the engine, Galt heard Jan's sigh from the back seat. Up over cottage country, Galt started to get his stomach back. But his whole body was still shaking. He tried to think of calming things. The family cottage next to D'Arnay's in the bay. The silence of the north while he worked at night, the only sound the fluttering of moths on the screen door. That was another reason why he took the job – he could live year-round at the cottage with Sally. The spousal hiring for her in Women's Studies was the crowning touch. They could both work at the same institution and be home together by nightfall. His partnership with Sally needed work; in the pressures of the Metropolitan University system, they had communicated more by e-mail than face-to-face.

Beep! Beep!

D'Arnay extracted his pocket phone and turned it on. "D'Arnay. What's up?"

The voice of the Acting President of Avalon, its avuncular suavity transmitted in digital bits to one of Andromeda's commercial satellites, then beamed and reconstituted in the PCS phone, seemed at once distant and close at hand. "Well, hello, dear colleagues. It's grand to see you up there. But you'll permit the comment: your arrival is a bit – how shall I say? – precipitous."

"Thought I'd let you know we're on time for the Board meeting," D'Arnay said dryly.

"To be sure! Yet I must say, we are receiving complaints from around the University ... "

"How fascinating!"

"The faculty union Head has ... ah ... suggested that you violated air space regulations ... "

D'Arnay looked across at Galt with a blank face. "Tell him we own that stretch of the river. Also the atmosphere above it. If they want to argue, they can call the university lawyer."

"Your wish is my concern, dear Chairman."

"You're goddam right it is, Giles." *Click.*

"Giles Rattenbury is an egregious twit," D'Arnay said. He trimmed the plane for an approach over the south shore of Stoney. Galt surveyed the islands, each with its little cottage and pine trees, standing in its own reflection. It was as if they were descending into a picture postcard.

"Do we really own it?"

D'Arnay shrugged. "Hell! – who knows? Now let's see. Any deadheads in the lake? Apart from your mother, I mean."

Jan groaned.

"Where is the bitch anyway?" D'Arnay wondered out loud as an afterthought.

The question didn't invite an answer. But Jan answered: "She's in London, heading for Spain."

"She still believes in civilization, the dumb broad!" D'Arnay confided to Galt, as if he was sharing the secret of a family illness.

Galt, his internal gyroscope staggering, said nothing.

D'Arnay changed his role from ex-husband to father. "At least, if you go to Avalon, you can live at the cottage. If the mice haven't eaten through the insulation."

"I'm not even sure I want to go to university," Jan said, continuing the tension. "I might go to Spain. Or Haida Gwaay."

D'Arnay conceded a mood of nonchalant resignation. "Your mother's right. Go to college. Pick up some skills. By the time you graduate, Avalon will be a world-class research center. Lean and keen. You'll have a degree you can be proud of – right, Cam?"

"Right!" said Galt distractedly. He had been checking his cottage. The dock was level in the water. The flag was flying. The bottoms of the trees were trimmed high. With last year's heavy winter, the deer, standing on high snow, had eaten the bottom branches of the cedars.

The plane glided on its ground-effect until one pontoon touched, then the other. The plane settled into the water. Jan gathered her knapsack and sleeping bag from the back. A few minutes later, they were at the D'Arnay cottage dock. D'Arnay switched off the engine. There was a sudden welcoming silence with the gurgling of water underneath the boat-house.

D'Arnay, dressed in an ancient brown leather jacket and jeans, sprang onto the dock with the rope. The others followed, Jan in an Oxford-cloth T-shirt with the Bishop Rye crest, and cutoffs, her blond hair blunt-cut above her shoulders – the perennial look of the private-school cottager. Galt was dressed incongruously in a business suit.

D'Arnay, checking the moorings of the float plane, was speaking over his shoulder. "Like I said – the infantile middle class sucking at the nipples of the Mommy-State is off the map. We shipped their jobs to the Third World. It's either joining the knowledge-producing elite, or flipping burgers at McDonald's.

"This is a fact of life your intractable mother fails to understand," he added.

Jan didn't seem to be listening to her father. She was standing at the end of the dock, looking out at the lake. Galt glanced at her briefly, taking in her long athletic legs. How many times had he seen those legs go by his cottage window, triumphant and capable on water skis? Galt appreciated acts of balance in every form.

D'Arnay led the way up the fieldstone steps, laid at the turn of another century by Godfrey Seton, Jan's great grandfather. "We're going to head back to the university. Want to come?"

"No thanks, Dad, I want to think for awhile."

"Okay."

"Bye Jan," Galt called ineffectually, for there was already no response.

Jan's solitude, Galt considered, was something her father could appreciate. He was an only child; she was the only child of an only child. She probably needed time to brood – like her father. Galt remembered times when the float plane would suddenly appear, dividing the peace of Stoney Lake, D'Arnay alone at the controls. The plane would touch down in a shower of spray. The lake would readjust itself to accept the intruder. But he'd stop the plane in the middle of the lake, to brood. Then, coming to a decision, he'd take off suddenly in a roar and be back at Andromeda Place in the city, in time for a board meeting hastily called from the plane. Next day, Galt and Sally would read in the paper about another newspaper or cablevision chain changing hands.

Galt took one last look at Jan alone on the dock. Then he turned his mind, as if on a swivel, to the task at hand. A Board meeting. Introductions. An informal airing of his academic restructuring ideas. Polite questions. He would be the senior academic officer at

Avalon. It was understood that he would run the university while the President was away, which most of the time he would be, doing alumni relations and corporate begging. Rattenbury was only Acting-President anyway, a longtime Avalonian and Founding Father plucked out of high-level government work to fill a gap. He would disappear back into his legend soon. Rattenbury was not the managerial type – he got too interested in peoples' ideas. Then Galt would become President.

All this had been communicated to Galt in the elliptical asides and body language of two gentlemen who had attended the same private school, and had judged each other's character on the playing field and at the college ball. Gentlemen who had adjacent cottages on Stoney Lake.

The university would be his. All his.

To serve, of course.

3

"There's no way I'm going in there straight," declared Jilaquns of the Qayahllaanas. Reaching into her medicine pouch, she produced an enormous joint. She lit it, inhaled deeply, and passed the cigarette to Jan. "Have some academic sherry."

Jan took the joint and inhaled. This was just like old times behind the gym at Bishop Rye School. But instead of the oh-so-cute Rye middy blouse with its absurd sailor's collar and the regulation navy skirt "three and one half inches above the knees when kneeling," Jilaquns was wearing frayed denim cutoffs, biker boots, and a mauve tank-top printed with the image of her clan totem, an eagle. She hardly needs the eagle symbol, Jan thought, since everything about Jilaquns – her cheekbones, her nose, her fierce eyes – was aquiline. The blue-black hair came down to her naked belly in perfect braids, each braid woven with the feather of a Red-shafted Flicker. And she was wearing a tribal lip ornament. Jan was still dressed in her cottage clothes. The two girls were seated under a pine tree outside Emma Goldman College.

The bell tower of the college rose up in three thin columns to unequal heights, climbing with the surrounding hills, not against them, seeming to tease down the sky. Like the rest of the university, the tower had fieldstone from the last Ice Age set in the concrete mix. The effect was to pull the landscape into the building. Sumac, maple and cedar had been planted to mirror the trees dotting the hillsides. And the ancient wilderness river flowed through the university village. Altogether, Avalon was inseparable from its natural environment.

"Someone is watching us," Jan said musically. Fifty feet away on the steps of the college, basking in the September sunlight, an ancient dog gazed along the length of its paws at the two women. The dog was a monstrous, rickety Irish Wolfhound, all black except for a grizzled muzzle. And it was frowning.

"I think it disapproves," Jilaquns said, taking another drag.

The sunlight dripped like honey on the two women and on the warm stone of the college steps where the dog lay. The afternoon was a fullness of silences. In each silence you could hear something growing. A chestnut fell from a tree in the middle of the quad.

"Who's Emma?" Jilaquns asked. She was reading a banner students had hung over the college door in preparation for Orientation Week. "Who's Emma?" the sign said; then in spirited italics the quotation: "*If I can't dance, I don't want to be in your Revolution.*"

"One of Mom's favourite sayings," Jan sighed. "Mom's everywhere."

"Who's Emma though?" Jilaquns repeated.

"Emma Goldman – you ignoramus. She was a garment worker in Metro in the Thirties."

"A safe symbol for the slumming aristocratic activist."

"Who's the Haida princess calling an aristocrat?"

"This place sounds promising."

It sounded promising to Jilaquns, alright, Jan thought. Jill was the long-legged star of the Rye modern dance class. Besides which, her politics were far left of the word "revolution." And she had a scholarship to study at Avalon's Center for the First Nations. For her part, Jan was not so focussed. What would her father think of her joining a college named for a Surrealist union organizer? Plus, was she even sure she wanted to go to college at all? She had driven down to Avalon quickly in response to Jill's call. She had agreed to check out the university to see if the right mixture of whims fell into place. The right mixture of whims was not falling into place. And the dog was obviously psycho. It seemed to be reading her thoughts.

"This college has been renamed so many times, no one knows what its original name is anymore," Jilaquns commented.

It was true. You could see where the old names had been painted out over the college door and new ones substituted, according to the prevailing ideology of the students who controlled its College Council. Now, depending on who you talked to, it was either Kropotkin College, to honour a founder of the Anarchist movement, or it was Leonard Pelletier College, for the martyr of the American Indian Movement, or it was Emma Goldman College, remembering a half-forgotten Surrealist. This year, the Surrealists seemed to be in the ascendancy.

Jan sat crosslegged, feeling the tingle of sunlight on her legs and her mind ascending to the cool beyond of utter choicelessness like an escaped balloon. If you have ever smoked fresh Gulf Islands Thunderbird grass in September, you will know what I mean. It helps you see things clearly. You can see with the omniscience of a visionary. You can see clear down the Georgia Strait to Seattle and the other side of Mount Baker. That is something like what Jan was seeing.

Well, she thought, the West Coast is out because Jilaquns is here. That left Spain – but she wasn't ready for her mother and her current companion. Other universities? They seemed remote, and she had no idea what she was going to major in anyway. Being a loner meant she needed her few friendships, including Jill. So, Avalon. Ecofreaks and folksy fiddle-playing men with their knees sticking out of their jeans, and saviours of the Third World, and anarchist animal rights vegans who ate seaweed. Over-parented superkids who had grown up in the back seats of Volvo station wagons, listening to tapes of Nana Mouskouri – the avant-garde fringe of high schools across the country. Avalon – where it was uncool to appear to be in a relationship with someone. Could she go to this place where her mother was some kind of a legend and her father was Chairman of the Board? Could she handle Jilaquns' fervent eyes? And her clothing styles which always matched her spirit perfectly. Like those artfully frayed denim cutoffs that were meant to look like they could fall off at any moment.

"Jill – how do you get your cutoffs to sag in just the right way?"

Jilaquns stood up and twisted her body around to look at her bum.

"Oh, you get a guy to sit in them. The guy's butt somehow stretches them out at the bottom – gives them that nice saggy thing. You look for sagginess there: they have to not fit tightly – they have to look schleppy. The guy has to have a nice pert bum to actually push them out. And then we put them on, and we're shaped differently, so they sag. You look like a prepubescent twelve-year-old boy."

The girls resumed their seat under the pine tree. Without lifting its great head, the dog wagged its tail when it saw them, *thump*, *thump*, against the warm cement.

"That dog's creeping me out," said Jilaquns, reaching into her medicine pouch and lighting another joint. Jan took the joint and resumed her dilemma.

Help! The dog was coming over to them. With a shuddering effort, the wolfhound had heaved itself up, stretched, yawned, and was walking stiff-legged towards them.

"The fucking thing is inside my mind!" Jilaquns said, pawing at her head.

The dog hovered over the two women. It sniffed Jilaquns' medicine pouch and gave a low earth-rumbling growl.

"Fuck-off! Those are tribal mysteries. They are none of your business."

"Nice doggie," Jan said ineffectually.

The dog gave Jan a determined sniff, then swung around and walked toward the college door. Then it paused. It looked back at the women, its tongue hanging out.

"We're meant to follow it," Jilaquns said.

"Whatever," sighed Jan, getting up from the lawn.

At the college door, the dog made a noise that was somewhere between a whine and a moan. Jan opened the big oak door. The dog padded under plants hanging from pine beams in shafts of sunlight, through the reception area. Jan watched the posters go by on the walls: clear-cut logging, date rape, genetically modified food, slum landlords, STDs, genocide in East Timor, world trade, and a type of non-commercial menstrual pad you washed and dried in the company of other women. There were no students around on the Friday before Orientation Week. Yet the university seemed ready to go. The dog led them to a door. On it was the lettering: "Faith Rackstraw – Classics. College Principal." The dog pawed at the door, adding a new scratch to years of scratch-marks under the door handle.

A grey-haired woman in a cashmere sweater and tweed suit answered the door.

"Ah, Clio – *good* doggie. You've found two more students for our ... ah ... *college*. Come in – shall we? – and do let us ... er ... *present* ourselves properly."

The accent was acquired somewhere in the mid-Atlantic between Radcliffe and Oxford. The affected laboring of phrases and the triumphant emphasis of a key word sounded to Jan's ears like a backhoe straining to suck buckets of mud out of a sewer-pipe trench. She was like one of those old biddies at Bishop Rye. Jan felt a high-pressure area form over Jilaquns. Oh god! – she's going to blow. Class war.

The girls went into the office, Jan leading.

"Do make yourselves comfortable, my dears. Here, I'll move these *c.v.*s off the chair for you."

Faith Rackstraw took a pile of resumés and put them on the floor, spreading them around with a laced Oxford shoe. "Clio, dear – you might begin on these. Give you something to do."

The dog's tail thumped amiably against the office desk as she proceeded to root through the *c.v.*s with her nose.

Jan took the seat vacated by the resumés. Jilaquns sat beside her, staring at the college principal, taking her in.

"Well, then. Let us introduce ourselves. I am Faith Rackstraw. And you are?"

"Jan D'Arnay."

"Ah. Jan D'Arnay indeed! Welcome to the college, my dear. You resemble your mother, if I may say so, though she wasn't at this college. She was at Lady Sears, if I remember correctly."

It's started, Jan thought. I am always going to be someone's daughter.

"And you, my dear?"

"You can call me Jilaquns. Aren't you going to offer us sherry or something? Or am I on the injun list?"

Rackstraw smiled pleasantly. "All in good order. One simply must keep some … er … *measure* with the sun – otherwise, all order is lost, isn't it, Clio?"

Clio's tail gave an affirming wag. The two girls paused to admire her.

"That's one fuck of a dog!" Jilaquns said appreciatively.

"Humanity's first friend."

"In our stories, whenever a dog appears weird things happen."

"Isn't that interesting? Perhaps hunter-gatherers remember the domestication of the dog uneasily."

Jilaquns stood up stiffly.

"I'm not at university five fucking minutes and I'm greeted with a racist slur! Who are you calling a 'hunter-gatherer' for fuck's sake? My people happen to be involved in legal battles to re-establish the fact that we are an advanced stratified nation engaged for at least three millennia in commercial fishing and long-distance trading. Shit! – we were making knives out of iron at least a thousand years before you whites came on the scene. The myth of the 'living primitive' has got to be the most racist Manifest Destiny imaginable."

Rackstraw smiled wearily. "Do compose yourself, my dear. Perhaps the sun is in the right position for sherry after all."

The Principal went over to a liquor cabinet and removed two glasses made of Waterford crystal and a bottle of Harvey's Shooting Sherry. She poured a glass and gave it to Jilaquns.

"I know you're not a paleolithic savage, dear. I was simply referring to the long memory of your storytellers, not to the state of your civilization. Yet it is … er … *an objective fact* that dogs are the only animals to be domesticated in the Mesolithic."

"Objective facts don't exist," Jilaquns stated, taking the glass and draining it in one swallow.

"Ah – you mean it is Jilaquns' opinion that objective facts don't exist."

"Facts are patriarchal world domination through the illusion of objectivity." The warmth of the sherry shot down to Jill's already buzzing toes, then bounced up and went out to her fingertips.

Faith Rackstraw poured a second glass of sherry and offered it to Jan. "Of course they are, dear. One couldn't agree with you more. Nonetheless, objectivity is an … er … *useful* fiction that one applies *hypothetically* for the sake of bringing different kinds of *knowledge* together at a university and comparing them."

"Sure," said Jilaquns, feeling suddenly mellower. "Whose knowledge?"

Rackstraw raised an eyebrow at the student.

"So-called 'facts' have no existence apart from my experience of them," Jilaquns went on. "And the political uses to which they can be put in my experience of them."

Rackstraw laughed pleasantly, her eyes twinkling. "I think that's delightfully … ah … post-Kantian of you. Tell me – if a tree falls in a forest and there's no one around to hear it fall, does it make a sound?"

Jilaquns seemed at a loss for a moment.

"Sure. It makes a sound. The spirits hear it."

Rackstraw laughed. "A brave answer – isn't it, Clio?"

The great dog wagged her tail some more and continued to snort through the *c.v.*s. The Principal poured another glass of sherry for Jilaquns and then one for herself.

Finally, Jan couldn't restrain the question any longer: "What's the dog doing?"

"Oh, Clio's short-listing part-time instructors for me. Aren't you, Clio, you wise old snout!"

The girls watched, amazed.

Rackstraw picked up the *curriculum vitae* that the dog had nudged aside. "See? Harvard. A fine Classics department. The candidate can probably read and write as well, if we're lucky. Clio never misses an educated teacher."

Rackstraw held the document under the dog's nose and watched its tail wag excitedly.

"The brute's nose can inhale a Sophoclean tragedy," Rackstraw explained. "And one shouldn't wonder. After all, her father was the weather god and her mother was the mountain spirit, Memory."

Rackstraw put the resumé on a pile on her desk. "That makes five – a good short-list. All commendable candidates, I'm sure." She glanced at Jilaquns conspiratorially. "Now, that's objectivity for you.

"I don't know why part-time instructors feel so hard done by," she added.

Jilaquns let out a peal of laughter. "Cool!"

"'Thought is blood moving around the heart.' Empedokles said that. Or moving around the nose in Clio's case."

Faith Rackstraw looked at Jilaquns mischievously. "Empedokles knew what he was talking about. He was a shaman, you see. They say his spirit flew into a volcano, so he must have been a shaman."

Jilaquns sipped her second sherry in the manner she had been taught at Bishop Rye. Then she stood up politely to leave. "It's been an event meeting you, Faith Rackstraw."

"I've enjoyed meeting you too, Jilaquns. You've come a long way from the Islands of the People. I hope you like it at Avalon."

"Oh, I'm sure it will be very interesting."

"And what about you, Jan? You've been sitting there silently. Making up your mind, I suppose. Do you think you want to come here and help give the place a new ... er ... *destiny*?"

Jan stood for a moment transfixed and giddy while the people who were inside her mind held a quick conference. "Sure. Why not?" she heard one of them say.

"We like to put our incoming students in residence for Orientation Week. That way they get to know the customs of Avalon. Clio will take you over to show you your rooms."

Rackstraw opened a filing cabinet, took out Jilaquns' registration form, and held it under Clio's nose. The dog made an identification that was more efficient and durable than any student account card. Then she began to plod out the door which the Principal held open.

"Do drop in anytime and we'll continue our talk," Rackstraw called out.

They followed the huge slow-moving dog through the lobby and out the oak door of Emma Goldman College. Then across the quad to the residence wing. Clio paused at the door to the residence, waiting for Jan to let her in. With a series of moans and sighs, the dog ascended the staircase, turning right at the top. *Click-clack*, her weary feet moved down the linoleum corridor until she came to the last room on the left. Clio scratched at the door with her huge paw. Jilaquns opened it and went in. Then Clio showed Jan a matching room across the corridor.

That is how Jan D'Arnay and Jilaquns of Qaysun came to be at Avalon University.

4

Universities are tied to the rhythm of the seasons. Academic study is portioned out according to the Fall Term, the Winter Term, and the Spring Term – and Summer School, the latter a frivolous anomaly that has never quite fitted the solemn measures of education. All across North America, universities close at the end of April, allowing students, it was originally intended, to return to their parents' farms and help put in the crops. Then in autumn, after getting the harvest in, the students go back to college. That is the rhythm of academic life consecrated in nineteenth-century agricultural America, the land of universal education. And so after Labour Day, after the fall fairs, the youth of America stream back to college with a sense of new beginnings.

Not many students are streaming back to Avalon University, however. Avalon is a small college anyway, as colleges go. With about 3400 full-time undergraduates, it is smaller than some high schools. And there is a recession on – one of the many caused by corporate restructuring. Not a severe recession, it is just sharp enough to make young people think twice about putting themselves in debt for the next twenty years for the dubious ideal of knowledge as its own reward. Since Avalon offers nothing but that ideal, many of its students are staying home, hanging onto what jobs they have. Of course, there are other factors, too various to analyze, which determine what young adults do with their lives in September.

Bud Lassiter, Registrar of Avalon University, is nevertheless analyzing those factors now for the benefit of Dean Galt. Lassiter understands the factors at work in Avalon's enrolment crisis. Those factors, in his mind, are largely the impotence of his high-school recruiting staff, a preppie man and woman with the upbeat air of camp counsellors who now stand together in front of the Registrar's desk, shifting from one foot to another uneasily. Galt is sitting casually to one side, taking notes. Bud Lassiter, for all his burly ebullience, is beginning to fray at the edges.

"Don't look good! Don't look good!" he mutters. Glancing at the incoming student figures, which he has noted on his wrist with a magic marker, he sees on the computer a matching dip in the number of returning students. Even calculating the eleventh-hour wavelet of adventurers waking up to a frosty morning in Alaska or running out of travellers' checks in Sri Lanka to decide they'd be better off at school, it looks like Avalon is going to be critically under-enrolled. Correspondingly, it will be critically underfunded according to the grant-per-head financing formula set by the legislature.

"No doubt about it, kiddies! We're taking a hit in the range of two hundred and sixty plus bodies. That's out of an anticipated first-year intake of one thousand. When the Board hears this, ye proverbial shit is going to hit ye fan."

"We did our best, chief!" This is the eternally buoyant Blake McCabe, senior high-school recruiter and former mainstay of the Avalon rowing team, whose sincerity even Lassiter finds terrifying. "Anyhow, we can still let in the holding tank."

Galt's face registers a complete loss.

"Ah, Mr. McCabe is referring to a pool of substandard applicants: senior citizens taking courses for recreation, high-schoolers with grades in the 60 to 69% range."

"We can't admit Cs without losing our position in the *Choosing Your College* rankings," Galt states flatly. "Even those C grades are pretty inflated, I imagine." In the university he has come from, he has never seen a C admission.

"That's for sure!" says Kayte Bubbins. Kayte is a clean-cut role model, former editor of the Avalon Student Yearbook, who even at this moment is pressing a clipboard against her chest as if to restrain her wholesomeness. "They can't even spell their names."

"They'll drop out of here by Christmas – before we report the enrolment totals to the government," McCabe says.

"Yeah – ouch! And the government is leaking the figures to the *Choosing Your College* special issue." Lassiter looks sorrowfully at Galt. "If our dropout rate gets published, we're roadkill."

Galt gazes thoughtfully out the window at the Library building, watching its lights making unstable reflections in the river.

Lassiter continues to glare over his beard at his staff, as if the sub-standard applicants were their fault. Kayte Bubbins regards her track shoes regretfully. Blake McCabe wishes he were far away, trying to persuade the one wacko student from Atikokan High to come to Avalon.

"You don't understand. It's like selling soap-flakes out there!" The Registrar looks meaningfully at Blake McCabe, waiting for him to take the cue.

On cue, McCabe takes a poster out of his briefcase. Printed in splashing colour, it shows a group of students arm-in-arm, free and easy in the summer of their youth. Just to have it on one's wall implies belonging to a teeming campus milieu with all its *bon temps* and sports event days. "That's what McMonster's putting out. It goes to anybody who even writes to the university for information. Now, look at this. Life at Country Club U."

Now McCabe has produced a magazine designed by an advertising agency, its cover done in metallic teal ink on laminated paper. Inside were pictures of students reading under trees, students shopping at a farmers' market, students in congenial groups like a beer commercial. Judging by the photographs, everything at Country Club U. was done in congenial loving groups.

"And here's what I have to give out," offered Kayte Bubbins, playing her part in the show. She held something at arm's length between thumb and forefinger, like a piece of detritus. *Be part of an adventure of learning with a community of scholars*, it read.

Lassiter slumped forward, his head in his hands in a posture of defeat. "It's Faith Rackstraw's phrasing. Why for the love of mike can't we get her off the Admissions Committee?" The Registrar glowered over his beard at the far wall, thinking particularly of

Faith Rackstraw and generally of faculty who encumbered every decision-making body of the university. Everybody at this faculty-governed institution wore two hats. And Rackstraw wore several. Not hats, but bonnets. With bees in them.

"That's what happens when you let tenured knowledge-retentives run a university," was Lassiter's comment. "Maybe the Admissions Committee should advise the Dean, instead of reporting to Senate."

Galt, taking the suggestion, nodded.

"You know," said Lassiter, brightening, "we can talk until the cows come home about 'learning with a community of scholars,' blah-blah … But it ain't gonna wash with the teenage masses." He banged a clenched fist against his teak tabletop. "We need a real recruiting budget, Mr. Dean. I've brought you here so you can see for yourself what it's like in the trenches."

"I get the picture," Galt said.

"Isn't the satellite campus working?" Ms. Bubbins asked helpfully.

"Oh yeah. The satellite campus. It is to laugh." With a convulsion of energy, Lassiter leapt from his chair, strode over to the far wall, grabbed a laser pointer, and activated his 40-inch flat-panel "plasma-vision" wall display which showed a map. The map was covered in arrows and circles drawn in bright colours. "You see here?" Lassiter pointed to a green circle at the bottom of the map where the road up to Severnville turned north from the industrial hinterland. Fluorescent canary yellow arrows seemed to be attacking the green circle, looking to Kayte Bubbins' eyes like so many spermatozoa attacking an unwilling ovum. "The green circle represents our satellite campus perimeter. We captured the lakeshore market in the Eighties. But the Country Club has counter-attacked, damn them! They're sweeping all the towns a hundred miles east of our satellite campus with storefront courses."

"What's this?" Galt asked, bemused. He indicated a phalanx of blue arrows closing in on the satellite campus from the west.

"That's your own Greater Metro University. You caught us in a classic pincer movement last year. Just as we were digging in on the northeast Metro sector. Pretty nifty work!" Lassiter nodded appreciatively at Galt. "To the north, that's Flakehead U. – outflanking us in cottage country. Our own backyard, for pete's sake! *We need money, guys.* Now look at this!" The Registrar pointed to a rash of tiny circles, near the center of the map, drawn in brilliant purple. "That's McMonster. They're parachuting right into our catchment-basin with their new electronic education initiatives. While we've been sitting on our butts talking about the integrity of professors personally marking their own students' essays ... "

The Registrar glared for no reason at Kayte Bubbins.

" ... *they've* developed interactive software for Distance Ed. Even as we speak, they're teaching courses on the Internet right here in Severnville. They sure caught us with our pants down."

"They've penetrated our defensive perimeter," McCabe observed sadly.

"It's too bad," remarked Kayte Bubbins, "that our Tutors-on-Snowmobiles project didn't work out."

They gazed at the situation map with its encirclements and turned flanks, counter-attacks and deep thrusts. In the middle of the map a green circle marked the location of Avalon University where the ancient glacial river plain met the antediluvian mountains.

Kayte Bubbins broke the silence abruptly. "Mr. D'Arnay is, like, head of Andromeda Networks? Why doesn't he buy an educational software firm; then we could get some serious educational technology at Av."

Lassiter's beard could not conceal his broad smile. For all her dismaying wholesomeness, Kayte was sometimes capable of insight. This was an insight.

"I'm sure it'll come," said the Dean coyly. "In the meantime ... "

" ... we're up shit creek," said McCabe, finishing Galt's sentence. He was mad at himself for not seeing the Andromeda connection before Kayte.

Lassiter slumped in his leather executive armchair, reorganizing his ebullience. "What to do? What to do?" His fingers drummed rapidly on his teak desktop. Then he smiled a hard-bitten smile.

"Well, staff. What do you do when you're surrounded on all sides?"

McCabe and Bubbins exchanged glances. The old guy had some trick up his sleeve – that's for sure!

"You fox the figures, boss," McCabe suggested stupidly.

"No way, José! We tried that once and we got burnt. There were government accountants crawling over us for weeks. No – what you do is … "

Here the Registrar looked up triumphantly from his desk.

" … you activate the Secret Doomsday File."

"What Secret Doomsday File?" asked Kayte.

Lassiter directed his explanation at Galt. "Oh – it's a little just-in-caser I worked out with the local Polytech. For use when their enrolment numbers are high and ours are low. Now, let's just take a gander and see where they're high."

The Registrar summoned data on his monitor. It showed the entire up-to-the-minute enrolment of the nearby Polytechnical College, divided according to areas of study. Lassiter began scrolling through the subject areas: *Accounting, Animal Care …*

Fascinated, Galt got up from where he was sitting and peered over Lassiter's shoulder.

"It's a little strategy of last resort my counterpart over there and yours truly fixed up in August," Lassiter explained. "When we were fishing at Stoney. You see – he's packing bodies in right up to the allowable threshold for funding. Just like we are. Or just like we're supposed to be doing." Lassiter glared at the recruiting staff from under his bushy eyebrows. "Any excess bodies, and he gets stung with a funding clawback for exceeding his enrolment maximum. So we take his excess students. And also some extras just to be on the safe side. That's why we set up this link."

"You mean, he's reading *our* figures too?" Bubbins asked.

"Sure. Why not? When we start losing our extra first-years at

Christmas, you guys can counsel them over to the Winter Term vocational courses at the Polytech. Then he can top up his totals before the Great Reckoning Day."

Cameron Galt found the phrase "win-win scenario" too clichéd to say. Instead he said, "The left hand washes the right, and both hands wash the face."

"Yeah – it's a win-win scenario," said the Registrar.

"I assume the Poly students have a limited number of elective courses in their study programs," Galt wondered out loud.

"Yep! When the elective courses are full over there, the Poly registration computer just feeds our courses onto each student's registration form. Ours are more difficult, but they count at par. Let's see – *Communication Arts*? Nothing there to take. *Dental Technician*? Nope! Looks like they're under across the board. Oh-ho! What's this?" Lassiter highlighted *Law and Security* with his cursor.

"Oh, no!" McCabe protested. "Not them! They're training to be penitentiary and corrections institute staff."

"Or police officers," Kayte add. "They, like, actually wear 'Law and Security' on their campus jacket sleeves. Then they strip off the words 'and Security' when they go to the bars. Can you imagine them in Cult-Studs 100?"

Kayte Bubbins, generous-minded as she was, anticipated the danger of law-and-order types in the Cultural Studies first-year course, which was notorious for its radical critique of the social vision of order.

"Well, what the heck! That's a hundred and fifty warm bodies over there they don't have teachers for. Must have been all the government brouhaha about public safety. Anyway, they don't have to take a Cult-Studs elective. They can take English 100. Read Geoffrey Chaucer. Now, lookee here!"

The screen was fixed on *Nursing*.

"I spy seventy-five Florence Nightingales who could surely benefit from our Psych 100."

"Yeah, but they'd drop out by Christmas – just after they hit the

Statistics mid–term," McCabe offered.

"Well, nurses ought to know Statistics." Lassiter countered. "Isn't that's what they do all day at the nursing stations? Anyhow, they changed Psych 100 this year. The Stats part of the course has been switched around. I arranged that with the Department. Stats doesn't hit till mid–March."

"That's after we report our enrolment totals to the government. How utterly cool!" McCabe said.

"Should I do it?" the Registrar asked. He looked around at the others impiously.

Galt glanced at his watch.

Lassiter pressed the command key. "Done with the press of a button. Crisis solved. Destinies diverted through the magic of tech-nology."

Cameron Galt, who had long since stopped taking notes, sat amazed. So this was how the small universities survived!

"You kiddies run off and learn some careers and counselling skills." Saying this, Lassiter felt like a minor diabolical functionary who had accidentally admitted two innocent souls into hell. Or was it a hundred and fifty plus seventy-five innocent souls? "I'm going to phone my buddy at the Poly. Oh, and Kayte – keep this under your bra, will you?"

5

Jan D'Arnay sat alone in her small residence room trying to decide which of her personalities she should be for Avalon. Consulting her inner council of ten advisors, she came up with no clear answer. She should look around some more – study the styles at the col-lege, they said. But the college was a riot of styles. With each soft September night, a heady mixture of alcohol, music and irrespon-sibility came over the residences. It seemed the first thing students did, on being shown their room by Clio, was to set up their sound system. Immediately the air was throbbing with various styles of music, each broadcasting the identity of its owner like so many mating calls – metalhead grunge from the first floor of "M" staircase, soulful women's blues from over there on the third floor of "C", Bach's six suites for solo cello played by some unique spirit high up in "K". Jan listened instead to the cosmopolitan hissing of her espresso-maker, trying not to notice the slamming doors, gigglings and scuttlings on the fire escape, and the other sounds of young adults away from home for the first time. She felt quite singular and alone. Typically, Jilaquns had disappeared.

By the end of Orientation Week, experience began falling into pattern for most of the incoming students. Bleary-eyed newcomers, who had huddled together in uncertain groups under the care of an *amiga* at the beginning of the week, discovered the prevailing dress codes they had earlier been anxious to identify. The college now broke out in every kind of alternative clothing style imaginable, as it had since the day its oak doors opened. Students seemed sure of themselves and their course choices now. They belonged. All had met with their Academic Advisors and were ready to begin an adventure of learning with a community of scholars.

All except Jan. Having no idea whatsoever of an academic plan, she had put off seeing her Advisor. This was just as well. Her Academic Advisor was nowhere to be found. A notice on his office door demonstrated that he existed, but just barely so, as an institutional functionary:

> *Since I do not wish to consume information, I am not on e-mail and my voice-recorder is disconnected. If you want to see me, please write a polite note in big round handwriting and put it in a scented floral envelope under my door, or come down to the Virtual Café, River Street and Lebanon Avenue, where I hold office hours.*
>
> *Jeremy Lewin*

The Virt was said to be the subcultural center of Severnville. The place called for subject position number four: the existentialist café-bar habituée. Jan put on her black minidress with complicated woven black wool stockings, and took *The Stranger* by Camus. This she held against a copy of the *New York Review*. There. She was ready. She had been carrying Camus all through Orientation Week in order to mark her difference from the mob that was being institutionalized, in that way meeting other *alienées* also hanging back from the process and making their particular statements of *revoltisme*.

Like many bars started during the Recession, the Virtual Café seemed to support the lifestyle of its owner rather than profitability. The lifestyle of its owner was decidedly countercultural. Jan found herself in a long narrow room plastered with framed magazine pictures of the Rolling Stones, self-portraits by Van Gogh, and images of Elvis. Over there above the bar was Marilyn Monroe side-by-side with a photograph of Baudelaire. There was no part of any wall that wasn't covered by a picture – even the ceiling had pictures. Eclectic to the point of being a parody of itself and of all subcultural oases from the Paris cafés of the 1860s to the beatnik cafés a century later, the Virt offered a haven to every category of the marginalized and the unstraight. Tables held upper-year Avalon students with studied attitudes of burnout. At the beer-keg handles, a woman in a black leather bra with a nose-ring answered Jan's query by gesturing wearily to the back of the bar. There, a short middle-aged man sat alone at a table by the pinball machine. He was wearing a black T-shirt and reading a copy of *Fanfare* magazine.

"Hi – I'm Jan D'Arnay. I'm supposed to be your advisee."

"Sit down, sit down," Lewin said with exaggerated graciousness. "May I get you a drink?"

"I don't usually drink before breakfast," Jan said sweetly. The clock on the wall said four in the afternoon. "But I'll have a beer."

Jan went and got her beer and sat opposite Professor Lewin, rubbing her stockings together.

"Camus? How droll!" Lewin glanced at Jan's dress with feigned appreciation. "Yet I can see that you have known a better world than this one. Have you, in fact, been to Paris?"

"Oh yes – many times." Jan lied brightly. "I could have been a great Paris bum."

"I can see you barefoot on the Champs Elysées selling the *New York Herald Tribune,* wearing a Vassar sweater."

Now this is pleasant, Jan thought. Her Academic Advisor, with his shaved whitening hair and earring, had an engaging worldliness. And he was the only person in five days who wasn't going to ask her if she liked it here at Avalon and what she planned to major in.

"It's Paris, you know, where the whole carnival of modernity got started." Lewin's manner was broad, authorial and self-parodic all at once. "The trace as virtual reality. Look at all these traces! The Beatles here, Jack Kerouac over there. That big photo over the beer refrigerator is Ford Madox Ford. The place is simply a museum of traces. You know Manet's painting 'The Bar at the Folies Bergères'? There's a copy in the ladies' can. Go and look at it. That mirror behind the bar-maid reflecting appearances. The Impressionists got the right take on things. Modern culture is simply a whirl of traces held together by the exchange of commodities at high speeds. And each commodity a sign: that's what reality is."

Jan, after a week of orientation, was herself dizzily uncertain about what reality was. So she asked: "The University too?"

"Oh sure. I don't know why anyone comes to university. We don't teach knowledge at university anymore – we simply move it around electronically. Like rearranging furniture, an endless intellectual redecoration." The professor's face suddenly assumed a diabolical grin. "Go out and have fun instead – that's my advice. In fact, young lady, as your Academic Advisor, let me give you this advice right now. *Leave this place at once!* Go back to Paris and walk around in your bare feet. Watch out for the poodle shit on the pavements. Hang out for a decade. Then come back here when you're thirty-something – old enough not to believe the crap we teach. Excuse me, I've got to smoke."

All the time he was talking, the professor was rolling a cigarette.

Jan watched with fascination as Lewin's busy fingers rolled the cigarette perfectly. If the raccoons at the cottage could roll cigarettes, they wouldn't be as dextrous as Lewin was. She wondered whether or not it was vulgar to ask the question that was uppermost in her mind. Subject position number four wasn't working too well. She would have to switch subjectivities. She asked the question anyway:

"What do you teach?"

"Teach? Are you crazy?" Lewin took an immense drag on the cigarette, held it in for an eternity, then exhaled audibly. To Jan's amazement, no smoke came out with the exhalation.

"I don't teach a fucking thing."

"What do you do then?"

"I turn."

"Turn? You mean like 'turn on'?"

Lewin smiled at her with affectionate scorn. Whoops! Wrong subject position again. This man was awesome at subjectivity switching. Faster than she was. "Turn. From the Greek *tropikos*, pertaining to the apparent turning of the sun at the solstice. Also *tropos*, meaning "figure of speech." From the Greek *tropos*, "turn," related to *trepein*, "to turn." There. Have I taught you something?"

"Yes."

"Don't believe it for a moment!"

"It was something about the sun turning and a figure of speech being a kind of turn."

"The sun doesn't turn – goon-child! The earth does."

Jan looked down at her woven black wool stockings, now so hideously out-of-context. Were the legs underneath them also unreal? She'd better revert to subject position zero – a dead set or holding window for her other identities. Chastened politeness.

"What do you turn around then?"

"The just now. *The right here and now.* Modernity, if you like." Lewin grinned impiously, then summoned up another display of self-mocking pedantry. "The word *modern* derives etymologically from the Latin *modernus*, which means *just now.* Look at Baudelaire: he taught us that."

Jan glanced over to where Lewin had pointed at one of dozens of similar pictures of Baudelaire which seemed to sound a sub-theme in the Virtual Café.

"*By modernity, I mean the ephemeral, the fugitive, the contingent, the half of art whose other half is the eternal and immutable,*" Lewin quoted. "That's Baudelaire."

"Then, if Baudelaire is right, the *just now* just went."

"Good girl."

"How do you catch the *just now* then?"

"Indeed." Lewin crossed his arms across his chest with a heavy authority, which he instantly undercut. "And who am I to catch it? After all, I just went too."

"Then you have nothing to teach!" Jan exclaimed.

"Of course! Don't you remember – I said 'I don't teach.' I just turn." Lewin took a final drag on his cigarette, then stubbed it out vigorously. Why do academics destroy their cigarette ends this way? Jan wondered.

"How from the position of not having a position to figure, to refigure, the *just now*? That is the question. Hamlet asked it." With that, Lewin put his fist to his forehead, thinking Hamlet-fashion. "Ah-ha! I will put an antic disposition on. You resort to appearances. You play roles. Act out traces of antiquities: antic, antique, lunatic – get it? 'Play's the thing, in which I'll catch the conscience of the king.'"

Jan was now thinking that Professor Lewin in his black T-shirt was, in fact, Hamlet-like. She felt outfoxed. He seemed to be reading her mind just as Hamlet read Ophelia's.

"You would make a good Ophelia, my dear."

All my Hamlets, Jan thought. Laying their heads in my lap and spouting their juvenile poetry. Leaving me to float downriver in my non-being, clutching a few certainties. The names of flowers.

"I think I'll have a cigarette after all."

Again the nimble hands were busy, and lo! A cigarette. Jan lit it and took a cautious drag.

"I am not, as you have now surmised, a boring academic. I am, in fact, a theatre director."

"Here — in Severnville?"

"You seem astonished, my dear. But Severnville is no larger than Athens was when Sophocles hit town. And, like Sophocles, I arrived and looked about me and said, 'Here is a city waiting for great drama.'"

"What sort of drama?"

"Oh, I suppose 'drama' gives the wrong idea! The play is called *Hamlet Turning*. The world's slowest, longest tragedy turned on itself. Demonumentalized, so to speak. You must go and see it. It's playing at the Emma Goldman theatre in November."

"I'll certainly go," Jan said. "If you've updated *Hamlet* to figure the true here and now."

"You understand so quickly, child. I do hope you're not taking Psych 100. It's full of dreadful law-and-order bozos. But I digress. Yes — it's a take on the condition of modernity refiguring itself. Just another humble take by yours untruly. You see, Shakespeare's was a take at the beginning of the modernist epoch. Mine is at the end. But it's the same condition. The dark castle of history riddled with ghosts and hypocrisies. Everything is an appearance. Is it real? Is Hamlet's Father's ghost real? Is action of any kind in fact possible in such a theatre-set of appearances?" Lewin let the question hang ponderously, indecisively, in the air, then changed his manner abruptly. "How old do you think Hamlet is, anyway?"

"I don't know. I think a young man in his twenties. Young enough to be a romantic."

Young enough to lay his head in my lap and spout romantic nonsense, Jan thought.

"Oh you poor thing! You poor deluded thing! You're too foxy to be a romantic. Or maybe you haven't been to Paris after all? I won't ask. 'The tragedy of a man who could not make up his mind.' What romantic crap! Read the play, dear. He is in his thirties. Just back from Wittenberg U., full of state-of-the-art essentialism and a fixed subject position Descartes would kill for. Assemble the evidence. Sift it carefully. Draw conclusions tentatively. And there you have him, wandering about a medieval Danish trace museum, striking essentialist poses. Traces everywhere! Just like here."

Lewin sat bolt upright with sudden inspiration. Inspired, he became theatrical. He stood up and prowled around the bar, examining the pictures suspiciously. Frowning, he investigated the pinball machine. "Hamlet in the Virtual Café. There's something rotten in the state of truth in the universe. Things are not what they seem. Then, inevitably, he starts fondling his essentialism. 'To be or not to be.' Hands off yourself, Hamlet, you pathological essentiophile!"

Lewin resumed his place at the table and looked deeply into Jan's eyes.

"Do you now know what Hamlet's tragedy was?"

"He couldn't … um, turn?"

"*He didn't know how to read traces!* That was his tragedy."

The comment cut Jan to the quick. She considered she was rather good at reading traces.

"He's hankering after the sublime, poor dear! Just as, I suspect, you are. Because, you see, another figuring of the modern is as an intensity, an intensifying, as a breaking of limits – of, in a word, *transgression*. You want to transgress, don't you?" Lewin winked at Jan conspiratorially. "Of course, you do! Everyone does. It's just that one doesn't know where to begin anymore." Lewin again resumed his professorial manner. "In any case, to carry on (I do hope I'm not boring your stockings off) – such an intensifying is *the sublime*. As for the *tropic* itself, since in its initial meaning it is related to the turning of the sun and hence the solstices, does it not make sense to say that the condition of modernity is in pursuit of light? The pursuit after light and the sublime seem to converge with modernity."

"I have no idea what you're saying," said Jan.

"Doesn't matter. I'm just talking nonsense anyway. When I have nothing to say, I lecture. Where was I? Oh yes."

Lewin got up from the table, and strode beside the bar, lecturing to three bemused students who were sitting there.

"Let us consider the sublime as a drive after the absolute, a quest after the zero degree of the sublime itself. 'There are more things in heaven and earth, Horatio, than are dreamt of in your philosophy.'"

"The sublime presents itself as what is on the other side of the transgression," Jan ventured.

"Indeed. Wise child. Modernity has its imaginary spaces. Is the Virtual Café *really* a transgressive space, or is it just another showcase of recycled modernity?"

Lewin glared at the students in the bar, heavy with attitude and attire. "Modernity on perpetual replay. And so the modern becomes a reflective discourse about itself. That is what, finally, we call *modernism*. Modernism as a restlessness for the new and the novel – as a restless reflection upon, and a restless reconfiguring of, the modern."

He's disappearing up his own sphincter, thought Jan.

"Then are we not led to our last tropic-slash-topic?" Lewin's arm cut down through the air to indicate the diagonal slash. "*The modern reflecting upon itself as modern*. Is there anything after the modern? What 'posts' the modern?"

Again, Lewin let the question hang portentously in the air as he did a little pirouette apparently under it, finally folding his hands before him.

"Oh fuck it anyway! I don't believe any of this," he said.

The professor looked so downcast and abject. Jan felt like giving him a hug. That was probably a transgression. She thought of the next best thing.

"I'd like to take *your* course."

"Would you? Really? You are so kind, my dear. You know, my

colleagues won't let me lecture in Cultural Studies 100. They think I'm unsound. But they're really afraid of something. Do you know what they're really afraid of?"

Jan smiled and shook her head.

"They're afraid I'll unmask their teaching. Pull them out of their intellectual closets. In fact, the poor dears can't make up their minds what to teach – neo-marxist pomposity or poststructuralist total heaviosity. Really, they *are* so solemn. They actually think they have something to teach! Yet they are virtually indistinguishable – I call them Rosencrantz and Guildenstern. Academics on the make. Thus I am reduced to conducting my own course within a course. You're quite welcome to join. The final assignment is to do a performance piece that deconstructs their lectures. A play within a play, so to speak."

Lewin, brightening into a version of one of his old selves, jumped up suddenly from the table.

"Come – let's away! Let us put an antic disposition on. Only by ascending to lies do we achieve the ring of truth."

He took Jan by the arm and led her out into the September sunshine.

"'Play's the thing, in which we'll catch the conscience of the king.'"

6

Cameron Galt gazed out his office window in Lady Sears College with a vague pride in his new university. He was beginning to bond with the place. Like the new students gathered in expectant groups on the college forecourt, his first and enduring wonder was the architecture and the sense it gave of a significant leisurely community. The buildings and walkways and footbridges played hide and seek with each other through the trees, bending back on their intentions mischievously, so that one felt in an Einsteinian universe present to itself in all places at once. The milieu, like the architecture, also had no center nor circumference but was present to itself everywhere at once as conversation. For yes – the place was an ongoing conversation. During an hour of office work, Galt had watched one upper-year student leave Sears College and cross the footbridge to Cabot College a hundred yards away. Over that hundred yards she had engaged in dozens of conversations as tiny societies formed and dissolved and formed again to talk. Each conversation began with joyful hugs – these seemed to be part of the ceremony of student life at Avalon. Even now the student was stalled in talk on the river bridge leading to the Ecology building and the Mall, her presumed destination, the site of more conversation. One couldn't move anywhere at this place without being caught in a morning's worth of talk. The university was held together by chatter. For the first time, Galt realized he had come, not to an institution, but to an oral village. He was to be Dean and Provost of an oral village.

This prospect excited him because his academic field was communications theory. Galt could practice what he had preached in his published PH.D. thesis on the differences between types of oral and technological messaging. In this he would be aided by his Executive Assistant who combined the art of gossip with an astonishing technological efficiency. It was time to call Sheena in to brief him on the crises at hand.

"Crises? No, nothing major. I guess you know we had an enrolment shortfall – but the numbers popped up mysteriously over the weekend … "

Galt listened to Sheena Meganetty's singsong voice, appreciating its power to calm unsettled faculty calling the dean's office about every petty thing. She was a woman of disguised middle age with intense green eyes and scarlet hair ablaze with henna. A plaited skirt of Indian cotton, patterned in browns, reached almost to her Birkenstocks – and what was this? A tattoo of a rose on her inner ankle. Around her neck she wore an amulet. Galt received a whiff of dark incense and the impression of small shops with chimes over the door where women bought self-enhancement books which they read in scented candlelit baths.

" … what else? Oh, A.W.C. … "

"A.W.C.?"

"The Avalon Women's Caucus. That's basically Hannah Janssen-Koeslag in Anthropology. They've issued a blacklist of courses they deem aren't positive for women and racial minorities. I'd just leave that one alone, if I were you. We've got a big Human Rights versus Academic Freedom row going on here."

Galt nodded appreciatively.

"Oh − and the Spanish Year Abroad Program has vanished off the face of the map."

"It's what?"

"It's gone. We can't find it."

Galt gave a waving motion with his hand, inviting elaboration.

"The Spanish Department runs a year abroad program in Mallorca for its majors. About twenty of them. We got a phone call last week from a student who'd flown over late to join the program. He found a sign at the university − we rent the facilities of the Universidad de las Palmas" (Sheena pronounced the Spanish perfectly) − "saying phone such-and-such a number for directions, which he did. Now he's disappeared along with the others."

"And the directions? Did you get the number?"

"Then the number disappeared too."

Galt slapped his knee with weary frustration. "Who's our staff member over there?"

"Jerónimo. We just call him Jerónimo. It's the name he uses officially. He's become a painter − you know, like Miró."

"Hmm!"

"His phone is disconnected."

"Any calls from anxious parents wondering where their kids are?"

"None."

"Let's hope they're off on a field-trip to Barcelona." With that remark Galt sealed the matter off for wait-and-see review. He was ready for the next crisis on his Assistant's list. But Sheena looked like she was containing something.

"There are levels to this," she said ominously.

Galt raised an eyebrow.

"Jenny Seton – I mean Jennifer D'Arnay. Do you know who she is?"

"Oh, indeed I do."

"She's Jerónimo's companion. They've been on and off for years, but people say they're an item now. What I suspect is they've set up a studio together in Granada."

"A studio together in Granada." Galt repeated slowly.

"So he can get away from his in-laws in Mallorca, you see. They are a prominent Mallorca family. They're out to kill him. Jerónimo probably had to get out of Las Palmas quickly, the poor dear!"

"Are you telling me the entire Spanish Year Abroad Program migrated to Granada overnight?"

"Yes."

"How do you know that?"

"Because the phone number Jerónimo left for the late student disappeared. That's the clue. Jerónimo can't be traced by his wife's family."

"Ah-ha! So I suppose the change of location of a part of Avalon University didn't receive the approval of Senate. Heavens! – did the matter go through any official body? Did it even go through the Spanish Department? I'm afraid to ask."

"No, of course not!" The way his Assistant said that suggested it was perfectly normal for programs to pack up and walk off overnight to another part of the map. As it was normal for an Avalon course to end abruptly because someone had murdered its instructor. Galt, from his graduate years in California, remembered a certain Hispanic style of arbitrariness. He began pondering the Board's reaction to this, especially D'Arnay's reaction, which would be another kind of arbitrariness.

"*Qué será, será!*" sang Sheena's voice suggestively, breaking in on his thoughts.

"Hmm, I suppose you're right. We'll just let Jennifer and Jerónimo and the Spanish Year Abroad quietly be — wherever they are." Then Galt changed his tone to one of administrative decision-making. "What appointments have I got?"

Sheena's eyes seemed to flash a brighter green at the change of tone. "A delegation from the Center for the First Nations — they'll be here shortly. Then the President of the Faculty Union at 9:30. Oh, and Bud Lassiter will be popping in with the late admissions list."

"Okay."

Galt leaned back in his armchair with a sense of satisfied authority while his Executive Assistant returned to the outer office. That was a good move, to greet the Center for the First Nations Council as his first formal act. The council represented more than just the rights of the many Native students at Avalon. It also claimed the earth on which the university was built. That earth, according to some contested treaty, was an ancestral hunting ground. It would be a good start to his provostship to have the Center for the First Nations on his side. On the other hand, Ruairi MacDonald, eternal head of the faculty union, was also a force to be reckoned with. The union spokesperson would normally be among the first people for a new dean to meet, the dean being technically head of the faculty. In any case, as provost and dean Galt was establishing his managerial double position. It would be one of balancing these two hats he wore against each other. And he had established his managerial style — a blend of decisiveness and the laid back. His Assistant had responded in kind. That style, which had worked so well at the Greater Metropolitan University, would with Sheena Meganetty's teamwork bring Avalon inevitably, irresistibly, implacably, under new management.

Sheena's iridescent red hair seemed to fill the doorway. "Joseph Waasagunackank is here with his people."

Cameron Galt rose from his chair to meet the delegation. Waasa-gunackank simply gave Galt one firm shake of the hand. "Joe," he said. "This here is Tom Baptiste." Galt shook hands with the Chair of the Center for the First Nations, a trim young academic in conventional tweed jacket and grey flannel pants and roll-neck sweater. He could be in any department, from Business Adminis-tration to Astrophysics, Galt thought. The third member of the delegation was different, however. She wore a studded black leather jacket over a black mini dress over long johns, with a single eagle feather separating her breasts and an ornament embedded in her lower lip. As she entered the office, she took off a motorcycle hel-met to reveal long black hair, which she shook out theatrically down to her waist. Joe introduced her, saying a long tribal name that came from the back of the throat, which Galt couldn't pro-nounce let alone remember.

"So," said Waasagunackank. "We welcome you to our land."

"I'm glad to be here," Galt said politely.

"We will begin with a smudging ceremony."

"Smudging ceremony?"

"Oh, yeah. We'll burn some sage and purify the place. The guy before you – he messed it up real good. Gotta tell the spirits who you are and why you're here. They already know that anyways – but we gotta ask them permission for you to use power in their land."

"Of course," said Galt.

The elder surveyed Galt with an easy gravity and a sly inturned wit.

"Then we'll talk about some things."

Galt tried to empty his mind of attitude. Yet he couldn't help wondering whether Sheena Meganetty would be pleased by this or not. The place already smelled of her sandalwood incense: pre-sumably, she had her own spirits to placate.

Joe looked up at the ceiling, found the smoke detector, and immediately de-activated it. Galt knew that this would cause a light to show red on the fire safety panel at the college Porter's Lodge and at Physical Plant and Maintenance. How long would it be before the maintenance staff showed up?

Joe was leisurely spreading his medicine on the seminar table in the middle of the room. This is where they sat: Joe at the head of the table in the dean's armchair, Tom Baptiste opposite him, and Galt at Joe's right hand. The woman took the seat opposite Galt and proceeded to stare at him profoundly.

Tumbling clouds of sage smoke filled the room. The three natives in turn waved the sweetness towards their faces, the student taking exceptional care to waft it in her jet-black hair and onto her long lean arms. Galt, thinking of what he would smell like at the upcoming Board meeting, did the same, pulling the scent onto his best blue suit. Doing so selfconsciously, he felt like every government agent who had ever sat across from a native chief in the history of the white expansion of America. But unlike those government officials, Galt now felt utterly powerless in his role as provost and dean – even more so when Joe, to Galt's astonishment, having waved the smoke in the four directions of the room, then carefully purified the dean's desk and his computer. All this time, Galt felt the level gaze of the woman burning into his mind. Her power seemed to be related in some way to the eagle feather which she was now holding. Galt tried not to notice the eagle feather.

"How can I help you?" is what he finally said when it was over.

The elder laughed suddenly. Great bellyfuls of mirth bubbled up inside him. "Ho, ho, ho!" he laughed. "That's funny. You tell him," he said, gesturing to Baptiste "how he can help us."

The First Nations Chair spoke in clipped efficient burst of information. Now this was a discourse Galt could deal with. He was beginning to feel some of his old power coming back to him – if only Eagle Woman would stop staring at him.

" ... among the issues unresolved from last year is the matter of Aboriginal membership on the Board of Governors. We have reserved the right to nominate our *own* representative, or representatives" – Professor Baptiste looked at the Dean over the top of his glasses meaningfully – "not *your* appointee."

"I'll put that to the Board this afternoon," Galt said pleasantly. "I can't see why they'd say no."

Professor Baptiste broke in impatiently. Apparently, it was Galt's role to listen to all the concerns, not comment on each one *seriatim*.

"The question of an enclosed First Nations study space on the third floor of the Library. The administration was supposed to construct this during the summer. But, regrettably, nothing has happened."

"Yeah," said the student. "We need our own space. We can't work in all that shit downstairs. We need windows that open too. We're used to being outdoors."

"Jilaquns of the Qayahllaanas is saying that our peoples need to be in touch with our Mother, the Earth, and the spirit-beings," Joe said gravely.

Galt looked at Jilaquns thoughtfully.

"Our proposed PH.D. in Aboriginal Metaphysics is held up at Senate," Baptiste continued. "A Native PH.D. program based on ancestral teachings, and someone is questioning its academic integrity."

"That someone is Ruairi MacDonald. Fascist doink!" added the student.

"It may be time to discuss our own academic decision-making structure," Baptiste warned.

"You mean a structure outside of Senate?"

"Yes."

Galt glanced over at Joe. The elder was pondering the matter impassively.

"The President of the Faculty Union is questioning our listing our tribal affiliations in university documents. It is offensive and explicitly racist of him to do that."

Galt sidestepped the accusation. "I've seen tribal affiliations listed in lots of college calendars. I don't see anything wrong with it. In fact, I think it's a good idea."

Joe nodded agreeably.

"But, about the Aboriginal study space in the Library. I don't see how we could replace the plexiglass windows and let some air in for you. They're built into the structure."

Galt wished as he said this that he could open a window in his own air-tight office. The sage smoke had risen to form a thick pall against the ceiling, like a mushroom cloud.

"That means you couldn't do ... ah, smudging ceremonies in there. But I personally don't see anything objectionable about a Native Studies Resource Area, though you might have to let non-Natives use it."

"We don't want whites in there," the student said flatly.

Galt, sensing his power as dean return to him, responded in his normal administrative style, which was a mixture of diplomatic reasoning and bullying.

"Then you'll have a discrimination issue, won't you?"

"I don't give a fuck," said the student.

"Maybe non-Natives can come in as our guests," Joe offered tactfully.

"Yeah — same as on reserves!" the student responded.

"That raises a larger issue," Professor Baptiste said, as if on cue. "The Faculty Union Executive is attacking the draft Anti-Harassment and Discrimination policy. That policy is our only protection against racist viewpoints in the classroom."

"You mean the clause about an environment conducive to dignity and self-esteem?" Galt countered. "That's been a touchy issue elsewhere, you know. The clause is as big as a barn door and dangerously vague. A racial slur — or at least a pattern of racist slurs — is offensive. Is a faculty member's Eurocentrism offensive in the same way?"

"Yes, it is," said the student, with a fed-up weariness. "You white liberals don't seem to get it! Let me explain. Rights don't fall from the sky — they are manufactured at staggering rates of exploitation. They're politically produced and enter the ethical mainstream by way of the checks and balances required for the stable problem-free exponential growth of the fascist democracies in the West."

Galt, without any difficulty this time, put on his best blank face.

"So what I'm saying is that a right like Academic Freedom is the ethical by-product of imperialism. Imperial Europe and North America produce and reproduce an acquired right like Freedom of Expression through the mass media. That's one way the acquired rights of *your* culture dominate the acquired rights of *my* culture. They dominate the ethical, cultural and political scene. The rights of others to produce new rights, ethics and freedoms don't stand a fucking chance."

The office seemed to fill up with guilty silence. Galt crossed and uncrossed his legs uneasily.

"Hey – she'd make a good professor," Joe said. "Why don't you give her a job here?"

The student couldn't restrain a small smile.

Galt, utterly defeated, resumed his role as institutional balancer. "Well, what can I say? We'll have to let the community fight it out at the policy language level. Speaking as Provost, we need a policy that allows marginalized voices to be heard and appreciated. Speaking as Dean, I can understand the Faculty Union's conviction about Academic Freedom."

The student threw up her hands with a sigh. "You still don't get it! Academic Freedom is merely a way of letting white racist bourgeois males spew out their colonialist bullshit. Profs have total power around here. Power needs to be accountable."

At that moment, there was a loud knocking on the dean's office door. Galt got up from the table and opened it. It was the College Porter peering in anxiously. "Everything all right here? The security board's showing red on your smoke-alarm system."

"Everything's okay, thank you. We were just ... er, cleansing the office."

"Sure," said the Porter doubtfully. He put his head in the door and peered around the room.

"Joe here was just burning some sage grass."

"Oh, I gotcha."

The Porter disappeared, leaving the door open between the dean's office and the outer office where the secretaries worked. Time was getting on. Galt had two more appointments before meeting the Board. Outside, he could hear uncontrollable sneezing and exclamations from the secretaries.

"I guess that's all we can do today."

The delegation rose to leave, Tom Baptiste first, clicking his briefcase shut, then the student, giving Galt a last unsteadying look, then Joe, who had made himself comfortable in the dean's chair and seemed unwilling to be moved quickly, if at all. Finally he got up and stretched out a thorny hand to Galt. "You can get to work now. The spirits are pleased to share their power with you."

"*Megwetj*," Galt said, cashing in his only word of Ojibway.

The sage smoke, hanging against the office ceiling like cloud cover, now drifted in purposeful wisps out the top of the door into the outer office. Lassiter came in jauntily, carrying a sheaf of computer printout. "Hi, guys! Smells like California in here."

Sheena was in the doorway. "Professor MacDonald is waiting to see you. Oh, and this smoke is going to … "

"We'll be quick," Galt said, cutting her off. "Now, what's the situation, Bud?"

Just then the sprinkler system went off in the outer office. Alarm bells rang simultaneously throughout the college. There were screams and frantic activity as the secretaries rushed to cover the computers. The delegation from the First Nations backed out of the drizzle into the dean's office. Outside Sheena was shouting directions.

"Try to get the equipment out into the corridor."

"This is too heavy – I can't move it. Oh *shit!*"

"The sprinklers are on in the corridor too!"

"Get it all in here then!" Galt bellowed. "The sprinkler's not working in my office."

A giant with a ponytail stood in Galt's doorway, carrying a laser printer. "*MacDonald!*" he shouted, emphasizing each syllable equally, proudly formal even in the midst of crisis. "Welcome to Avalon. A Third-World university with state-of-the-art technology. Ha!"

"We'll talk later," Galt said.

"The late admissions records!" Sheena screamed.

Two secretaries, hair bedraggled, make-up streaming down their faces, were dashing back and forth between the offices, carrying disc trays and printout. MacDonald was now pushing Sheena's entire desk with its built-in computer towards the dean's office. With a soggy ponytail and water dripping off his beard, he was puffing and wheezing terribly. The native delegates had resumed their places at the dean's table, Joe looking relaxed again in Galt's armchair and grinning with mirth. Outside, the fire alarms rang idiotically. A steady drizzle rained down from the sprinklers which were still spraying the outer office.

"Just like home in the Islands," Jilaquns remarked.

The College Porter was back, taking in the situation. "We'll have to shut 'er off at the mains."

"Better call the Fire Station first," Sheena suggested.

"Oh yeah," said the Porter.

But it was too late. Already Galt could hear the distant sirens as trucks from the North Severnville Fire Station responded to the fire alarm signal that had rung through automatically to their status board.

"It's okay – they're radio dispatched. We can phone in and cancel the alarm. You'd better do it." Sheena, cool in any emergency, handed Galt's phone to the Porter. The Porter pounded the buttons frantically.

"Phone's dead," he announced.

"Go out there in the rain and call them."

The Porter held a file folder over his head for protection and went to the outer office. He tried the phones. "Nothin' workin' out here neither."

"I must have pulled all the wires out of the wall when I was moving the desk," MacDonald confessed apologetically.

"I'll go call on my cell," the Porter said, leaving the room.

Galt stood dripping wet and powerless in his office, surrounded by his Executive Assistant, the two secretaries, the three members of the First Nations Center, the Registrar and the Head of the Faculty Union. Glancing out the window, he saw a crowd of excited students gathering on the forecourt of Sears. More students were streaming out of the building, carrying their sound systems. Galt was aware that the group behind him was also looking out the window. He turned around and put on his best diplomatic manner.

"Does everybody here know each other?"

Professor MacDonald, at the forefront of any social situation involving formality, surveyed the faces before him, bowing courteously to each one in turn. "I don't believe I've had the pleasure of meeting the young lady."

"Jilaquns of the Sealion clan of Qaysun of Haida Gwaay," the student said noncommittally.

MacDonald stretched out a giant hand to Jilaquns. "Ruairi Mac-Donald of Clanranald of Moindart and the Isle of Rhum."

"You can fuck off," Jilaquns said.

"Sure, lassie. And the same to you."

"Okay, take it easy," Galt said sharply. "We're all in this rain-filled boat together."

"And you, sir, if I'm not mistaken, are a descendant on your mother's side of … " MacDonald paused to let the great syllables gather, each carrying its explosive historical weight " … of the illustrious Iain Garbh Cameron – he who bore our wounded chieftain, Grant of Curriemony, on his back all the way to Glenurquhart after the slaughter at Culloden on that terrible sixteenth of April, seventeen hundred and forty-six."

"Yes, my mother's name was Cameron," Galt offered weakly.

"Then shake the hand of your kinsman," boomed MacDonald extending his great hand again. "I can tell a guid Cameron across the glen."

Returning the handshake, Galt now felt humbled by another kind of presence. He stood silently, shaking hands with a giant whose own hand would not let go of his, but seemed to infuse a historic warmth. Still MacDonald held his hand in a vice-like grip of feudal allegiance, his eyes rolling wildly.

"It never rains but it pours," Sheena Meganetty said with a nervous gaiety. "Now where are those late admissions files?"

"I didn't see them," said one of the secretaries.

"I didn't either," said the other.

Fire trucks had now pulled up outside the window. Firefighters in full gear complete with oxygen tanks were charging into the building. Soon they were in the outer office, gazing up at the sprinklers. The fire station chief had a lean red face and a bushy moustache; water dripped off the eaves of his helmet. In his hands, a waterproof laptop computer showed the safety plan of the college. "Bill, you go down and shut it off. It's control point blue zero-zero-one, at the Porter's Lodge. What the hell's a porter, anyway?" Then he strode into the dean's inner office. "You people alright? Having a party, are you?"

"Well, not exactly … " Galt said.

"Okay – everyone outside. We'll do a preliminary damage assessment so you can alert your insurer."

Outside on the forecourt of Sears, Galt stood in his limp blue suit, enduring the analysis of a crowd of students and faculty. The red light on the pumper truck swung round and round. More students were calling down anxiously from upper-story residence windows. Galt heard a familiar voice in the crowd behind him. It was the voice of Faith Rackstraw. She was explaining as if to a first-year seminar a subtle point of textual interpretation. "Débâcle. That's the word for it. To be … er, *correct*, you want to spell it with the *French* acute accent and the circumflex. You know, the word refers originally to a sudden rush of water, like a flood. Then it has come to mean … er, a *stampede*, a rout, and by one of those curious extensions of etymology, a downfall, as in the *downfall* of a government."

Then a mirthful aged voice beside Galt.

"I guess we cleansed your office real good." Joe said. "Ho, ho."

7

"D'Arnay thought it was pretty funny," Galt said to Sally. "And the Board appreciated my initiative in making an effort with the natives."

"Umm."

In the cool September night, the fire was drawing well, though the fireplace had not been used since the spring.

"I notice Hugh didn't invite us over to his cottage for drinks," Sally observed. "That's what I would have expected for your first week as Dean."

She extended her stockinged leg from the wicker chair until her toes touched Cameron's toes with a decisive nudge. Wifely solicitude, with just a hint of reproach.

"His daughter's taken over the cottage," Galt said. "She's at Avalon, you know. Do you remember Jan?"

"Yes – Jan the water skier. You seemed to like her legs, if I recall."

Again the hint of warning. Sally had her sexual politics antennae up, that was for certain. Is this what Avalon did to people?

Outside the loon called across the bay.

Cameron remembered Jan slaloming expertly past the boat dock. That was … how many summers ago? It seemed like yesterday. He had brought Sally to the cottage for the first time that summer, both of them with PH.D.s complete and ready to begin their academic careers at Metro. Sally, free at last from the hothouse of her family, was all excitement and new beginnings. The cottage suddenly lost its mustiness – it had been a kind of prolonged honeymoon. Then work came, and with work the wordless division of roles of modern relationships, so that they were not husband and wife – they had never been that – nor even partners; they were more like what D'Arnay had called them during the job interview – a team, an academic team. Galt and Galt – like a law firm. At least Sally had put her family name along with her entire family behind her. Yet Cameron felt a distance from Sally which he hoped living together at the cottage would diminish. The cottage closed everything up: summer succeeded summer here in the eternal coherence of place. The place of his boyhood. It would be a sanctuary from the overstimulation of Avalon. Even now, Galt felt the pull of the institution like an immense vortex. He understood why so many faculty and students actually became Avalon.

"Hannah has an absolutely super policy in the works on Sexual Harassment," Sally was saying. "It's the best in the country. It's going to give Avalon a model gender-relations environment. And look at the Student Union Executive! Every one of them a woman, and most of them from visible minorities."

"Well, old Ruairi won't like the policy much. He'll be dragged into it kicking and screaming"

"Maybe he'll take Early Retirement and let us rebuild Avalon from the ground up."

This wasn't precisely Cameron's sentiment. Not being a revolutionary by nature, the suggestion of radical change triggered every one of his cautious administrative reflexes. He had an applecart to guide through a hectic marketplace. He observed again that Sally was full of the political enthusiasm that seemed to infect everybody at Avalon. He had never seen her quite like this before. The spirit of change and the spirit of traditionalism – these seemed the strongest forces at Avalon, stronger than research, stronger even than teaching.

Again the loon called. This time the sound came from around the point. The loon called with a timelessness oblivious to human change or human fixity.

"The loon's still here," he said.

"What about the Board meeting?" Sally asked, pressing him further back into the day.

"Oh – it went okay. There's a lot of fuss about the *Choosing Your College* magazine rankings. We're going to have to do a proper job on promotion next year. All the Board is concerned about is Avalon coming out on top of the small university category in the ratings."

"The Anti-Discrimination and Harassment policy will certainly put us on that map."

"Maybe. But you've got to find the thin line. The policy could cost us some alumni donations."

"C'mon – let's go to bed," Sally said. "I'll help you find your thin line."

★　★　★

"Don't put the roach in the fire," Jilaquns said. "Fire is one of the portals to the spirit world." She reached into Jan's fireplace with an arm apparently insensitive to flame, plucked the marijuana end out, and gave it back to Jan. "You don't want to give the spirits your waste. It sends the wrong message."

Jan giggled, far beyond solemnity or etiquette. "Sorry! I thought they'd like a toke. After all, they gave us the stuff to use."

"They appreciate tobacco," Jill replied sternly. "Especially with clamshells. But then you offer it as a gift."

Outside, the September night in complete stillness curved like a womb around the cottage. The stars were ripe fruit on the axletree of the universe. Around the point from the bay a loon babbled insanity in the night.

"The Dean is a nematode," Jill announced. "The Head of the Faculty Union is a Hudson's Bay Company trader. And the faculty are dead white males, except for a few bourgeois feminist profs. We've got a lot of work to do here."

Jan, zoned out on grass, didn't feel much like doing work. She didn't feel like politics either, for that matter. Dope had the opposite effect, however, on Jilaquns. She was rippling with galvanic currents of energy.

"You heard I'm Aboriginal Affairs Commissioner on the Student Union Executive? The sisterhood appointed me. Now the majority of the Executive is aboriginal. And some of them are two-spirited."

Two-spirited was Jill's term for lesbian.

"Anyway — there's a vacancy for a member-at-large. You sure you don't want it?"

"I'm not even sure I'll be here by Christmas."

"Oh Jan — stop being a ruling-class flake!"

"I'm not a flake — you know that! It's just that there's nothing to learn here. They don't teach knowledge. I mean there doesn't seem to be a thing called knowledge anymore — just attitudes and approaches to it. Knowledge management. Nothing to grow inside."

Jan paused. The effort of making the statement collapsed her mellowness, like air escaping from a balloon. "What are you taking anyway?"

"Who's here to study? I'm here to repossess this place for aboriginal civilization."

"What about your scholarship?"

"Fuck scholarships. They're for elitist twits."

"Jill — you're a grade A, class one, turbo-driven fruitcake."

Jilaquns laughed one of her body laughs — she could sound like a loon sometimes. "We've got to get you on the Union Executive! Then we can swing you onto Senate as a student rep when the Anti-Harassment and Discrimination policy comes up for debate."

"I don't know," Jan replied. Really she did not know. Beneath the power of the British Columbia Thunderbird Jill had produced from her medicine pouch, grass which was now making Jan's consciousness expand omnidirectionally to the farthest reaches of space-time, she heard the faint voices of ancestral obligation like a receding chorus. Public service was in her genes, she knew. But also canny unconscious political trip-wires, one of which was sounding now. This would not be a good use to put the D'Arnay name to. What if she got into a political situation with her father?

The loon called again, rounding the point. A cry that was the voice of wilderness itself. The primal.

"Loon Woman," Jill said. "If she hadn't heard the homeless spirits crying, the Gull-White Elder wouldn't have created this world to make a place for them. It's a woman who starts things, as usual. If it weren't for her, the Great Spirit would still be dreaming."

That's more like the old Jilaquns, Jan thought. It was a kind of womanhood she could relate to. Soft and mystical and eternal. It was why she'd invited Jill, herself a sort of homeless spirit, to live with her at the cottage. Jan wanted to be free of men for awhile, especially the men she had met so far at Avalon. At best, they were shaggy Ecology-Philosophy majors with their knees protruding with a studied indifference through holes they'd carefully ripped in their jeans. Sensitive stud-muffins concealing beneath a generous friendliness the age-old patriarchal hatreds. The kind who would patiently delay and delay the intended seduction, then swiftly take away from Jan the feminine mellowness she was feeling tonight. Her being relaxed again at the thought of that femininity. All she wanted was to be at one with the cosmos, at one with her lake, at one with her friend Jill.

"I need a boy-toy," Jilaquns announced.

Jan wandered out to the porch to be under the stars. From the porch, she found herself somehow on the boat dock, the place of her happiest and most secure moments. The water gurgling underneath the dock sang of a permanence of cottage summers reaching back to earliest childhood memory. The stars came closer to watch her. Loon Woman called again – a gothic chant that made the flesh tingle. Jan felt she could reach up and squeeze the stars until silvery star-juice ran down her arms.

"We don't see them much where I come from." Jill was beside her now. The two women stood together under the cavern of the heavens. Lake water lapped gently under the boat-dock.

"*Oda-Ka-Daun Anakwak.* Those three stars there."

"Orion's Belt. We call them Orion's Belt."

"The people here call them the Stern Paddler. He circles around *Nemetahamum*, the Bow Paddler. You see, the sky is a giant canoe."

"Which is the Bow Paddler?"

"The one you call the North Star. Polaris."

"It's beautiful, isn't it?"

"And look – there's the Girls Who Married Stars, and those are their Star Husbands. The sky is full of stories. And Fisher – *Ojig.* You call him The Big Dipper."

"Or *Ursa Major* – the Great Bear. We have a story too, or at least the Greeks did. *Kallisto*, the Bear Woman. She was the daughter of the Wolf Chief, *Lykaon*. The story is up there now, with yours. The Cub and the Great Bear."

"Fisher. See? – he has a broken tail. Joe told me he broke his tail getting the Girls Who Married Stars out of the tallest tree in the world. They fell into that tree one day when Spider Woman was letting them down."

"Which one is Spider Woman?"

"I don't know. Joe didn't say."

Jan looked down at the lake, every star reflected perfectly in its stillness. "C'mon – let's take a dip in the Milky Way!"

She started to take her clothes off. Jill took hers off too. In the silence of the north, under the pageant of the stars, that pageant reflected in the lake's abeyance, the two girls stood. Then they dove together. One, leggy and blond, dove into the Great Bear; the other, slim and dark with raven hair, into the Bow Paddler.

Part Two
NOVEMBER

8

September gave everything it had to the promise of education. It was a long drawn-out autumn that year at Avalon, with night frosts taking the trees as if in stop-action frames through stages of florid protest. Jan, making the drive every day from her cottage through the boreal forest, and coming to know some of the trees as individuals, felt she could see them in the very act of turning. Some trees shook off their leaves in one decisive gesture, plunging headlong into winter to meet their fate with a suicidal clarity. Others hung back and hung back as if remembering summer romances, those green memories reddening by degrees at the edges until memory itself was lost. One familiar maple, standing in its leaves at the lip of the Severnville Valley, went brilliantly insane just as Jan's van passed it. She put this sign of mutability behind her in the rearview mirror, and forged on with a renewed if fragile purpose. Shopping at the outdoor farmers' market with the other students, and sharing in their buoyant shaping of new lives for themselves, she was gradually becoming part of the community of Avalon.

Then the October rains came to take education through another of its moods. Long stains of moisture darkened the rubble surface of the college walls. Mists rose up from the river in the morning, making the students hurrying between classes seem like ghosts. Essay topics and lab assignments had been given out now; a sense of obligation framed the earlier dream of freedom. But still the obligation seemed remote to undergraduates who were redefining themselves almost daily in the social complexities of community. Jan, previously aware of people as stereotypes, began to know them by the stories they attracted. This was Ashley Tiffin, the nursing student from the Polytech, who had carried an injured team-mate on her shoulders off the rugger field and all the way to the Health Center. That was Victor Bosko, who had caused a shock-wave throughout the campus by challenging the Student Union Executive to end funding of "special interest groups" – and then he had gone on to list them: the Gay Collective, the Ecology Garden, Day Care, Take Back the Nite March, the Womyns' Center, and the Aboriginal Students' Association at Avalon. How quickly stories attached themselves to people here! Jan wondered what stories would attach themselves to her. Nothing so absolute as the narratives that burdened others, she hoped. She changed her identity daily in order to shrug off the pressing weight of stories.

October became November. Trees that had pressed their redness against the morning mists now seemed transfixed in their death agonies, clawing at the sky for warmth and light. And still the Avalon students went on talking, standing in the first snowflakes in their sandals. Jan realized Avalon was not like the other universities where people came out of their lectures with blank faces, jettisoned into the daily world of traffic and aloneness. Here at Avalon, going to classes was an interruption of a conversation – a conversation that was resumed, with some new faces, an hour later. Jan, alone at the cottage, began to miss the conversation. Jilaquns was not there for Jan to share her education with.

Where was Jill anyway? Jill was a good friend, but the trouble was she was a nomad. She couldn't seem to decide whether to stay at the cottage with Jan or find her own place. So she did both, coming and going unpredictably. Sometimes she would be gone for a week, then suddenly she would be blasting along the shoreline on her motorcycle just in time for dinner, resuming a monologue as if she had just stepped out for an hour. The monologue involved protecting the student union from "that fascist doink" Victor Bosko and his counter-revolution of Nursing students.

"The syringe-heads are at college for the first time, and they think university's one huge mindless party – you know, football games and beer and cheerleaders and rah! rah! college."

"Maybe we can educate our keepers," Jan suggested.

"Educate? Get real! They're not here for education."

Jan found this remark of Jill's incredibly funny.

"They've already turned the Library into a sorority," Jilaquns went on. "Sitting around and striking Buffyish poses. Shit! – it's, like, a soap opera exploded out of a TV set, and nobody can find a way to stuff it back in the box … "

Jilaquns' voice was approaching a growl.

" … plus they're in our faces about student union accountability."

"Well, you said yourself, power needs to be accountable."

"Why the fuck should marginalized others be accountable? If Bosko doesn't like what we're doing, he can impeach us." Jilaquns angrily dumped a log into the woodstove, sending up an explosion of sparks and smoke. Jan was nestled in her wicker chair with her morning coffee. She gazed out at a faint November sun struggling to rise far down the lake to the south. The islands, with their cottages closed for the winter, seemed separate and alone. Over on the other side of the world, civilization was awake and halfway through a day. She decided to check her e-mail.

"Oh god! A letter from Mom! Are you ready for this?"

"I can take it!" Jilaquns declared, arranging her legs in the other wicker chair.

"She's in London," Jan said. Then she settled in to read the letter out loud:

Dear Daughter:

Your Errant Mother confesses to a keen discomfort with neo-conservative London with its knock-offs of her erstwhile husband everywhere in the ascendancy, if anything leaner and meaner while lacking his redeeming capriciousness. Noting that post-Thatcherite, Tony Blair let-'er-rip capitalism does nothing for the classic English mind-body split except exaggerate that disjunction to the point of national crisis, she is inclined to avoid the company of gentlemen altogether, the better to exercise that highmindedness that is so becoming to womanhood. Even now as she sits in a pub, typing on her faithful laptop companion and trying not to resemble an intellectual Hampstead crumpet, your Errant Mom is being checked out by two Thames Television producers with vengeance in their eyes and confusion in their balls. Ah me! The ceremony of innocence is drowned here, as everywhere, in global capitalism. Nevertheless she is bemused by the resilient continuities of English life — the smells of diesel fumes, fish and chips, curry; the paganism of Church of England vicars; tabloid sexuality; the Royal soap opera; the battle of Europhiles *versus* Europhobes; intelligent TV; the singsong elegy of wind and weather and seasons of the year in the voices of an island people. Nonetheless, your Wayward Mom is not long for this place with its muggings in the streets and its steady drip-drip-drip of rain on north London brick. She will correspond next from Paris — this with some guilt in her heart, it being a particular defect of her parenting that she never introduced her Gentle Daughter to the pleasures of Paris — *tant pis!* — an omission that will be rectified by the magic of facsimile and electronic mail.

"Is this woman for real?" Jilaquns remarked.
Jan smiled and continued reading:

To reply to your query — yes, your Errant Mom's reunion with Lynda Rideout served only to remind both erstwhile classmates of the passage of the years. Rideout, in spite of two decades' residency in the British Isles, four apple-cheeked brats full of a pesky pertinency and marriage to a Bank of England C.E.O., failed to show even the slightest crack in her Bishop Rye Head Girl

manner. This was predictable. Having dropped more
LSD than her entire graduating year at Bishop Rye, there
was no discernible effect even then on a manner which
today she flaunted as the two of us, braiding each other's
dyed hair nostalgically in red, yellow and blue ribbon,
went shopping at Claridges. It was Rideout, your Errant
Mom recalls, who introduced your E. M. to The Grate-
ful Dead at a concert where Lynda, overcome by the
phallic pulse of the first giant California speakers erect-
ed in Metro, took off her blouse and danced naked before the appreciative and loving masses, swinging her
already matronly breasts to the music in a monstrous
display of *noblesse oblig*e – at once a random act of kindness and a senseless act of beauty. To tell the truth,
Lynda still takes the death of Jerry Garcia badly and,
last night in his honour, the two of us rolled one of
those enormous English doobies that resemble dyna-
mite sticks and blew our brains out perfectly.

"I don't believe this woman," Jilaquns said, shaking her head in
awe.

Your Errant Mother approves of her Beloved Daughter's decision to go to university. She confesses to being
taken abruptly by the news that her ex has added the
Chairship of Avalon to his already swollen holdings –
hardly the jewel in his diadem, but the opportunity,
doubtless, to introduce a new sex-toy into his sterile
relationship with that Tartar mistress while exacting
further recrimination against his former wife and all
that she represents in terms of a lost eroto-ontology.
Your Mother evinces a certain wonder at the turning
of the wheel that has brought her Gentle Daughter to
Avalon University, there to frustrate his ill-founded urge

to privatize the known universe. All the work of Ms.
Fortuna, no doubt!

To your query about the efficacy of university education, your Mother can only recall a few glimpses of
her own, leading her to counsel that the actual process
of education takes place mysteriously outside the formal
structures of what is taught. She observes that while undergraduates at the earliest universities were meant to
study the *Posterior Analytics* of Aristotle, what they actually read were the love poems of Ovid. And while your
Mom in her day was supposed to study the *Anatomy of
Criticism* by Northrop Frye, what she in fact read were
the love poems of Leonard Cohen – these recited aloud
around the kitchen table of the Student Housing Co-op
under a naked lightbulb. Thus Eros subverts the ways of
power, and universities carry out the immemorial duties
of higher education in spite of themselves. Your Mother
is not being entirely cynical when she suggests that the
only purpose of the university is to provide a relatively
safe laboratory in which the young adult can experiment with her new-found freedom – in a word, to grow.
How this surrogate parenting happens is yet a mystery,
secure from the accountability formulas and performance indicators of the Hugh D'Arnays of this world.

Lastly, your ever-concerned and solicitious Mom
expresses her anxiety about her Beloved Daughter's decision to live at the cottage. Out there, will she not feel
isolated from the propaedeutic milieu (see above)? Yet if
you insist on living at the lake, she asks you always to
bear in mind that this was *our* family cottage – the
Setons' – long before the D'Arnays bought *our* manners
with their money. Thus you must make it your own
home, especially after the weather gets cold in November. And do remember to feed the descendants of that

first Seton chipmunk whose teeth-marks, dating from the year 1907, are still on your grandfather's porch screen door.

Blessings and Best Love,
Jennifer

Mutely the girls sat in the silence which the letter commanded.

"It sounds like something out of George Bernard Shaw," was Jilaquns comment.

"Yes, she's quite mad," agreed Jan.

"She still thinks prose is a useful weapon in the struggle."

Jan smiled. "I should never have given her that laptop as a going-away present. It brings out the worst in her."

9

If you've been out of university for ten or twenty years, you'll find things are pretty much the same – but the institution has changed in one important way. That change is the emphasis given to research. There is almost a fervency to the research done by faculty nowadays. The new research effort is a consequence of all the corporate partnerships and endowed chairs, and it is a consequence of governments suddenly taking an interest in the universities. Having been neglected by the state for some nine hundred years, the university as a social institution is now expected to show results.

I mean results that you can measure, such as the number of articles published in respected journals or the number of papers given at conferences. How young people grow up to be beautiful adults after putting intellect and imagination at the center of their lives for four years – that is not a result; it is a serendipity. Results are what counts, and so every year research funding officials, civil servants and politicians pore over a university's research output before deciding how many funds to award the university for the next fiscal year.

Results — but I don't want to use such a crude term as this for things of mind and spirit. Deans call it "quality and quantity of published scholarship." Government agencies call it "research productivity." Politicians, in one of those high-sounding phrases politicians have, call it "More bang for your education buck."

And so professors are hard at it everywhere, banging away at their research. The professors of Avalon are no exception. For instance, you will see Faith Rackstraw in the Senior Common Room taking her morning coffee and banging away at the *Times*. Everybody knows she is taking the pulse of civilization and its decline since Parmenides enunciated νοεῖν as a mental principle. At the tables in the Food Court, Professor Leland (Philosophy) is banging away with a Bic pen, putting the finishing touches to his great opus on avian signs of a spiritual universe. Called *Birds of the Kenomagaywakon Valley: A Metaphysician's Odyssey*, this original work promises to be a revaluation of what the whole field of Metaphysics and Ornithology can be about. Leland has been putting the finishing touches to this book for eighteen years, and so the work is exceptionally promising.

Meanwhile down at the Virtual Café, Professor Jeremy Lewin, having finished a great breakfast, is banging away at the latest posthumous book by Foucault. The fact that Lewin has not published a single scholarly article in twenty years cannot be held against him, for his research production consists in living fully what he calls "the life of the mind." And this he is virtually doing at the moment, negotiating another of the waves of cultural theory that have redefined the Humanities today. Negotiating successive waves of theory is what Jerry Lewin has done since that year he washed up on the beaches of Avalon University, his head still ringing from the 1968 Democratic Convention in Chicago and his body wasted from Woodstock. In those days he read Herbert Marcuse. But Marcuse's brilliant problematization of the one-dimensional society led him to

SEAN KANE

the brilliant critique of instrumental reason by the Frankfurt School
theorists Adorno and Horkheimer. Then there had been that brief
fling with the brilliant fading sunset of Hermeneutics represented
by Ricoeur. Then, just when he was ready to write something on
Ricoeur, there came a wave of thought from Jacques Lacan with his
brilliant revaluation of the Freudian unconscious in terms of the
repressed signifier. Then Derrida, whose brilliant deconstruction of
speech and writing rendered Lacan *passé*. Then came Baudrillard's
brilliant take on commodity-semiosis and *la société de consummation*
which Lewin's slower-moving colleagues were even yet teaching in
tedious lectures in Cultural Studies 100. But Lewin had moved on,
because the brilliance of Michel Foucault hit him like a late-break-
ing seismic wave, and he pondered the new critique of Enlightenment modernity with the same rising excitement with which he
had once pondered Ricoeur. Then, when he was ready to publish on
Foucault, along came the second generation of post-structuralists,
Deleuze and Lyotard, whose brilliance he interrogated avidly at the
back of the Virtual Café. Like a tidal wave, the major postcolonial-
ist thinkers gathered complexity and washed over Lewin with their
phosphorescent brilliance. He read them all.

There. Have I not persuaded you that Jeremy Lewin has been
living a life of the mind? Lately, he has been putting his energy into
theatre-directing, trying to convince a skeptical dean that the earliest philosophical discourses were oral and took the form of drama.

I don't mean to suggest by these examples that Avalon lags behind the Metropolitan University in its research. On the coffee
table in his office, Dean Galt has examples of research published by
his faculty. The examples are there to impress visitors; they especially impress colleagues who come in to ask for a sabbatical in
order to complete some research. There on the table is the paper by
Nglesi Mwangulu (Economics) on "The Least Squares Estimator in
Dynamic Models Showing Heteroscedastic Errors." Even the first
page of this paper will take you off at the knees, I promise you. And
of course there is a slew of articles in the field of Ecology in which

85

Avalon has a reputation – I won't bore you with their titles. Because there looming above them all like a Roman temple is Ruairi MacDonald's two-volume work bound in blue with gold lettering: *History of Trade in the Era of European Expansion.* To this pile, Cameron Galt has modestly added his own publication *How We Frame Messages.*

It is a good display for a small university, Galt thinks. His new policy of Performance Indicators should compel more publication by faculty, however. The Dean surveys his policy, almost ready for distribution. But first the day's e-mail.

From Professor Emeritus Jacob D. Weisberg to the Association of Retired Professors:

> *Our series of noon-hour "Lectures by the Fountain" begins in the Food Court next week with Nglesi's topic, "Who Is The Real You Beneath the Shopper?" The idea is that this would be an analysis of the construction of human identity as consumer, as well as a critique of the consumer culture, designed to appeal to housewives and teenagers. Each retired professor will speak on the topic for five minutes. Correct formal academic regalia should be worn for these lectures. We won't pass a hat at the lecture; instead, a mortarboard or academic cap can be placed discreetly at the foot of the lectern, with a sign indicating that donations to the Retired Professors Dental Plan would be welcome.*

Galt frowned at the message, then let it go by. The second e-mail was from Ruairi MacDonald:

> *The Union's position is that we will accept Performance Indicators for anonymous statistical-gathering purposes only, on the condition that the Employer agrees to promote a research atmosphere of Free Expression and Inquiry, by affirming the Union's Declaration of Academic Freedom at November Senate.*

All in the life of a dean, Galt thought buoyantly.

The next message was from Hannah Janssen-Koeslag on behalf of the Avalon Women's Caucus:

> *AWC agrees to Performance Indicators for publicity purposes only, provided the Administration pledges to maintain a research environment untainted by sexism, racism or other forms of discrimination. Your commitment can be signalled by your affirming the Caucus's proposed Anti-Harassment and Discrimination Policy at November Senate.*

Very interesting, Galt thought. The institutional pressures were reaching an intensity that made his mind sing. As administrator, he was coming up to concert pitch. To be good at it, you had to have a feel, not for the issues themselves, but for the way they sounded a chord. That was where the particular music of an institution lay. Academic Freedom *versus* Human Rights: to most people these might seem like wrong notes, but to a dean's ear, to Galt's ear, they struck an interesting chord. The trick was not to dampen down that chord by trying to negotiate a compromise. Let the chord play itself out. The outcome would be a split faculty. A split faculty, going into a contract negotiating year, was just what any administrator wanted. Cameron Galt thought these things, listening to the patterns which the music of the university made in his soul.

"Mr. Victor Bosko to see you."

Sheena's head withdrew from the doorway and was replaced by a tall and strikingly handsome young man wearing a white shirt and tie beneath a brand-new Avalon University jacket. The words "Law and Security" stood out brightly on his arm. He was carrying a leather attaché case with the letters v.b. in gold. This, after sitting down, he immediately clicked open as if to signal a quick moment of Higher Business between corporate equals. Galt decided to take the bait.

"So, Mr. Bosko. What's cooking?"

"Just thought I'd drop by and introduce myself," the student said breezily. He took a booklet out of his briefcase and laid it with a decisive slap on the dean's coffee table. *The Common Sense Revolution Comes to Education*, it read. Galt did not take that bait.

Bosko was making himself right at home at the coffee table reserved for decanal *têtes à têtes.* "I've done an institutional analysis. As a client and consumer of the products this corporation has to sell, I set up a personal user-satisfaction model. So I can map personal outcomes against expectations, you understand."

Sets of computerized spread-sheets unfolded from Bosko's apparently bottomless briefcase.

Galt said nothing. Much of his job as dean was to be a bemused listener.

"I thought if you got the other students here to use this model, we could adapt Avalon to The New Reality."

"Ah-hmm!" Galt said. "What's your take on the place?" He managed with some effort to eliminate any patronizing tone from the question.

Bosko brightened immediately. "To put it in a nutshell, this institution subscribes to obsolete assumptions. Statist socialistic assumptions — I guess you know that. That's why you're here to change it."

Bosko smiled a quick conspiratorial smile. He held up the first spread-sheet showing the various departments of the university in coloured boxes. "Look at these static, unitary, Fordist assembly-line production units! They reflect an old-fashioned resource-based economy protecting its urban areas behind a national trade policy."

"Ah-hmm!"

"It's totally out-to-lunch," Bosko said, suddenly lapsing into the vernacular. "The New Reality involves acquired skills and technology, competing globally. What's needed are Just-in-Time Learning Systems to provide knowledge as needed when needed."

Galt leaned back, as if pinned to his chair by the clichés. His face went blank.

"As you know, computer-mediated communications are facilitating the emergence of federated flexible production coalitions," Bosko went on obliviously. "A de-institutionalized interactive team approach to knowledge. Not just JITOLS but NCUS."

"NCUS?"

"Non-Curricular Units involving D.N.D – Delivery, not Distribution."

"Of course."

"Implying access by the end-user, not acquisition by the institution. The cost of accessing electronic knowledge is a fraction of the cost of its present wasteful distribution." Bosko looked at Galt accusingly. "But I don't see any evidence of Avalon outsourcing for JITOLS and NCUS."

Galt, remembering his days as a teacher, decided to coax the human being out from behind the display of jargon. "Tell me, Vic – where do you fit into all this?"

"Me?" The student's manner suddenly dissolved. There was a shy grin, as if it rarely occurred to Victor Bosko to think of himself at all. Galt sensed a decent, well-brought-up young man.

"I mean, what brings you to Avalon?"

Vic pondered the question, then began speaking spontaneously. "Oh, I was enrolled at the Poly – doing a sort of pre-Law program. Then I suddenly got switched here. And I'm glad too – I always wanted to be at university." This Vic said proudly. It seemed to Galt that Vic carried the hopes of a large struggling family, as if the whole family were enrolled at Avalon by proxy in its one representative.

"I hope Avalon serves you well."

"I know it will!" Vic said eagerly. "I'm a little older than the other students here, you know. I've been working as a field-organizer for the Reform Party. But I feel like I fit right in here."

"Good!"

Bosko noticed the materials he had put on the table, now apparently left out of the conversation. His manner changed sharply.

"Even though Av is way behind the rest of the world. Tell me, Mr. Dean – how does your organization define a Total Quality Management initiative consisting of Customer Focus, Continuous Improvement and Employee Involvement? Is it one that includes the euphoria of cross-functional teamwork and process-flow mapping?"

"C'mon, Vic – stop talking like that!"

"Like what?" Afraid of having given offence, Bosko seemed genuinely confused.

"You're sounding like an executive training manual."

"Am I? Sorry. Sometimes I can't help it. Look – I'll just leave these things with you."

Bosko held up a second spread-sheet with quite a different organizational plan on it. The man certainly had a state-of-the-art computer, Galt thought.

"Applying marketing logic, I've identified which courses here are (i) cash cows (they're in red), and (ii) cyclical (in blue) and (iii) niche-hunters (green). I thought this might be useful to you."

"Well, thank you. I'm sure your work will prove … ah … interesting to the Academic Planning Committee."

"But that's a subcommittee of Senate."

"Of course. Academic decision-making is traditionally the responsibility of Senate."

"I guess I've got a lot to learn," Vic offered willingly. There was another shy smile. "But I don't see how your organization can adapt to The New Common Sense Reality without a Total Quality Management initiative in place at the Chief Executive level."

"Well, we're working on Performance Indicators," Galt suggested. Now he was sounding patronizing.

"If we don't adjust quickly to Just-in-Time Learning Systems and Non-Curricular Units, then we're going to miss The Common Sense boat. Courses won't be taught by professors; they'll be delivered by educational software firms bidding for the right through outsourcing."

Out came a handshake. Then a business card.

"If I can be of further help to you, just give me a call."

Victor Bosko left the room in haste as if he was catching the mid-morning shuttle to Washington.

Galt, after a slight hesitation, put the material in the shredder.

He looked out his office window at the rainclouds over the Mall. Then his eye was caught by the flicker of a camp fire. Squatting beside the camp fire, in a light misty rain, was Joe Waasagunackank. Galt put the Research Performance Indicators document face-down on his desk. "Think I'll go out and see what Joe's doing," he said to Sheena, taking his umbrella from the outer office coat-rack. Research Indicators could wait, he thought, as he made his way to the front door of Sears, then to the forecourt outside.

"Ho! Sit down, Cameron. Talk to me for a while. You can see I'm holding office hours."

"Out here?"

"Sure. I'm no good inside four walls. This is where I'm comfortable. I can do some teaching. Someone comes along, sits down – maybe I can tell them something."

Galt sat down on a log beside the lean, weathered figure. He stared into the fire. Those were birch logs taken by Joe from the Senior Common Room fireplace.

"I always stand somewheres in sight of a lake," Joe said whimsically.

Galt had no idea what to make of this. He said nothing.

"That's what the birch logs are saying – in the fire there. They don't want to be in a room neither. They are saying, 'I always stand somewheres in sight of a lake.' Now, maybe, I'm sending them back to their lake."

Galt looked at the plume of birch smoke ascending in the mist. Joe looked across at him and smiled.

"That's what the birch tree said one day to Nanabozho."

"I'd like to hear the story sometime, Joe."

"Sure. That was when Nanabozho had this caribou head stuck on his own head. He turned himself into a snake so's he could eat the caribou brains, because the wolves had eaten all the rest, eh? Then somethin' went wrong – somethin's always going wrong on Nanabozho, you know – and now he's got caribou horns stuck on his head and he can't see nothin'."

Joe paused and looked up from the fire, feeling the power of the story returning to him.

"Ah, well what was he to do? He bumped into a tree. 'What sort of a tree are you, my little brother?'

'Oh, I always stand deep in the forest.'

'Oh, my little brother, you must be a tamarack.'

'Yes,' he was told.

Again he bumped into a tree.

'What kind of tree are you, my little brother?'

'I always stand on the mountain.'

'Oh, you must be a pine.'

Again he bumps into a tree.

'What kind of tree are you?'

'I always stand somewheres in sight of a lake.'

'My little brother, you must be a birch.'

"So, you see, Cameron. That's how we know our trees. We tell this story. Listen – I'll tell you some more.

"Well, he continued going along like that. Again he bumped against a tree.

'What kind of tree are you, my little brother?'

'I always stand somewheres near a lake, a short way back in the forest.'

'Oh, my little brother, you must be a poplar.'

'Yes.'

Again he continued going along. Again he bumped against a tree.

'What kind of tree are you, my little brother?'

'I always stand by the bank of a lake.'

'Oh, my little brother, you must be a cedar.'

'Yes,' he was told."

Joe stopped the story abruptly. He gave Galt a hearty clap on his shoulder.

"The story goes on. I'll tell you the rest of it sometime. Nanabozho stories – they just run on into each other, eh?"

Galt got up from the fire slowly. He rubbed some mist off his face.

"Thanks for the story, Joe. That was a privilege. I realize I don't know much about trees."

Joe laughed. "You come back here sometime and I'll tell you some more. I guess you just had some First Nations research." Joe gestured with a slow wave of his hand across the landscape. "Out here in Turtle Island. That's what we call the world of time and space, you know. The Turtle carries the world on her back. Ho, ho! I'm researchin' out here in the University of Turtle Island."

Back in his office, Galt found that he could not deal with the Research Performance Indicators document. Not even noon, he decided to call it a day and drove home.

IO

The Registrar enjoyed the appearance of being pulled away from important work. Now in charge of promoting Avalon in the media, he let himself be discovered examining the *Choosing Your College: the Nation's Best Universities* issue which had just come out. He looked up from the magazine into a pair of brilliant blue eyes set in a wide-cheekboned face.

The librarian's hair was black and cut in a page-boy. Except for the whitest of faces and a white-coloured blouse, everything else about her was black – sweater, corduroy slacks and boots. A young member of the faculty, she conveyed an air of purity and competence. Bud Lassiter couldn't make sense of the prepossessive coolness she conveyed. What motivated her, and her entire generation, was a mystery. They seemed to have been beamed here from a distant planet.

"Ah, Ms. Endicott. Pull up a stool and make yourself at home." Lassiter gestured toward a chair beside his desk. Anyone sitting there gained a view of Lassiter framed by the picture window, behind him, the Kenomagaywakon river flowing past in subdued majesty. On the far side of the river was the Library ringed by the Humanities Colleges: Cabot, Sears and whatever the heck it was the students now called it – Goldman College?

Robyn Endicott continued to stand.

"I was just glancing at the *Choosing Your College* issue. And, as you know, Avalon would have been in first place among the small liberal arts colleges if it weren't for our poor showing in just two categories. One is scholarships. We placed at the bottom of the goddam heap. I intend to rectify that immediately. I'm personally asking D'Arnay to put a hundred thousand dollars into scholarships. A world-class institution should have world-class scholars."

Ms. Endicott looked out over the river and showed no sign of agreement. She did not even blink. Lassiter examined her white skin. Finally, he located two or three freckles around her nose and felt more comfortable.

"The other category is library holdings. We placed thirteenth. The other universities must have boosted their holdings suddenly."

Lassiter eyed Endicott as if it were her fault that the university showed so dismally in its library holdings. Again, Endicott gave no trace of expression.

"Do you happen to know precisely what the extent of our holdings is at the moment?"

"Of course I do."

The Registrar waited for the librarian to give him the totals. They were not forthcoming.

"What are they then?"

"Total holdings vary according to the assumed access protocols. There are seven of them. You should ask the Chief Librarian for the operational categories desired."

Lassiter groaned as if the burden of promotion was suddenly too much. "I did. He says he doesn't know."

Endicott's eyes widened imperceptibly.

"Something about how government documents are organized," Lassiter went on. "They might or might not be included in the gross figure depending on the circumstances. Now I'm asking *you* about this – you're in charge of on-line services."

Endicott paused for a moment to collect her thoughts. "What the Chief Librarian means is that such items as government documents are organized into large units. A series of volumes within a report, for example. We purchase the several volumes as one item."

"Ah-ha! Then you catalogue them as one item, right?"

"Yes. As much as we can of them. At present there's a backlog of govdocs waiting to be catalogued and put on-line. You'll find them in boxes in the staff room on the fourth floor."

"Very interesting. Ms. Endicott – is there any way we could … ah … quickly increase our official holdings in this important area?"

"I have no idea what you're speaking of."

"What I'm saying is these important … ah … *volumes* appear to be sitting around in boxes or arranged as unitary sets rather than being correctly identified and entered into the computer totals as *individual* items. A lot of them, I'd guess."

"Yes, there is. But there's not much demand for government reports, really."

"Yet if they could be differentiated immediately, on a crash basis, you know," Lassiter went on, "our gross library holdings would increase, like, dramatically."

"Yes, they would."

"Then why not catalogue them as individual items and get them on-line?"

"Because it would mischaracterize our holdings to do so. Users seek the complete set, not the particular volume in the set. Also because we have no money to waste on statistical cosmetics."

Lassiter made a hopeless gesture with his hands, which he hoped Endicott understood. "It's a darn shame the library staff allocation has been set. It's Board policy to hold the line on library services. I guess the library is always the soft underbelly of the university when it comes to cost-cutting."

"Yes, it is. Like scholarships."

Now it was the Registrar's turn to look out the window. He looked out the window for a long time. Finally he spoke: "Would two Full-Time Equivalent positions do it?"

Endicott jumped as if she had been bitten by a mosquito.

"Yes. That would be very helpful."

"I'll take it to the Board tomorrow."

"A world-class institution deserves a world-class library," Endicott observed.

"Er ... for sure! And if I get you the two FTES, you'll have the separate volumes all on-line by Christmas? That's when Andromeda needs our figures for the next *Choosing Your College* issue."

"Yes. But I wonder why the media is interested in total holdings when so little of it circulates. Why not report the number of items circulated per capita student? And then there's not only our physical contents but our ability to provide information from outside our walls. We could be leading the country in our user rates."

"That's a good idea, Ms. Endicott. Not much for a student to do up here in the boonies except read books."

"Thank you."

Endicott left the room with a trace of a smile on her face. Lassiter, glad to be rid of her sphinx-like self-containment, relaxed. He e-mailed D'Arnay at Andromeda Networks about interesting his magazine staff in the access and circulation rates of materials per enrolled student. Then he picked up the *Choosing Your College* special issue and examined Avalon's ranking in the category of upper-year class sizes. He lifted the phone to call the dean's office.

★   ★   ★

Sally Galt did not notice the waning of noise in the office corridor as the afternoon wore on. She did not hear the click of the locking door as the secretary left at five o'clock nor the babble as the students lined up for the dining hall at six. At eight, the cleaning staff came with the vacuum cleaners. Sally Galt worked on.

Anxiety and excitement exploding on her nerve-ends drove her on. The anxiety came from a fear of not being taken seriously – of not being taken seriously as an individual, an academic and a woman. The anxiety had its further source in her boisterous family, each one jostling for attention, and Sally the middle one, the studious one. This analysis, even as she was reminded of it, she rejected as unforgivably essentialist and deterministic, like all psychology. Truth is momentary and political. And the truth was that Sally had outpublished all her contemporaries in the field while still failing, until now, to land a tenure-track job. Evidently the gate-keepers of a masculinist academic world were threatened by her three biographies of woman authors and by her expertise in the field of Life Writing – literature from or about the feminist self. Even her new tenure-track position at Avalon was undercut by the fact that she was a spousal hiring, the partner of a dean.

She would just have to prove herself – that's all there was to it! And this was where the excitement came from – for at last she had a chance to establish her own authority and reputation. Here was a university that was relatively free of sexist coding – in fact, the preponderance of women students gave the place the air of a learned matriarchy. Here, students listened to what she had to say. Her brilliant performance yesterday at the lecture in Women's Studies 100 was the talk of the University. The length and professionalism of her course syllabus had increased the course enrolment overnight. Her faculty web-site was a thing to envy. And Hannah was pleased with her and so were Hannah's colleagues in the Women's Caucus. At last, Sally Galt was a star, if a rather insecure star, in the firmament. She faced her computer and typed fervently.

Knock, knock!

It came again – *knock, knock!*

"Come in."

It was most likely that Nursing student – what was her name? – Ashley Tiffin, who had sent an e-mail about suffering "a groin injury" while playing for the Women's Rugby team. The student stood unapologetically by the door, a picture of health in her overalls and damp brown hair. She looked like she had just come out of the shower.

"Hi – I'm Ashley Tiffin. You wanted to see me?"

Sally Galt eyed Ashley Tiffin severely over her monitor. She made out the button that was pinned to the strap on the student's overalls above her breast. "You'll have to marry me first!" it said.

"You missed your seminar presentation."

"I'm sorry. It's like I can't walk."

"You walked here."

"Yes, but I can't concentrate. It hurts like crazy."

"You're letting your gender position down."

Tiffin blinked, innocent of this reasoning.

"I just want you to consider the extent to which your seminar partners feel let down when you don't show up. As your facilitator, I also feel let down."

"I guess I made a big mistake not attending," Ashley conceded. "I meant to come."

"A mistake? You meant to? That's too easy, Ms. Tiffin. It's a misframing. Let me re-frame it for you. Re-frame it not in relation to your intentions but in relation to the consequences. Look at the consequences of your absence. A seminar topic on which you were to be the presenter goes unpresented. Your co-workers in the seminar have done their reading so as to be able to support you. You volunteered for the topic and you're not here. You're somewhere else."

"It was a bad judgment call, I guess," Ashley offered helplessly. "I'm sorry."

"Sorry? That's simply not good enough, Ms. Tiffin. An apology is the easy liberal out – it's like a politician caught in a sex scandal.

Big apology, redemption, the air is cleared; it all goes away as if it never happened in the first place."

Ashley Tiffin shifted her weight from one leg to the other to show that the bruised *Gluteus maximus* was the real cause of the situation. What was this about sex scandals?

"I'll try and do better next time."

"The intentional subject being a myth tied to so-called 'objective' morality" (Sally made the quote marks in the air with her fingers), "I'm not very interested in your subject position."

"Well, I can't think what else I'm supposed to say," Ashley said, showing a natural belligerence. "I took a boot in the crotch – that's all I know."

"Forget about your body, Ms. Tiffin. Instead, analyze the outlook which circumscribes the sensitivity you ought to have shown to the group. What is there in your ideological set that at present restricts your view of the consequences of your act on an other or others?"

Ashley Tiffin thought for a moment. "I have no idea."

"Okay, Ashley. Go home and consider the larger politics of your actions."

Tiffin left, moving slowly, confused.

Sally wondered if she had been too hard on the student. No, she was in the right. Theory put her in the right. The myth of the intentional subject meant individuals could get away with murder, abuse, everything. "I didn't mean to do it." History was littered with these naive apologies of a regretful individualism. What if Nurse Tiffin accidentally doubled the dose of Digoxin on an infant with a heart defect? "I'm sorry – I didn't mean to do it – I'll try to do better next time." Actions can only be judged by their consequences.

Sally got back to work.

"You're working too hard!"

The rooted radiance of Hannah Janssen-Koeslag filled the office door like a great chestnut tree. Chestnut ringlets tumbling down over warm freckled shoulders. A smell of sun-warmed earth after rain, a natural body smell. Suddenly, Sally's whole being subsided and she sighed. Hannah had a centering effect on her. She was like an entire sisterhood – countless sisters all in harmony inside that one honest body. Sally gazed at Hannah and blinked. Her contact lenses needed moisture in this dry office. Maybe she had done enough work for one day.

"C'mon over to my place and we'll have a bite and relax. It looks like you haven't eaten."

Sally nodded and gathered her papers together gladly. She clicked her briefcase shut. Last of all, she shut down her computer.

"MacDonald's going to pull an Academic Freedom stunt and derail our Human Rights policy," Hannah declared. "I can smell it. I can tell what that old Tyrannosaur is thinking any time of day."

"Shouldn't we be calling a meeting of the Women's Caucus?"

Hannah subsumed the idea into her easy grace, yet it was clear the idea had not occurred to her.

"Good idea. Get the jump on the dinosaurs. You know – if you've been in a Mesozoic theme-park with the same colleagues for twenty years, you get to know their tricks. Mac's going to try to chew up my Anti-Harassment and Discrimination policy at Senate. I just know it."

How easily politics collapses into the personal here, Sally thought. Issues that are too important to personalize become personal vendettas. Sally had a vision of Ruairi MacDonald and Hannah Janssen-Koeslag locked like two ancient mesozöon reptiles in an eternal death-struggle. Yet it seemed more like a minuet, a game, a friendly rivalry played out over twenty years. Was there no outside to this place? Did the real world never get in?

"It's like this university is a single mind," Sally offered. "Everybody knows what everybody else is thinking. There's no reference to the real world."

"This *is* the real world, honey."

Hannah, exuding her matriarchal warmth, took Sally by the arm.

"We can go over the Anti-Harassment and Discrimination policy. Then we'll watch a chick-flick."

I I

"Professor Lewin?" It was Ashley Tiffin (Nursing I) trying doggedly to further her education by ending each of her utterances on a
rising note of doubt, as if Ashley Tiffin's whole existence was a
question mark. "What did the lecturer mean this morning when he
said ... " Ashley flicked through voluminous notes in the ring-
binder on the seminar table before her until she finally found the
quotation. " ... *that Cultural Studies has revived the spectre of a capitalism that has finally mastered its own historicity ...* "

"Which has found a way of recreating itself minute-by-minute
apparently outside of time," translated Lewin.

Ashley nodded doubtfully " ... *and therefore liquidated any endogenous capacity it may have once had for redemptive self-transformation.*"

"Means it can't do a take on itself anymore. Therefore 'the' revolution ... " (Lewin touched the air in front of him with extended
forefingers to mark the disparaged definite article) " ... is no longer
to be seen as the built-in inevitable outcome of capitalism."

"Why not, sir?"

"Don't call me 'sir'! I can't stand it. Don't even call doctors 'sirs'
when you get to do their work for them. Because for Marxists the
Enlightenment model of a social structure progressing dialectically
to its end-point no longer applies. It never applied in the first place,
poor dears!"

"How are we supposed to describe capitalism then?" Ashley Tiffin, star fullback of the Avalon Women's Rugby Team, was being a
good sport, Jan thought.

"As *a code-dominated order of generalized exchange,*" put in Victor
Bosko. The hairy Bosko (Law & Security I), now growing his idea
of an academic's beard in order to disguise his hair-trigger oppor-
tunism, was looking at Jan triumphantly. Or, rather, was now looking at Jan's thighs. "That's what last week's lecturer said."

"Yeah, yeah," Lewin said offhandedly.

"Oh, right – I get it. *Commodity semiosis*?" Ashley said, glancing appreciatively at Bosko. But Ashley as usual ended the statement in the interrogative. Jan was sure Ashley did not get it, in spite of the Nursing student's new black Cult-Studs T-shirt out of which her freckled arms extended in a jangle of bracelets.

Lewin was pretending to be a Grade One teacher: "Now, class, new word. *Commodity semiosis*. Who can remind us what *commodity semiosis* means?"

The students looked at the floor. Tiffin was busy rifling through her notes. Bosko smiled as if he knew the answer. Jan surveyed Lewin's office where the seminar was taking place. A squash racket tucked in the bookcase. A pile of unmarked essays probably from years back. A photograph of a young moustached Lewin as skip on an Oxford rowing shell. Hanging on the back of the door, the red-and-blue Oxford D. PHIL. robes which, Lewin claimed, were for a thesis he had written on Wittgenstein in six weeks after waking up from a year-long depression about his homosexuality. There was other storage attic memorabilia having mainly to do with theatre, such as those Greek theatre masks. "Debris left behind by the angel of History," Lewin called it.

"Well, like you said last week," Bosko finally answered, as if assuming an unwilling leadership.

"I didn't say – Rosencrantz said," corrected Lewin.

"Okay, like Rosen ... like the lecturer said: commodities-assigns. Capitalism recreates itself daily through the high-speed circulation of commodities which have become signs."

"Become?" frowned Lewin.

"Oh, alright – they always were signs," Bosko replied testily.

"Thank you."

"I remember," Ashley Tiffin said gaily. "The Coke bottle sells a way of life. Coke points to McDonald's hamburgers, and McDonald's points to Batman toys, which point to Disneyland, which points back to Coke."

"An endless circularity," observed Bosko gravely and knowingly.

"Very good, class. And, you see, there's no center or margin to this recirculation of signs. No depth or surface. Those structuralist metaphors don't apply."

The seminar fell silent. Everyone was trying to imagine a something that had no center or margin, no depth or surface, no structure whatsoever.

"The Blob!" exclaimed Ashley Tiffin suddenly, starting to giggle.

"Interesting," Lewin replied. "Ms. Tiffin perceives it as a threat." Lewin turned to face Ashley Tiffin. "Your allusion, no doubt, is to the 1958 horror film directed by Irwin Yeaworth that launched Steve McQueen's career. Has anybody seen it?"

Some nods.

"It evolved into a cult classic," Lewin went on. "The people-consuming gelatinous mass eats all the great American icons. It eats the local diner. It eats the local movie theatre. It first appears at the local make-out joint. It's glorious because it puts you completely in a teenage juvenile delinquent mind-set. Yeah, and yet — this is interesting — Irwin Yeaworth, the director, was primarily a religious broadcaster. He made Christian educational films — can you believe? And a TV series offering moral lessons for preschoolers."

"I guess he saw popular culture as a threat to the capitalist way of life," Victor Bosko pronounced carefully, not taking a position on the question.

Ashley straightened her back, innocent of any juvenile delinquent mind-set. "I think something that is shapeless is a threat to any way of life. There's no up or down — everything is something else."

"Don't be afraid of it, my dear. One day you're going to be dealing with Cystic Fibrosis. Or, properly speaking, with the Cystic Fibrosis gene, which is part of an endless recirculation of signs called the human genetic material."

Ashley Tiffin, confused yet patronized, sat expectantly with her lips open, waiting for the inevitable question.

"Would you say, Ms. Tiffin, that having a copy of the gene for Cystic Fibrosis is a good thing?"

103

"No, it isn't – because there's a mess-up in the flow of salts and fluids in the cells lining the airways. CF kids get a lot of mucus in their lungs. Poor kids! Bacterial infections. Some don't live past their forties."

"I said a copy of the gene for Cystic Fibrosis, my dear young lady. *One* copy."

"So?"

"I didn't say *two* copies."

"Oh I see. Two copies of the gene – one from each parent."

"Then you've got CF – mucus in the lungs. But if you inherit only *one* copy – and one in every twenty people of European extraction does – you've got better protection against cholera. Isn't it funny? Cholera causes loss of fluid; CF causes retention of fluid. It looks like one CF gene protects against asthma too. Yet asthma causes a narrowing of the airways; so does a double copy CF gene. Maybe a single CF gene protects against other diseases. I'm sure I'm a single CF gene carrier."

The seminar laughed.

"So, you see, a sign (and a gene is a sign) does contradictory things. It all depends on context. Heavy smokers don't get Parkinson's disease so much because smoking depresses the inhibitor of Dopamine in the brain. How can you say a particular thing is absolutely 'good' or 'bad'? Every sign circulates into other signs."

Victor Bosko nodded with feigned approval. Ashley Tiffin was noting something frantically in her ring-binder. Jan glared across the seminar table at Bosko. The role he was playing in class seemed meant to impress her. The dork was probably hitting on her.

"Come now, my dear students. Shall we get onto something more edifying? What about your performance pieces? Any new proposals?"

"I have a question," Jan said.

Jerry Lewin raised his eyebrows.

"The two course lecturers sound the same. What is it that's making them sound the same?"

"Ah, ha!" Lewin exclaimed.

"They're like a double copy of the same gene." Ashley, surprised and delighted at her sudden wit, was the last to join in the laughter.

"They're putting mucus in my neural receptor sites," she went on.

"And what, pray, is that same gene?" Lewin asked.

"Patriarchal theorizing," Jan answered. "The more they argue, the more they resemble each other. They're like Tweedledum and Tweedledee. I think pretty soon they're going to switch positions completely without knowing it, and still go on arguing with each other."

"They're a structure," said Ashley, her bracelets jangling suddenly. She was pleased with herself today. The interrogative note had fallen from her utterances. "So – what is the blob they're afraid of?"

Jan felt the beginnings of a sisterhood with the star fullback of the Women's Rugby Team. "They're arguing in order to take their minds off the black shape in the forest which is going to carry them away."

"What is that black shape?" Bosko asked ignorantly, struggling to reassume the role of omniscient.

Jan turned on Bosko with a practiced and gracious *hauteur*: "The freedom and expressivity of women. I haven't heard the unfreedom of women mentioned once in the lectures, except as an example of the *hierarchical family system maintained by the code of capitalist order*."

"Yes, they're making the whole problem so totally abstract," Ashley sighed.

"Don't blame the gene," Lewin said to Jan. "Power speaks the same language everywhere." Then he turned to face Ashley. "To learn its ways of disguising itself, you have to pitch your camp in the network of signs. Cultural theory is what creates that site for you. It's the nomad's tool that makes the lines of power visible in any situation. And then that tool will help you warp to another site. Remember – we are intellectual nomads of the information age."

"Intellectual nomads of the information age," wrote Ashley Tiffin in generous round letters across the top of her page.

In the end Jan left the seminar with an idea for her performance piece. Bosko caught up with her by the front door of Goldman.

"I just wanted to say – that was a great comment you just made in the seminar. About those sexist lectures."

Jan studied Victor Bosko in his white shirt and tie, his college jacket slung over his shoulder casually.

"I also wanted to notify you," Bosko went on, "that I'm on Senate as Cabot Student Council rep. I'm ... uh ... prepared to support the Student Union delegation on this Human Rights thing. Profs have too much academic freedom. They're responsible to no one. Tell Jilaquns that's my position. In fact, you can tell her I've got the votes of the college council reps in my pocket. I can deliver."

"Sure, Victor."

Bosko continued to stand in front of her as if he had something more on his mind. "How about you and I doing lunch together sometime, and we can discuss it."

"I don't know, Victor. I'm pretty busy."

"Well, whatever."

Jan, appalled, shrugged off the oily Bosko and headed towards the parking lot.

"Take care," he called after her.

12

"You have a meeting with the Faculty Union leaders today at noon. That's MacDonald, Lewin and Endicott. Then, Senate tomorrow afternoon – which you're chairing, by the way. President Rattenbury has to be at an alumni gathering in the city."

Galt groaned and held out his hands helplessly.

"I'll take that as a yes," Sheena continued. "Then you meet with D'Arnay and Lassiter on Friday at four. The meeting's in the lounge at the local airport."

"Wow! D'Arnay's flying up for a meeting. I wonder what's up."

"Jupiter is in conjunction with Saturn," Sheena advised. "Expect a big corporate donation."

Now how on earth did Sheena know that? Not even Rattenbury had been told about the chance of landing a large donation to the Ecology Center. It was top-secret. D'Arnay had even disguised his flight to Hong Kong last month. Galt looked vacant. He was having difficulty getting used to the otherworldliness of his Assistant and her ability to read the mind of the institution. This she did by means of a horoscope program on her computer, keyed to the hour of Avalon's being given the right to grant degrees. Well, if one lived and breathed the rhythms of the university as fully as Sheena did, one did not have to draw on the organization of the cosmos for prescience.

With this rationalization, Galt was free of the suspicion that Sheena's control of his itinerary – and through it his whole personal life – had something to do with her toe-ring.

It was a ring of fine braided silver on the fourth toe of Sheena's left foot, visible now above her Birkenstock.

"You're wondering about my toe-ring, aren't you?"

"Well, yes – it is kind of curious."

"It's on my fourth toe – that's the toe of Venus. It's like the powers of the fingers, really. A ring on the first finger is the ring of power – the finger you use to point with." Sheena pointed her first finger at Galt. "That's Jupiter's finger. The Pope's ring is on the first finger when you kneel to kiss it."

Had Sheena once kissed the Pope's finger?

"Incidentally, D'Arnay has a ring on his power finger. Then, a ring on the second finger indicates a person with caution. If you wore a ring, you'd wear it on your Saturn finger."

Galt laughed. "Or on my Saturn toe."

"A ring on the third finger means a person inclined to love. The Venus finger. That's where wedding rings go."

"I see. And the little finger?"

"The finger of Mercury. Those people are good with words."

"What about a ring on the thumb?"

"A thumb-ring means the person is just plain weird. Incidentally, speaking of Venus – she's coming in strong on your chart this week. I'd watch out for a beautiful acquaintance, if I were you."

Sheena turned and padded out of the room. Galt was left thinking about his love-life, such as it was. He didn't know any beautiful acquaintances – at least, none that mattered. There were none in his past. Sally was beautiful – in her thin tall way, but she was hardly a mere acquaintance. Or was she getting to be less familiar to him? Galt sent a memo down to his feelings; up came a quick appraisal. Certainly the move to the cottage had been good. There, they were free of ringing telephones, free of neighbours with large growing families asking for Sally's bread recipe. Free as they always had been of children, they were now free even of the decision they'd made not to have children, there being none of them up at the lake in the fall to offer a noisy reproach to the way of life he and Sally had chosen. And that simple efficient way of life was proving its worth. He had never felt as close to Sally as he did now. At the cottage, he would watch the rain splatter against the picture window of the winterized sun-room, while Sally tapped with muffled purpose on her computer. Another lecture for Women's Studies, another biography of a woman writer. Sally was moving from strength to strength. And so was he. They were functioning together perfectly as a professional team, rotating around each other like one of those double stars in the galaxy.

But where *was* Sally? Galt couldn't feel her reassuring gravitational tug. He checked again: she hadn't sent her usual morning e-mail, which she did after answering her own overnight messages. Probably she had forgotten. Involved as she was in the intensity of a liberal arts and science college, she would work into the night, then crash on the couch by the computer. Sometimes, when she had a lecture to give early the next morning, she stayed at Hannah Janssen-Koeslag's.

Galt watched the raindrops on his office window playing tag with each other like excited children. He ought to read over this Research Performance Indicators policy. But something was making him restless. He decided to take a walk to the Senior Common Room and bring back a coffee.

The s.c.r. at Sears had skylights that sent shafts of light onto cactus plants and potted vines. Paintings by the wife of a past president of Avalon graced the walls. Supported by beams of redcedar the low cozy roof seemed designed for the rainy weather. The fireplace was roaring. Around it, secretaries from the various offices in the college were taking a coffee break, resuming a daily conversation about children, hospitalizations and bargains at Wal-Mart — an ongoing conversation that seemed interrupted by the distraction of work. There by the coffee-maker was Giles Rattenbury in a striped shirt and three-piece navy suit.

Galt had only spoken once to Rattenbury — it was during a coffee break at a meeting of the Board. For the duration of the meeting itself, the Acting President had said nothing. He had brought no briefcase or paperwork, giving the impression of existing at a level above such things. Resting his shaggy head on his hands, he had gazed off into the future, looking precisely like the figurehead he was.

"Well, hello, dear colleague!" Rattenbury's manner was at once affectionate and stately. "You know, I was just coming from the campus book store, and I saw your book there. And my what a fine work it is! I must say, you have much to tell us about the messages we intend for each other and the bias of the particular medium that conveys them."

"Thank-you, Mr. President," Galt said. Rattenbury's messages, he considered, were biased by an accent that conveyed ancestral civility. Warm and folksy, it spoke of wooden homes on the coast, set among old-growth trees — houses with dozens of windows, each one a different size, each one sporting its own striped awning.

"Coffee? But of course you will!" Without waiting for a reply, Rattenbury poured a cup just the way Galt took it: double cream, no sugar. He motioned Galt to a round pine table set in a nook beneath a skylight. Round tables were a motif at Avalon, left over from the founding of the university in its extravagance of Arthurian symbolism.

"But I do hope, Mr. Dean, that you aren't going to expect us all to match that quality of research."

Rattenbury looked across at Galt and seemed almost to be winking. Galt felt flattered and challenged both at once.

"Well, as you know, Mr. President … "

"Ah, Giles, I think."

"Yes. As you know, Giles, we're losing research infrastructure funds to the large universities. We're being left behind in the rush. My hope is that Avalon – that the community, I mean – can begin a process of renewal." Then Galt added, "Under your leadership."

"Me? Ah, you're too kind. But who am I? I am merely the smiling face of old Avalon until Mr. D'Arnay finds us a president. My role is to speak nostalgically, at alumni get-togethers, of the University our graduates know and love. But research? Oh, I don't do that sort of thing anymore." The Acting President leaned forward when he said this, confiding the disagreeable secret to Galt.

Likely true, Galt thought. As a symbol of the old Avalon, Rattenbury was one of those great teachers who seemed legendary here.

"But I do know this," Rattenbury broke in. "There are two kinds of faculty members at a university, here as elsewhere. There are those who teach and those who research. The teachers are so excited by reading everybody else's books they never write their own. The researchers are so excited by their own book they don't read anybody else's. This, I venture to say, is a melancholy fact of life. There's nothing you, dear colleague, can do to change it."

Galt took the opportunity to sip at his coffee. He did not want to be argumentative. Argumentativeness was not the managerial style, which was best executed through memos neutral in tone but far-reaching in their detail.

"The mistake every administrator makes is that he tries to change things." Rattenbury smiled at Galt with an innocent savagery. "We dispatch our administrators rather quickly here, you know. We send them off to the Food Court."

"But how can you not try to do something?" Galt asked politely and carefully. He realized he was being made to feel very much Rattenbury's junior. Rattenbury's civility had that effect; so did the impression the man gave of a weary defeated wisdom. "The University can't just muddle through this funding crisis."

"Perhaps not. Yet I dare say that if anyone tries to do something about it, he'll just make it worse."

"Why's that?" Galt asked, now genuinely intrigued.

"Because the University runs entirely on hearsay. If a person issues a report in the morning, by mid-afternoon there are a thousand versions of it. Nobody ever reads the report — nobody ever reads anything here. Everybody just hears about it from everybody else. The original report, whatever it was, is clean forgotten."

Giles Rattenbury laughed gently to himself. Galt was listening carefully. There was a benign self-mocking side to the old man's observations. They seemed half-meant. Yet Rattenbury might actually be telling him something.

"That's why I say — don't do a thing. May I repeat myself? Don't do a thing. One only has to make sure the place keeps chattering away to itself — then it runs perfectly well on its own. What one must do is simply walk around the place all day, from common room to common room — just as I'm doing now, keeping the university talking. Be the perfect host who, if I may quote Lao-Tzu, seeming to appear the least, appears the most."

Galt saw something to this remark. The ideal manager should be anonymous. But those observations about walking around and talking all day — they made no sense at all.

"That is why one must not keep any minutes of meetings. No records at all. Don't ever write anything down. Then when somebody comes up to you saying you promised them something, you won't remember; neither will anybody else."

That was funny, Galt thought. The whole discourse was funny. Rattenbury, catching Galt's smile, continued: "And don't ever be in your office where people can find you. Indeed, it's preferable if nobody knows where your office is. Do you know where my office is?"

"It's in the Library somewhere."

"Somewhere! But you see, dear colleague, I'm never in it. I am walking around all day talking to people and cherishing thoughts that depend on nothing."

"I see," said Galt, frowning. He did not see at all. "But what if ways need to be changed ... well, too quickly for the community to talk it through?"

"Ah," said Rattenbury. "The Rules of Sound Administration. Number one: encourage dissent. However, a person ought not ever to encourage it personally. Number two: let it build up to a point of unison. Number three: act before it destroys you."

"Don't encourage it *personally*?"

"Oh, no!" said Rattenbury, frowning. "What you must do is you tell person 'A' your idea. Then you tell person 'B' the same idea. Tell 'B' that you heard it from 'A.' Then, go back and tell 'A' that 'B' agrees with his idea. After a while, people will forget you told them the idea in the first place. People begin to think it's their own idea. Eventually they'll come to tell you about it. Then, of course, you must say that the idea is totally impractical – quite out of the question. That way, you build up resistance to the original idea. That way, more people become involved. Then at a precise point in time, you give way gracefully and the idea gets triumphantly implemented."

This time it was Galt's turn to laugh. Old Rattenbury made a kind of wacky sense.

"Well, Mr. Dean – I suppose you must get back to your office and amount to something." Giles Rattenbury rose, extending his hand in a hearty handshake. "Remember what I say: only a man with no hands can re-order the world. No hands. That's the way to make things happen at a university."

Back in the sanity of his office, Galt felt a familiar habit-energy waiting for him. It seemed for an instant that he saw himself sitting in his office armchair, a set of habits in the shape of a dean. And it seemed that he then stepped back into himself, the two bodies becoming one. Yes, it was just an illusion; it was a trick of the eye. Had Rattenbury done this to him? "Cherish thoughts that depend on nothing" – now what on earth did that mean? Everything here depended on everything else. One would have to have an infinitely clear mind in order to negotiate all the complexity. One tiny mistake and it could all come crashing down. Yet the complexity was self-sustaining to a degree. It was like the complexity said to be built into the design of a passenger jet: say, fourteen certain things had to go wrong, and they had to go wrong all in a certain order, for the thing to crash. Yet one couldn't rely on the power of complexity to sustain itself; the tragic chain of circumstance depended on some initial pilot error. Had he made any errors yet? Galt reassessed his performance carefully and could think of none. Then, he took the Research Performance Indicators plan out to Sheena's office.

"Could you set this up as a Board Executive memo from me? Usual Avalon format. It's the P.I. plan – better mark it confidential. I'll just make a copy first – for the cottage."

Galt walked over to the photocopier and put the document in the machine. One of his good habits as an administrator was occasionally doing the photocopying himself. He knew that secretaries appreciated the courtesy. He pressed the start button.

Nothing happened.

All the lights were on and they showed green. He pressed the button again. The machine made its complicated humming sounds, then fell back into inexplicable silence. He looked: there was lots of paper in the tray.

"The machine isn't working for me."

A presence of sandalwood perfume came up to Galt from behind.

"That's because you haven't introduced yourself to the photocopier. I'll introduce you."

Sheena bent over the photocopier, a cascade of red hair tumbling down. Putting her forehead to the photocopier, she whispered something inaudibly. Suddenly, the machine came to life and dutifully made its copy.

Sheena smiled her Mona Lisa smile. "There's a *diva* in the machine, you see. You have to be courteous to the *diva* or she won't work for you."

"I see." Galt took the photocopy and put it in his briefcase, giving the original to Sheena.

"Don't forget to say 'thank you'," Sheena said in a motherly voice.

"Thank you, Sheena."

"No – I mean to the machine."

"Oh, alright. Uh – thank you, machine. Is it proper to call it just 'machine'?"

"Yes, that's okay. She has a name, of course, but the names of the *divas* are secret unto themselves."

Galt returned to his desk, confused, trying to think of what it would be like to have no hands and re-order the world. He checked his e-mail. There was a new message. It was from Hugh D'Arnay at Andromeda Place. In contrast to D'Arnay's usual grandiloquence, the message was clear and simple: *Where is the Spanish Year Abroad Program?*

13

The kitchen, hearth-womb of the motherhome. Five free-spirited women, having consumed a huge Lebanese feast which they have made together, are sitting in the warm light of a heavy gold-fringed lampshade which hangs just above eye level from the ceiling. They are: Hannah Janssen-Koeslag (Anthropology) whose home this is; Sally Galt (Women's Studies), a probationary tenure-track appointee, though no one doubts that she is going to get tenure, because (a) she has an intimidating mass of publications on women writing from or about the self, (b) she is a woman in a university where women are in the ascendancy, (c) she is the Dean's partner. Rita Solomon is also there – Rita is the Human Rights Officer of Avalon University, the person entrusted with processing complaints and recommending appropriate disciplinary action under the interim Anti-Harassment and Discrimination Policy, Draft 3, which these women are hoping will soon become Draft 4 and the official policy of the institution. Also in attendance are Jilaquns of the Haida First Nation and Jan D'Arnay, her friend.

Such a convergence of female power at the institution has never before been assembled under one roof. Janssen-Koeslag is on Senate now, and she's got herself on the Board of Governors as faculty representative. Rita, a woman of colour, is also a political force, partly because she is in touch with Human Rights officers with similar views to hers all across the country. Jilaquns, of course, is from one of the most marginalized of peoples, the aboriginal people of America. She is a member of Senate representing the Student Union Executive, where she is Aboriginal Rights Commissioner. And everyone knows who Sally is. Jan, too, for that matter. Their connections run to every office of the University.

They are, in fact, with the exception of Jan and Jilaquns who are guests tonight, the inner core of the Avalon Women's Caucus, a group that meets regularly to plan the passage through Senate of a real zero-tolerance Human Rights policy.

"One that will cut the balls off Ruairi MacDonald," Sally Galt declares.

"What's the dirt on him, anyway?" Rita Solomon, as the university's Human Rights Officer, is supposed to be impartial. However, part of her job description, as she sees it, is to promote an institutional atmosphere untainted by sexism, and she has never, she thinks, found herself in a more flagrantly masculinist place than Avalon University. And, for her, the symbol of that masculinist freedom is Ruairi MacDonald.

"There's no doubt he's a *peña parada*," agrees Hannah, using a term of the South-American peasant women's movement usually applied to male government officials.

"But he's too sloshed to follow through!" laughs Jilaquns.

"But he's been married three times," exclaims Sally.

"So what? I have too," Hannah replies.

"That's okay," says Rita. "I mean – I don't think it's okay for him to marry his students, but one must assume that at the inception the affairs were free-consenting acts, even if between unequals."

Rita is trying to be neutral. Ambiguity, however, is more her manner. That is what Jan, watcher from the corners, thinks. Solomon is a lyrically thin woman with frizzy hair cut almost to the scalp, short enough to suggest a critique of contemporary gender positions, yet suiting her long shapely neck, and certainly just right for a responsible officer of the university.

"That's not the point," argues Sally. "He was in a position with each of his wives, when they were originally his students, to withhold a benefit or favour."

"Nobody complained," Rita said.

"There was no one to complain to," Sally pointed out.

"Have some *kibbi*," Jan said.

"Can't. I'm too fat," said Hannah.

Hannah Janssen-Koeslag has gorgeous tumbling curly chestnut hair and a milk-fed complexion. Her formidable bodice is covered with a huge beaded necklace from Ecuador. Under full sail, she is majestic to the point of being intimidating, and they say that Janssen-Koeslag once made the *Sendero Luminoso* back down in the mountains of Peru. Jan thinks that Hannah is going to be a grandmotherly curmudgeon in her old age, displaying a corpulent near-nakedness and shrewd off-the-hip counsel.

"Is he looking down women's blouses, or what?" Sally asks, rekindling the topic. "Are his lectures contaminated by his obvious, blatant transparent sexism?"

Hannah's body giggles from top to toe. "Honey – have you ever heard him lecture? There's nothing very sexist about cargo tonnage statistics of ships trading between Norwich and Antwerp in the early 1600s."

Sally is quick to reply: "Unless, of course, the whole economic history viewpoint is sexist, which unarguably it is. Have you ever heard a woman talking about mercantile tonnages?"

"Other important things happened in the 1600s too," observed Jilaquns flatly. "Like robbing the Aztec people of gold and emeralds."

"Well, I grant you, he is hideously eurocentric," Hannah said.

"But he calls us 'lassies'!" argued Sally, pressing the point. "That is so totally demeaning."

"Take it easy and eat your *baqlaawa*," Hannah suggested. "Who's for *cappuccino*?"

"The fuckhead called me 'lassie' right in the Dean's office," Jilaquns said.

There was silence at this. Nobody wanted to ask how the Dean, Sally's partner, dealt with it.

"You could file a complaint under the interim complaint procedures," Rita offered. "That might rattle his cage. He'd have it on his file. After a bit, a few other quote-unquote 'lassies' might add to the file, and then we'd have him."

"He'd come back at us by arguing that the Gaelic for 'lassie' is a historic term of respect or some damn thing in the Highlands, not implying endearment." Deep in her manifold being, Hannah, it must be confessed, had a certain affection for Ruairi MacDonald, a man of principle even if he was a slob. "Anyway, I think Ruairi calling Jilaquns 'lassie' is kind of funny."

"I don't think it's funny," said Jill.

"Maybe we need to lighten up more," Hannah suggested.

"Yes," agreed Rita. "Laughter can be an effective tool in political awareness and social change. The role of humour in feminism is an effective way to lighten our lives, help us deal with our anger and hurt, and bring us together in community."

"In any case, we need a better target if we're going to create a climate of political necessity for Draft 4. What we need is a real below-the-belt, low-down-in-the-groin harassment." Hannah, upon second thought, helped herself to a huge portion of *baqlaawa*.

"The truth is, we don't have much on anybody," Rita lamented. "And yet the place is so flagrantly out-to-lunch on teaching that concerns women. Look at the Politics Department. One woman. Look at First Nations … "

"The Center for the First Nations is off-limits," Hannah remarked.

"Thank you," said Jilaquns.

"Well, look at Cultural Studies then," Sally put in. "Sixties males who think that Theory is the summit of learning."

"Yeah — unfit for womenfolk and those feeble and infirm of wit," laughed Hannah.

"But the classes are full of women," Jan volunteered. "Everybody takes Cult-Studs."

"That's the sad thing, isn't it?" Hannah said wearily. "Where were women in the protest movements of the Sixties, anyway? They were giving head to student leaders — that's what they were doing."

"Ugh!" Sally shivered.

"You know, the men have cleaned up their act considerably since the early days," Hannah went on. "We can give ourselves a hug for that! You wouldn't believe what it was like here in the Seventies. Young male faculty coming here straight out of the graduate schools — in effect, the same generational age as their students. All swimming in the same post-Sixties current. Sex, drugs, rock n' roll, and Marcuse." Hannah, as usual, was pulling historical rank. It had been she, singlehandedly, who had started the Women's Studies Department at Avalon.

"I guess that what we need to do is be in a position to debate Academic Freedom at November Senate," Rita said, bringing the discussion back to the present.

"Absolutely," agreed Sally. "MacDonald pulled a fast one, slipping in that motion affirming Academic Freedom."

"The man's cunning — you've got to give him that!" Hannah said. "If the Academic Freedom declaration passes, it's going to be like the fucking Rock of Gibraltar. It's an obstacle to any easy passage of Draft 4."

"MacDonald's motion commits the Administration to promoting an environment of Academic Freedom," Rita explained. "For the whole University, I mean — not just for the faculty."

"What are we going to do then?" Sally asked.

"You understand, my role in this has got to be low-profile," Rita said.

"Yours too, I suspect," Hannah said, nodding at Sally.

"No way! Everybody knows where *I* stand," said Sally Galt.

Jan, at the corner of the table, just outside the magic circle of lamplight, wasn't sure if she liked Sally Galt or not. Her contact lenses, sparkling in the lamplight, made her seem at once intense and vulnerable. She remembered Mrs. Galt from years ago at the cottage, a tall thin child-bride, full of nervous energy and self-consciousness — an unlikely partner for the clear-eyed bachelor Jan used to watch through half-closed eyes while sunbathing on the dock. Now, Sally was a more professional version of herself. Jan, testing her feminist subject position against the array of feminist subjectivities present at the table, found Sally Galt's manner brittle. She was feeling like a wiser older sister to Ms. Galt. Hannah, on the other hand, had an organic heartiness, a blend of commitment and insouciance, that Jan couldn't get her mind around. This woman ate the right food. She was historic. She was deep and capable.

Hannah licked the *cappuccino* foam off her coffee spoon reflectively. "What I think is this. The faculty votes on Senate are going to be solid either way. Aboriginals and women faculty against the classic liberals and libertarians. Even with the Administration representatives supporting us, we're going to be outnumbered. That means it's all up to the students."

"The Union Executive representatives are pledged to defeat the motion," Jilaquns reported. She nodded at Jan who nodded back.

"Okay, that's six votes," Hannah said. "Then there's the College Council reps – two student senators from each college. That's twelve votes."

"The Common Sense Revolution," Jilaquns said. "They're controlled by Bosko."

"Not the Goldman senators," Jan added. "They're controlled by no one."

"Jilaquns," said Hannah sweetly. "It seems to me you're going to have to forge an *alliance à temps* with Mr. Bosko. Stretch out the tentacles of friendship, as they say."

"No way! The dork hates us injuns."

"Maybe he does, maybe he doesn't," Hannah replied. "You don't know that for sure, do you? What you do know is that he's holding down all the College Council reps, except Goldman College. And his recent e-mail seems to be running in the direction of a Harassment/Discrimination policy."

"There'll be a price for his support," Jan said thoughtfully.

"Agh – you can start negotiating with him, at least," Hannah countered. "Students need to speak with one voice around here if they're going to be effective. He'd buy that. Maybe give him a position on the Student Union. Something about having an enemy in the inside of your tent pissing out instead of on the outside of the tent pissing in?"

"He'd be inside, pissing in," Jilaquns retorted.

"Well, you see my point. Tie him up in negotiations just long enough to get his votes. All we need to do is force back the Academic Freedom affirmation. Then we're home-free."

"We'll see what we can do," Jilaquns said. "But we're not touching the Common Sense Revolution, are we Jan?"

Jan shook her head vigorously.

"Let's talk about course content," Sally said. "I brought the book list for Cultural Studies 100. Not a single notable woman on the reading list."

"Does your balloon never come down, Sally?" Hannah Janssen-

SEAN KANE

Koeslag sighed deeply. "I admire your panache, dear. But it would be dangerous to do that at this point, don't you think? If we go after people's teaching now, we're just going to antagonize them. They'll all crowd under the Academic Freedom banner."

"Yes," said Rita Solomon. "Let's get Draft 4 adopted, then we'll go after their teaching."

"We shall be the scourge of the lazy and the patriarchal," announced Hannah. "But right now I'm kicking you out – I'm going to bed. I've got four children to face in the morning and then I have to see a lawyer about getting more support for them from their various fathers. Don't do the dishes. We can stay up late some other night, Sally."

The meeting ended in a ritual of hugs. Driving home to the cottage with Jill, Jan wondered to herself if the subject position of concerned activist student was holding up. She had not contributed much to the meeting. On the other hand, Avalon was becoming a more interesting place by the hour. In the car, she told Jilaquns that she'd accept the position of Student Union Executive member-at-large and vote at tomorrow's meeting of Senate.

14

Even universities much larger than Avalon are academic communities, having traditions of collegial decision-making that pre-date democracy itself. For collegial decision-making to work, information must be spread quickly and evenly, and for information to be properly dispersed, universities have evolved their unique system of committees. The most important business is dealt with in closed session in these committees. That assures everybody in the university receives the information within an hour. However, if really important information has to be circulated quickly through the community, it is put in a report marked *Confidential*. If the information is vitally important and has to spread like wild-fire, it is marked *Strictly Confidential*.

Yet there is one committee at Avalon where information moves in the opposite direction to the normal flow of news in the university. Here, information goes in and nothing comes out. I refer, of course, to the Joint Committee. It is a small body – three from the Administration, three from the Faculty Union – which looks at problems of employment that arise in the life of the university. Officially, the Joint Committee is responsible for interpreting the clauses of the Collective Agreement between management and teaching staff. Normally, interpreting the Agreement means resolving complaints before they develop into full-fledged grievances. And this informal resolution of complaints involves a certain amount of favour-trading between the Union and Administration leaders. Today, especially, Dean Galt, flanked by Bud Lassiter and Sheena Meganetty, were here to trade favours.

Opposite Galt sat Ruairi MacDonald, with Jerry Lewin, his right-hand man, who took the Minutes, and Robyn Endicott, who did the mathematics. It was going to be an interesting meeting because the dean was caught in the Classics department scandal, in return for an escape from which, MacDonald reasoned, the dean might talk about – or be tricked into talking about – his plan for institutional downsizing. Of course, negotiations about changes to the Collective Agreement fell outside the purview of the Joint Committee. Yet ground could be broken informally between two parties who meeting regularly over the years enjoyed the intimacy of co-evolution.

"Our turn to chair the meeting," declared Ruairi MacDonald. "Stimulants? Sustenance? All are called to dine at the table of the Union."

MacDonald gestured magnanimously toward a side-table spread with muffins, Danish pastries, sliced cantaloupe, grapes and strawberries for the health-conscious, coffee (caffeinated and decaf), and the makings for tea. The snacks were paid for out of faculty union funds, and were considerably more lavish than those provided by the dean a month before. MacDonald's lavish spread made a statement about the size of the union's strike fund. Galt's frugal offerings had made their own kind of statement too.

"A wee matter first, to test our wits," MacDonald announced. "We understand you're seeking the Union's agreement to your automatically reappointing a Level II librarian at present on a limited-term replacement contract – this without advertising the position as required by Clauses III.5.0 to III.5.3 of the Collective Agreement. *Right?*"

"Right," Galt repeated. "The renewal would be for another eight months until the regular librarian, whom the person in question is replacing, returns from an unexpected maternity leave which she is now taking following her research leave."

"Which I happen to know she spent in the south of France," added Lewin. "Where Venus still walks the earth, and *caroles* are sung to the goddess in whose steps flowers spring up. *Dolce* France!"

"I dinni think wimmen should be taking government research funds in order to start sprogs – but ah well!" MacDonald muttered.

"The replacement is fully trained in Serials and Microforms, as well as Paper Technologies," Robyn Endicott said. Robyn, with her athletic body filling a white blouse and black slacks, and with her black hair, struck MacDonald as a leader-in-waiting – perhaps, with her command of numbers, the next president of the Union. But what in the name of hell were "paper technologies?"

"What in the name of hell are 'paper technologies'?"

"Books and periodicals."

"Buiks! Then why not say 'buiks,' woman?"

"The proposed replacement has done a good job, and she knows where everything is in the Library," put in Sheena Meganetty.

"I'm glad someone does," MacDonald grunted.

Everyone laughed except for Robyn Endicott. Ms. Endicott still did not understand that banter was the way of the Joint Committee, its members common survivors in a lifeboat propelled into the future by gusts of gossip.

"Well?" MacDonald rested his huge head on his hands and seemed to inhale the silence. The members of the committee looked around the room. They looked at a bright red tartan kilt hanging on the back of the office door, at an old steel-engraving of a Scottish castle, at a photograph of an antique Harley-Davidson motorcycle, at rows and rows of books on trade and navigation, full of statistics and thoroughly unreadable. MacDonald would have to give on this. What would be the price? MacDonald stroked his beard thoughtfully. "We allowed this sort of exemption in 1976, 1989, and 1993, as I recall."

The Dean, his Executive Assistant, and the Registrar looked at each other blankly. So did Professor Lewin and Ms. Endicott.

"I remember the 1976 case," Sheena said. She also had a meticulous institutional memory. "That was the automatic replacement in Psychology when Jack Scanlon died — rest his soul!"

The atmosphere in MacDonald's office changed suddenly. Far away, on the other side of the world, storm clouds gathered over a mountaintop in the Hebrides.

"Aye — puir Jack Scanlon!" MacDonald seemed to be plunged into a sorrowful remembrance of the departed colleague. The room sat in nervous respectful silence while a distant *pibroch* played in MacDonald's complex soul.

"And then the limited-term replacement *suddenly* and *mystairiously* received tenure, to become a pairmanent member o' this Univairsity without advairtisement, interview or due process of hiring, contrary to III.5.5.1 of the Collective Agreement." MacDonald roared. "*Disgraceful!* A year later — lo and behold! — he joins the Administration, being promoted to Vice-President of Student Services. Aye, and the sun shines streght oot his mooth!" MacDonald pounded the table top with a gnarled fist. "I was in a dwam. If my second wife hadna' bin divorcing me at the time, I woulda' haid the wit to put a stop to it!"

Sheena Meganetty took an interest in an uncomfortable sandal underneath the table.

"Be that as it may," Galt countered, "we can promise no tenure-track position for this limited-term replacement."

"Mind whit ye say, mind whit ye dae! Ye won't change the duties of the regular librarian sudden-like when she returns from maternity leave, and then *mystariously* create a tenureable position for her replacement because she has turned out to be God's gift to Serials and Microforms?"

"I'm not creating tenure-track positions for anybody – you can count on it."

"An' you can mak a kirk or a mill of that!" MacDonald reflected for a moment. "But I'll allow the exemption. Draw up the Letter of Understanding, will you Jerry? The wording should say that this is a one-time only exemption agreed to in the unusual circumstances of the limited-term appointee having expertise specific to Serials and Microforms. What other surprises d'ye have for us?"

Cameron Galt felt uneasy in the contradiction between legal formality and oral gossip. He was having trouble gauging the working style of a committee that was by turns collegial and confrontational. He chose to err on the side of the oral. It brought parties together. Certainly, the two sides would have to be together on this next item.

"Well, it seems the Classics department has been conducting a review of a candidate for tenure – last one they'll ever see! And the department chair evidently decides that comments made in confidence by a particular faculty member on the department's tenure review committee are intemperate to the point of ... well, let us say, *showing prejudice* against the candidate."

"Faith Rackstraw!" exclaimed Lewin with glee. "Faith Rackstraw blows it again!"

Galt ignored the interjection. "Apparently feeling that the representatives on the committee might have been influenced by the faculty member's prejudice, and the candidate cast thereby in an unfair light, the Chair asked the committee members to resign."

"Noo whatever did she do that for?" asked MacDonald, with a sweet false innocence.

"To make way for a new Tenure Review Committee."

"Ah-ha!" MacDonald growled.

Once again there was silence in the meeting. It was not the silence of options being explored. It was the silence of an invisible bolt of power sliding from Galt's side of the table to MacDonald's.

"So why the difficulty with this candidate's tenure award, any-way?" Lewin asked. "I hear she's got a great publication record in feminist theory."

"Evidently, doubts were raised about her teaching – and her general collegial compatibility," Galt reported.

Bang! The table shook under MacDonald's fist. "That is not the point!" *Bang!* Again, the fist came down on the table top. MacDon-ald took a deep breath. "We are not concairned with the candidate in question – we dinna give a hoot about her research profile or her teaching promise. Least of all are we concerned with the question of her *com-pat-i-bility*. There is only one thing that concairrns us here today."

MacDonald paused to let the silence gather. The Dean looked distinctly uncomfortable.

"We are concairrned only with the integrity of the peer review process, the immemorial academic custom of judgment by one's colleagues, fellow specialists in a branch of knowledge. Peers have the Academic Freedom to say whatever they want tae aboot an ini-tiate."

Galt regarded his hands helplessly. "Look – I inherited this one – it happened before I got here – and I don't think any of us will get to the bottom of who said what. But please see this. If the candidate is an outspoken feminist, and a preponderantly male tenure review committee is uneasy about her teaching – I won't even go into the issue of her compatibility – and the Chair of the committee, who is female, has apprehensions about prejudice, then we have a situation. The University will explode over this. There's too much Human Rights tension in the air already."

MacDonald let out a great sigh that filled everybody in the room so that even the conference table itself seemed to sigh.

"Again, ye've missed the point, laddie. The candidate's views? That's nary our concairn. The views of people in the Univairsity? That's nay our concairn either. If the candidate does not like the outcome of the peer-review process, she is free to appeal it. Provision is made for an appeal under III.6.4.3. The point you keep missing, sir, is that the *Academic Right of Freedom of Expression* was violated by the departmental chair acting as an officer of the Univairsity." MacDonald rolled a baleful eye at the Dean. "In other words, sir, the Chair, as *your* surrogate, forced on a peer review process − where colleagues ought to be free to express their opinions − a climate opposed to Academic Freedom. We will not stand for this! The Union will not stand for this!"

Again there was a terrifying silence around the table. Raindrops beat a frenzied pattern against MacDonald's office window.

"I wouldn't touch this one with a barge pole," remarked Lewin.

"But surely," Galt persisted, "people can't make injurious comments about a person behind her back."

"Oh, we do that all the time around here," Lewin said gaily.

"But apparently massive prejudice was displayed."

"Says who?" demanded Lewin.

"Says Faith Rackstraw."

"Says Faith's dog. It didn't like the smell of the committee."

"Professor Rackstraw reported that she hadn't heard comments as extreme as this in twenty years."

"Oh, Faith's just being her usual effete self," Lewin exclaimed.

MacDonald considered this might be true. He couldn't abide Rackstraw. Her affected laboring of phrases sounded like a *sasunnach* prelate. He turned towards his apprentice. "Robyn − how many grievances d'ye count comin' oot of this one?"

"Three," said Endicott. "Plus a lawsuit against the University."

"Yons a right fankle!" Ruairi MacDonald seemed delighted. He clapped his hands together. "Coffee anyone? A slice of fresh cantaloupe perhaps? I could go tea and scones and raspberry jam."

The Dean shook his head ruefully. The Registrar made a tight-lipped smile and rolled his eyes in defeat towards the ceiling. Only Sheena Meganetty, at the Administration's side of the table, was at ease: she knew the next act that was coming in MacDonald's theatre. The wait was long, for first MacDonald had to go laboriously over to the side-table and pour himself a cup of tea, which he drank while gazing at the steel-engraving of the castle in Scotland. Finally, he turned and faced the representatives of the Administration.

"Mr. Dean – maybe we can give ye a way oot."

"Yes?" said Galt, faintly, expectantly.

"Now, the committee members who were forced to resign: have their resignations been received?"

"Sheena?"

"Yes, the resignations were extended – under protest, of course. Faith evidently scared the committee to bits with the suggestion that the disadvantaged candidate might sue."

"And so she might! So she might!" Resuming his seat, Mac-Donald had brought a pitcher of icewater to the table and was pouring himself a glass. "What's a wee lawsuit noo and then, eh?" Apparently, Ruairi MacDonald, unlike the faint-hearted members of the tenure committee, flourished in an atmosphere of litigation. "But listen to my question, will ye? My question was – did the committee members in fact resign? Have their resignations bin in fact received by any univairsity body?"

"Oh, I don't know," said Galt, exasperated. He couldn't see what MacDonald was driving at. "This mess has been the talk of the University since last spring. Who knows who did what anymore?"

Sheena spoke up. "Except for Faith Rackstraw, nobody from the tenure committee has notified the Dean's Office yet."

"Then no one's resigned," MacDonald said, softly and meaningfully.

"No one's come to us with a grievance either," reported Endicott, catching on to the game. "It's all around the University, yet no one's come to us with a grievance."

"And d'ye know why no one's came to us? No one's came to us because, technically speaking, *nothin' has happened.*"

Lassiter, who had been silent until now, finally exploded. "How can you say nothing has happened, for pete's sake? A shit-storm has happened, that's all!"

"Look," said MacDonald with finely measured impatience. He sounded like he was addressing a first-year History seminar that had not done its reading. "At this point in time – at precisely this point in the process, if the resignations are retracted – no clause in the Collective Agreement has been broken – *right*? The resignations have not been officially received, and therefore the members of the committee cannot be said to have resigned. The committee is still in place. Academic Freedom has not been violated."

"But it has!" Lewin interjected.

MacDonald put up a great restraining hand. "Naw, laddie – if ye run the situation backward in time, *as far as the Union is concerned*, Academic Freedom has not been violated. If, however, you run the situation forward, electing a new Tenure Review Committee and so forth, the mess is incalculable and novel. Grievances no matter which way ye turn. Was the candidate's tenure earned? Or did she achieve it by circumstance? Will future candidates achieve tenure on a technicality that their Human Rights have been violated? Then we may as well not have a peer review process."

"It stinks to high heaven," admitted Lassiter. "Like a goddam pig farm."

"The Human Rights atmosphere is making everyone jumpy," Sheena offered.

"Of course it is, lassie! At the merest suggestion an individual's Human Rights have been threatened, Academic Freedom goes oot the window." MacDonald glared a bloodshot eye across the table at the Dean.

"I hear what you're, saying," Galt said, meekly.

"Dinna wheenge, son – I'm giving ye the way oot. Take it. Roll the situation backwards just a wee bit. Faith Rackstraw must apologize to the peer review committee for threatening its members. She has made a griff. Now, she has sober second thoughts about the intemperate impulse of asking them to tender their resignations. The integrity of the committee is preserved. Academic Freedom is preserved. With the resignations withdrawn, the members of the committee can come to a decision. The decision can be appealed and only strictly evidential grounds of teaching and research will be allowed. The Union is not involved in a divisive situation. Piece of duff!"

"Alright," Galt agreed.

"We won't minute this, will we?" Lewin said.

"Naw – it didna happen."

"Mum's the word," agreed Lassiter.

"A closed mouth gathers no foot," said Sheena Meganetty.

"Indeed, it may happen, now that the committee's confidentiality is broken, that members of the committee have had second, more positive thoughts about the candidate's teaching." MacDonald sighed and reached for the satisfaction of a cigar before remembering that the university's smoke-free policy applied even to his own office.

"Now let's move on to something major," he said ominously.

There was a rustling of paper and scraping of chairs against the floor as the members of the Joint Committee prepared themselves for the new item.

"Academic Freedom," MacDonald announced.

The Dean looked up, startled.

"I believe Professor MacDonald wants the Administration to formally endorse our declaration of Academic Freedom at tomorrow's Senate," explained Robyn Endicott.

Galt shook his head wanly. "I understand your position. I also understand the position of the Women's Caucus. I hear from the Caucus about this almost daily, you know." The Dean grinned. The members of the Joint Committee grinned with him. "But the Administration can't afford to support one position over the other in a split community. I hope you appreciate that. The Administration's position is to be neutral."

MacDonald nodded. "Off the record. Let's go outside so I can smoke. The meeting of the Joint Committee is now concluded."

Outside in the chilly November afternoon the rain had stopped. Ice was forming on the puddles of the Cabot College walkway. MacDonald lit a cigar. "I'll take a daunder with ye over to Sears."

The Dean and the President of the Faculty Union picked their way through crowds of students rushing along the bridges between classes.

"We've been trying to negotiate a Voluntary Early Retirement plan with your Hugh D'Arnay for a year now. But he keeps fending it off."

"Well, you understand we're in a period of transition with upper management."

"Aye. And would I be right in assuming, sir, that it is a consequence of the transition to undertake a major downsizing of the faculty?"

"The assumption is correct. But even with an Early Retirement Plan, I'm not going to be able to balance the faculty salaries side of the operation."

"D'Arnay's damned command economics. He gives ye yer academic budget and it's skint, and ye have to balance it. No way to run a univairsity."

"In any case, we may still not have enough money to downsize through Early Retirement." Galt warned.

MacDonald paused at the footbridge leading over to the forecourt of Sears. His gabardine raincoat billowed in a sudden gust of wind from down the river. He stamped out his cigar.

"Supposin', sir, I were to find you, say, forty faculty who want to take Early Retirement. Now, jist supposin'. Forty, I say, including Rackstraw and her soddin' dog. And jist supposin' that their early retirement would be paid for out of the faculty side of the Pension Plan Surplus."

"Hmm. Forty. That's the entire senior professorate at Avalon. Experienced leaders in the University."

"We're all knackered, laddie. We're useless tits."

"What's in the Surplus for medical benefits for the ones who are left? Not to mention the ones who are hanging around the Mall?" Galt quivered at the prospect of forty more retired faculty added to the group at the Mall. "And what if there's a significant government funding cutback two years up the road, and we have no Pension Plan Surplus to deal with the layoffs?"

"You can sell more Univairsity property. Hell, mon, you can sell the Univairsity, since there won't be much left of it if there's a big funding cutback."

"I'm listening."

"Say, forty faculty. Spread all over, you see. Then we can preserve the core of Avalon in good nick tae a better day."

"There may not be a better day, Ruairi."

"Laddie, I know why you're here. Ye're here to bring in pure researcher and pure teacher streams. It worked at the Metropolitan University. It won't work here – can't ye understaun? It won't work here because there aren't enough researchers spread around all the Humanities departments. I can count the researchers on the fingers of one hand. I can, laddie. It will only work if you want to shrink the University down around an Ecology Research Center. And I dinna think you want to do that, do you now?"

"No, I'm with you. Avalon is nothing without the Humanities."

"Good! Weel then – if you replace those forty expensive senior professors with forty top-notch faculty at the beginning of their careers, you can renew the place."

"Forty faculty, you say?"

"Aye."

"And you'll let us have your Pension Plan Surplus to work this with?"

"I'll do the calculations for you. I'm the only one around here who knows how the Pension Plan works, anyway."

"Alright – I'll see what I can do."

"You're a good man, Cam." MacDonald seized Galt's hand in another unending handshake.

Galt took advantage of the bonding ceremony to get something off his mind.

"Ruairi – I don't want a strike this year."

"Neither do I, Cam. And, I assure you, neither do the forty faculty leaders who will be retiring fra the fray."

MacDonald withdrew his hand from Galt's. "I'll see you at Senate," he said. "*Beannacht leat!*"

Galt waved goodbye and made his way to the Dean's Office.

MacDonald disappeared in the direction of Faith Rackstraw's flat in Goldman College.

15

AVALON ASSOCIATION OF RETIRED PROFESSORS

4 November

Dear Fellows:

Those of you conducting Remedial Spelling classes in the Food Court should announce to your groups *The Great January Bargain Days Spell-off Tournament* which is sponsored by our Association and takes place in the Mall from 10:00 a.m. to 12:00 noon on January 9. Here are the rules:

1. Five teams are participating, as follows:

> The Dyslexic Collective
> Aboriginal Aphasiacs
> The Queens of Illiteracy
> Orthomorphs
> Spellers from Hell

2. Teams will set out at 10:00 a.m. from the Food Court looking for spelling mistakes in the signs and notices of shops in the Mall. Thanks to cooperating merchants there will be approximately 150 spelling mistakes to be found.

3. Teams are awarded one point for every spelling error located.

4. Teams are awarded a further point for each spelling error successfully corrected.

5. Inadvertent spelling mistakes which are found anywhere in the Mall, and which are not on the list, have a value of four points if found and corrected.

6. The Prizes are:

> First Prize: for members of the winning team, coupons representing a 20% discount on any purchase from the merchants participating in the event.
> Second Prize: for the runner-up team, a 10% discount on any purchases made at the Mall.
> Other Prizes: food vouchers for participating teams redeemable at any outlet in the Food Court.

7. Pocket computers with spell-checkers may not be used. Persons over 30 years of age should be discouraged from participating. Avalon Association of Retired Professors tutors may not be involved beyond the point of cheering their respective teams on. Any betting should be done discreetly.

8. Teams are invited to stay at the Food Court after the event for a Cultural Studies 100 performance piece involving trapeze work by Jilaquns and Jan D'Arnay.

★   ★   ★

AVALON UNIVERSITY
Office of the Provost and Dean of Arts and Science

To: Hugh D'Arnay
From: Cameron Galt
Date: 5 November
Re: University Heights Mall

<u>Confidential</u>

1. Following up yours of 23 October, I have checked into the situation you mention, and advise that serious repercussions would ensue if retired professors of Avalon were charged with loitering at the Food Court Mall. Apart from the fact that they are citizens and customers of the various fast-food outlets at the Mall, the professors evidently enjoy the respect and loyalty of the student population at Avalon, which would be sure to picket the Mall if the professors in question were removed.

2. The merchants consider the retired professors a welcome presence in the Mall. Evidently, they are bringing in business, not only from students but from housewives, teenagers, etc., who have been seen attending lectures and taking classes from the retirees. Incidentally, the retirees are also offering a free babysitting service to Mall patrons.

3. Bud Lassiter reports that the retired professors are assisting in no small way in the overall Avalon enrolment picture.

★   ★   ★

Date: 5 November
To: all faculty
From: Sheena Meganetty (Dean's Office)

At a recent meeting of Senate, the following motion was approved:
Students who wish to observe their cultural or religious holidays should notify their instructor so that tests, exams, field-trips and significant class events can be rescheduled.

For your information, the following list indicates the major religious observances in the Fall Term. A further list of Faith Days in the Spring Term will be issued in January.

September
6   Rosh Hashanah (Judaism)
10   Ullamabana (Buddhist – Mahayanist)
12   Ghambar Paitishem (Zoroastrian) begins
15   Yom Kippur (Judaism)
18   Ananta-chaturdasi (Jainist) holiest day of Dashalaksani-parva
19   Ksamavani (Jainist)
20   Sukkot (Judaism) begins
28   Simhat Torah (Judaism)
October
12   Ghambar Ayathrem (Zoroastrian) begin
14   Dassehra (Hinduism)
19   Pavarana (Buddhist – Theravada and Mahayana Schools)
20   Birth of Báb (Baha'i)
31   Samhain (Celtic – Wicca)
November
2   Mahavira Nirvana (Jainist) or Dipavali
3   Diwali (Hindu, Sikh)
12   Birth of Bahá'u'lláh (Baha'i)
18   Birthday of Gura Nanak Dev Ji (Sikhism)
26   Day of the Covenant (Baha'i)

28   The Ascension of 'Abdul–Bahá (Baha'i)

28   Hanukkah (Judaism) first day, until December 5

December

3   First Sunday of Advent (Christian)

12   Maunajiyaras (Jainist)

25   Christmas (Christian – Gregorian calendar)

26   Death of Zarathustra (Zoroastrian)

28   Birth of Gura Gobind Singh Ji (Sikh)

29   Mi'rāj al–Nabīy (Islam) begins in evening

31   Ghambar Maidyarem (Zoroastrian) begins

★   ★   ★

AVALON UNIVERSITY
Office of the Registrar
5 November

Welcome to Avalon University's new Touchtone Registration
System (TRS). This service is provided to you by the Office of the
Registrar and has been developed to make the course registration
process easier and faster for you. When you use this system our
computer will communicate with you using voice messages and
voice prompts. You can respond to these prompts and messages by
pressing the appropriate key on your touchtone phone.

Using any touchtone phone that emits different tones for each
key that is pressed, you will be able to:

• Register for courses
• Withdraw from courses
• List your course registrations

PERSONAL ACCESS CODE

Each time you use the TRS you will be required to enter your six
digit Personal Identification Number (PIN). The first time you use
the TRS your PIN will be your birthdate and you will be asked to

enter your birthdate in the form YYMMDD. For example, if your birthdate is 31 December, 1980, you would enter 801231. Before you will be able to proceed, the system will request that you change your PIN. We recommend that you choose a familiar number for your six digit PIN. From then on, you must use this PIN to access the system.

IF YOU MAKE AN ERROR

If you should make an error when keying in a number, complete the entry. The TRS system will respond by repeating the number you have entered and ask you to confirm if the number is correct. If the number is incorrect and you have responded by pressing '2' the system will ask you to re-enter the correct number.

The system will allow you three chances to enter the information correctly. After the third failure the session will be terminated.

BEFORE USING THE TOUCHTONE SYSTEM

Review the *Course Registration* and *Course Offerings* section of this calendar.

Select the Avalon University course you wish to register in or withdraw from.

Check the section entitled SPECIAL INSTRUCTIONAL FEATURES to determine if there are any restrictions, eg. required start dates, prerequisites, professor's approval, limited to Nursing students, etc.

PAYMENT PROCESS

Avalon University requires that all services be paid in full prior to being provided. Payment may be made by entering your credit card number. If you currently owe money to Avalon University, you will receive a voice prompt to that effect. Unless you respond to the voice prompt indicating how you may pay outstanding fees and service charges by entering your credit card number, the session will be terminated.

★   ★   ★

6 November

Bud
Dear ~~Registrar~~,

I am writing to convey to you the protest of students at Goldman College, as well as my own dismay, at the proposed "Touchtone Registration System." At Avalon, your education is a <u>personal</u> adventure of learning with a community of scholars, and with the guidance of Academic Advisors who counsel each student about her or his course choices within an unfolding academic plan of study. That is the Avalon way. That has always been the Avalon way. The proposed "Touchtone Registration System" strikes at the heart of Avalon's uniqueness as a community devoted to learning.

For this reason, the Council of Emma Goldman College has voted unanimously to encourage students *not* to participate in the computerized registration system. Course changes made by students at this College will be done in the traditional way with their Academic Advisors. Then the paperwork will be gathered by us and mailed to you, and you can process it all yourself!

Yours sincerely,
Faith Rackstraw
Principal
Goldman College

cc. Cameron Galt
Provost and Dean of Arts and Science.

★　★　★

7 November

Cameron Galt
Dean of Arts and Science

Cameron Galt:

Greetings! I am writing to inform you that at a recent meeting of the Center, it was decided to award the degree of Doctor of Philosophy in Aboriginal Metaphysics and Healing to Mr. Joseph Waasagunackank, Elder of the Anishnaabe People.

This decision has the outcome of honouring Waasagunackank's deep knowledge of the wisdom of the Earth, as well as his stature among the Aboriginal Peoples of America. Our intention is to bestow the Degree at a special one hour and forty-five minute ceremony at the commencement of the Spring Convocation, before the national anthem, with drummers and singers from the Anishnaabe and other First Nations participating.

Although Avalon University does not yet have official accreditation to grant the degree of PH.D., I wish to remind you that the Center for the First Nations has final authority in matters involving aboriginal education, and it has reserved the right to determine soundness of learning in all matters involving Aboriginal knowledge. Accordingly, I am writing now to inform you of our intention and to ask your office for cooperation.

Megwetj,
Tom Baptiste

★ ★ ★

This message is for all faculty from Sheena Meganetty in the Dean's Office. Further to our memo of 5 Nov., the list of Important Faith Days is not – repeat not – inclusive of all faith traditions in the world. For Native students, a listing of important dates and times (e.g. December = Moon of the Little Spirits – Anishnaabe) will be available from the Center for the First Nations, and such celebrations and significant times (such as the beginning of the hunting season) may be brought to the instructor's attention by students concerned. Thank you.

★　　★　　★

Riing! Riing! Riing!
Click

This is the telephone number of Sally M. Galt and Cameron Galt. We're sorry – we cannot come to the phone to take your call right now. Please leave a brief message after the tone. Thank you.

"Ah, it's Sally, Cam. Looks like I'm at this meeting late and can't make it up to the cottage. Easier to stay over at Hannah's and do the Womens Studies 100 lecture in the morning. There's last night's lasagna in the fridge – it's better the second night. See ya."

Click

★　　★　　★

This message is for all faculty from Sheena in the Dean's Office. Further correction to our memo of 5 Nov. re: important faith days. The term "Celtic" does not connote a recognized world religion. It applies to ethnically and linguistically diverse peoples of European extraction united originally by common sets of customs. One of these was respect for the fertility cycle of our Mother Earth, which was honoured in her 4 phases on the night before each entry into the next phase: *Samhain* (eve of the first of November); *Night of the Goddess* (= Brigit) (eve of the first of February); *Beltain* (eve of the first of May); *Lughnassa*, dedicated to the harvest sun-god Lugh (eve of the first of August). This is important since students identifying themselves as either Worshippers of the Goddess or as *wiccas* may ask for and should be given special exemptions from tests, exams, etc. on these nights of worship. Thanks.

★　　★　　★

7 November

Gentle Daughter,

It was while having wine outside Le Mabillon on the Blvd St-Germain, happily watching Paris be Paris, that your Errant Mother read your e-mail, and therefore with laughter and delight that she read your last sentence, wishing that she be in a café. Happily, she was there with a gentleman who could share her delight in both the letter and the café.

Ah, Paris, which believes it has invented culture. It is everywhere rampant. On the R&R shuttle from Charles de Gaulle Airport, a young girl plays charming Renaissance airs on a recorder. She passes the hat with a smile and a curtsy, and your E.M. gives her a couple of francs. The musician gets off two stations down the line, and her place is taken by a guy with a guitar. He sings old Bob Dylan songs nicely. And his accent is irresistible. At the spectacular La Défense business, shopping and sightseeing complex, there are fountains that dance to piped classical music. The post office there has chairs at each counter so you can actually rest your feet while you buy your stamps. At Au Trou Gascon on the rue Taine, your Mother asks for a *Marc de Bourgogne* as a *digestif*. The waiter brings a list of *Marcs* five pages long.

Yet your Errant Mother is not one to be taken in by this display of civilization, which is in fact a display of consumerism. She all too readily sees its nether side. Here it is midnight, and outside on the streets of the Left Bank all the children of the Western World (and those who wish they were) are pouring out their energy, in search of the world they have lost, which is the world their elders sold from under their cradles. Thinking this makes your Delinquent Parent quite sad. Slumming yuppie that she is, she has been learning what she can from the streets. And what she sees are the hustlers and prancers getting by on inborn talent because that is all they have – that, and the heaps of broken images and ideas they can amass from the rubbish of history. Paris – capital of the 19th century, slum of the 21st. Every-where, beneath their *esprit gallique*, your E.M. sees poor lost children: they have not had the luxury of a real cul-ture or (the next best thing to a culture, and its usual substitute) an education. And if the young – raised under the constant spray of spiritual defoliants of a high-tech, mass-mediated civilization – come to believe erroneously that culture is inborn and innate, who can blame them? What else could they believe, given the conditions in which parents like me and their titular leaders and *émarques* have abandoned them?

Ah me! Your Delinquent Mom is heavy with a regret which this excellent late-night Burgundy does nothing to dispel. If cultures have been smashed to smithereens, perhaps it is true that this ever was the case – that culture (I hesitate to use quotation marks as highlighters) is merely the spoils of the victor. Yet the schools that once did duty in place of real culture are being methodically trashed, and with an alarming, almost proud and visceral haste, by the Hugh D'Arnays of this world, who wish to sell pasteurized ideas in smart tin cans and plastic take-out bags. What then will take the place of the schools of learning? Little *ad hoc* cultures hobbled together by nomadic bands moving, either suavely or desperately, from garbage heap to garbage heap? Probably so, *hélas*. Your E. Mother, in her worst Arnoldian-Eliotean moments, concludes that a nomadic band is fine if it is allowed to mellow like the Burgundy she is imbibing. Without such mellowing, the brew might be a little shrill and raw.

Coming to Paris, as you see, has not cast a rosy glow over your Mother's view of things. Indeed, she is inclined to view modern European culture as essentially a habit of conversation linked rhythmically to the consumption of stimulants and depressants, namely coffee and wine. In other words, culture exists to give people something to talk about in a society of *alienées*. This may be especially true of the three café society countries whose inhabitants take breakfast out in the morning. I refer to Spain, Italy and Hungary (where the custom produces extra-sociable superficialities like the Magyar cream-puff who has caught your father's fancy). Why the people of Paris do not similarly hit the cafés in the morning, there to prolong their endless chatter about politics and film, is a question which the gentleman who is with your mother now is at some difficulty to explain. (The issue seems to turn on the traditional polygamy of these urban people, and the need to touch base each morning with one's spouse over a familiar stick of French bread.)

To your query about joining your Erstwhile Mom

over the Christmas Break in Granada, where she is going in order to study the Moorish garden as a site of contemplation, you would be very welcome company. As always.

To the proposal to do a trapeze performance in a mall with Jilaquns (please give my fondest wishes to dear Jill), your Concerned Mother counsels that it is a long time since her Athletic Daughter did competitive gymnastics and waterskiing, and Jill's background in modern dance, however accomplished it is, may not be adequate preparation for erotic exercises on the high bar.

To the idle curiosity as to which professor of Avalon it was that your mother mingled with during her checkered past, your moral mother advises that it is, of course, impolite to ask such a question, a lady's affairs being strictly her own.

To the news of achieving a seat on the Senate of Avalon University, your Mother advises her Daughter, similarly, to try to keep her mouth shut.

Peace, Love, Happiness,
Jennifer

★   ★   ★

MEMO TO: Members of Avalon Women's Caucus

As you are no doubt aware, the first male backlash against our Anti-Harassment/Discrimination policy (Draft 3) takes place at Senate tomorrow at 13:00 hours in the form of an institutional endorsement of Academic Freedom in a motion to be moved by MacDonald/Lewin. It is important that all women at Avalon try to attend this meeting of Senate. Even if you are not a member of Senate, your presence at the meeting is vital, especially for the student senators who will be contesting the MacDonald motion. Please try to attend.

Many thanks!
Hannah.

★   ★   ★

AVALON UNIVERSITY FACULTY UNION
8 November

Dear Brothers and Sisters,

Tomorrow afternoon at Senate, a motion will be put by me as President of the Union, seconded by Professor Jeremy Lewin, affirming the Declaration of Academic Freedom which makes up the Preamble to the present Collective Agreement. When this Motion carries tomorrow, it will become the responsibility of <u>everyone</u> at the University – faculty, students, support staff AND administration – to commit themselves to promoting as the first aim of Avalon University a climate conducive to Free Inquiry and the Free Expression of Opinion. The principle of Academic Freedom is the foundation of everything we do at Avalon. It is the basis of our profession as scholars and teachers.

Please try to come to this important Meeting. A show of force from the faculty will ensure that the Motion succeeds.

Slainthe,

Ruairi MacDonald
President,
Avalon Faculty Union

★   ★   ★

CONFEDERATION OF COLLEGE COUNCILS

from the desk of Victor Bosko

8 November

Dear College Council Members:

Tomorrow is a very important day for the Common Sense Revolution at Avalon! Now that all the college councils (with the exception of Emma Goldman College) are speaking with one voice, and that voice is the voice of the Common Sense Revolution, it is time for us as students to assert our rights as the client-user sector of the University. As consumers, we have the right to determine the quality of the educational products being sold to us through the tuition fees we pay. Heretofore, professors living in ivory tower isolation from the real corporate world (where we are going to find jobs and careers) have been the ones to decide what is best for us to learn. Entrenched in their autonomous, not publicly accountable disciplines, they have the power to pass down irrelevant specialized knowledge (through their control of curriculum, journals, conferences, etc.), they have the power to regenerate themselves, and the power to control entrance into their midst (through Ph.Ds and tenure-track hirings). Thus, these disciplines have developed with the obsolete industrialized assembly-line production unit model of society, with its bureaucratic self-maintenance, inertia, and rule-orientation instead of goal-orientation. Tomorrow at Senate, the Faculty Union is trying to protect its unaccountable, statist, socialistic bureaucracy of knowledge by passing a motion in favour of Academic Freedom.

However, we students know differently! We know that real learning only happens when *diverse students from various backgrounds* pool what they know and join in a common effort to accomplish *something that needs to be done.* Thus, we in the Confederation of College Councils are voting against Academic Freedom and Privilege so as to make room for the new Anti-Harassment/Discrimination policy which underlies the user-friendly, interactive model of learning and ensures that our diverse voices will actually be heard in our own education. Bring as many friends as you can from your college to show that students claim the right to control their own education.

Yours sincerely,
Victor Bosko

P.S.   The Student Union Executive members on Senate have agreed to vote with us in defeating Academic Freedom

★   ★   ★

This memo is for all faculty from Sheena Meganetty (Dean's Office). Further to the e-mail of 8 Nov. yesterday re: faith days, it has been brought to my attention that a court recently ruled that *wiccas* (witches) do not constitute a religious worship system involving formal observance customs, and therefore unfortunately do not qualify for the exemption stated in the Important Faith Days memo of 5 Nov. from this office.

★   ★   ★

16

Jan examined the faces of the members of Senate as they trooped into the Council Chamber. Or, rather, she examined their reflections. For the room jutted out into the river like a ship's prow, and what Jan saw against a black November afternoon were the faces reflected in the fluorescent light that was flung against the windowpanes. They looked like jovial ghosts in a ship of glass sailing into the night. Outside, the ocean of hills rolled away to infinity.

There was tension in the room, broken by the forced jocularity of faculty hanging up their raincoats and umbrellas in the hall outside. It was like the tension before a public execution, Jan thought. Victor Bosko, chief executioner, was already in position. Wearing a pin-striped blue suit that bunched at the shoulders, and with a laptop and printer before him on the varnished pine table top, he had picked a strategic position directly opposite the Chair of Senate, and sat there dark, portentious and forbidding. Filling the row beside Bosko were the student reps from the colleges – the Common Sense Revolutionaries. Mostly first-year students, they wore college jackets with their majors spelled out on their left arm – and one of the women wore a pink angora angel-fluff sweater. And another woman was dressed in a blue suit with oversized imitation pearls like something out of *Ally McBeal*. Had she really had her hair done for the occasion? Ashley Tiffin, on the other hand, over there beside the wall, broke ranks altogether in her black tights and long black sweater. Cultural Studies was having an effect on her.

Bosko looked across at Jan who sat at right angles to him with the other Student Union reps. Jan glanced away from his reflection and looked him in the eyes. Whereupon Bosko winked confidently.

Jan as member-at-large *pro tem* was the only white among a phalanx of women from the First Nations and other visible minorities. Six solid votes. So with the Bosko minions onside, the students were going into the meeting with sixteen Human Rights votes.

The Emma Goldman anarchists in high grunge – who knew which way they were going to fall? Even the optimistic Jilaquns had put question marks beside their names which she had written on a serviette. The faculty members of Senate were entrenched, of course, behind Academic Freedom: two from each college – that's twelve votes, except that three of them were Women's Caucus members supported by students who sat in a nervous group on the other side of the room. Nine votes then. Sally Galt was there, in the visitors' seats, along with an excited crowd of students from the Gays and Lesbians Collective. But Hannah Janssen-Koeslag had a vote alright. There she was taking her seat with a majestic bustle among the three Women's Caucus members, who were clearing a place for her. Joe Waasagunackank and Tom Baptiste from the First Nations Center apparently had seats on Senate. Joe, wearing his dark blue windbreaker and jeans, seemed lost in thought. Tom Baptiste took his seat with an executive manager's ease, and promptly began scanning the Minutes. The Natives faced the senior officers of the university who sat in a row close to the center of authority in the room. This group, comprising the six college heads, would presumably support Human Rights over Academic Freedom. If a student is in a situation of harassment or discrimination, where is her Academic Freedom? However, there was no telling how Faith Rackstraw would vote. Probably her vote depended on the intuition of Clio who at this moment was scratching her fleas, making the vast council table shake.

There was a bustle outside the room, then a hush of awe as Ruairi MacDonald entered. As head of the Faculty Union, he also had a vote. So did Professor Lewin by his side with the top of his head coming to MacDonald's shoulder. Lewin, for some reason, had chosen to wear a grey suit that was too long in the sleeves and too wide at the lapels. Beneath it, he wore a black shirt with a mostly white floral tie, looking, Jan thought, like an Italian film-director. Sunglasses, which he wore against the glare of the fluorescent lights, completed the illusion.

Jilaquns was nervously putting a series of tick marks beside a column of names which she had titled "Reactionaries." Two more ticks. That made fourteen. And fourteen very articulate votes. Led by "The Laird," the faculty were here to defend the basis of their profession.

The Chair of Senate broke off a rushed conversation he was having at the coffee urn with the Registrar. Today's chair was not President Rattenbury – it was Dean Galt.

He seemed much younger than when Jan had gazed up at him through the eyes of a teenager. Now, instead of cottage shorts and sandals, he was wearing a suit – a dark-blue suit – and of all the men in the room he was the only one whose clothes were tailored perfectly. The neat trimmed beard – she had not seen that beard before. His hair, which used to be black, now had a gentle greyness in it. Jan had a picture of elegance and power coloured in hues of blue and silver. How would he call this issue if forced to cast the deciding vote? Would he support the equality of all races and sexual persuasions? Or would he defend the ancient freedom of academics to criticize society without fear of reprisal?

Jan looked out into the November gloom and pondered the issue. Human Rights appealed to her because she was a woman. Yet since she had never once in her life been discriminated against or harassed – unless you counted Victor Bosko's lugubrious advances by voice-recorder and e-mail as a form of harassment – she felt personally removed from the issue. Human Rights was very much Jilaquns' concern, and Jan had heard many reasons why. Jan felt duty-bound to support the principle, and not just because she was now part of the official student leadership. Avalon led the country in the health of its environment of gender relations. This was a university where gender rarely intruded on professional relationships.

Academic Freedom, on the other hand, commanded her loyalty too. Obviously, free thought and free speech was more than a male professor's license to be an all-out creep. It was a traditional freedom from accountability for one's opinions, like the exemption enjoyed to a certain limit by judges and politicians – other professionals who couldn't do their jobs properly if they were to be fired for their statements. Academic Freedom allowed professors to do daring research, research that criticized the will of corporations that were taking over the world, and the universities with it. Moreover, the exuberant idiosyncrasies of Avalon – Professor Lewin's playful irreverence, for example – were rooted in the right of Academic Freedom. Jan wondered how she might vote if she weren't bound by the resolve of the Student Union Executive to vote as a block for Human Rights. Professors have power; power must be accountable.

November Senate droned on in the background of Jan's thinking, with speakers raising tiny nervous points in anticipation of the main agenda item. Beside her, Jilaquns was drawing mythcreatures on her empty styrofoam coffee container in elegant formlines. Outside, the dark hills conferred among themselves.

Now what was this? Someone – it was Professor MacDonald – had changed the order of business, bringing Academic Freedom to the top of the Senate agenda. And now he had moved his motion affirming Academic Freedom; Jerry Lewin had seconded the motion. Hannah Janssen–Koeslag had the floor, chestnut ringlets tumbling down to her dimpled elbows.

"Mr. Chair – there is absolutely no reason why Senate needs to affirm Academic Freedom. It is already in the Collective Agreement. I object to this time-consuming piece of mischief tactically inserted into the agenda of Senate to block the natural evolution of a Human Rights policy at Avalon."

Janssen-Koeslag resumed her seat after smiling grimly to the applause which came from the visitors' seats behind her and from the Student Union Executive. The Common Sense Revolutionaries rapped their knuckles on the table top with judicious approval, but stopped when they saw that Bosko himself was immobile.

"Mistairr Chairrman!" Now the deep tones of Ruairi MacDonald, his vowels rich with history and his consonants spat out decisively. "As my dear colleague herself knows well, the articles of the Collective Agreement do not apply to the Univairsity as a whole. Academic Freedom does not, at the present time, extend to teaching assistants nor to faculty hired on contract. So consequently, they have no guarantee against reprisal for the free speaking of their views. Most regrettable of all, sir, the principle of Academic Freedom does not extend to the *students* of Avalon. But they are also members of a community that is devoted – a community that *should* be devoted – to free enquiry after the truth and free expression of the truth, no matter how disturbing the truth may be. What of a student who, let us say, writes a critique in his term paper, let us suppose, of the growing power of Andromeda Networks in the nation's media and who is then cautioned for his views? Now, I know such recrimination would never happen here ... " MacDonald turned effortfully and let one of his eyes fix on Hannah Janssen-Koeslag " ... yet reprisal against a student for his or her views ... " now MacDonald turned slowly and faced Victor Bosko " ... has occurred at other universities, where students have stuck their heads out beyond the safety of current social pieties, and then, like Socrates, have had to swallow the hemlock."

Cries of protest came from the visitors' gallery. MacDonald forged on regardless.

"Aye, Mistairr Chairman. Students and faculty have been denied careers at other places because they have protested the commercialization of the university and the new corporate embrace. Administrators everywhere are bowing to pressure from big corporate donors, like our Mr. D'Arnay. No – Academic Freedom is a principle which *all* of us – faculty, students and administrators – must swear to uphold if we are still to have an autonomous university. And so, by affirming Academic Freedom today, we are affirming for our Univairsity the basic principle which since time immemorial has encouraged free enquiry as the foundation of scholarly life."

MacDonald, as if enlarged by his speech, stood for a moment, then sat down ponderously, gruffly waving off scattered applause from the faculty. Jan noticed Sally Galt rolling her eyes to the ceiling in the body language of an aggrieved teenager.

"Right on!" said Jerry Lewin.

"May I respond to that?" Hannah got to her feet again, exuding a disarming radiance.

"If you ask me, Mr. Chairperson, it is the obligation of the Administration to uphold the law of the land. And the law of the land, as passed by the Legislature, stipulates that each workplace of each public agency — and that's us — shall have an environment of zero tolerance of discrimination and harassment … "

"Zero tolerance equals intolerance!" yelled Lewin suddenly.

Hannah, with a portentous certainty, rotated to face Jerry Lewin. It was the certainty of a tank training its gun turret on a small, unforeseen and irritating pillbox.

"Well, that is the law, my young friend, and you will just have to live with it. The intellectual free ride is over. You've had your fun. In fact, you've had your fun at the expense of women and colonized others since the Late Neolithic. Now it is time for you to grow up. Our goal should be to have the cleanest gender and interracial environment in the country — one that is safe and supportive for everyone to responsibly express their views in. Safe and supportive for women, lesbian and gay people, members of visible minorities, people with disabilities, people of the First Nations. We will no longer be silenced by power codes defined by and for liberal white bourgeois males. That is what I mean by Academic Freedom!"

Thunderous applause from all sides of the room. Jan realized she was applauding too. But what was Bosko doing? Again, he was transfixed. This time he was transfixed by his laptop into which he seemed to be entering something of utmost importance. His printer delivered a printout which Bosko frowned at undecidedly.

"Permit me, Mr. Chairman!" It was Jerry Lewin rising to speak, the effect of authority undercut by his short height and dark glasses so that he looked to Jan like a pugilistic beetle.

"On the contrary, intolerance of harassment and discrimination is *not* the law of the land. It is simply a well-meaning but ill-worded act passed by the Legislature, which crudely transects the Freedom of Speech provisions of the Constitution, which *is* the law of the land. Indeed, in every contest between Human Rights and Freedom of Speech that has come before the courts, the judiciary has ruled, quite properly, in favour of the Constitutional safeguards of Free Speech. And any sane person can see why. Without Freedom of Thought and Expression there is no free society."

Lewin remained on his feet, looking sternly around the room in a manner that blended Oxford debating style with a theatrical soliloquy. "I do not wish to live inside somebody else's agenda. Not Professor Janssen-Koeslag's nor anyone else's."

"Freedom has responsibilities! Have you ever considered *that*, Professor Lewin?"

Members of Senate turned in their seats to identify the brash new voice from behind them. The speaker was Sally Galt. She was standing up and speaking from the visitors' gallery.

"Mr. Chairman! Order!"

"Professor Galt is not a member of Senate."

Dean and Provost Cameron Galt smiled benignly at the meeting. "The Chair is in no position to deny anyone their freedom to speak or be heard. Least of all Professor Galt," he added smoothly.

There was nervous laughter.

"Thank you … Mr. Chairperson," said Sally, smiling back with a formal sweetness. "My point is simply that freedom of speech does not carry with it a freedom to offend. Professors do not have the right to hurt others by their remarks, do they? They do not have a license to poison a person's well-being or environment of productive study by making a comment that creates negativity for individuals or groups … "

"A comment?" Lewin asked.

"Yes, *one* comment, Professor Lewin. Just like one vulgar piece of washroom graffiti, one offensive sign hung from a residence window, one demeaning cartoon in the student newspaper, one obnoxious T-shirt image, one instance of exclusion. A word can kill. It just takes one comment to offend."

"That's crazy!" said Lewin, throwing up his hands.

"See, Mr. Chairperson? That's precisely what I mean. The male backlash stereotypes me as crazy. Irrational – just like all women."

Jan could see that Sally Galt was livid. Her voice was losing its forced evenness.

"Irrational, he calls me – for simply suggesting that faculty do not have the right to drop sexist remarks. Intemperate – for simply proposing that males do not have the right to make a woman uncomfortable for pursuing a major that used to be reserved exclusively for males. Hysterical – for simply saying that liberal white males no longer have the freedom to teach women and minorities out of history, out of politics, out of literature, out of culture."

Flushed with conviction and passion, Sally turned to address her husband.

"Mr. Chairperson, in an effort to break down barriers created by imbalances of power that exist between groups at this University, I move an amendment to the main motion … "

"Mr. Chairman!"

"Out of order, Mr. Chairman!"

" … adding the words. 'This right of Academic Freedom will be deemed to apply only to matters involving the actual research expertise or teaching duties of faculty, and provided … '"

"Mr. Chairman, the amendment is hostile!"

"Professor Galt is not a senator!"

Sally Galt stood up in the visitors' seats firm and determined. "Would you please bring this meeting to order, Provost Galt?"

"*Order, please.*"

"Thank you. As I was saying, 'provided the view or conduct exemplified is not unwelcome, unwanted, offensive, intimidating, hostile or inappropriate.'"

"Professor Galt is not a senator," called Lewin. "She can't move an amendment."

"Well, *I* am, and I'll move it instead," declared Hannah Janssen-Koeslag. "I move that the following amendment be added to the main motion … "

"But the amendment is hostile," bellowed Ruairi MacDonald.

"You haven't heard it yet," Hannah replied, without turning her head.

"We just heard it from Sally," Lewin yelled.

"*Order! Order!* The speaker has to be allowed to introduce the amendment before I can rule on its admissibility."

Hannah studiously resumed her manner. "The amendment has two parts. The point of the first part is that Academic Freedom will be restricted to matters of faculty research and teaching expertise only …. "

"Are ye so daft, woman?" MacDonald roared. "Yon amendment will turn us all into compliant zombies!" MacDonald turned to the other senators, imploring their support. "Look – one's opinions are to be restricted now to the course content, the nuts and bolts of a subject. Academics are no longer to hae' the will to speak oot on the broad issues touching the direction of a society. Instead, we are to be wee microprocessors in some univairsal rational computer, wi' each microprocessor restricted to its bittie o' expertise. Not on yer nelly! It is the deith of the univairsity, I tell ye. Tis the deith of the univairsity as a place for the public discourse because it is the repression of free will and individual conscience."

MacDonald's eyes were staring wildly in every direction. He seemed ready to explode with exasperated indignation. But he was not the only one who was agitated. Jan felt Jilaquns shifting in her seat beside her. Was Jill going to speak to the motion? God help us if Jill speaks to the motion.

And what was this? A note had been passed along the table to her, from student to student. Jan viewed it discreetly. A computer graphic of a couple dancing the jitterbug cheek-to-cheek. Then the words that had been processed through Victor Bosko's laptop computer:

"After the vote, what say you and I blow this popstand. Dinner at Rugantino's. We got some real things to talk about. Signed, Victor B." Beneath the signature was a graphic of a happy face, like the ones put on kids' finger paintings by kindergarten teachers.

Screw this! Jan thought. Is this the price of support from the Common Sense Revolution? Suddenly, clearly, Jan D'Arnay assumed the right she had to take care of herself. She had a voice.

Dean Galt was speaking. "I take it the mover and seconder of the main motion regard Professor Janssen-Koeslag's amendment as unfriendly."

"You're darn right it's unfriendly," Lewin exclaimed. "It's also moronic."

"Apparently the amendment is not acceptable to the movers of the motion," the Chair reported neutrally, looking at Hannah Janssen-Koeslag. "You are free, of course, to vote against the motion when it is put."

Janssen-Koeslag shrugged her shoulders resignedly.

And now Vic Bosko was speaking. Or at least, Bosko's new suit seemed to be speaking, making practiced courtroom gestures that seemed detached from his script. For he was pretending not to read from his script.

"Good afternoon, Mr. Provost. I'm Victor Bosko speaking for the Confederation of College Councils. Mr. Chairman, we in the Confederation of College Councils, representing the Common Sense Revolution at Avalon, hereby signal our intention to vote *against* the motion as it is presented. We hold the view that no right is absolute and universal, because each right is defined and qualified by each other right within a relational system."

Heavens, thought Jan. This is straight out of Cultural Studies 100. Where are this guy's politics anyway?

"Accordingly, the application of any one right depends upon its precise circumstances. The limits of a right are determinable only at the point at which any view expressed allegedly gives offence to others. As consumers of education, we support the user-friendly model of accountability provided by Human Rights."

Bosko bowed solemnly to the Chair, then sat down to uncertain applause from his benches. That was the moment Jan D'Arnay decided to vote for Academic Freedom. She did not want to live in an airtight litigational world managed by would-be lawyers like Bosko.

She felt Jilaquns rising to her feet even before Bosko had folded up his statement. Oh-oh! Jill was holding her eagle feather.

Jilaquns of the Qayahllaanas let the silence in the room gather until all eyes were upon her standing in her all-in-one black leather catsuit. "I don't know what the previous speaker said," she began in a quiet even voice. "He sounds like a government lawyer to me. But I want to say something to the piston-brain that spoke before him. He went on and on about the death of the university. I say so what the fuck! If a university full of racism and sexism is his idea of a nice place for students to be in, well then … let it die! In fact, it has already died because it never lived. The university as a social institution has been a pit of systemic discrimination since the word go. For eight centuries women weren't even allowed in the great male bastion … "

Across the room, Professor MacDonald smiled wryly at this historical fact. He appreciated the use of facts in argumentation, whatever the speaker's position.

" … for fear that their menstrual fluids would interfere with the study of Divine Philosophy."

Jan, suddenly, got a fit of the giggles.

Sensing she had hit home, Jilaquns relaxed. Relaxed, she found a comfortable anger.

"And that eight-century tradition of impotent moribund patriarchy continues to the present day. And now, in this present day, I am here to tell you as a woman that I am sick and tired of being discriminated against in my own University. I've had it with jock assholes … "

"Mr. Chairman! Mr. Chairman!"

"Order, please!"

" ... seducing first-year women during Orientation Week. Also, I'm through with being a silent pretty face in seminars, or, conversely ... "

Jan hid her face in her hands.

" ... having to rest my boobs on the seminar table just to let a male prof know I exist ... "

"Mr. Chairman!"

" ... not to mention the cultural dignity of my people being conveniently forgotten in the classroom, not to mention the backhanded sneering any of us have to put up with if we choose an alternative sexuality."

Jilaquns faced Ruairi MacDonald coolly.

"I want to ask Professor MacDonald one question: where the fuck was Academic Freedom when Aboriginal people were being oppressed?"

"Mr. Chairman!"

"The truth is, Academic Freedom is the clothing of the white liberal bourgeois male," Jilaquns continued. "It is a right acquired by political force and is inextricably glued to imperialist expansion which continually overturns the rights of others. Farmers in India who had the right to grow a wide variety of food in the 1700s had to grow just cotton – cotton which was used to fuel the Industrial Revolution. 'Freedom of Expression' and 'Academic Freedom' are rights that follow from the industrial epoch. Now, they are used to protect the white male's self-serving reading of history and prop up his worldview from the balls up."

Jilaquns paused, looking straight ahead of her.

"Those are some *facts* for Professor MacDonald who abuses us with facts in order to have his way with history. That is all I have to say."

There was thunderous applause from the students crowded into the visitors' gallery. Jilaquns took her seat.

Afterwards, there were a number of speakers, mostly from the faculty side of the debate. One speaker gravely reminded senators of the history of the institution of the university as a traditional place of dissent, mentioning its pivotal role in the self-determination of European nations in 1848 and its continuing influence in Latin-American politics today. Jerry Lewin, not to be outdone, spoke elegiacally of how the campus protest movements brought the Vietnam War to an end in the Seventies. Then Faith Rackstraw spoke fondly of the churchbell of St. Mary's in Oxford, and of how at its sound students and their teaching masters rushed out eagerly to oppose civil authority during the Middle Ages. Jan, listening to all of this, measured it against a speech that was being composed by her inner councillors, much to the discomfort of her body. Would her body please behave itself when it was time for her to stand up and speak – an inevitability that was just making her heart bounce harder. This was terrifying. The glass ship was becoming real.

"Mr. Moderator – It is time to put on record the views of the Center for the First Nations on the motion moved by the Avalon University Faculty Union Executive."

Tom Baptiste remained sitting while he spoke, shyly supporting his spectacles with one hand. He spoke softly, almost wistfully, from a position that seemed outside the arena of the debate, if not removed from white civilization altogether. Senators gave him their complete attention. Jan broke off struggling with her body and listened too.

"Academic Freedom is what we, here in the First Nations Center, call a white man's law. It belongs to the eurocentric notion of universalist premises of behaviour. These have been the means by which aboriginal peoples have been systematically silenced around the globe. Today, speaking on behalf of silenced indigenous peoples, we are voting against any reaffirmation of those claims. We don't want anyone to think that we are negative or defensive in doing so. Actually, we are voting for something that is very positive. We are voting for the original ideal of the university as a place where various nations, speaking their own languages, housed in their own accommodations which later came to be called 'colleges,' joined together to study. Such a community of communities implies a meeting place where views can be exchanged without discomfort or fear of reprisal to the various nations. That is how we explain Academic Freedom to ourselves, Mr. Moderator. It is honest enquiry restrained by thinking of the hurt which attitudes can do – which attitudes have done – to others. That is the way we have always respected the customs and ceremonies of others among the councils of the First Nations."

Ruairi MacDonald stormed to his feet.

"I have a speaker's list," Provost Galt said. "The next speaker is, I believe, Ms. D'Arnay. She had her hand up."

Jan felt a cold fear extend from her gut down through her flexors to her knees. Gymnastics finals had been easier than this. Perhaps she'd do a line of handsprings across the Senate table.

"Let me say this now, sir, to rebut my dear colleague who needs a lesson in history," MacDonald persisted. "The lesson of history is that Freedom of Expression and Thought gave minorities a voice that was denied them by autocracy. Indeed, my colleague from the First Nations would not be sitting here, were it not for that Freedom – *right*? He speaks about *his* people being written out of history. Weel, let me tell ye about *my* people! My people were written out of history too, don't ye know? They were driven off the glens and the land that was theirs since time immemorial. Forbidden to wear the bonnet and the neck-cloth and the coarse plaid, so they were. Forbidden to sing the holy Psalms in Gaelic or run the stills to make the ancient whiskey. Driven to the emigrant ships bound for Americay. Driven into the king's regiments to be cannon fodder during Bonaparte's wars. Driven to the coal pits and the salt pans and to the building of the Caledonian Canal. And d'ye know why my people were driven off the land in the great Clearances? Tae make way for a lot of *sasunnach* sheep! Tae clear the land so the sheep of the Englishmen could graze."

Ruairi MacDonald stared woefully at members of the senior administration as if the Highland clearances had been their doing.

Then he lifted his gaze and stared out beyond the river into history.

"Och, those homes burning in the vale of Strathnaven on that bitterly cold fifteenth of December, eighteen hundred and thirteen! The crying of the uncomprehending wimmen. The barking of dogs. And the two thousand people of Kildonan – all gone, except for three farmers. Think of it, will ye? The fifteen thousand men an' mithers an' helpless weans evicted fra the glens of Sutherland between the year eighteen hundred and ten and eighteen hundred and twenty. In point o' fact, seven hundred and ninety-four thousand puir dumfounert souls evicted from the Highlands which they had possessed since the beginnings of clan history, so that the rich could have pastures for their sheep. 'Twas nae better, Ms. Jilaquns, than India and its cotton. Then, some of us were given back some scunnered land at a tax of two shillings and sixpence per acre – aye, we had our reservations too! The sudden silence in the glens. When the remaining people fell into the poverty and alcoholism that was intended for them, they were offered relief. Relief in the amount of five pounds per year for every one thousand souls! D'ye not know that? Why d'ye not know that? Ask yourselves that question!"

MacDonald shifted his gaze from the river and looked forlornly at the ceiling, his eyes blank and unfocused.

"And now let me talk about *my* people," he said softly. "My people – the MacDonalds of Skye and the Outer Isles. Five thousand of my people lost to their homes after the year 1801. Our wimmen are reduced to gatherin' seaweed on the shore. Och, it goes on. Two thirds of the people of Caithness, Sutherland and Inverness – they're bin uprooted and dispairsed so that the new lords can shoot deer. And then the epidemics are comin' – the cholera of eighteen hundred and thirty-two. The famine of eighteen hundred and forty-six!"

MacDonald's eye caught Cameron Galt looking uncomfortable at the front of the room.

"And what of the Camerons? – *yer* people, Mr. Provost and Dean.

Sheep scattered more of them than fell to the bayonets of Barrett's Regiment at Culloden. *Tha mo chlann air a bhi air am murt!* they cried. My children, my children are being murdered!"

MacDonald's huge body stood swaying, held in pastness. The Council Chamber seemed to fill up with regret. Someone coughed.

MacDonald opened his eyes. He spoke in a small sorrowful voice now.

"We had nothing except our dream of Freedom, ye see."

He paused again, letting his eyes sweep the room.

"The Universal Declaration of the Rights of Man."

Ruairi stood immobile, trying to release himself from memory.

"We are all uprooted children of History. Let us therefore speak to each other from the basis of our common deprival."

Ruairi MacDonald sat down awkwardly and stared at the table before him. There was no applause this time. The heavy silence of the ages fell upon the room.

"Call the question!" Lewin said suddenly. "Call the question before I tell you about *my* people." Lewin took his sunglasses off. "In fact, I *will* tell you about my people. Six million … "

"Hold your horses, Senator Lewin. Did you want to speak, Senator D'Arnay?"

Jan D'Arnay never knew what compelled her to speak in Senate that day. Was it rage at Vic Bosko's shifty compromise of radicalism and the corporate order? Was it some deep collision in her genes of the Setons and the D'Arnays? Whatever it was, two powerful energies met the right way in her. At least, that is how she explained it to Jilaquns afterward at the Food Court. Her intervention seemed scripted for her, yet it was everything she wanted to say — all ten of her inner councillors were behind her — and for weeks afterward, as her remarks replayed themselves in her memory, she felt no wish to change a single word. This is what, at first faltering, then with growing confidence, Jan said:

"I've listened to both sides of the debate — and I admit I've listened as a first-year student who hasn't really thought these things through. So maybe my response is naive? But I want to say that nothing that's been said today really makes it clear for me what universities are actually for and why we have them at all. That phrase of Professor MacDonald's – 'enquiry for truth'? It sounds very noble, but it doesn't do much for me – it doesn't do all that much for my generation. What is true anymore? Do the universities know what is true anymore?"

It was when she said this, Jan remembered afterward, that people began to listen. To her. A group getting coffee at the side-table had put down their cups and were standing, listening to her. She saw an approving smile on Sally Galt's face, a frown on MacDonald's. Bosko was gazing up at her like a puppy. All this she saw in the vivid clarity of being, perhaps for the first time in her life, completely vulnerable, as if she were totally naked in front of the senators. And this was a funny feeling because it was also when she had asked that basic question that she realized she had gapped out – she had shifted out of her body. She could feel her feet firm on the carpet, but between her feet and her head there was nothing but space. She was sailing.

"Nowadays, we believe something different. We believe that there isn't one single truth we can all aim at anymore. That single truth turns out to be an illusion manufactured by the dominant group in a society that controls how you manufacture and distribute truth."

Now Professor MacDonald was really scowling. But Jerry Lewin, by his side, had a sweet impious smile. Jan went on.

"So one group's truth is another group's oppression. The fact is that each group, each people, each individual, has its own truth. Where does that leave the universities?"

Jan paused to let the question gather an answer. In reality, she paused because she had no idea what she was going to say next. But suddenly her body was coming back to her. She could feel her arms and legs and torso re-attaching.

"I think Vic Bosko hit it right on. Because truth is relative to each user-group, there is no highest truth left anymore. The highest truth, if that's a truth, is how to *negotiate* among different peoples' truths. Bosko said it: we become truth-managers, truth-lawyers – we have become bureaucrats. Is that why we're at university – to become bureaucrats?"

Jan sighed and let herself breathe deeply. Now, Sally Galt was starting to frown. Bosko was trying to avoid her eyes. Only Lewin's smile was unchanged. She realized that during the whole speech so far, she had been twisting and untwisting a strand of her hair.

"So universities are no different from the corporate bureaucracies. There's no truth in the business world now except negotiating between different truths belonging to different consumer-groups. When one truth doesn't work anymore, you dump it and just outsource another. And the universities are like that too. Knowledge has become a disposable commodity. Maybe that's why the universities have lost their mission. How can we criticize society? We've become the very thing that we're supposed to criticize."

Jerry Lewin was smiling broadly now. But some of the other senators looked puzzled; a few had lost interest. Jan realized, however, that Dean Galt was looking at her intently. Bud Lassiter, sitting at the Dean's right hand, had tuned out and had even stopped taking minutes.

"We don't even have our own language at the university now," Jan continued. "Which means we're going to have to invent one. Maybe it'll come from Body – I mean, the truths of real personal experience. If we're going to define the university as an entity apart from the corporate world, we're going to have to do some extreme things. We're going to have to do some extreme things with our bodies. People are going to be offended. Especially the corporate world is going to be offended – but other people are too. So I guess what I'm saying is we need academic freedom in order to find a language for the universities. We need the freedom to find ourselves again as critical enquirers."

Jan was forced gently into her seat by the same invisible hand that had pulled her out of it. Then her knees started to shake – it was like she was waterskiing flat-out on broken water. There was no applause, except from a beaming Jerry Lewin, who stopped clapping when he realized he was clapping alone.

"What the fuck … ?"

"Ssh, Jill – I'll explain later."

"Are you ready for the question?"

"May we hear the motion again?"

Jan, as if in a trance, vaguely heard the phrases go by as they were read out loud by the Registrar. Each phrase seemed to squeeze through the glass and lose itself in the black November hills. "*The common good of society depends upon free enquiry and the free exposition of knowledge. Academic Freedom in universities is essential to both these purposes. Consequently, all members of the academic community at Avalon are entitled, regardless of prescribed doctrine, to freedom in carrying out their research, freedom of teaching and of discussion, freedom to criticize the University, and freedom of censorship by the institution.*"

"Bonny words!" MacDonald said in a loud voice to Lewin. "I wrote them masel'."

"It supports mischief as a form of intellectual play," responded Lewin.

"All in favour of the motion."

Not a forest, but scattered groves of hands went up: most of the faculty senators; Faith Rackstraw, alone among the administrators; one of the Goldman student reps. Jan's own arm rose in the air as if it had a mind of its own. Bud Lassiter, as Secretary of Senate, was prodding the air with his forefinger, counting the votes. Everybody looked over to where the students were sitting. They would be the key to the outcome. Slowly, trying to look disinterested, even bored, Victor Bosko cocked his arm in the air, his elbow resting on the table. There was confusion and whispering up and down his row. Eventually, in ones and twos, the members of his caucus all followed his example – all, except for Ashley Tiffin.

"I don't believe it!" Jilaquns shouted across the floor to Vic Bosko. "You just spoke in favour of Human Rights!"

"Wrong! I spoke in favour of the commutability of values."

Jilaquns leaped to her feet, her leather catsuit gleaming in the fluorescent light. "Mr. Chairman, point of order while Vic Bosko does us the favour of resigning."

"Chill out, Jilaquns. I'm not resigning."

"Resign!" Jilaquns retorted. "You were in charge and you did not have the courage to lead ... "

"*Order, please!*"

Jilaquns addressed her explanation to Senate as a whole. "I want everyone here to know that the train of Vic Bosko's life has just left the station without Vic Bosko on board. His story will be told without him. He therefore has failed to leave any impression at all. He will barely even have amused us with his presence."

"Order! May we continue with the voting?"

Jilaquns resumed her seat and folded her arms with satisfaction against her chest.

"All against the motion please signify by raising your hands."

These hands looked more like a forest, but a very small forest: the Women's Caucus senators; the Student Union Executive, except Jan; the administration reps, except Faith Rackstraw; the two Natives from the Center for the First Nations; the other Goldman College rep; and Ashley Tiffin. But except for Ashley, whose arm extended defiantly like a flagpole, the arms went up in a posture of defeat for it was clear that Human Rights had lost.

The Registrar whispered the outcome of the vote to the Chair.

"The motion carries," declared Dean Galt.

"Yahoo!" exclaimed Jerry Lewin. He started to shake MacDonald's hand. But MacDonald, whether through modesty or through the sense of just another routine victory achieved among hundreds, gave Lewin a clap on the back, and clipped his briefcase shut.

A crashing sound came from the direction of the Women's Caucus. It was the sound of an attaché case slamming shut violently. It was Sally Galt's attaché case. And Sally was now storming out of the room, with Hannah following her. Next, Jan heard the sounds of women's voices remonstrating in the corridor. "Common deprival! Did you ever hear such crap?" came Sally's voice. "And what did they do with their precious little Declaration of the Rights of *Man*? They used it to suppress the indigenous people of every country they expanded into on the back of the Industrial Revolution." Jan couldn't make out Hannah's replay. It seemed to be low-voiced, soothing. "And their women never got a crack at that Freedom of Speech," continued Sally's voice. "They had to sweep the friggin' kitchen for another two hundred years until they finally hit the streets as suffragettes."

Sally's voice was lost in the hubbub of conversation as senators took advantage of the break to stretch and talk. The Student Union Executive had gone into a huddle. Jan, with her knees doing an insane skeleton dance, resumed her gaze out the window, watching the river slide by into nothingness. A shape like a ghost was approaching her from behind. The reflection in the glass materialized into the form of Victor Bosko.

"Your speech was cool. I want to say it was influential on how I voted."

"Fuck off, Bosko," Jan said without turning her head.

The reflection vanished. Jan gazed again on the motion of the river until she felt the room moving like a ship through the night. Another ghost was approaching her in the mirror, a tall bearded ghost in a perfectly tailored suit. This time Jan turned her head and looked up. She looked up at him through the eyes of an adult.

"I appreciated your intervention," said Cameron Galt.

"Thanks. I don't think anyone understood it though."

"It had to be said."

"Thanks anyway."

Dean Galt returned to his place at the front of the room. Jan returned to her communion with the wilderness. Maybe the river understood, but it carried away everything it knew.

17

"The virtual university," said the Registrar.

"The virtual university?"

"Yeah, center everywhere, circumference nowhere, like God. I found three more of them of them on the web this a.m."

Galt found Lassiter's hip blend of technospeak and vulgarity unsettling, yet he pursued the topic distractedly.

"No campuses anymore, I suppose."

"You betcha! No more factory-style universities. The whole Industrial Revolution model of education is gone the way of the dodo. Instead, people educate themselves on the web. You pay a fee to register for a course, you get a password, then you use file transfer protocol to download course materials which the prof has put on the web. Students chat away electronically and e-mail the prof in charge."

"Prof? I should think profs are dodos too."

"For sure! They're just there to design the courses. The learners really communicate with teaching assistants on contract."

Galt eased the car around a small lake that had accumulated near the Library steps. Then he proceeded down the main drive of the university on his way to the airport. Driving in this storm was going to be difficult. He wondered what flying from Metro would be like for Hugh D'Arnay.

"A few research-intensive professors and lots of cheap contract labour," Galt mused. "And those few professors pull in research funds. The university pays for itself."

"Right on! It's totally privatized."

"But a university would have to specialize to get itself on the map."

"You know, we're doggone lucky we got into the Ecology game in the Seventies. We've got the labs and the expertise. Students actually have to come here for hands-on experience in the labs. We don't have much else."

"Except beautiful buildings."

"Like, beautiful *expensive* buildings. Now that D'Arnay's cable companies have got high-speed internet access into the homes, students can get a university education dirt cheap. They don't have to pay ceiling-high tuition fees just to come here and gawk at nature for three years."

Galt slowed the car down when a torrent of rain lashed the windshield. The wipers worked doggedly, allowing sporadic glimpses of the River Road.

"How can D'Arnay fly through this crud?"

"D'Arnay can fly through anything," Galt responded.

They drove moodily at a pace set by the weather. In the time it would take them to get through town to the airport, D'Arnay, high above the clouds, would already have made the trip from Metro.

"That was fun yesterday at Senate."

"Yeah, right. Real hoot. Like watching Jurassic Park. Fat lot of good Academic Freedom's going to do them when the sky falls."

When's the sky going to fall? Galt thought. Has it fallen already? He went over in his mind the downsizing plans he'd brought for D'Arnay's inspection. The Voluntary Early Retirement proposal had enormous up-front buyout costs. And the Academic Restructuring plan also had costs. There would have to be external reviews, department by department, individual by individual, all based on performance indicators. It was like cutting back a small forest that was all tangled and overgrown – taking out the dead wood, trimming the green wood in just the right places. The trick was not to lose anything essential. Could he hang on to the college system, for example? It was a key to the personality of Avalon. Would D'Arnay agree to mount a deficit? Probably not. What if the government hit the university with a funding cut? Each one percent decrease meant $250,000 which he would have to axe out of the academic budgets. And what about enrolment?

"What's next year's enrolment picture looking like, Bud?"

"Don't look good. Demographics are as flat as a nun's chest for the next five years. Everybody's tripping ass-over-tea-kettle to get state-of-the-art recruitment plans in place. McMonster's sending CD-ROMs with incredible video windows to all the counselling and careers offices in the high schools."

Galt absorbed the suggestion. It would be up to him and Bud to make a CD-ROM that could compete with the propaganda put out by the other universities. Now that High-School Liaison had been pried out of Faith Rackstraw's hands to report directly to him, it would be easier to undertake a real promotion campaign.

"With a system-wide enrolment slump, we get hit the hardest because we're so damn small," the Registrar explained. "Education is expensive now. Students are hunkering down in their parents' basements to save money. And we don't have many students in our catchment basin to pull in. Which means we have to go national to find our niche-market."

Galt managed the car carefully on the River Road through blinding cloudbursts, then down the main street of Severnville, now drab in the off-season. With the tourists and cottagers gone, the town had reverted to its role as a small manufacturing center. The corporate globalization that had changed the complexion of the workforce across America had taken its toll here. You couldn't see it in the rain, but there was poverty in Severnville. Corporate restructuring had crashed like a wave across business and government agencies; its power unspent, the wave had crashed over the universities – except for Avalon which was insulated by its insignificance. Now, even Avalon had to adapt or go under. Galt's role was to make the adaptation smooth so that Avalon could retain its character as a quality university. One that would attract students who still wanted a traditional personal milieu. He had to get Avalon to the top of the small universities column in the *Choosing Your College* rankings. The first step had been taken. He had bargained MacDonald out of a faculty strike. Students would come to a university that seemed happy with itself.

Ping! Ping!

Galt picked up the car phone. "Cameron Galt speaking."

"D'Arnay here. Look — I'm just circling a cumulus pillar over Bethany. Where are you guys?"

"Pulling out of town on a straight run to the airport. We'll be there in fifteen minutes."

"Great. See you in the cafeteria."

Twenty minutes later, Galt and Lassiter dashed through the rain from the parking lot to find D'Arnay in an empty cafeteria with his daughter. Jan wore a yellow rainslicker and rubber boots. The image of her speaking at Senate played in Galt's mind with an earlier image of her waterskiing past his cottage. A strong straight back. The two images balanced together briefly in Galt's mind, then toppled together as they were erased.

D'Arnay, in a leather bomber jacket and jeans, rose to meet them. "Hello, gentlemen. You know my daughter?"

"You should have seen her at Senate yesterday," Galt said.

"I was just hearing about it. Wished I'd been there. All in the family tradition of public service, I guess."

Jan smiled and said nothing. She was clutching a bottle of brandy.

"I brought up a bottle of *Marc* for the cottage." D'Arnay explained. "I have a daughter who brushes her teeth with *Marc de Bourgogne*. Sorry it got bruised flying through that squall line."

Galt laughed. D'Arnay, among other things a racer of six-meter sloops at the Metro Yacht Club, knew all about squall lines.

"I'd better fly myself," Jan said on cue. "Before the road in to the cottage floods out. Nice to meet you, Mr. Lassiter. Bye, Dean Galt. Bye, Dad."

"See you later, alligator," called out father to daughter.

Jan strode out of the building, leaving the three men to talk.

"And now to business," D'Arnay said briskly. "We'll have to be nimble. I want to get out before the next storm. Bud tells me he found the Spanish Year Abroad program. It's in Granada."

With a member of his own class, Galt could afford to take the matter lightly. Yet he was still surprised. The Registrar had not told him about this. Did Lassiter have a direct line to D'Arnay, whose eyes were now piercing like an inquisitor's? The Year Abroad Program was clearly a matter of personal interest to the Chairman of the Board.

"At least, I now know where the thing is!" Galt said, lightly.

"I saw the gas receipts for the course mini-van on the computer," Lassiter explained. "Looks like they went on a field trip and ran out of gas in Granada."

"It won't be going anywhere after this!" muttered D'Arnay. "Time to downsize. I'm sure you don't want to hang onto this vexatious and intractable arabesque." Having come to a decision, D'Arnay was now relaxing into grandiosity.

"Not at all." Galt shook his head. "What do you think, Bud? Should we keep it?"

Lassiter gave the thumbs down sign.

Galt realized that with three quick words he had condemned the Spanish Year Abroad Program and its twenty-year history to oblivion. Or the program had condemned itself. Irresponsible! Business had to be routed through Senate.

"I'd go over there at Christmas break and end it, if I were you," D'Arnay suggested gravely. "Before the idiot in charge – what's his name … ?"

"Jerónimo."

" … before Geronimo runs up a slew of desperate termination expenses."

"You have to disentangle the godforsaken thing from the cost-sharing arrangement with the host university over there," echoed the Registrar. "I figure the program students can slip into January half-courses to make up their missing credits."

"Apocalypse Now for the Year Abroad Program," said D'Arnay, giggling. "Go over there and terminate that guy's command."

Lassiter laughed. "Terminate. With extreme prejudice."

The coded exchanges among members of the same managerial elite were clear. Galt would have to fly over at the Christmas Break.

However, Christmas in Spain with Sally might be fun, he considered.

"And now the good news." The expression on D'Arnay's face was like a four-year-old child's, finding a toy fire-engine underneath the Christmas tree. "The good news is … "

D'Arnay paused for a sip of coffee.

" … we have a corporate sponsor. He's a Mr. Wu from Hong Kong. The environmental education toy manufacturer. He's leading the fight for environmentally-conscious industrial practices in south China. Now he's bought into educational software for primary school kids. He likes our world-class Ecology Center."

"Good," said Galt. "How much?"

"How much does he like it? He likes it about seven million dollars for starters – and he'll go higher. But he wants more info."

"What kind of information?"

"Oh, the usual. Profile of the institution. Assets, especially land assets. The Chinese are very interested in land, you know. And our management plan."

"You mean the downsizing plan?"

"Right! Let's take a look at it. We'll probably have to give the guy an honorary degree as well."

Galt took the document out of his briefcase. The file was slim. This was the way business was done among upper-level managers, he thought. It was done quickly and orally. Tedious accountability forms and laborious committee processes were for underlings. "You understand it's not content-specific," Galt explained. "No departments are mentioned. This is just the machinery for downsizing."

"Sure," D'Arnay said. "If actual departments get mentioned, Ruairi will blow his fuses and call a strike. Then we'll be at the bottom of the ratings."

"Wu won't give his yen to a third-class U.," Lassiter said, seeing a joke.

D'Arnay flicked through the pages quickly, reading bottom lines with an eagle's eye. "Ah-ha! A voluntary early retirement plan with a job-redefinition scheme as a follow-up. That'll make them hop!

It looks like it's going to take some time though. It's not the way we do things in the real world."

"Well," Galt explained, "you have to assess the departments by using external appraisers. So everybody knows what the benchmarks are. Cost per graduate indicators and learner-satisfaction indexes. If departments aren't performing up to scratch, we ... ah, terminate their command. Our goal should be to retain and build on departments that rank up there with the Ecocenter."

"How do you close them down?"

"You give them three years so the majors already in the discipline can pass through. Then you pool the redundant teachers into a general interdisciplinary program – call it 'Humanities.' Put the research-performers into an interdisciplinary graduate school and pay them partly through government research grants."

"Hey! We become the first totally interdisciplinary small university," Lassiter exclaimed. "That'll look good in the *Choosing Your College* rankings."

"You can turn a small ship around faster," D'Arnay observed. "But this might not be fast enough." D'Arnay's eyes had assumed the level keenness of that first meeting at the Yacht Club when Galt had been hired.

"I don't see how we can turn her around faster," Galt said finally. "Consider the up-front costs. The external appraisal teams are going to be a heavy expense item. Early retirement buyouts will be costly – even if we paid out from the faculty side of the Pension Surplus for that. And grievances – there will be lots of grievances. They cost twelve grand each just to reach the formal conciliation stage."

D'Arnay seemed to be balancing alternatives in his mind. A tautness came over his sun-tanned face. Should he sail in a holding pattern downwind, then crash the start line at full sail in the position of advantage just as the gun sounded? Or should he nose along the start line in a half luff, then head up when the gun went off?

His conclusion was addressed to the Registrar. "Bud, can the place really stand another seven or eight years of Chinese torture? You have a very militant employee group."

"Dunno' if it can," Lassiter agreed. "We'd better get the pain and gain over with *tout de suite*, then start from scratch. Apocalypse Now."

"What do you think, Cam?"

"I've made a gentlemen's agreement with the Union to solve it with voluntary retirements. The *quid pro quo* is no strike."

"Hmm."

D'Arnay had already decided – Galt knew that.

"Okay, gentlemen. I'll take the downsizing plan and get it keyed to funding and enrolment variables. Maybe there's a way through this. You ... " D'Arnay pointed to Galt, " ... keep a lid on a strike. And you ... " now he pointed to Lassiter, " ... press-gang some bodies into the place; I don't care where you get them from. And I'll ... maybe I'll get interested in this *Choosing Your College* special issue."

Lassiter laughed. The hollow chuckle of a yes-man. For the first time that day, Galt felt the sky brightening. Yet with every decision D'Arnay made, there was a hidden quick-retreat option. Galt wondered what the hidden quick-retreat option was here.

"You'd better send me department-specific cuts – oh, what the hell! – employee-specific cuts. Be as micro as you can. I'll fill in the blanks. Handwritten – no copies. Our China-desk wallah can translate them for the venerable Wu."

"He's going to see these?"

"Why not? He won't give money to a university that isn't in charge of itself. He might bargain to bring in an Academic Management Organization."

Galt caught the note of warning.

D'Arnay rose from the table quickly and glanced out the window at a complex sky. "Looks interesting," he said. D'Arnay sounded relaxed now; evidently, the tension had disappeared with the decision, and he was assessing the more engaging challenge of flying through a major winter thunderstorm to Metro. "By the way, who is a Mr. Vic Bosko, who faxes me his up-to-the-minute ideas on Avalon? A student leader? Is he working for you guys?"

Galt made a long face.

"The kid's going to be a crank, if he ever grows up," D'Arnay said, "yet I can't resist reading his stuff. He's pulling some interesting data out of the Reform Party policy files and applying it. Not entirely without merit."

"I get his stuff too," confided Lassiter.

"Wu wants to tour the Ecology Centre in January. We'll have to give him dinner afterward," D'Arnay went on.

"Rugantino's – in the Mall. I'll make a reservation. How many?"

"The four of us, on our side – we'd better include Rattenbury. Then on the other side, Wu, and his number-cruncher. Plus his translator – he'll probably bring a translator, just for theatrics. Say, seven. That's for the ninth of January – you got that?"

Lassiter entered the information in his Palm Pilot. Galt wrote the date on a serviette and put it in his pocket.

"Something else is happening on the ninth, but I can't think what the hell it is," D'Arnay muttered. "Better mark me down as doubtful. But Wu and company can use one of the Andromeda planes."

"Excellent," said Galt. "Thank you."

D'Arnay took another look at the sky. "That's some heavy-duty cumulus! An easterly. Temperature's dropping too. I'd better punch through it now so I don't have to de-ice."

Cameron Galt and Bud Lassiter got up quickly from the chairs. Hugh D'Arnay seemed to be gone even before he'd shaken their hands. As the Dean and the Registrar drove back through the rolling farmlands south of Severnville, they heard the roar of a Lear jet, then saw a brilliant arrow of purpose overheard, disappearing into low clouds.

"I don't think I could live like that – flying by the seat of my pants," Galt said.

"May have to," the Registrar responded.

Ping! Ping!

"Galt speaking."

"A little bumpy up here, guys," said D'Arnay's voice. "But I can see Metro. Look – will one of you check with City Hall and see if we can start building on the fields east of the Ecology Center? Sewers, electricity – the whole works. Tell them to run it out to us and we'll build. Thanks."

"Aye, aye!" said Galt.

The voice was gone.

"Now, what's he up to?" mused Lassiter.

"I really don't know. That land has been disposable ever since we got the Mall."

Galt reflected for a moment, then he asked: "Tell me, Bud – is there anything D'Arnay hasn't got his finger in? I thought Board Chairs just came up for meetings and ate their Restigouche salmon lunches and smiled benignly."

"It's MacDonald's fault," Lassiter replied. "He made it impossible for anyone to want to run this zoo. So the Board got fed up and brought in D'Arnay, and he just sort of took over."

Driving to the university, they rehashed the meeting of Senate. Galt dropped Lassiter off at the Library steps, then headed north through the rain to the cottage.

18

The car phone pinged again just as Galt had pulled the Jeep to the roadside to wait out a blinding downpour.

"It's me. Where are you anyway?"

"Trying to find the cottage road."

"Look, there's no way I'm going to make it up in this weather. I'll stay over at Hannah's ... You alright? I can hardly hear you."

"Yeah, I'm okay."

"I'll come up tomorrow morning – dark and early."

"Okay."

"Stay warm."

"You too."

"Bye."

"Bye."

Galt replaced the phone in its bracket and listened to the rain hammering on the roof of his Jeep. Communication with Sally was merely informational, he reflected. Just the essential data for cohabitation and the coordination of careers. That is what the trend to privatization has done to people. The whole world is becoming privatized. Even husbands and wives have become privatized unto themselves.

The downpour showed no sign of diminishing. And now there were lightning flashes. Knowing the way to the cottage from child-hood, Galt decided to push through the storm before the road in became a mud slide. He soon found the turnoff to the cottages, a road cut like a tunnel through second-growth trees, some of them almost a century old. The wire gate at the entrance to the road was banging wickedly in the wind; someone had left it open – proba-bly the girls up at the lake. Galt didn't feel like getting out of his Jeep in this weather and closing it.

A thunderclap destroyed the sky at the end of the lake. Galt an-ticipated a night with no power. Torrents of water ran down the road through fresh tire tracks. He came to the clearing where roads branched out leading to cottages along the shoreline. Tiny hand-painted signs hung at odd angles from a birch tree, each one bearing the name of a cottage-owner. *Seton* – that was the oldest sign. With small black letters burned into pine that had once been varnished, now barely visible among the overhanging branches and high up on the trunk of a tree that had grown over the years, this topmost sign spoke with a discreet hush. Under it, a new sign – *D'Arnay* – flashed in the lightning. The sign, like the man, spoke in italics, Galt thought. And there was his own sign – *Galt* – which he had carved when he was ten at his father's knee. Galt took the road in.

Once inside the cottage, he heated up a can of turkey vegetable soup, although he didn't feel like eating in this storm. The faces of his ancestors stared severely down at him from ancient cottage photographs. Then a lightning fork took the power out. The thunderclap lifted the lake and dropped it. Humming nervously to himself, Galt located the flashlight and rounded up the candles and began to place them around the room until the cottage looked like a shrine. Good – the soup had had enough time to warm. Holding the soup in a coffee mug, he peered out the window at the lake, watching diagonal slashes of rain cut through the air like a kindergarten finger painting. He'd better make a fire.

There was a loud banging at the door.

It was Jan in her yellow rainslicker, her blond hair dripping water down to her cottage rubber boots. "Hi! The power's out. I thought I should come over – do you mind? I don't want to be alone in this."

In her hand she was holding the bottle of brandy D'Arnay had given to her, now half drunk.

"Sure. C'mon in, Jan."

"The weather report says severe storm warning all down the Kenomagaywakon Valley."

"Don't worry – I've seen worse."

Jan stripped off her rainslicker, giving it a shake before hanging it on the top of a canoe paddle by the door. She was wearing a green Avalon sweater with the sword in white, point up, and black tights and grey wool socks.

"Oh, that's my comforter – I always need it for thunderstorms."

"*Marc de Bourgogne?*"

"Dad gets it for me at the rare wines store at Harbourfront. *Marc* is the only thing Mom and Dad agree on anymore. Want some?"

"Thanks."

Jan padded over to the kitchen area in her wool socks, opened Galt's cupboard, pulled out a glass, and poured a generous dollop of brandy into it, and gave it to him. "Cheers!"

"Thanks. Here, have a blanket. Sit by the wood stove and watch the lake. Keep an eye on the lightning strikes. I'll just get changed, then light a fire."

"Where's Sally?"

"Oh, she couldn't make it up in the storm."

"She's at Hannah's," Jan said matter-of-factly. Then she looked quickly out the window.

Galt was startled. He thought he caught a note of warning in Jan's response. He worried it briefly, then lost it among more immediate concerns. He checked the flashlight by the door, his rubber boots, the phone. The phone was dead. But then, he thought, the response of Jan's wasn't unusual: everybody at Avalon knew where everybody else was at any time of day. In the bedroom he found a pair of track pants and a hooded track top which he put on. Coming over near Jan to start a fire in the wood stove, he smelled rain on her skin through a haze of brandy. The fire in the stove flared quickly drawn by crazy gusts that sped through the chimney top. The cottage was trembling in the wind. Another thunderclap close by. Jan took a pull of brandy straight from the bottle, leaned her head back in the wicker chair she had chosen, and hiccupped violently.

"This stuff tastes like sperm."

Galt blinked, then took a discreet sip from his glass, letting the warmth of the brandy make a tunnel down his throat. It seemed to make him larger from the inside. And it did taste – well, fertile.

"Like a forest floor," he offered.

"I think I could get pregnant from *Marc*."

Galt took the other chair by the wood stove and tried to think of something less familiar to say. But all he could do was worry about the storm. The wind was blasting through the trees like an express train. The cedars by the lake were doing a macabre dance. He had not told the truth to Jan a minute ago. In fact, he had not seen a worse storm than this – at least not in November when one usually got steady drizzle.

"I thought you were good at Senate," Jan said, starting a conversation.

"Good? But I didn't say anything."

"You let the horses run around the paddock."

"Well, the issue *is* important. Academics are trying to define what a university should be in the new century."

"So are a lot of other people."

"You mean politicians."

"And CEOs. If Daddy has his way, Avalon will resemble an anthill. Everybody doing their functions silently, with the whole place run by an Academic Management Organization."

"It's going to be hard to hold our own against that corporate vision," Galt probed cautiously.

Jan seemed indifferent, almost detached from Galt's concern. "Maybe it doesn't matter at the big knowledge factories where everyone's anonymous. But Av is so human!"

Jan took a sip from the bottle and began to muse. Beyond the space of her musing, a thousand shrieking winds tore at the roof shingles. Water gurgled and choked in the evestrough downspout.

"You know, you'll have to get off the backs of the faculty. Let them be the total wackos they are," Jan said.

"Wackos? Yeah, well, I guess. You understand, a dean is supposed to hope that his faculty will occasionally take a break from being wackos and actually produce some research. Advance knowledge and so on."

Jan giggled from top to toe. "You know what your mistake is? Your mistake is you think Avalon is a university. It's not a university − it's a community at play with itself."

How accurate she is, Galt thought. She has her father's casual, almost distracted cogency, but passed through the eccentricity of her dingbat mother. Galt decided to change the conversation.

"How's your mother, by the way?"

"She's okay, I guess. She's in Granada right now. I'm going over at Christmas to see her." Jan took another swig on the bottle and collapsed into a choking giggle. "Sorry – *Marc* gives me the giggles. What was I saying? Oh yes – Mom wants to celebrate my birthday over there."

Jan bunched her body up on the chair, suddenly becoming loquacious.

"I was supposed to be a Christmas present, you see, but I came late – on January the ninth. That meant I voided a deduction for dependents on Dad's income tax return for the fiscal year before. Dad was so angry! Mom thought it was so funny she named me 'January.' I think she did it just to send Dad further up the wall. Isn't that grotesque?"

Galt smiled, wanting to say nothing that would interrupt the impromptu soliloquy.

"Jilaquns is named after a river goddess, for heaven's sake! Imagine being named after a river goddess! My name stands for a stupid joke between parents who are separated."

Jan, in self-pity, surveyed the few mouthfuls of liquor remaining in the bottle.

"You know, you have a god in your name too," Galt pointed out encouragingly. You're Janus – god of thresholds."

Jan D'Arnay brightened at the suggestion. She'd obviously never thought of it before. She took it into her inner pools of silence. Thresholds. Boundaries. It suited her. Galt, not wanting to intrude on her reflection, got up and poked the fire. Rain was drumming on the roof like a tribe of hallucinating drummers. When he took his seat again, Jan was lying back in her wicker chair with her knees up, gazing at him. The gaze seemed to come from within her being.

"You were wondering what good is a university that's always experimenting with itself," she said, reading his mind uncannily. "Do you remember, in the back of Dad's float plane I called it 'play school.' Dad's right, in a way. We don't take education seriously."

Galt took what he hoped seemed like a thoughtful sip of his brandy and waited for the next swerve in the stream of intuition.

"Only morons take education seriously," Jan continued. "People who believe in facts. But there aren't any facts — at least, not in the Humanities."

"No facts?" repeated Galt, trying not to sound like a moron.

"No — only embodiments. What you say — I mean, your discourse, your way of talking about something … "

Galt could see that Jan was plainly having trouble with her own discourse. But then she'd drunk most of the bottle of brandy.

" … your discourse depends on your body — where it is in space and time, where you are in relation to your body, whether you're deep in your body or abstracted from it. So it's not the discourse — it's not what someone says — that's important. It's their body music. Do you understand?"

Jan's eyes searched Galt's eyes with care.

"You don't, do you?"

Galt shook his head with a slow smile.

"Okay — I'll try again." She paused for a second, trying to locate a current of inspiration. "Right! — I've got it!" Jan sat up abruptly in the chair. "Years after you graduate, what would you still like to know? Are you going to take just this one way of seeing things or that one way of seeing things? No. You might as well not come to college at all if you're going to be stuck inside some social cliché. Those are the students who get Ds. Then at the next level there's the Vic Bosko type. He's going to graduate on your Dean's List because he's clever and he can compare more than two discourses. But he doesn't know zot about their social functions. He doesn't know how the system manipulates these two or more discourses he's busy hacking. He wants to be a lawyer but the truth is he's going to end up as a middle manager somewhere in the system. Now, take Dad. Dad knows how to compare all sorts of discourses and switch them when he needs to. And he knows how the system works — the system of discourses. But he doesn't know *why* it works, and he's not interested in finding out because the system is paying him big bucks. Then, at the next higher level, there are the graduates who crack the controlling discourse of the system – the discourse that controls all the others."

"What happens to them?"

Jan smiled. "They go on to be professors."

She collapsed into the wicker chair as if the stream of perception had exhausted itself. Seeing Jan in the chair, Galt realized for the first time how out-of-place those wicker chairs were. They were not the thick unpainted wicker of cottages of old, but machine-woven Hong Kong wicker, with hideous sapphire-blue floral cushions. They belonged in a suburban sunroom. Sally had bought them.

"Are you going to be a professor?" he asked.

Jan laughed. "No."

"Why not?"

"There's a level above discourse-hacking, you know – where you question discourse altogether. Saraha says: 'There is only one word now worth knowing, and I do not know its name.'"

"Only a man with no hands can reorder the world," said Galt, remembering Rattenbury's quotation.

Jan's face was like a child's brightening. "Or a woman with no hands. I'll probably end up a frustrated artist like Mom."

"You could do worse," Galt offered.

"I'm taking Professor Lewin's course just so I can watch his hands."

"An embodiment."

"Sure – that's what you remember years after you graduate, isn't it? You remember a sort of connection between a discourse and its teacher. And other discourses and other teachers. You don't re-member what they taught, but you remember how they think things through. So, years later, you're a walking university. You come at things through the minds of a bunch of virtual teachers who sit inside your memory."

"An embodied university." Now it was Galt's turn to laugh.

"But isn't that what you remember?" Jan insisted. "Not what they said – but the way they said it. What do you remember?"

Galt reflected for a long moment. He had a clear picture of the teacher at Metro who had propelled him into Communications Theory. One of Marshall McLuhan's protégés, the man had brought an intellectual, almost a technical care to the magnesium-flare brilliance of the media guru's thinking. But he hadn't taught how bodies frame messages.

"I see what you mean. 'Style is a way of seeing,'" Galt said, quoting McLuhan quoting – who was it? – Seneca.

"But hard to sell to the public, right?"

Galt chuckled. He was thoroughly enjoying this conversation. It was the first real conversation he'd had with an Avalon student. He hadn't even had such a conversation with Sally. But then Sally wasn't a conversationalist; she was an achiever. She knew exactly where she was going in her world of women's self-construction of gender through meta-fictional discourse. Was that a style you'd remember thirty years down the road? At least you'd have some good critical and research skills.

"Yes, hard to sell to the public," he agreed. "We bought them off with beautiful buildings thirty years ago. Now we have to buy them off with technology."

"No technology can beat face-to-face teaching," Jan said.

"Face-to-face teaching – what a novel concept!" Galt mused ironically. "Maybe some educational planner high up in the Department of Education will discover it. 'Spoken language – the new *techné*. And gesture. How to utilize language and gesture in face-to-face teaching to cut down on soaring educational delivery computing costs by bringing learners together in actual interactive physical scenarios.'"

Jan's whole body dissolved in a chuckle. "'Recent studies conducted at a small university called Avalon have shown that you can get more bang for your educational buck by actually transporting learners to a centralized, intensified learning location.'"

"'Termed the *Carnival of Style Approach to Learning*,'" Galt continued, "'such an instantaneous, transparent, interfacial experiential center has the decided advantage of laying down adaptive multi-purpose perspectives in three quick years, which a student can apply independently to a multitude of later discovery-situations that may subsequently arise, instead of prolonging a series of *ad hoc* educational retooling sessions expensively over a lifetime.'"

Galt laughed until he almost spilt his brandy. He hadn't had this much fun in years. In fact, he didn't know he even had this playful side to his personality. Outside, the winds, as if catching the mirth, whistled through the screened-in porch like shrieking spirits. Jan was surveying him over the top of the brandy bottle.

"Want to smoke some grass? Grass is really good with *Marc de Bourgogne*."

Galt shook his head wistfully.

"You smoked it once, but you didn't inhale – right?"

He laughed again. He hadn't smoked a joint for twenty years. Now, for the first time the idea crossed his mind. It was a temptation. But what he felt even more than the joint was the temptation behind the temptation. Not the long body-stockinged legs drawn up comfortably under Jan's chin, but body itself and all the playful subjectivities racing around inside it like children at recess. Galt quoted to himself one of his own memos from the Metro University: 'A correct professional distance is arm's length, plus an inch.'

"I usually have one before I crash," Jan said. "Do you mind?"

"No. Go ahead."

Jan went out to the hallway and brought back her stash from the pocket of her rainslicker. Soon the pungent smell of marijuana filled the room.

"I wish we had some music."

In the candlelit space they listened instead to the pattern of rain on the roof and the crackling of logs in the wood stove. Galt suddenly felt ageless, at peace. After a while, Jan opened her eyes.

"I fell asleep."

"You can use the guest room. Down at the end of the hall, past Sally's room."

Sally's bedroom, in sad fact. How privatized even their bodies had become! Mobile mainframes for various software programs.

Jan uncoiled herself from the chair and took a candle and the bottle of brandy. "Goodnight. Don't let the bedbugs bite!" she said sleepily.

She disappeared in an aura of candlelight down the hallway.

He put more logs in the wood stove, then went around the room blowing the candles out. Then he went to bed, thinking strange tumbling thoughts. He half hoped Jan would come tip-toeing into his room. If she did, what would he do? He wrestled with the idea until in the struggle he became two Cameron Galts lying on the bed and staring at the ceiling. But she never came. Galt 1 and Galt 2 listened to the rain drumming like tiny fingers on the roof, until sleep came and dragged him down and made him one.

Part Three
JANUARY

19

With the beginning of Christmas Break came the first big snowfall of the year. Snow hung in fantastic shapes on the parapets and ledges of the colleges so that the whole university resembled a dream castle from a children's storybook. After the dons' parties and the snowball fights in the quad, after the frantic shopping at the Mall, the students turned off the coloured lights they had kept burning in their windows, and went home to friends and parents, leaving Avalon University silent and empty like some ruin of civilization held in an Ice Age.

Faith Rackstraw used the first day of the Break to give a party for the cleaning staff; then she took Clio and the book she was writing to a chapter house in the country where the nuns of Mother Church provided her usual room to work in, as well as the familiar discipline of Advent. Joe went back to his Nation and did the trap lines and the ice-fishing. Ruairi MacDonald flew to Edinburgh to give a paper on the rise of Scottish mercantilism, then to Glasgow University where he prowled the archives which he knew like the back of his hand. Jeremy Lewin flew to San Francisco, losing a bunch of Cultural Studies essays on the plane. Sheena Meganetty, wary of flying because of an astrological prediction on her computer, took buses and trains instead – to a self-healing session in Colorado in order to regain touch with the goddess within.

Jilaquns, already a born-again goddess, stayed for a while with Jan in Metro, where she made jokes about Jan's father's condominium and hung out at the inner-city bars with artists and rock performers who had parties in studios converted from old warehouses. Then she flew home to the Islands of the People. Jan, with her father and Erzsébet away in the Bahamas, was able to be alone for most of the time. While doing her Christmas shopping, she kept luncheon appointments with old classmates from Bishop Rye, now worlds apart from her at the Greater Metropolitan University. She went to a couple of parties and left early both times. She spent part of Christmas morning on the phone with her father, turning down an invitation to fly down to Nassau. The next day, she took a flight to London, changing at Heathrow for a flight to Málaga, crowded with drunken English sun-worshippers on holiday. Then she took a peaceful late-morning bus up through the Sierra Nevada to be with her mother in Granada.

Cameron and Sally Galt stayed at the cottage on Stoney. Sally typed a paper that she was to give at a conference with Hannah. Cameron worked on the retirement and restructuring plan. Listening to Christmas carols from faraway places on the radio, they ate the customary dinner they prepared together for Christmas Eve, and exchanged token presents. Early Christmas morning they drove down to Sally's parents in Metro for a second Christmas dinner, noisy with Sally's sisters and their excited children. Cameron called his father and mother in Florida, then spent the next day in the guest bedroom, brushing up on his Spanish with the dictionary Sally had given him, and preparing for his overnight flight to London.

20

He was halfway across the Atlantic when the image hit him full-force. His stomach went empty as if the plane had plunged a hundred feet down an air-pocket. His perspectives went haywire as if an inertial navigation system had been scrambled by a space-time singularity. Fighting for stability, he discovered all his backup systems missing. Only with a great effort of will was Galt able to find his mental horizon and recover altitude.

"Shit!" he said.

The passenger beside him, a young Korean executive, woke from his sleep, stared blankly at Galt, then put on a set of headphones.

The image of Sally and Hannah who had driven him to the Metro airport. Goodbye, goodbye. Have a great conference. Hope it doesn't rain in Spain. Ta ta, etc. *Flight 601 for London is now ready for boarding. Would passengers please proceed to departure lounge 36 and have their passports ready.* A light hug which was not really a hug but a hand patting his shoulder. A withheld hug, unwilling, a consolation. Galt passing through the metal detector, his arm extended in a nonchalant goodbye wave over his head. And on into the endless corridor to the departure lounge. The freedom of beginning a journey alone. Just a minute! He's forgotten to give Sally the address and phone number in Spain. Could she get it from the university? No – Sheena would be away; this would be easier.

Galt now racing back along the corridor sheepishly, against an amused flow of travellers. She had forgotten to ask for it and he had forgotten to give it to her. How silly! Where are they? They can't be far.

There they are in the middle of the concourse beneath its huge glass canopy roof. Two women looking like schoolgirls beginning a holiday, jumping up and down in uncontainable excitement, eagerness, anticipation. And freedom. They are hugging – long giving hugs in which beings are exchanged. And yes – they are kissing.

Galt turned away, confused. No – this couldn't be happening.

He looked again. The two women walking towards the car-park exit, arm-in-arm, then Sally skipping, practically dancing around Hannah in a spirit of release. Release from what? From the single-mindedness of a workaholic trajectory? The endless continuity of dutiful intercourse with a single body (male)? The perpetuity of life in an empire of men over women? Or release from him, Cameron Galt.

His instinctual reaction in a crisis was to do nothing until the outlines of the crisis declared itself fully. Doing nothing, Galt turned and went back through the metal detector, his arms limp at his sides. Down the now empty corridor to begin his lonely voyage into the night.

All those non-communications – you don't notice them because what they communicate is nothing. All those consolation hugs, ungiving light taps on the shoulders. Those nights when Sally, working late, phoned to say she was staying at Hannah's.

Galt found his seat on the plane and then began a process of mourning.

The full outline of the crisis failed to disclose itself. That was because, Galt concluded, the crisis had already happened – it had passed into the irreversibility of time. What he was left with were the consequences. The consequences told in an image.

The image hit him full-force on the nerve-ends. Then it hit him again and again, but with diminishing effect, like a ball dropped on the floor, losing power with each bounce, losing its power to the gravity of the inevitable.

Galt could not bring his well-honed problem-solving mind to bear on the event. Thus his second conditioned reflex to a crisis failed to work for him. Instead, he began to hate the University and everything it stood for. In this mood, he spent seven hundred miles redrawing the crash downsizing plan in his head, letting his body be carried along with its sorrow by the plane while his mind plotted a delicious revenge against the institution that had betrayed him.

The Korean executive beside him had disappeared, finding a seat elsewhere.

Galt reached into his briefcase, took out the resumé of Jerónimo, and glared at it with scorn. No matter how much any academic manages to conceal his ambition, the self-pride will show on the *curriculum vitae*. It is the Achilles heel of every academic, Galt thought. Yet the *c.v.* before him broke the rule. Typed by what was probably an ancient Olivetti typewriter with its "o" key silted in and its "e" key simply missing, the document regarded its surveyor with a matching scorn. Letters missing or above the line, mistakes blanked out with a row of fervent "x's", the upper-case "E" substituted for the missing lower-case, Spanish superscripts inserted with a Rapidograph, and its author's name written with a great flourish across the top: *JERÓNIMO*. What was the date of all this negative mischief? Galt checked the entries to find that the *curriculum vitae*, if such it was, had not been updated in nine years. "That's it for tenure and any kind of job security for you!" Galt thought savagely. Apocalypse Now. The entries were unclassified according to refereed and non-refereed publications; most of them were in Spanish; they followed no logic except the crude logic of chronology. The idiot had evidently typed the resumé quickly by memory, x-ing out publications attributed to the wrong year or adding them in an afterthought.

Cameron Galt, Provost and Dean of an irresponsible university, looked out the window and exchanged blackness with the Atlantic night. The other passengers had settled down to sleep. The cabin assistants had disappeared. The image of betrayal stabbed him some more.

Off the west coast of Ireland, with morning brightening the wingtip of the plane, Galt's mood changed. It changed from "don't get mad – get even" to another sentiment that was similar. "If you can't beat them, join them," Galt thought, modulating revenge into subversion. Why not? The arrival of a continental breakfast helped to alter his mood. So did another image. It was the image of Jan D'Arnay with her legs tucked thoughtfully under her chin, sitting in Sally's hideous chair. Didn't Jan say she would be in Granada with her mother? The image seemed to draw the plane towards Europe; the blast of jets pushed the other image behind him. Suddenly, whatever allegiance Galt had to Human Rights went out the window. Take that, Women's Caucus! What would they think of a dean who got too close to a student? Sally hadn't seemed bothered by Jan's overnight stay. When Sally had arrived the next morning, looking fresh and happy, she'd treated the bleary-eyed Jan with a sisterly tenderness. Maybe Sally had had a good night with Hannah and didn't care about anything. Well, she would care about this!

Galt ate his *croissant* and reflected on what he perceived to be the hypocrisy of Sally's position on responsible relationships. If she enjoyed a double standard, why couldn't he? Or why have double standards at all? He toyed with the idea of an institution without double standards of freedom. The image came to him of hosts of Avalon students supporting him on policy initiatives. And faculty too! He, Cameron Galt, the center of popularity in a university devoted to the freedom of each of its members to become themselves fully. To become themselves fully, so long as they didn't hurt another person in the process, restricting that other's freedom also to grow.

In this anarchic libertarian spirit Galt waved aside the London papers that were being offered him by the cabin assistant. Passengers were opening their window blinds and the plane was suddenly full of light, activity and destination. When his breakfast tray had been removed, Galt saw that Jerónimo's resumé was still on his lap.

Well, what use had this man made of his freedom? Galt surveyed the life accomplishments of this most insouciant of colleagues in a new light. Mostly art exhibitions over the last several years – in Barcelona, Madrid, even one in New York. Jerónimo was apparently a well-known painter. He was also, like many artists, cunning – cunning enough to be cross-appointed during that time to the Cultural Studies Department where "cultural production" counted on a par with scholarly publication. Working forwards through the resumé, Galt worked backwards in time. He located two years in which the employee had nothing to report. A dry spell, maybe? A marriage breakdown? These things happen, Galt thought grimly. Then he began to discover a second Jerónimo hidden in time beneath the pages of the first. The author of a torrent of critical essays in leading journals in both languages, of book-length studies of Hispanic literature, of critical biographies of major Spanish poets and painters, and of several books of his own poetry published throughout the Spanish-speaking world. And the editor of some anthologies. Good heavens – Jerónimo was a man-of-letters, to use that quaint phrase. He was apparently an admired and respected figure in the Spanish literary world during the last period of the Franco regime. His publications record also listed lines of praise from the great painters

and poets of twentieth-century Spain – Miró, Alberti. He had accomplished more in one incandescent burst of activity in his youth
than most scholars do in a lifetime. At the beginning of it all was a
law degree from Zaragosa. Galt wondered what it would be like to
be taught by this embodiment of civilization.

"Excuse me. Are you Dr. Galt? There's a videoconference call for
you."

Galt glanced up at the flight attendant. Heavy eye makeup concealing perpetual jet-lag in her face. Who would be calling him at
this hour? Of course, it would be late at night behind him.

"The call is from a Mr. Hugh D'Arnay. We can feed it into the
videoscreen here – just use these earphones. Or you can come up
to the communications center if you want privacy."

D'Arnay – who stayed up late into the night. And who believed
in face-to-face exchanges between upper-level managers. Or virtual exchanges by videophone – the next best thing.

"I'll come forward."

What could this be about?

Galt settled himself into a private communications alcove, with
its computer surmounted by a videocamera.

"Just press this call-back button," said the flight attendant. Galt
did. Then the Andromeda Networks logo came onto his screen,
followed by the image of a tired-looking Hugh D'Arnay.

"I see you loud and clear," said the digitalized image of D'Arnay.
"Good flight?"

"Up and down."

"Look, Cam – I've just got the government funding figure. It's
going to be announced on Monday. We're going to be taking a hit
in the 10% range. Not big enough to crush us, but big enough to
switch us into the crash downsizing scenario."

D'Arnay paused.

"I'm afraid we'll have to ditch your Renewal through Voluntary
Early Retirement plan."

"They'll strike."

"Let them."

"But I thought we agreed we could do staged faculty renewal even at the 10% cut level."

"Did we? Well, I'm afraid that may have to be toast, as they say. The government – bless their wicked commonsense hearts! – evidently wants to force the universities off tenure."

Below camera view, where D'Arnay couldn't see him, Cameron Galt clenched his fists grimly.

"It doesn't need to force *us* off tenure! Don't you see? All the other universities can be in strike and turmoil, and we can sail upwind of them all. That'll look good in the university excellence ratings. Solves our admissions problem too."

Galt felt a cold fury building in him.

"That's why I costed out the Faculty Renewal plan right up to the 15% funding cut level. *We can do it!*"

D'Arnay's level eyes flickered for a second. A second's hesitation.

"Cam, we're obviously coming at this from different perspectives. That's okay. We've got time to sort it out. The announcement's coming down the pipe on Monday. It's Thursday here now – Friday for you. Can you terminate – what's his name? – Geronimo and get back here by Sunday? We can figure out what to do on Sunday night."

"Yes, I can do that. But why the rush?"

"Wu – remember? We've got to have something in place for Mr. Wu. He's on his way – probably left Hong Kong already. And I think I've got a corporation to partner with Wu if we have to top up the donation."

"What's the corporation?"

"Can't say right now – it's a numbered company. But the government will pitch in too with some capital development funds, if we pull it off. In any case, you've got to be here to read the riot act to the faculty when the you-know-what hits the fan."

"Rattenbury ... "

"I don't want him to do it. He's passable at fundraising but he's egregiously inept at crowd control. Can't handle the air pockets of history."

Well, *there's* a streak of trust! Galt thought. And it looks like Apocalypse Now for Rattenbury. D'Arnay was holding something in his hands.

"These are the crash plans. I've fine-tuned them a little. Can you look them over for Sunday?"

"Sure."

D'Arnay's hands disappeared from view; almost immediately the printer beside Galt delivered five pages.

"I received five pages – right?"

"Right."

"All transmitted clearly."

"Good. See you at Andromeda Place on Sunday. Phone when you see the east coast and we'll send a limo out to get you."

Hugh D'Arnay's image disappeared from the screen, to be replaced for a second by the Andromeda Spiral logo. Then the screen resumed its whimsical off-use pattern.

Galt returned to his seat as the airplane began its slow descent path over Cornwall to Heathrow. Galt, betrayed twice in one quick night, did not have the strength to look at D'Arnay's transmission. He sat in a state of turmoil, watching the tight patchwork of greens and browns of the English countryside play hide and seek with the broken cloud cover.

"Would you please fasten your seat belt, sir?"

Oh yes – the flight attendant with the eye makeup.

"Sorry." He fastened his seat belt quickly. Betrayed twice in one night. *Clunk!* What was that? Of course, the wheels coming down for landing. The resistance of air drag. The plane became clumsy as powerful forces met on the wing surfaces and fuselage. Then it was out of the sun and beneath the cloud cover of a busy European Friday morning.

Galt's mood changed again once he boarded the holiday flight to Málaga with a host of English holiday-makers. He barely noticed

the festivity. Feeling instead a sort of Nietzschean tragic joy, Galt —
or at least the administrator busy inside the hollow shell of Galt —
was prioritizing his sacrifice. He would try to persuade D'Arnay to
hold off the downsizing for a year. That would buy time. There
were too many incommensurables. With D'Arnay's plan, a strike
was inevitable, and a strike on top of the agony of institutional redefinition would mean an enrolment slump as the market waited to
see what Avalon stood for. An enrolment crash would entail a large
deficit. If D'Arnay's Board had to carry a deficit why not apply that
cost instead to a slower, more extended institutional redefinition?
Even then, D'Arnay would be courting a strike. It depended on the
list of "voluntary" early retirements. Who would they be?

Galt finally looked at D'Arnay's five-page memo. Yes, it was as
bad as he thought. The man hadn't fine-tuned Galt's work at all —
he had pushed it one stage further. Now, the Humanities and Social
Sciences were to be dissolved into a small interdisciplinary catch-all
annexed to a core of Ecology and Environmental Studies. Any
Humanities course that could be redesigned to support the study of
the environment was kept as an "interdisciplinary support course."
All the others were wiped off the books. Ruairi's "European Trade
History," for example, was gone. So! D'Arnay had taken Galt's idea
of an interdisciplinary university, but he had shrunk it down to a
research park. A large graduate school was prominent — in fact, there
were even hiring slots in the plan for unnamed research specialists
to be lured away from other universities. Presumably, these specialists would be cutting-edge researchers who would haul in industrial grants. The researchers would attract graduate students who as
teaching assistants would do the actual undergraduate instruction
dirt-cheap using course material the research professors had up-
loaded on the Web. The virtual university. It would work, alright.
The environmental scientists would support it. As for the Humanities and Social Sciences faculty, if they went out on strike there
would be no jobs for them to return to. Was that why D'Arnay had
said "let them strike"? Altogether, it was a neat bit of corporate

downsizing. An effectively privatized university. Someone must have helped D'Arnay with this. Bud Lassiter? Yes, the crash downsizing plan had Lassiter's vacuous enthusiasm all over it. The Registrar had betrayed him too! Three betrayals in one night! Yet the plan would work. The sacrifice to be made was the end of Avalon as a liberal arts college with a personality all its own. Did D'Arnay really believe in the liberal arts at all?

How to save the liberal arts identity of Avalon? Galt thought furiously with the mind of someone D'Arnay was not – an academic. Trained to look for the compromise in any confused situation, Galt scanned the downsizing plan, ignoring the costing figures and concentrating on the departmental groupings. If he could only find the compromise! Maybe he could protect the collegial core of Avalon, holding it intact until a better day, a better government. Galt noted that the Humanities courses D'Arnay had retained lay in domestic and local subject areas involving the Kenomagaywakon Valley region. These were courses that couldn't be duplicated by other universities or by the educational software firms. Courses that gave Avalon identity as a regional center. Think globally, act locally. But Avalon wasn't a regional center: it was one of the best small universities in the nation. Was the Center for the First Nations retained? Ah, there it was – but only as a minor degree in T.E.K. – traditional environmental knowledge. Everything in D'Arnay's plan supported the Environmental Sciences. But what was a region anyway? Had that concept ever been settled? What, come to think of it, was the natural environment? Nowhere in D'Arnay's thinking – or was it Lassiter's thinking? – was there room for people to reflect on what it was they were doing in the name of Ecology and Environmental Consciousness.

Ah – that was it! Galt sat bolt upright when he saw the compromise, almost upsetting the beer of a soccer-shirted holidayer beside him. What use is Ecology without a critical reflection on the subject itself? The history of ecological thought down through the ages. Galt quickly made a sketch on a Sunflight serviette. History –

the account of mercantile expansion and the plundering of the colonial margins for the imperial center which sustains North-South inequality. That would keep Ruairi at Avalon, if he wanted to stay. Philosophy and Cultural Studies – what is "Nature"? First Nations teaching – of course, keep that! Literature – I wonder …. Galt noticed that D'Arnay had transferred Avalon's literature courses over to the Polytech, where they were called 'Communication Arts.' Yep! – Lassiter's fingerprints were all over this. Hmm – a school of wilderness studies, say. No one else had that! And there was plenty of wilderness around Avalon to study. Geography – issues of parks, policy and ecotourism, as well as all the statistical science courses D'Arnay had kept. Politics – yes. Economics – yes. Sociology – yes. Women's Studies – no! There were departments of Women's Studies everywhere. Take that, Sally! Classics would be gone: also Psychology and Anthropology (that meant Hannah). Modern Languages could become introductory courses in various global languages taught by the international students Av attracted.

Galt looked with a diabolical glee at his sketch and saw that he had retained a Humanities core big enough to balance the Sciences core. Enough of the original departments remained to nourish the project of non-scientific study. And these were subjects with a good potential for interdisciplinary alliances. That would keep the liberal arts configuration strong. A leaner, stronger Humanities aiming its interdisciplinary critical thought at the social vision of an age dominated by global and ecological concerns. It was a Humanities leaning forward into the futuristic work of the twenty-first century. Think globally, act locally. How many great ideas, Galt wondered, had been sketched quickly with a Bic pen on a serviette?

As the plane circled over the Mediterranean for its final approach to Málaga, Galt balanced absurd hope against the actual process of persuading a stick-in-the-mud faculty to downsize in any way at all. And what about persuading D'Arnay and the board which he controlled? As before, any redefinition process would carry phase-out costs and job-retraining costs that D'Arnay wouldn't be willing to pay. Maybe the counterthrust was useless.

In the taxi to the bus station, Galt sank back into the mid-Atlantic gloom which his fervent effort of rationalization had failed to dispel. He thought about Sally again. His few words of guidebook Spanish provoked a good-natured and incomprehensible monologue from his taxi-driver as they drove through the run-down tenement buildings of Málaga, with washing hanging from every balcony.

He was one of three passengers on the late-morning bus to Granada. To the throb of pan-European rock music coming out of the bus driver's radio, Galt composed his resignation letter. High up in the Sierra Nevada, two teenage girls with hip-hop skirts and gypsy hoop earrings got on and talked volubly, apparently about an all-night party they were coming home from. Galt stopped phrasing his sacrifice and began to take a cursory interest in his surroundings.

About two hours later, he got off the bus and peered around a choking, exhaust-filled bus terminal in Granada. A short figure materialized in the smoke like a demon from hell. Galt felt his hand caught in a large brown hand, and saw a bearded, heavily-spectacled face gazing up at him.

"So? Welcome to Andalusia."

The tone was warm, casual, even nonchalant, yet with a sense of event.

"Jerónimo?"

"Yes – I am Jerónimo."

There was a note of mirth in his voice, as if it were a funny thing to be Jerónimo. A hand took his luggage, and Galt followed the figure out of the garage into the bright morning streets of Granada. Perhaps it *was* a funny thing to be Jerónimo, Galt thought, following this man who appeared more decrepit than even he himself felt. Jerónimo was wearing a shapeless black overcoat. His hair, black with streaks of white, was caught in a ponytail, some of it falling over his face. Galt smelled a scent of Gaulloise cigarettes and the wine, fever and cynicism of the European avant-garde. How-

ever, Jerónimo felt more ancient than that. With his squat sturdi-
ness, he might have been a *conquistador* or a Roman centurion,
veteran of a hundred campaigns, retired to this most prized of the
empire's provinces.

"We will go to a café. It is better to stay up all day and pay your
– how you call? – sleep debt at night."

Jerónimo's battered car sped through narrow cobblestone streets
up a steep hill as if it knew its own way home, drunk, from a party.
Galt, feeling the inertia of an all-night traveller, could not have cared
less if Jerónimo had in fact taken out the entire row of motorbikes
parked at the last corner. White houses rising above walls whizzed
by. Jerónimo was keeping up a friendly running commentary.

"This is the Albaicín – the old Moorish quarter. See? It is on a
hill facing the Alhambra. We'll show you the Alhambra later. This
is where the mother of the caliph lived. Now it is for tourists and
artists."

Galt absorbed this information abstractly. He was having difficulty with his host's pronunciation of the "th" sound which buzzed
in Galt's ears like a fly. Of all the modes of transportation of the last
several hours – Sally's car, airplane, moving sidewalk, plane, taxi and
bus – this was the most dizzying. The car swerved suddenly, avoid-
ing an oncoming car by centimeters at a bend in the cobbled lane.

"*Idjiot!*" Jerónimo shouted over his shoulder, still driving at full
tilt. "That man – he cannot drive! He should not be driving a car,
eh? He is supposed to honk at the bend in the road."

Much to Galt's relief, the car screeched to a stop in a little square
completely shaded by trees. The square was enclosed by buildings
with second-floor balconies of elaborate wrought iron. Suddenly,
an oasis of peace unfolded like the petals of a rose. People were sitting on benches in the shade, talking. A small market seemed to be
in progress. In one of the buildings was a dark doorway with a sign
over it – Aixa's Café.

"Your travel is over," Jerónimo announced. "Now you are going
to meet some friends."

21

To Galt's surprise, Jan D'Arnay made her way across the café and gave him an immense hug. She was wearing a green college T-shirt and jeans – the Avalon undergraduate uniform right here in Granada. But she had added huge gypsy hoop earrings. Barely had one of those silver hoops disengaged itself from his shirt collar and the warm impress of her body left him, when the other woman turned away from the bar to greet him. Of course, it was Jennifer D'Arnay. However, Mrs. D'Arnay, unlike her daughter, was dressed for an occasion. Galt had an impression of baby-fine blond hair caught back in a bun, perfect skin, a tiny diamond stud in each ear, and a single diamond on a thin gold chain around her neck. She was wearing black crepe flared trousers and a plain matching top.

"Cameron, how very good to see you!" she breathed in his ear, giving him not just a hug but a kiss on both cheeks in the Latin manner. Galt, confused, stood immobile. Over Mrs. D'Arnay's elegant black shoulder, he saw Jerónimo grinning like a diabolical child.

"Hello, Jennifer – it's been a long time," Galt said weakly, trying to regain a sense of context.

"*Café con leche y una tostada!*" bellowed Jerónimo above the voices of other patrons clamoring for attention.

One of four servers behind the counter nodded in mid-activity. There was the hiss of espresso machines, the smell of steamed milk. And talk! Everywhere people were locked in dialogue, facing each other, only inches apart. Galt, hemmed in by the press of bodies at Aixa's café, stood on a floor littered with discarded sugar wrappers.

"You must be very tired from your journey," Jennifer said sympathetically.

"Yes, I suppose I am. In any case, I'm very glad to be here."

Galt replied automatically. He felt pulled to the floor by a gravity of sorrow while around him, as if on the outside of a bubble, a surreal carnival was going full-blast. The dark smoky café was packed with bodies – bodies arguing, bodies gesticulating, bodies filling themselves with food and drink. A man beside him at the counter stared sternly at an oily mixture of brandy and some other kind of alcohol, then downed the whole potion in a single swallow. With a shout of triumph, the man waved goodbye and went off to work. Over in the corner, a lottery machine woke up and played a lunatic melody. Galt found a metal foot-rest under the bar and put a tired leg on it. Jan took the place of the brandy-swallower on his left. To his right stood Jennifer, a golden pillar of grace. Beside her, level with her shoulder, was the head of Jerónimo. A piece of toasted bread spread with margarine and marmalade appeared before him. Then a thick small glass of coffee beside it.

"One sip of this and the lights come on all over Europe," Jennifer declared.

Galt dutifully drank some coffee and immediately felt himself coming into focus. "Well, now what are the plans?" he said stupidly. Even as he said them, he heard the words flutter to the floor like used sugar wrappers.

"Plans? What means this – plans?"

"I think the plan should be to try to keep you awake," Jennifer laughed. "If you sleep now, you'll be *hors de combat* for three days."

"We've got some time to kill. Why don't we take him to the Alhambra?" Jan offered.

"Kill time? What an unutterable concept!" Jennifer shot at her daughter severely. "Never, ever, use that expression!"

"I think the expression comes from the First World War – no? The soldiers in the trenches have nothing to do. They are always waiting for something to happen."

" 'It is time that beats in the breast,' " said Jennifer D'Arnay, cocking her head in the direction of a stream of memory:

> *Time is a horse that runs in the heart, a horse*
> *Without a rider on a road at night.*
> *The mind sits listening and hears it pass.*

"When she quotes Wallace Stevens, watch out!" Jan advised. "Wallace Stevens makes her horny."

"No, my contumacious and refractory daughter, it is not Wallace Stevens that fills the spirit. Rather it is doing something beautiful for its own sake. *L'art pour l'art*."

"Which equals doing zot-all," Jan said crossly. "Nothing seems to happen in Granada – not until night, that is, when the bars open."

"But in fact something is happening at this very minute," Jennifer retorted. "We are drinking coffee in Aixa's Café and welcoming Dean Cameron Galt, which is an act of civilization quite opposed to the barbarity and emptiness of war."

"Oh, Mom – come off it!"

Jerónimo looked across at Galt and winked. "I don't understand mothers and daughters."

"Certainly – I'd like to see the Alhambra," Galt cut in. "But Jerónimo and I have some business to discuss."

"'Nowhere so bisy a man as he ther nas. And yit he seemed bisier than he was,'" quoted Jennifer in Chaucerian English.

"It is not necessary to worry about the Spanish Year Abroad. Already I made arrangement to end it."

Once again Galt looked blank.

"So now there is nothing for you to do here, eh? – except give birth to time." Jerónimo giggled at the idea.

Give birth to time? Galt pondered the concept with a rising irritation. "Speaking of which – we do have to talk about something, I'm afraid. There is a new Early Retirement scheme. I need to explain it to you. I hope you'll consider it."

"I consider it already. No problem. I retired ten years ago."

Then Jerónimo's eyes flashed with a remembered rage and his "th" sounds began to buzz like a thousand angry bees.

"It was when they try to put me in the first-year course. Introductory Spanish! Can you imagine this? I have to wake up at eight in the morning to hold a Spanish conversation class with first-year students. We talk about the current events, but they no read the newspapers – so we talk about their cats. And boyfriends. And birth control."

Jerónimo shuddered at the thought of it. Arms waving in the air, he was getting more excited.

"Then finally we can talk no more about the birth control and safe sex. And so there is nothing left to talk about. So I read to them poetry by César Vallejo. At eight in the morning, I am reading Vallejo's poetry. They don't want to understand."

Jerónimo proceeded to extend the remembered indignity as if to the point of orgasm. His arms waved wildly so that Galt had to protect his coffee glass.

"Even worse – then I have to read all their first-year essays in Spanish."

Jerónimo rolled his eyes to the ceiling in despair.

"Finally, I give them all Cs – I didn't read them. Instead I read the – how you say? – appeals."

"And how is Avalon?" Jennifer said, changing the topic adroitly. "And Sally – is she liking it there?"

Galt didn't know how to answer the question. The heavy mood suddenly jumped on his shoulders, sinking him to the floor. He opened and closed his mouth like a goldfish in a tank.

"Oh, you are unhappy," Jennifer D'Arnay determined. Changing her mood she dissolved into sympathy. She put her arm around his shoulder. "Something is terribly wrong, dear, isn't it?"

At that motherly tenderness, Galt nodded his head like a child, choking back tears. He looked down at the gutted sugar wrappers at his feet.

"This man is sorely wounded," Jennifer announced. She turned to her daughter. "What is the duty of a lady to a gentleman who is grievously wounded?"

"Give him a brandy?"

"The first duty of a woman is to nurse the afflicted individual back to health," Jennifer corrected.

"Oh, Mom, you are such a sexist – I don't believe it!"

"Nonsense! I am not a sexist. I am a liberal bourgeois intellectual which I consider the summit of human achievement."

Jan threw up her hands in mock defeat. "She is an incurable sexist goddess," she confided to Galt as if explaining the problem apologetically to one of her own generation. "Her consciousness was formed in the age of James Bond and the Italian cinema minx."

"It is at least superior to that of the new international genderless proletariat," Jennifer retorted. She shoved her glass of wine away on the counter and took Galt by the arm. "Come – let's go for a walk in the fresh air. *Un paseo.* You will note that the Spanish have perfected the art of walking. Of walking in order to be seen. Notice their gait, their deportment, the attention they give to their carriage. Jerónimo will buy the wine for tonight – won't you, dear? Thoroughly unpalatable volcanic detritus – however, it will rekindle our sagging spirits. I intend to induct you into the mysteries of the Sufi meditational garden."

An hour later, Jennifer D'Arnay was still holding his arm as they meandered through the gardens of the Alhambra. Each garden varied in the colours of its roses and fountain pool tiles from the garden they had just left. Each garden precisely similar in design to the one they had just left. Each garden offering four exits from its rectangle to four other gardens, and those four opening out pointlessly to sixteen others, and those sixteen …

"While the Goths were banging each other on the heads with swords, the Moors were contemplating the sensuous pleasures of infinity," Jennifer announced with her usual note of heightened matter-of-factness. An afternoon sun stood in the bluest of skies, but a cold breeze was blowing off the snows of the Sierra Nevada. Galt stared at yet another small fountain at the end of its rectangular pool, bubbling up just enough water to break the surface.

"To the ear of the Moor, there is no more beautiful sound in the world than the bubbling of a spring in an oasis," Jerónimo explained. "And the most beautiful taste – it is also water. They were connoisseurs of water. In Granada not long ago, there were water stalls in the streets. You could buy water with different fragrances."

Jennifer nudged Galt into yet another garden. This one had yellow roses. Blue and green fountain tiles. Cypresses and orange and lemon trees. How many gardens had that been? He had lost count. Why did he feel he had to keep a count of everything? The meandering from one corner of paradise to another also seemed liquid in its motion. Altogether, this was putting him in a trance. Disoriented by jet-lag, two, possibly three betrayals, and a day that had jumped right into the middle of the next, Galt was further disoriented by the gentle insistent nudging of Jenny D'Arnay's breast against his arm.

"How tiny are the purposes of man beside the infinite ways of Allah," she said serenely, guiding him to yet another garden.

This one had enormous crimson roses. The scent of pecan and avocado pear. Yes, there was the ubiquitous fountain. The tiles were black and green this time. They were in a labyrinth that led to no significant center, that guarded no inner meaning, that had no end in view. Delicately patterned repetition, a design that invited no unravelling.

Galt thought of the theory of frames and their importance to early Communications Theory. Logical levels and hypertexts.

Jan thought of the endless decorativeness of Persian carpets and the hypnotic flute music of North Africa.

Jennifer thought of the *One Thousand and One Nights*, where each story had characters who were storytellers, each of them telling a story within the story until you were splendidly lost in the narrative. In this case, guiding Cameron through the Generalife, she was Queen Shahrazad healing a traumatized King Shahriyar.

Jerónimo thought of endless sexual bliss in an Islamic heaven, ministered to by dark-eyed *houris*.

"It truly is an aesthetic culture," Jennifer observed. "Everything is done under the rule of poetry – the poetry of eating, the poetry of walking, the poetry of conversation. It is a pity we cannot see the Medina of Zahra. Four thousand marble columns – can you imagine that? All of those columns gleaming with bronze and gold and silver. The Chamber of the Caliphs had thirty-two doors, each one decorated in gold and ivory, hanging on pillars of transparent crystal. And the marble of the roof was cut so fine that you could see light through it. Just think – light passing through sheets of differently coloured marble!"

"Where was it? Was it around here?" Galt asked.

"No, it was at Córdova."

"It was built by Abderrahma the Third, the greatest of the Spanish caliphs," added Jerónimo. "The Berbers destroyed it. Later its stones were used to build a monastery. Now there is nothing left."

"Did you like the fountain in the Court of the Lions back in the Alhambra?" Jennifer asked. "The Palace at Zahra had a fountain that was filled, not with water, but with mercury. Set in motion, it dazzled the onlooker with flashes of light and colour."

"Thirteen thousand servants lived in the palace," said Jerónimo. "To feed all the fish in the garden tanks, it took twelve thousand loaves of bread."

"Beautiful!" Jennifer declared. "A culture of poetry and story-telling and faith."

"'There is no document of civilization which is not at the same time a document of barbarism,'" Jan stated in her best Cultural Studies voice. "What about the Hall of the Abencerrages back there where Aben somebody or other woke up one day, had a paranoia attack, and offed thirty-six members of his family? The heads of his wives and children rolling right beside the marble fountain of the Court of the Lions."

"A minor domestic incident," replied Jennifer. "Don't exaggerate it out of proportion. Remember – these Moorish caliphs were tolerant of the Jews. They allowed a Jewish culture of great learning to flourish. Not so the Visigoths who castrated everyone who was circumcised."

"What about the sex-slaves, then? What about the concubines? All the women hidden away behind their veils?"

"Veils? Here is a culture where a woman is free of the anxiety of her beauty. She does not have to manipulate it to please men."

"See? She's absolutely incurable," Jan said, taking Galt's other arm. "What about the belly dancers, Mom?"

"It is a mystical diversion. Like flamenco dancing. *Duende*. The spirit of God in a room. And a God who is not insensitive to the beauties of the body."

"Bodies moving seductively for the reclining *pasha* eating his dates and belching and farting," replied Jan. "It is striptease and you know it!"

"I don't go to watch the flamenco dancers anymore. It is like the world heavyweight wrestling," Jerónimo reported.

"I like to belly dance," Jennifer said. "I'll put on my costume and dance for you tonight."

Jan rolled her eyes to the Andalusian sky.

"One needs constantly to refute the terrifying puritanical solemnity of the young," Jennifer said.

They came to an ancient stairway tunneling under a canopy of trees where streams of water ran in troughs down each stone handrail. Again, Jerónimo explained:

"They knew how to keep the temperature cool with water and trees. In the summer it gets so hot here. You can taste the heat. Sometimes there blows across a red dust from Africa and covers everything.

"Time for some wine," he added, as if considering that hot summer dust.

From the gardens of the Alhambra, they went to the bars of Granada. "It is a university city," Jerónimo explained to Galt as a group of students thronged by in the night street, arm-in-arm singing. Young people were calling to each other from motorbikes. Everywhere there was a Latin air of carnival. "And we are a young country," he said, in a tone that suggested how out of place he felt in the new European Spain. A country of the young. And so all the bars. There were whole streets of them. How many? Oh, maybe two thousand of them altogether.

They went from one bar to the next until Galt had the impression each bar opened out to another in the same dilatory way as the gardens of the Alhambra. There was a café bar that showed films; there was one that doubled as a bookstore, another as a pharmacy. There were upmarket postmodern bars and there were ancient gypsy bars where Jerónimo was welcomed like a member of the family.

"I go to their weddings and funerals."

There was a bar that had an art gallery downstairs, and Jerónimo, after surveying an exhibition of photographs, began a spirited dialogue with a young woman with flashing eyes who was standing alone by the door.

"Those eyes could send a message at thirty yards," Jennifer remarked critically.

"Look at her neck and shoulders. She must have spent an hour on her hair," Jan said.

"Good that she did," Jennifer replied, "because then you don't notice her squat legs."

At this, both mother and daughter seemed to stand an inch taller.

"What on earth are they talking about?" Galt asked.

Jennifer attempted a running translation of the dialogue, catching all of its elegance: "'It seems to me, Señorita, that the wonderfully perceptive photographs I have just seen downstairs are yours, because it is not difficult to discern in them the eye of a mature woman. Would you speak of the camera as a particular artistic medium having a feminine eye, if I may use the term?'

"He's such a rake," Jennifer confided. "He has the mind and body of Dante. I love him. 'Thank you,' the woman is replying. 'That is very kind of you. But no – in fact, those are not my photographs: they are done by a friend. Yet with respect to the question you are raising about the feminine lens of the camera – its affection for detail, if I understand you rightly – yes, I would say ... '"

"They talk so beautifully in the bars," Jan concluded. "And with such conviction about everything. But then when you translate it, you find they're saying absolutely zero."

"My dear daughter – they are simply keeping alive the dream of civilization. What they are saying to each other in so many ways is *Gracias*. Thank you for responding to my individuality. And thank you for acknowledging my otherness as shown in my artistic self-expression. *Alteritas* – Otheration, if you like. That is what civilization is. It can be counted in all the relationships of trust a society has. And associations and agencies based on the principle of trust. Trust, I say – not manipulation of the other for profit. That is why I love Jerónimo. He is something especially rare – a gentleman."

"Actually, Mom, he is trying to seduce that woman."

"No, he is flirting. I am of the opinion that heaven is a state of endless flirtation."

"It looks like a seduction to me."

"So? Maybe he will succeed." Jennifer D'Arnay shrugged her shoulders. "In any case, that also is civilization – perhaps its most intense form."

"She calls sex civilization," Jan remarked dryly. "Everything comes down to sex in the end."

"No, rather, everything ascends to self-esteem, my intractable child! *Pundonor.* Having a good opinion of oneself. It is the flower which Rome planted in Iberia, and which took in this realistic soil better than it took anywhere else – and for which, alas, we have no equivalent in English. *Nobleza.* As I say, he is a *caballero.*"

"He's Don Quixote if he thinks he's going to score with that woman."

Jennifer D'Arnay turned, looked into her daughter's eyes, smiled faintly, and said nothing.

"I really shouldn't have any more of this wine." Another glass of *rioja* had appeared magically in front of Galt.

"But, my dear, you simply must! We are only just getting started. Besides, the wine seems to be a favour from the table in the corner."

Galt saw a table full of young people in the corner, giggling and whispering to each other. About *him*. The girls were heavily made up, with hoop earrings. The boys were dressed in black. Then he saw the Avalon sword logo peeping from a T-shirt under the leather jacket of one of the boys. Of course, they were Avalon students in the Year Abroad Program. Gone native. He raised the glass of wine and saluted them.

Then he felt the urge to go to the men's room. *Caballeros*, not *Hombres*. He hoped the toilet wasn't like the one in the last bar – a Moorish hole in the floor with walls that dripped ooze. No, this one was clean and, to Galt's mind, civilized. Jerónimo was there, peeing with enormous flair, not into a urinal, but into a toilet.

"You see that name?"

Jerónimo pointed out the name of the manufacturer inside the toilet bowl with a stream of livid pee.

"I was going out with the daughter of that capitalista."

He spat out the word with a vehemence worthy of the Spanish Civil War.

"He makes toilets for all the resort hotels on the coast. Also, he makes the hotels. And then, he did not like me because he found out I was a communista. He send his agents after me – the idjiot! So I have to leave Mallorca in the middle of the night – wake up the students and put them in the van. Then I come here. That is why the Year Abroad Program is in Granada."

Jerónimo looked over his shoulder at Galt.

"Now I have the satisfaction to pee over his name. See? I pee on his name!"

Jerónimo did up his fly with triumph.

"It was not a success in Mallorca anyway, the Year Abroad. They don't speak Spanish in Las Palmas – they speak Catalán. The students were not even learning Catalán. They were learning Danish and German from the girls on the beach."

Jerónimo gave Galt a melancholy pat on the shoulder. "I don't know why I even had the Spanish Year Abroad in Mallorca anyway.

Only that that girl was there."

After another two bars, Galt decided to stop drinking wine. However, there was evidently no limit to the volume of wine Jerónimo was consuming. And Jennifer too; her *hauteur* was dissolving into wild snorts of laughter. Jan was talking earnestly with the group of Avalon students who had joined them. The roving party eventually found its way to Jerónimo's house high up in the Albaicín.

"I had it restored," Jerónimo explained with obvious pride. "We found the ninth-century foundations and we built it up again in the Moorish style."

Galt, looking down from a second-story balcony, admired the patio that the house was built around. There were potted ferns and flowers delicately placed on the tile floor. The fountain at the center gurgled its welcome of peace and refreshment for the homecomer, hot off the dusty streets. Crimson roses, illuminated by lights placed in the flowerbeds, were climbing a white-washed wall. Over that wall, he could see the palace of the Alhambra, also illuminated, on the opposite hill. Galt blinked his eyes. The mirage did not go away. How impossibly romantic, Galt thought. Even under this January sky with a cold wind from the Atlantic shaking the stars, he could feel the dolorous melancholy and inner solitude beneath the opulence of the place. Down on the patio, Jennifer D'Arnay, dressed in see-through Arab girl trousers and a gold-laced brassiere, was talking animatedly with the students.

In the library, he found Jan sitting alone beneath one of Jerónimo's paintings.

"My mom is quite mad," she said.

Unartistic as he was, Galt, couldn't help admiring the painting. It showed a naked couple. The graceful outlines of a woman were clinging intently to a male figure; his face, turned toward the viewer, was a confusion of frantic brush strokes. Strong racy lines in black acrylic fell ironically on a white-washed canvas surface.

Jennifer and the group of laughing students came in from the garden. "Jerónimo," she announced gaily. "I am about to dance."

"Oh, Mom – you're not going to. *Please!*"

"Why not?"

"Because you are a complete tart!"

"I am merely celebrating the joy of my womanhood. I don't see how that is substantially different from hanging upside-down from a trapeze in a skin-tight body stocking with Jilaquns."

Jerónimo lay back in his ancient leather armchair with his feet propped up on a Moorish cushion, and chuckled. Every cell in his body seemed to contain a giggle.

"Jerónimo – I would like to hear you read some more of your poetry," Jan said diplomatically.

Jerónimo smiled gravely at the suggestion, then shrugged his shoulders. "Sure. Why not? We can dance later."

He took a volume from the bookshelf and put on a pair of heavy-framed reading glasses.

"You see," he explained to Galt, "this is when usually we have our classes in the Year Abroad program. At midnight, when it is civilized. I am going to read the poems of my friend Rafael Alberti. I have been educating the Señora D'Arnay in Hispanic literatura."

"Yet I regard literature in the English language as the greatest secular achievement of the human race," said Jennifer archly, re-playing a familiar argument.

"Pah! So much writing, and so little painting. Turner – if you like the sublime. I don't like much the sublime. The Pre-Raphaelites. This is not painting."

"Well, there are writers who draw and paint," Jennifer replied. "Why do we have them? Blake, Rossetti, Morris, Lear, Beerbohm – and John Ruskin, a superb draftsman. And yes – Mervyn Peake, Michael Ayrton, Wyndham Lewis, David Jones."

Jerónimo shook his head noncommittally. "I don't know. Water-colour artists – and wood-engraving, maybe. Those are your arts, no? The arts of the anxious foreheads of the English, full of care and fussiness. Nobody who can stand up and paint the face of God."

Galt had difficulty remembering what happened next. Jerónimo started reading poetry – line after galloping line of it in a mournful inward voice. Then there had been dancing to feverish flute music from Morocco. Jerónimo had danced the peasant dance done at the running-of-the-bulls festival in Pamplona. Each of the women students had taken a turn to dance with Galt, who for the first time in his life knew no selfconsciousness. Jennifer was in the middle of it all with a pair of castanets, her long blond hair released from its bun weaving lyrically with the motions of her belly.

Then Galt dashed outdoors to throw up in the fountain.

"You're perfectly right to throw up," Jan said, kneeling beside him and wiping the vomit from his mouth with a tea towel. "My mother is such an animal."

"I'm sorry," Galt sputtered, watching his vomit make slow meditative spirals in the Andalusian fountain.

"It's okay. Come inside and get warm. It's going to rain."

The students were saying elaborate goodbyes at the door in Spanish. Jerónimo had lit a fire. Jennifer was sitting cross-legged like a *yoghina* on the divan. Jerónimo returned and sat down beside her. The night settled into the friendly after-repose of civilization.

"I think Cameron has something to tell us about the University," Jennifer suggested tactfully at last. "What's the matter? Has Hugh sold it to the devil?"

"Oh, you know," Galt replied vaguely. "Cutbacks." He was on his own ground again, or what was left of it. But his mouth and his brain were not on speaking terms with each other, all his internal organs were in different time zones, and the diplomatic clichés fell apart as fast as he constructed them. "It's the same everywhere. The government is using command economics to force the universities to be accountable to corporate priorities."

"Accountants! The whole universe is being run by accountants," said Jerónimo.

"And lawyers," Jan added, thinking of Victor Bosko.

"'Lawyers were the first things to emerge from the mouth of Chaos,'" said Jennifer.

"Ah – Pico della Mirandola," Jerónimo said, recognizing the quotation. "He claimed that he would reconcile Plato and Aristotle, Paganism and Christianity. I don't think Giovanni Pico della Mirandola would exist in the university today."

"The golden-haired Renaissance phenomenon," sighed Jennifer.

At the display of erudition, Jan looked askance at Galt. They were sitting beside each other on a sofa draped with Moroccan rugs. Jennifer saw Jan's glance and brought the conversation firmly back to its topic.

"If Hugh D'Arnay had his way, he'd turn all the universities into one-stop convenience stores selling wage-work indentures."

"That has happened at other places," Galt said gravely.

"The whole world is becoming privatized," said Jerónimo.

"Yeah – well he couldn't privatize me," Jennifer declared. " 'Two things a man cannot control – Destiny and a woman's soul.' Too bad he never read the *Arabian Nights*."

"So? You are Dean. Why do you not do something?" Jerónimo's mood had suddenly become grave.

Galt wondered what to say. "Well, there's not much I can do, Jerónimo. The university is owned, technically, by the Board of Governors, and the Board hasn't much choice except to pass a fifteen percent funding cut down to the faculty. We can't raise tuition fees any higher to take the edge off the cut. That means voluntary retirements, if we're lucky."

Galt paused, gathering in detail.

"I'm afraid it may be a lot worse."

"How much worse?" Jennifer searched Galt's eyes.

"I'm afraid Hugh wants to scale Avalon down to a regional research center. Specializing in environmental work."

"Studying the distribution of frog larvae," Jan said.

"How perfectly insipid! Just like the unimaginative thug!" remarked Jennifer.

"He will be making us be in our offices at eight o'clock in the morning," Jerónimo said with a shudder. "And wearing business suits and ties. Like Rattenbury."

"Well, we're not embalmed yet!" Jennifer stated, rising in an easy gesture from the divan. "More wine? Who is on the Board these days, anyway?"

"Small-town businessmen, real-estate developers, D'Arnay worshippers. They lick his boots." Saying this, Galt realized he no longer had any loyalty to D'Arnay or the Board.

"D'Arnay! That man is a cretin!" Jerónimo agreed.

"When is it going to happen?" Jan asked.

"On the ninth. Two days from now. That's why I have to be back. I'll have to talk the faculty out of a strike, if I can."

Jerónimo laughed waving his arms like an excited crow. "Ruairi wants to strike again. Ha, ha. All he wants to do is have a strike. Ever since he stop drinking, he has wanted to strike. In fact, every time that Ruairi feels he wants to drink again, he puts the whole university on strike. The place gets *delirium tremens*. You know – he is very clever, that man Ruairi. Each strike makes us one big family again. The older faculty – how you say? – induct the young. On the picket lines the senior professors pass on to the junior professors the tradition of resistance."

"There's a bright side," Galt remembered. "Hugh's flying in a corporate donor – a big one – from Hong Kong. The donation may be big enough to save the place."

"Save the place, my ass!" Jennifer jangled her ankle bells impatiently. "Hugh doesn't want to save the place – he wants to privatize it. His ambition is to privatize all known reality out to the farthest reaches of space-time. I know that – I lived with the jerk."

"Who is this generous capitalist?"

"Mr. Wu. I'm not supposed to tell you this – but what the heck! He makes environmentally conscious toys. And D'Arnay says he's got another corporation to partner with Wu. And some government research infrastructure funds to glue the deal together."

"Very interesting." Jennifer walked across the room, ankle bells jingling. She went into the kitchen and came back with a bottle of brandy and sat down again beside Jerónimo. "So why would Mr. Wu want to put his money in an obscure university in nowheresville? What's in it for him? And who's the corporate partner – I'd like to know."

Jan looked at Cameron. Cameron looked at Jerónimo who was frowning. Cameron Galt felt cold steel slide into his gut.

"Mr. Wu is *buying* the Environmental Sciences operation, isn't he?" Jennifer said. "He's going to run it as a for-profit private university. Or he's fronting for someone else who will. Probably an Academic Management Organization or a software consortium. The rest of the university can go to hell as far as Hugh is concerned, so long as he can privatize the one part of Avalon that is profitable."

Again, Galt felt devastated. He gulped. Why hadn't he twigged to this? Nowhere over the Atlantic, countering D'Arnay's downsizing plan, had he thought of this possibility. While he was reacting to the surface betrayal, the larger, deeper one was taking shape around him invisibly. Of course it was a possibility! It had the imprint of Andromeda Networks on it.

"Why didn't you tell us that before? We are your friends, Cam."

"I didn't tell you, Jerónimo, because … because the idea never occurred to me until just now. I never thought Hugh would go to such lengths … "

"Hugh will go to any lengths, the fuckhead! Forgive me, dear daughter, for referring to your sperm donor in these terms. He has given you a beautiful mouth and, if you chose ever to use makeup, bewitching eyes. And basically he is a very fine man. Once, he was a gentleman. But now, sadly, his higher reasoning processes are contaminated by the virus of capitalism in its cancer stage. He is full of the hatred of our times."

Jennifer jumped up from the divan and strode to the hall, her ankle bells jangling furiously. She came back with her purse, and held an address book up ominously.

"It's all my fault. He is trying to settle an old score. I wounded him, you see, and now he is trying to make me pay."

"What on earth are you doing, Mom?"

"What am I doing? What are *we* doing? – you should say. You, daughter, are going to go back immediately and bring the students out on the picket lines beside their esteemed teachers."

Jennifer turned to address Galt.

"And you are going to mediate between the Board and a University that is out on strike. We'll tie the place up for a month. No entrepreneur will invest in the sort of instability and havoc we're going to set loose. Perhaps we can scare him off. As for me – I am about to call my ex."

"Mother – don't!"

"I'm not sure that will be very helpful," Galt added.

"I want to speak to the idjiot too!"

"Where is his private emergency-use number? Oh yes – here it is." Jennifer punched the buttons on the console. She grinned wickedly at Jerónimo. "This was the number we used for side-table deals when we were litigating."

Jennifer held her brandy in the air and tapped her foot impatiently, making the ankle bells ring like a galloping camel train.

"Hugh? … Hugh. Yes, it's me alright … Why am I calling? I'm calling to point out to you what a miserable thatch of shit you are. Shit in a silk stocking, as Bonaparte said to Talleyrand – however, you lack Talleyrand's cultural graces, not to mention his flair for trimming his sheets to the next wind. You're stuck in late twentieth-century kneejerk piddle-down economics … Where am I? It's none of your goddamned business where I am … Yes, as a matter of fact I have been enjoying a little brandy – but that's beside the point. The point is, reality is passing you by, Hugh. The French, having *le sens civique* which you so sadly lack, are investing more than ten billion dollars a year in culture and the arts, and you're trying to sell some popstand of a university … How do I know about it? I can see through your dime-store Machiavellianism halfway across the planet. Now *listen!* If you sell Avalon to some offshore carpetbagger, you will go down in obscure regional history as

224

the first of the twentieth-first century Visigoths … No, don't c'mon me – you will be forever branded in that part of the media you cannot control as a barbarian. Furthermore, I will personally see to it that the Rideouts resign from your Board and henceforth have nothing more to do with you … *Yes I will*. I'll phone Lynda and who knows who else. I will tell them what a corporate scrotum you are … Well, what if Wu changes his mind and the deal falls through – then where'll you be? Nobody will buy the damn place. You'll just have to swallow a deficit. That'll hurt, I'm sure. The great Hugh D'Arnay, controller of God knows how many ventures, stuck with a money-losing lemonade stand he can't sell … What's that? No – this is not some personal vendetta. You can tell that obese Hungarian creamcheese beside you that this is straight business … She can have what's left of your fucking body – I'm doing business with your soul. How is it going to feel in your dotage – having sold your daughter's university right out from under her, and she having to explain this to her classmates – how's it going to feel to look back and realize that you have achieved nothing but utter destruction? All the money in the world and a black bituminous gorge of inner emptiness that your Hungarian *crémache* is unable to fill … No, I will never fail to remind you of it, you uptight stick! … Well, yes, as a matter of fact I am achieving quite a bit. Using your money, I have discovered the meaning of life. I'll shoot it to you in a fax sometime. Meanwhile, if you try to sell any part of … Fine! *Goodbye!*"

Jennifer D'Arnay slammed down the receiver.

"There! It won't do any good, but at least I feel better. He won't be able to have an orgasm for three weeks."

"I don't think we can save a university this way," Galt giggled. "Besides, he'll have my head."

"Don't worry, dear. You can threaten him with a half million dollar severance settlement. I'll give you my lawyer's number.

"And now," Jennifer announced, "I feel like dancing. Unrepressed eros is the energy of history."

Galt remembered little after that. The thrilling mesmerizing flute music began again. Jenny danced like a dervish – an unlikely dervish holding a bottle of brandy and drinking from it each time the rhythm of the music changed. Jerónimo watched from the divan, feeling perfect. Finally, Galt toppled over, like a statue, senseless onto the sofa.

22

A finger was tracing arabesques on his tummy.

"Your obstetrician was left-handed."

Jan continued to draw whimsical spirals around Galt's belly button. "I have a private theory about belly buttons. Innies are created by right-handed doctors. Outies are the result of left-handed doctors. Yours is an outie."

Galt felt the accumulated hospitality of at least fourteen bars like lead shot in his brain. All the cells in his body were tiny dragons breathing *rioja*. Red acidic dragonbreath. He wondered how Jan could stand him. He tried to lift his head from the sofa. It fell back with a thud. Galt groaned.

"C'mon, get up! We're going to see Lorca's grave, then we're catching the next plane home."

Galt wondered at her easy familiarity. Then he wondered at the way she said "home." He extended a tentative leg out from underneath a Moroccan blanket. Jan was now slipping last night's jeans on, arching her back over the sofa to slide them over the length of her thighs. Galt, blinking at the still naked top half of her body, was suddenly hit by another after-effect. It was a collision of guilt, dismay, and a wonderful wicked pleasure. A rooster broke the morning into fragments. Out on the patio the Moorish fountain bubbled its eternal idiotic noise.

★　★　★

"It's very hard for Jerónimo to do this," Jennifer said, twisting around to face Galt in the back seat.

"Yes – it is very sad," Jerónimo said. "These hills are full of blood."

The car climbed into the mountains, following sharp curves in the road around stone-walled terraces holding tiny fields of wheat and olive trees. They passed the village of Víznar.

"I don't want to go in there."

"It was a Falangist village," Jennifer explained. "They took the prisoners in trucks up here. A priest gave them confession. Then they were shot. They lie in the *barrancos* – the ravines around here."

"How many died?"

Jerónimo shrugged his shoulders. "Who knows? In Granada, they kept official lists. Eight thousand names. Many more were brought up here."

He glanced back at Galt and smiled painfully.

"And now the history books in the high schools, they hardly mention the Civil War, eh? Just a paragraph – no more. We are so happy to belong in the new Europe. To put the past behind us and forget. Me, I cannot forget. It is hard to be an old man in Spain today."

They were high up on a road that snaked through the mountains. Bare slopes of grey clay with a few dried bushes. To the left, the mountain plunged down to a river and its little villages. To the right, it rose like a forbidding wall, twisted and sharp. A few stunted pines. In the back seat beside Galt, Jan was deep in thought.

"That house there. It is where they took him the night before. With the others. He had done nothing wrong. Except to be an artist."

Then some yards further, at a hairpin turn in the road where a stream bed channelled down the eroded shale cliff, there was a bridge. They got out of the car there, and walked up a gentle slope into some trees. There were rushes and thin grasses and moss, a few blue flowers. The ground was dreadfully uneven. Lorca had had to dig his own shallow grave in this place. They stood over it – a patch of earth on which someone had arranged small rocks in the shape of a cross. One of the rocks was splattered with wax where a candle had been lit.

"Here is the grave of a poet." Jerónimo's voice was full of sorrow.

They looked down at the grave for a long time. Then Jerónimo turned away – Jennifer gave him a big hug from behind. The valley far below with its villages, and in the distance a mountain. Morning breaking over these mountains where Lorca had been a child. The cry of a rooster coming up from the valley. Then, for Lorca, nothing.

Jerónimo, following a personal custom, was picking up some litter that people had left behind in this sanctuary – empty Coke cans and some fast-food wrappers. Galt and Jan and Jennifer saw what he was doing and did the same. Soon the grave of Federico García Lorca was clean again – clean and holy, because it was remembered.

Jerónimo began the procession back to the car. Silently, they drove back to Granada.

At the bus station, Jerónimo embraced Galt.

"Well, my friend – now you have seen Granada," he said with his usual plain-stated sense of occasion, handing Galt his cabin bag and attaché case. "Come back here whenever you can – you are always welcome. *Mi casa es tu casa.* And I wish you good luck at Avalon. Try to save it – it gave me so many happy times."

"Thank you, Jerónimo. You have been very kind."

"We'll be back before the winter is over," Jennifer said. She gave Galt a big Latin hug and kisses on both cheeks. "If you see D'Arnay, don't forget to tell him he's going to have to deal with me. I will be his scourge until the day he dies."

Then mother and daughter exchanged hugs. "I'm sorry your pre-birthday celebration got a little mawkish. Send me the videotape of you and Jill on the trapeze. And don't do any back fly-aways."

"I won't, Mom," Jan replied in her dutiful daughter voice.

"Have a good flight, kids!"

★   ★   ★

Later, on the plane, Cameron Galt fought off waves of sleep with coffee and tried to think about where he was in political and moral space. Returning over the Atlantic was a reversal of his earlier mood. He did not feel avenged – he was not a recriminating person. Nor did he feel especially determined about anything. There, with Jan's blond head dozing on his shoulder, and gliding over the clouds of the Atlantic, he felt just a little ennobled. This was not a feeling he should make much of. It would exist forever as a memory, held in secret, having the strength of a narrative withheld. And he was good at withholding, at cultivating a reserve.

Approaching the Canadian coast, he arranged to send D'Arnay a fax apologizing for having to miss the strategy meeting and asking him to hold off any announcement of downsizing. "Let's wait a week and see how the big universities react first. We can then set our tuition fees accordingly," he suggested deviously. That would keep the lid on until he was on the ground and could do something. Galt considered what that something might be.

"Your mind is noisy – please turn it off," Jan murmured.

"I'm sorry – I can't help worrying. That's what I'm paid to do – worry. This Avalon thing is too big for me."

Jan lifted her head, shook out her hair, and looked out the window.

"You're not you paid to worry about Sally," she said, speaking to the clouds.

Oh god, she knew. So they all knew. Then last night – was it just … ?

"And as for the Avalon problem, if it's too big for you then it's not your problem, is it? It's all of our problem. Look, we'll give it a really good fight, and when it's all over we'll say we did our best."

How like her mother she sounded!

Jan snuggled into his shoulder again. "Anyway, the universe is unfolding perfectly. And the sun is in Capricorn – the sign of the sea-goat. And in two days it's my birthday! So things are starting to happen. Jerónimo already called Professor MacDonald. Last night,

229

after you passed out in my lap."

"Oh no – he didn't! Shit!"

Galt collapsed back into his seat, powerless in the hands of so much fortune.

23

Cameron Galt, Provost and Dean, strode into Sheena's office with authority springing like flames from his shoulders.

"Give me the crises in order of magnitude."

Sheena stroked her long red hair. "Well, the Sun is in Capricorn and there's a strange energy coming, I think, from Mars … "

"Maybe you could tell me what appointments you've made."

Sheena licked her lips and straightened her back. "Professor MacDonald. I said you'd contact him as soon as you got in."

"Good."

"Mr. D'Arnay wants you to call him at his office."

"Okay."

"The Registrar wants you to phone him. He says enrolments are crashing across the system because of the tuition fee hike."

"Of course they are!"

"Incidentally, some hacker has put a virus in our new Touchtone Phone Registration System. We've had to reprint the old forms."

"What else?"

"The First Nations Center has circulated a manifesto declaring the First Nations students and faculty a distinct and separate college within the University."

"Oh yeah? What's its name?"

"I can't pronounce it – it's very long and it's in Ojibway."

"Anything else?"

"You've got a Mr. Wu and party touring the Ecology Center. The President and the Registrar attending. That's at eleven."

Cameron Galt let out an insane giddy laugh. His Executive Assistant glanced at him apprehensively.

"Then lunch at Rugantino's, right?"

"Right. Mr. D'Arnay has e-mailed his regrets."

"By the way, what's going on at the Food Court today?"

Sheena consulted her computer. "The Great January Bargain Days Spell-off Tournament; usual classes in Philosophy, Politics, Economics; 'Lectures by the Fountain Series' resumes with a talk on 'International Trade and Your Shopping Dollar'; a performance piece by two students in Cultural Studies."

"What time's that – the performance piece, I mean?"

"Eleven thirty."

"Oh, oh! That's when Wu is in the Mall."

Galt looked out his window at a picture postcard view of the university, framed by icicles that hung like chimes from the college roof. Snow-blowers were flinging snow from the footbridges. The river had iced over. Behind the Ecology Center, the lights of the Mall flashed red. Galt wondered if he should ask the question:

"Anything from Sally?"

Sheena's eyes skittered to the floor. Yes, everybody knew.

"No. No messages from Professor Galt."

Was there a trace of pity in Sheena's voice?

"Thanks, Sheena."

"I'm glad you're back, Cam."

★　★　★

The members of the Avalon Faculty Union Executive stared at the empty office chair where Ruairi MacDonald was supposed to be.

"He's never been late for a meeting in his life," said Faith Rackstraw.

"He must have been here this morning because he left his office door open," Jerry Lewin said. "Maybe we should start anyway – we're in a serious mess."

"Who's chairing the meeting?" Faith asked. It was impossible for the members to conceive of anyone but Ruairi MacDonald chairing a meeting of the Faculty Union Executive.

"I'll chair it," said Robyn Endicott.

"The minutes will record that Ms. Endicott chaired the first emergency meeting of the year," Lewin intoned.

"Our problem, as I see it," Endicott began coolly, "is that the government has announced a funding cutback of ten percent for the post-secondary educational system. Concurrently, they have de-clared that tuition fees can rise, but they can't rise to a level to cover the funding loss. In this context, we have heard a rumour ... " Endicott emphasized the word judiciously.

"What do you mean 'a rumour'?" Lewin broke in. "Ruairi said last night that Jerónimo called him from Spain saying the place was going to be sold ... "

"It is only, at this stage, a rumour," Robyn repeated firmly. "We have to treat it as such."

"Robyn's absolutely right," Faith said. "The air is full of ru-mours. Why, coming out here I heard students on the shuttlebus saying that Emma Goldman College was going to be closed. What utter nonsense! Nobody has consulted *me* about it! And I can tell you – over my dead body it will be closed. The atmosphere is sim-ply rife with rumours of all kinds. We must disregard them. We must face the crisis at hand with a clear mind and a high heart. That is the Avalon way."

"Agreed, then? I'll issue a circular immediately. Faculty should disregard unsubstantiated rumours and should not pass any on. Whose authority should I send it out under?"

At that moment, there was an explosion of noise in the quad. *Po-ta-toe, po-ta-toe.* It was the patented sound of an antique Harley-Davidson with dual exhausts. The noise reverberated off the stone-work of Cabot College, sending two pigeons flying into the sky in terror. Then the noise came right into the office corridor.

Faith Rackstraw put her hands over her ears. "Heavens above! –

is he going to drive that thing right into the office?"

"He's running his Harley in January! – he's got to be crazy!" Lewin said.

The motorcycle engine sputtered to a stop, backfiring in the cold air. There was an ominous pause. Then an earth-shaking crash as Ruairi MacDonald lurched through his office door. The door banged against the coat-rack, knocking over a dress kilt and academic robes which hung there. MacDonald glared around the room with a bloodshot eye. Then, directed by decades of habit, he found his chair at the head of the table and collapsed into it.

"*Gille ghille is measa na'an diobhal!*"

"What's that, Mac?"

"The servant of the servant is worse than the devil."

MacDonald put his motorcycle helmet on the table and leaned on it with his great arms. Then, in a voice that seemed to come from another age, he said, "The grey shepherds hae' ta'en us over. *Crughain*. D'eil a one o' us shall remain."

"Good heavens, man! Pull yourself together! It's not the end of the world," said Faith Rackstraw.

"Och, but it is!" MacDonald lifted his huge head up. "Ye dinna understaun? They're cutting us jist right to force us off tenure and Academic Freedom. Everythin' we stood for. More than that and they'd hae' th' whole univairsity system on strike. They've hit us just enough – the cunning bastards! It's no richt! And they'll do the same again next year until they have us. Then Hugh D'Arnay, the *traitor!*" – MacDonald yelled the word so that it rang off his office walls – "has ta'en advantage of th' opportunity in order to sell us oot. I cuid hae' ta'en on wan or t'ither of the scoundrels – the government or that quisling – but not the both of 'em."

MacDonald slumped over his motorcycle helmet and wailed a moist Gaelic lament.

"O my children – hae' I not focht for our ain hame wi' every fiber of my soul since whan I was a loon? Hae' I not ge'in it my utmost? Every ruim in th' univairisity is like a friend to me. The laughter that happened in them, the great occasions, the exchanges of ideas. I kinna gae inta a ruim without but the memories of the years comin' tae mind. What a bonny place this was! Now tis wabbit, dumfounert, forjeskit. I'm awfy sorry."

"Professor MacDonald is drunk," Faith Rackstraw declared.

"That means there'll be no strike," Lewin whispered.

"What should we do?" Robyn asked.

"Cain't ye see? It's all by wi now. There's nothin' left to do. We have no Union namore. The clan is broken."

★　★　★

"Yes, slowly now − 2, 3, 4, 5, 6. Now our tummies touch. Good. Then slow wide circles with the arms − 7, 8, 9, 10. Now our hands touch lovingly. Now, grip."

Jilaquns' arm came slowly down to meet Jan's arm. Jilaquns' knee hooked the bar of the single wide trapeze, her other foot catching the rope higher up. On the other side of the trapeze, Jan's legs did the same.

"I think we've got it!" Jan said, hanging upside down and facing the upside-down Jill.

Outside the cottage window, the ice of Stoney Lake was now the sky. The sky, with low cloud cover, was now the lake.

"Doesn't it get you behind the knees?"

"Capricorns have good knees."

"Oh yes − I forgot. Happy Birthday, Jan."

Jill's head moved closer to Jan's and gave her a kiss.

"Thanks. Okay, let's practice the you-on-top-of-me routine once more. Then we can go over and set up at the Mall."

The phone rang. Jan skilfully extracted her legs from the ropes, fell head-first into a somersault landing, bounded to her feet and started for the phone. The voice-recorder clicked in.

"It's Victor Bosko calling ... um ... with birthday wishes for the most attractive woman at Avalon. That's you, January. Happy birthday, and ...

ah, yeah … give me a call sometime. Bye."

Click.

"How in the fuck did he know it was your birthday?" Jilaquns asked, still hanging upside-down from the trapeze.

"The dork probably has everybody's birthdates on his computer," Jan sighed.

"He's such a stain," Jilaquns agreed. She fell to the mat like a feather and did a handspring. "So it's your birthday. I've got a great present for you tonight."

"January the ninth is also the last date for dropping courses without a penalty," Jan reminded her.

"Shit! I forgot. I'd better drop them now before they ding me with a row of Fs."

Jilaquns went over to the telephone and consulted the Avalon Touchtone Registration Guide. She stared at it for a minute, nodded, then lifted the handset and punched the Avalon University number into the console.

"Welcome to Avalon University. Press 'One' for the Office of the Registrar, press 'Two' for … "

Jilaquns pressed 'one.'

"Welcome to the Avalon University Telephone Registration System. Please enter your 7–digit student identification number."

Jilaquns entered 2002505.

"You have entered … 2 … 0 … 0 … 2 …5 … 0 … 5. Press 'One' if this is correct. Or press 'Two' if this is incorrect."

Jilaquns pressed 'one.'

"Please enter your 6-digit birthdate by entering two digits each for the year, the month, and the day."

"How can I tell the machine I was born in the Moon of the Little Spirits?" Jilaquns said, punching in her birthdate in the form YYMMDD.

"As you have not recently used the Avalon University Touchtone Registration System, we require that you provide your own Personal Identification Number. This number must be six digits and will be used every

time you use the TRS in the future. Your PIN is considered private information, so do not give it or show it to anyone. Please enter your Personal Identification Number now."

"Jan – what's your favourite number?"

"Oh, I don't know. Give it the number of the Beast of the Apocalypse."

"What's that?"

"Six, six, six. Then repeat it."

"I think the fucking system can go fuck itself!"

"As you have not recently used the Avalon University Touchtone Registration System ... " repeated the voice. Only then did it occur to Jilaquns to identify the disembodied voice as female.

"You don't have to wait out the whole prompt," Jan advised. "Anyway, you can take it easy. The system is designed to monitor your response time. Dad has one at Andromeda Networks."

Jilaquns pressed the numbers.

"Please re-enter your Personal Identification Number to verify it."

Jilaquns repeated the number.

"You have entered six six six six six six. Press 'One' if this is ... "

"Well, you could at least say 'THANK YOU!'" Jill yelled into the phone.

" ... correct. Or press 'Two' if this is ... "

"Courtesy. Will not compute," Jan said sarcastically.

" ... incorrect."

Jilaquns of the Sealion Clan of the Eagles of Qaysun pressed 'one.'

There was a pause. Another voice came out of the machine. It was the voice of Bud Lassiter. *"Please press 'One' to register in a course ... "*

"The egomaniac has put himself on the audio – I don't believe it!" said Jilaquns.

" ... Press 'Two' to withdraw from a course. Press 'Three' to list your registration. Press 'Four' to pay for courses that you have requested. Press 'Five' to terminate the call and exit the system."

"I'm exiting your whole fucking system!" Jilaquns said. However, the number she pressed was 'two' – withdrawal from a course.

"I am sorry. You currently owe Avalon University money … "

"No way!"

" … Your registration requests will be cancelled if you do not make a complete payment during this telephone session. Please press 'One' if you wish to exit the system and cancel your registration requests. Or press 'Zero' if you would like to continue the session."

"I would like to continue the torture, cyborgbrain!"

Jilaquns pressed 'zero.'

"The total amount you owe Avalon University is … eight … dollars … and seventy … three … cents. Press 'One' if you are paying with VISA. Press 'Two' if you are making a payment using an Avalon University account reference number … "

Jilaquns pressed 'two.'

"Please enter your 13-digit Avalon University account reference number."

Jilaquns scrambled for her medicine bag. It was hanging from the back of a chair in the hallway.

"Please enter your 13-digit Avalon University account reference number."

"Wait, you son of a bitch!" Jill pleaded, pulling the contents out of her bag, trying to find the account number.

"Please enter your 13-digit Avalon University account reference number, or your session will be terminated."

Jilaquns punched the numbers madly into the console.

"Your Avalon University account reference number was accepted. Please allow two business days for your registration requests to become official. Now, enter the 4-digit course catalogue number of the first course from which you would like to withdraw."

Jilaquns punched in the catalogue number of the first course.

"This is totally crazy and inhuman!"

Suddenly, a new voice came on the phone. Instead of the robotic tones of Bud Lassiter trying his best to be neutral and distinct, this voice was alive with energy, alive with theatricality, alive with a glorious mad cheerfulness. It sounded like the voice of a king arousing the troops to action in the battle scene of a history play by Shakespeare.

"Congratulations! You have just been dehumanized by the Avalon University administration. Avalon is a university under occupation. The face of that occupation is the technology that has just demeaned you. The base camp of that occupation is the office of the Chairman of the Board of Governors. In a moment I will give you his private phone number at Andromeda Networks so that you can record your complaint. Do you have a pencil and paper handy? Don't forget the combined universities demonstration at the Legislature in Metro to protest the funding cuts. Students! Intellectual workers! Unite with your professors to save the university!"

Jan, amazed, listened in to the receiver with Jilaquns.

"It's Jerry Lewin. He's trying to disguise his voice."

24

It seemed like Saturday morning at the Mall — the place was so busy. In fact, it was only a weekday, but what made the Mall and especially the Food Court so crowded were students taking classes at the True University of Avalon, as it had come to be called. The True U. was in full session. By the statue of the Lady of the Lake was a sign giving the day's events: the "Lectures by the Fountain" series; the Spelling Tournament; new seminars in Philosophy, Politics, Economics. All around the Food Court the emeritus professors, dressed in brilliant academic regalia, were holding seminars for groups of teenagers, new mothers, and senior citizens — as well as regular Avalon students. Over by the McDonald's outlet, Waasagunackank was telling stories as part of the retired faculty's baby-sitting service. The Great January Bargain Days Spell-off Tournament had just gotten underway, supervised by Professor Nglesi Mwangulu wearing a faded maroon University of London academic gown over his white tennis sweater and grey flannel trousers. "Remember the rules, please" he said to five teams of excited students bunched and ready to go. "No spell-checks. You have an hour to find up to a hundred and fifty spelling errors we've put in the signs of co-operating merchants in the Mall. One point for every identification of a spelling mistake. One more point if you get the correct spelling right. Are you ready, teams?"

The professor held a stopwatch in his hand and put a whistle to his lips. The members of the spelling teams wore T-shirts proclaiming their affiliations: "The Dyslexic Collective," "The Aboriginal Aphasiacs," "The Queens of Illiteracy," "Orthomorphs," and "Spellers from Hell."

The professor blew his whistle. "Now, go!"

The teams dashed off to find spelling mistakes in the Mall.

"Just as well I'm retired," declared Jake Weisberg over his hamburger and fries. "I couldn't live a life of the mind with chicks like that in my class." He gestured towards Jan and Jilaquns, who had set up their trapeze in the Food Court and were now taking off their sweatsuits to reveal skin-tight body stockings. Jill's was white, and her long raven hair hung down over it in perfect strands. Jan's was black, and her blond hair, shorter than Jill's, flashed gold.

"I never could anyway," confessed Tony Leland. He tapped a boney finger against his wispy skull. "I got girls in the attic."

Nglesi Mwangulu, joining them, smiled shyly and said nothing.

"C'mon, Nig – show some postcolonial energy!" said Jake, hitting Nglesi on the shoulder.

Nglesi grinned broadly.

Jake Weisberg put his long-distance spectacles on. "I'm as blind as a bat, but even from here I can see the folds of babyfat … "

"Now cut that out!" Leland implored.

" … and maidenhair delicate as fern fronds," continued Jake mischievously. "And yes, for the benefit of those among us who are erotically challenged, I can just make out a small damp zone under the armpit elastic, as slippery and salty as a tidal pool."

"Leave us retire in our dignity," Professor Leland persisted.

"Dignity? You call giving lectures on the Political Economy of Shopping dignity? And for this?" Jake indicated his Columbia

University mortarboard, upside-down on the floor, half full of money. Above it on the cafeteria table was a sign: "Donations to the Avalon University Retired Professors Dental Plan would be appreciated."

"It has always been a perquisite of our profession to enjoy the carnal spectacle of youth. So why not now?"

"I don't understand why they wear those black boots," Leland wondered, looking down at his carpet slippers.

"Well, I'll tell you, Tony. Those are called Doc Martens. They're for in case you get too close. Imagine with me, please. The girls are in your seminar, dressed just like that while you're going on about a difficult passage in Kant's *Critique of Pure Reason*. And then your eyes begin to fixate on the female nipple. Not on the nipple, rather, but on the hair-pores that surround their … what in hell are those things called?"

"Oreos," suggested Professor Mwangulu.

"No, you idiot! That's a kind of cookie."

"They do look remarkably similar though," Leland admitted.

"Wait! − I've got it! Aureoles. Yes, that's it − aureoles. And then, just when you get riveted on each pore in the aureole, one of those Doc Martens comes up and hits you swiftly right in the begonias."

Leland flinched in his wheelchair. "No, I couldn't teach them − that's for certain."

"Me neither," agreed Mwangulu. "Look at their bums."

The women had tested the trapeze for the last time. It hung on long ropes from a fixture way up beside the skylight, normally used for suspending Christmas decorations. Just a few feet beneath the trapeze was a gym mat. Ashley Tiffin, handling the sound system, nodded to say she was ready.

Jerry Lewin strolled into the Food Court, saw the retired professors, and joined them. "No doubt, you are here to witness that overflowing of Eros into Divine Philosophy that Plato speaks of."

"Hi, Jerry. These your students?"

"The one in the black is. The other one is her friend. They're doing a performance piece for Cult–Studs."

"I regret I ever went into Philosophy." Leland remarked sadly.

Jan came forward and made a mock curtsy in the direction of the professors, then spoke to the crowd.

"May I have your attention, please? I'm Jan D'Arnay; this is Jilaquns of Qaysun. We're going to be doing a short performance piece for you. It's called 'The Place of the Body in Modern Patriarchal Cultural Theory'."

Jan took her position at one side of the trapeze, Jilaquns at the other. At an invisible signal, both women swung themselves onto the bar. Each clutching a rope with one hand, and each with one foot on the bar, they hung outwards, their free arms and legs extending like wings.

The speakers coughed into life. *"The field of Cultural Studies has revived the Frankfurt School's spectre of a capitalism that has finally mastered its own historicity and thereby liquidated any endogenous capacity it may have once had for redemptive self-transformation ... "*

Slowly, the two women circled their arms inwards, their bodies curling up together like the petals of a flower at night.

"And the last avatars of this stormy entelechy, emerging from France, identify the culprit in the story of Enlightenment's ineluctable progress towards total unfreedom as commodity semiosis and the universalized commutability of values in the reinforced world of 'la société de consummation.' "

Now the women were beginning the first of a series of slow intertwinings, black against white, white against black, until they looked like a hermaphroditic union.

"Good heavens!" exclaimed Professor Leland.

"It sure beats Dynamic Models with Heteroscedastic Errors, doesn't it, Nglesi?" said Jake Weisberg.

A second voice now came through the speakers, as portentous and arid as the first, while the two gymnasts languidly ran their hands down each other's backs to the thighs.

"The more the structural law of value desiccates social space, the more its unsatisfied reciprocity is invested with repressed libidinal energy, coming to

haunt the receptive dumb-show of social life."

"To think that I spent forty years marking Politics essays when I could have been doing this!" Weisberg declared.

Now Jan and Jill were in the upside-down position they had rehearsed earlier, each hooking a back of the knee around the trapeze bar, with the other foot hooked around the ropes. Their bellies, then their breasts, touched; arms extending slowly down to the floor, each grasped the other's hand.

"The freedom of women to circulate on the same economic and social terms as men has been resisted, not just because it challenges the entrenched system of power and privilege, but also because the patriarchal ideology that justifies that resistance has continued, through the vicissitudes of cultural liberalization, to play a crucial role in the valorization of an asymmetrical gender code in the maintenance of the hierarchical family–slash–class system which the code of capitalist order underwrites ... "

The women assumed an even more erotic form. Now it was impossible to tell where arms and legs began and ended. Cheek molding perfectly into cheek, their hair fell in a blended waterfall of black and blond. Professor Weisberg readjusted a suspender strap and scratched his crotch. Professor Leland stared, immobile like a welded cafeteria fixture. Professor Mwangulu, immaculate in his white tennis sweater under his University of London gown, stirred uneasily in his cafeteria chair. Jerry Lewin was taking notes on a McDonald's serviette.

The first of the Great January Bargain Days Spell-off teams was finding its way back along the Mall thoroughfare. They were standing in their black miniskirts and Doc Martens and yellow Queens of Illiteracy T-shirts to watch. Coming down the escalator from the top level were the Aboriginal Aphasiacs wearing headbands and red T-shirts with the Thunderbird symbol. At the cafeteria tables the emeritus professors lent brilliant colour to the Mall with their rainbow of academic robes.

At this point, Acting President Rattenbury came through the Food Court arch, escorting a perfectly dressed, blue-suited, white-haired Chinese gentleman; a young woman, also Chinese; and another man carrying a briefcase with gold hinges and locks. Following them was Dean Galt looking grumpy and singular. Then the burly Registrar dressed in a too-tight sports jacket and over-large grey flannel trousers.

"You should have warned me of this," hissed Lassiter to Galt.

Mr. Wu saw the large sign that was placed on the Mall information desk and motioned a hand towards it, asking for the translation. "Welcome to the True University of Avalon," said the sign. The interpreter, dressed in a trim navy-blue suit and pearls, translated the statement for Wu, who nodded, frowning. Then he stopped to gaze at the trapeze where Jan, swinging on her belly on the bar, arms and legs extended, was surmounted by Jill crouching on her back.

"Indeed, because of the complexity of the process wherein cultural politics arises, the rectilinear relation its issues bear to matters of class hegemonic control, and the potentially self-undermining character of any transparently instrumental intervention into hot zones of consciousness, we must say that the Revolution (if the term retains any meaning) has perhaps permanently missed the historical boat."

Jake Weisberg, sometime marxist in the New Republic mode, fell into a profound depression at the thought of the lost revolution. In the silence, he could hear the dripping of water off the sword in the Food Court fountain.

"Oh, oh! That looks like the buyer from Hong Kong," Lewin warned.

"What's he buying?" Weisberg asked.

"Us!"

Jan, sitting astride the trapeze bar, and noticing Cameron Galt in the party, raised an elegant arm and blew him a kiss. Jilaquns, thinking this was part of the performance, copied the gesture, blowing her kiss into the face of Mr. Wu.

Lassiter was trying to hurry the party into Rugantino's. Now the Orthomorphs were arriving in their exaggerated mohawk hair styles and motorcycle chains.

"Against the positive deployment of transcapitalist discourse and symbology, and with the cultural dialectic of commodification having, as we saw, no truly inner principle of sublation ... "

The women on the trapeze had begun a symmetrical dance in the air that looked for all the world like an autoerotic striptease.

" ... one must, on the plane of normative consciousness and in a spirit of pre-revolutionary attentisme *wait with the transcendental cultural resources lying at hand ... "*

Mr. Wu, flanked by one of the Queens of Illiteracy, watched as if in a spirit of pre-revolutionary *attentisme* as the performance came to an end and the two women somersaulted simultaneously off the trapeze.

" ... then, when some fresh round of superstructural troubles breaks out, the more likely it is that something truly human will ... "

At this point, the audiotape seemed to be broken.

" ... strive ... to ... emerge, striiive ... too ... eemerrge, striiive ... tooo ... emeerrge," it said, with a voice slowed down mechanically and deepened to the point of utter senility.

Jan and Jill made deep bows to applause that resounded all around the Food Court and from the upper level of the Mall. Young mothers with their infants in strollers applauded. So did members of the Dyslexic Collective, carrying their skateboards under their arms and wearing enlarged sun glasses and baseball caps turned backwards. Jake Weisberg, who had just seen four perfect female breasts in a row, also applauded. "For God's sake, Jerry, give them an A plus!"

Jerry Lewin grinned one of his sly sideways grins.

Mr. Wu was puzzling over an elaborate explanatory translation offered by his pert translator. Finally, she threw up her hands and shrugged. Wu shrugged his shoulders as well. Lassiter was trying to push the visitor in the direction of Rugantino's. Mr. Wu, however, seemed to want to be introduced to the distinguished Faculty of Avalon, who had apparently showed up in their full academic regalia especially to greet him.

"Alright, bets please, gentlemen," said Weisberg. "I'll spot ten Big Macs on the Queens of Illiteracy."

"That's just because you want to sniff up their miniskirts, you lecherous dog," Leland replied. "I'll bet you five Remedial Mathematics classes on the Orthomorphs."

"All of next week's lectures on Postcolonial Trade and Bargain Shopping on the Spellers from Hell," offered Mwangulu, raising the ante.

Everywhere, people were lining up at the fast-food outlets for lunch. Lassiter whispered a message to the beautiful interpreter. "Tell him that if he were to put the factory in the field we just saw, right next to the Ecology Center, the Food Court could serve his workforce."

Wu waved off the translation. "Your University ... very alive," he said to President Rattenbury.

Safely inside Rugantino's, Galt took his seat at the table marked "Reserved," and scanned the restaurant for further signs of danger. Rugantino's was crowded to capacity. The waiters and waitresses, Avalon students making money on the side, were skipping as they took orders.

"Mineral water: Badoit, Perrier, San Pellegrino ... "

The place was bedlam. Standing in a group waiting for a table, The Spellers from Hell team, carrying pompoms and dressed like cheerleaders at a football game, gave their team yell.

What the hell
If we can't spell?
We're the sexy
Belles from hell!
That's Belles:
B.e.l.l.e.s.
(Disease-free,
No apostrophe).

Wu had ordered a dish of plain noodles, on top of which he was delicately arranging selected vegetables from his salad. Giles Rattenbury, dressed as if for an affair of state, ordered veal massalla. Wu's interpreter picked sparingly at a dish of rice and chicken salad. Bud Lassiter had ordered an immense seafood linguini which he was attacking with gusto. The accountant from Hong Kong, in a moment of panic disguised as diplomacy, had duplicated Lassiter's order, and was now staring in dismay at a huge dish plunked down by a waiter still wearing his Dyslexic Collective T-shirt with its quotation from Nietzsche: "So long as there is syntax, I am still persuaded there is a God."

"I've spoken to the mayor of Severnville," Lassiter was saying, "and also the guy who owns the Mall ... " The Registrar waited for the translator to translate the phrases for Mr. Wu " ... and they agree it will be easy to run services out here for your new buildings."

Wu had a forkful of noodles at his mouth when Galt saw a sight that filled him with dread. It was Ruairi MacDonald, back turned to the diners, drinking alone in a dark corner by the washrooms. Ruairi looked around and met Galt's eyes simultaneously. MacDonald rose from his table, upsetting a glass of whiskey. His eyes rolled with a will of their own in his great head, while white hair fell down to his shoulders over his Harley Davidson T-shirt.

"*Cameron Galt!*" he bellowed. He bellowed Galt's name so loud that someone at the next table dropped a fork. "D'ye know what yer distinguished ancestor Cameron did at the Battle of Culloden on that sixteenth day of April, seventeen hundred and forty-six?"

There was a sudden hush throughout the restaurant. In the kitchen, someone clattered some dishes. Then even the clattering fell silent. Everyone in the restaurant paused to listen. MacDonald was swaying on his feet, spit running from his mouth onto his beard.

"He led the charge – fro' the centairr of the line, wi' Clan Chattan, and the MacLeans and Lochlann MacLachlan beside him ... "

Galt prayed that he could disappear under the red-and-white

checkered tablecloth.

" ... and he went up to that *sasunnach* bastairrd and wi' his clay-more he unseamed him from his nave to his chaps until his *guts* fell steaming before him on the heather."

Lassiter, beside him, made a choking sound and stared down at his linguini. Wu leaned over to hear the translation, then pursed his lips together. Rattenbury's body began to heave with deep inaudible laughter. Lassiter was shooting blank shots of hate Galt.

"Aye!" repeated MacDonald, relishing the power of the image. "His *GUTS* steamin' on the heather."

He had moved over to their table now and was towering over them. Like King Lear on the heath, one eye fixed on Galt, the rest of him scattered throughout time and history.

"We cuid hae won it, you know," he said in a soft mournful voice. "That December at Derby, one hundred and thirty miles from London." MacDonald saw Mr. Wu regarding him with amazement. "The Bank of England was paying in sixpences," he explained earnestly to Wu. "There was panic in the city. That bastairrd King George the Second was preparring to go back to Hanover. D'ye know why the Highland Army didna press on and take London?"

The diners in the restaurant looked into each other's faces for the answer.

"*They had run oot of oats!*" bellowed MacDonald. "*There was narry an oat left in their sporrans.*"

Cameron Galt got up from his chair and put an arm around MacDonald's shoulder trying to lead him out of the restaurant.

"And I, too, hae run oot of oats. I am nae guid ta' thee. *Comma leat misse, mas toil leat do bheatha thoin'n arrigh dhuit fhein.*"

Galt pushed MacDonald to the door just as Jerry Lewin was coming in. Lewin took the hulking dejected figure of MacDonald under his care.

"Do not think o' me," the Laird said, going out the door. "Take care o' yourself if ye value your life."

There was a forced return to conversation throughout the restaurant. Much shrugging of shoulders and an atmosphere of confused concern. Galt resumed his place at the table. Then Lewin burst in the door and came over to where the delegation was sitting.

"He is sitting sobbing by the fountain," Lewin reported, glaring at Lassiter. "Because you and D'Arnay have sold his University right out from under him, to turn it into a research-and-development arm for an offshore capitalist who is buying into kiddie software."

"Professor Lewin – I'd like you to meet Mr. Wu. He is considering being a corporate sponsor of the university." Lassiter made the introduction quickly, delicately emphasizing the word "sponsor."

"Sponsor, my ass! He wants to buy the place – don't you Wu? Listen, Wu – here's some shrewd investment advice. Don't buy the place! Do you read me? *Don't. buy. the. place!* It will bring you nothing but trouble."

For the second time, Galt felt a tragic hush come over the restaurant as he escorted a member of his faculty to the door.

"Better you should buy some town in the Russian Republic," Lewin yelled over his shoulder. "You'll lose your shirt here."

Mr. Wu smiled patiently at Giles Rattenbury. "I think many children would like toys that come from here. It is like Santa's Village."

Outside in the Food Court, Galt found Professor MacDonald by the fountain, looking happier, flanked like bookends by Jilaquns and Jan. MacDonald rose and reached out one huge tribal hand and held Galt's hand with the clinging warmth of a drunk.

"You're the new laird now," MacDonald said smiling weakly. "Cameron of Avalon."

Part Four

FEBRUARY

25

At most universities, change happens quietly and efficiently, and a faculty member first reads of it in the university gazette – a new endowed chair here, a department terminated there, a new building, a flurry of early retirements. Those institutions are so large and subdivided that any change feels remote and already in the past: it has happened to someone else in some other part of the system. So a faculty member notes the change and gets back to the important things that concern him, which is reading his e-mail and his pay slip. That is how change happens at the large universities – as natural and inevitable as the winter snowfall.

Change at Avalon, however, is immediate, anticipatory and, riding the crest of rumour, it touches everybody. That is because Avalon is not a normal university – it is an academic community, and perhaps as with the first communities of Christian believers, change here is felt as apocalyptic. It was especially apocalyptic that bitter February of a year when the corporate jaws closed on Avalon, and the University fought back with everything it had.

What Avalon has most of is the power of talk. In a crisis, talk is no inconsiderable power. If you have spent most of your life in a true academic community as I have, you'll understand the unique feeling of empowerment that comes to the many through talk. First of all, talk allows the threat to be seem precisely for what it is so that it can be dealt with by the entire community. "There's going to be a corporate takeover of the Ecology Center." "No, you moron – it's a *sponsorship*. I heard it from Sally Galt and she must have gotten it straight from the Dean himself." "But Sally dumped the Dean – didn't you hear? She's bought a house with Hannah Koeslag, so that takeover thing must be just a rumour." "It's not a sponsorship, anyway – I heard it's just a corporate *donation*." "A donation! – are you crazy?" "No – it's a donation. One of the secretaries in the Registrar's Office said so, and the secretaries around here know everything." "There aren't any secretaries in the Registrar's Office – dummy! They were terminated and replaced by the fucking Touchstone Registration System." "So? The System's not working: they had to hire the secretaries back." "If it's only a donation, why does the copy for next year's University Prospectus say the 'Avalon Institute of Ecology and Environmental Science?'" "It does? How do you know that?" "I know that because Ashley Tiffin – you know Ashley? – she was on the rugby team but now she's Ms. Total Scholar Girl – anyway, Ashley has a friend who got paid to typeset the Prospectus." "Students won't be coming to any Ecology Institute because there's going to be a Strike." "A Strike? Are you wacko or something? How's there going to be a Strike if there's no Union?" "There *is* a Union – it's just that Big Mac's not running it." "Yeah – I hear he's on Sick Leave." "So who's running the Union?" "Jerry Lewin." "Jerry Lewin? Get real! Jerry couldn't run a bar mitzvah."

Do you see what I mean? Through talk, a community comes together effectively to take the measure of a crisis.

★　　★　　★

Cameron Galt rolled up his sleeping bag and hid it under his office desk. He had taken to working late in his office, not bothering to make the difficult drive up to the lake in the February snows. The cottage seemed empty anyway without Sally. "It's best for me just to stay in town" was all she had said, speaking the coded language of separation which does not have to explain anything. Galt did not have the strength to contest that coding since there was nothing he could do about the situation anyway. But he took from it the idea of staying in town as well. And there had been no communication from Jan to suggest that his staying at the cottage might be worthwhile. So Galt, shaving off his beard and starting to wear jeans like a student, disappeared into work as was his habit. At night, kept awake by the fax and teleconferencer machines in Sheena's office, he thought of Jan D'Arnay's legs and their muscle tone. In the mornings, he greeted the cadre of student protesters who had begun an occupation of the outer office.

"Hi, Ashley. So what day's it now?"

"Hey, Mr. Dean. This is Day Three of the Occupation."

Ashley Tiffin, with her gigantic teddy bear, was rolling up her sleeping bag. Over those three days, Ashley and the Dean had acquired for each other the wary affectionate respect of biological symbionts. This was especially so because Galt had cooperated with the occupation by appearing, to all effect, to be personally imprisoned in his office, and the protesters had cooperated in turn by not disrupting the work of the Dean's secretaries. Biological proximity had its uses. Still, it was beginning to smell a little ripe in here, Galt thought, as we watched the seven other students sorting out their various sleeping bags, flutes, drums and guitars scattered among last night's pizza boxes. Sheena had taken to burning incense when she came in in the morning, and she was clearly irritated at having to enter her office by a rope ladder through the window, the students having chained the door to filing cabinets and ceiling fixtures designed to fall on the heads of police if they crashed in.

"Okay if we begin our seminar?" said Ashley. The protesters had been having an endless seminar on Cardinal Newman's *The Idea of a University*. "After we brush our teeth, I mean."

"Sure. Just keep it down to a dull roar."

"Any reply yet from the Board?" one of the students asked.

"Well, the Board wants you out of here. They say you're a safety hazard. But I told D'Arnay that it would be hard to get all of you out until he agrees to talk."

"Yay! Way to go!"

"And he's agreed to talk — but just with me. I'm going down to Andromeda Place today."

The Avalon Eight, as they'd come to be called, gave a cheer on behalf of many.

★ ★ ★

Later that day, from the top floor of the Andromeda Place tower, Galt looked down on the lawns and buildings of the Legislature while D'Arnay took only a brush-off interest in Galt's plan for re-structuring the University. The notion of downsizing through early retirement similarly ran into a wall of good-natured vagueness. Even the subject of privatizing the Ecology Center D'Arnay waved away offhandedly into the clouds that were rolling up from the harbour outside the floor-to-ceiling office window. Instead, D'Arnay talked about educational software. It became clear that there was nothing to talk about.

Galt finally had to interrupt him:

"Are you able to confirm or deny, for the benefit of an agitated university, that Wu is negotiating to buy the Ecology Center?"

"Forget Wu. He's not a player in this."

Not a player? Galt thought. But he just toured the Ecocenter.

"'There is a tide in the affairs of men which taken at its flood leads on to fortune,'" D'Arnay went on. "Do you remember studying that goddam play at Colborne? Every year we did that same lugubrious Shakespeare play. And now that's the only line I remember from it."

Galt chuckled at the memory of English classes at Colborne College long ago. Then, D'Arnay was a laid-back, laconic shit-disturber. Secure in his social class, he smoothly tested the irrelevance of high-school teachers until he could graduate and assume the world.

"Timing is everything," D'Arnay continued. "You've got to know when to jump and when to hold back."

Nothing D'Arnay said removed Galt's frown.

"Look – we're finally on top in the *Choosing Your College* ratings." D'Arnay waved the special magazine issue in the air as he spoke. "Thanks to our funds available for scholarships and our total library holdings. We moved way up in those two categories. Means we can go off a universal tuition fee structure and start raising the fees of each career-oriented program."

Galt understood that the phrase *career-oriented program* did not mean the Humanities which in D'Arnay's mind led nowhere. He was referring to the Ecological Sciences.

"All you have to do, Cam, is hold the ship of state together for a few more weeks. Until summer, when no one's around. Look like you're doing something constructive. Wave. Smile in all directions. Hold off a strike. And get the radicals out of your office, will you? They're giving managerial efficiency a black eye."

"I can't do that without calling in the police. They say they'd have to pop the outside window at night when there are no student supporters around. Special tactics squad, strip-searches, the whole works. It's standard containment policy."

D'Arnay rose from his desk signalling the end, not of an interview, but of an object lesson in managerial vagueness. "Cam — you've been through a lot lately." It was D'Arnay's Head Prefect's voice. "I went through it too with Jennifer. And still the insufferable bitch won't leave me alone." Chuckle. "Just try to keep your act together. Look — if Colborne College did anything for us, it trained us to punch through the squalls and ride out the gales. Right?"

A big hand on his shoulder. Galt now knew precisely the amount of pressure that determined an empty consolation touch on the shoulder and a touch with genuine human warmth. He felt no genuine human warmth from D'Arnay. Meeting over.

★   ★   ★

That evening Galt looked up from his desk into the blue eyes of Robyn Endicott. She had come up the rope ladder and through the outer office silently, almost magically, and was standing in front of him wearing a black parka trimmed with white imitation fur. She looked at once preppy, athletic and uniformed. Galt motioned toward the two armchairs that were arranged around the coffee table, the place for decanal heart-to-heart discussions.

"Thank's for seeing me on such short notice. I have to tell you that Professor MacDonald is in hospital."

"Oh, God! What happened?"

"A motorcycle accident. Nobody else was hurt – but Professor MacDonald has a broken leg. Undetermined internal injuries. Also a cracked skull. He wasn't wearing his motorcycle helmet."

Robyn Endicott, as she said this, did not break eye contact with Galt. She did not even seem to blink.

"He was drunk," she added.

"I'll arrange for replacement staffing in his courses."

"Professor MacDonald doesn't wish to be replaced," Endicott said. "He wishes to continue teaching."

"From his hospital bed? How can he teach?"

Endicott's face showed no change of expression. "Professor Mac-Donald claims his mind is unaffected. He'll give his lectures into a camcorder. Professor Lewin is going to be taping him. Then Lewin will rush the lectures over to A-V Services, and they'll be shown on the screen at the regular time in the lecture hall."

"What about his seminars?"

"The students are supposed to come in groups to his hospital room. The first group went this afternoon. They brought heaps of flowers. The place looks like a Hindu shrine."

At last, Robyn's face cracked a smile.

Galt decided to reflect Ms. Endicott's cool formality. "Please convey my deepest sympathy and concern. I'll be in to visit him as soon as I can."

"Thank you. I want to take this opportunity to inform you that I am Acting President of the Avalon Faculty Union."

"Congratulations! How can I help you?"

"The combined universities' Day of Protest at the Legislature is this Friday. The faculty wish to be relieved of normal teaching duties that day so they can join their students at the demonstration."

"I'll send out the e-mail immediately."

Endicott blinked. "Don't you have to run it past D'Arnay?"

Galt smiled a wry conspiratorial smile. "Anything else?"

"Thank-you. That's all for now."

After Robyn had left, Galt pondered the style of the new faculty spokeswoman, which seemed to combine a gentle reasonableness with a distancing of self. Perhaps Robyn has no self, he thought. No, that's not true: her monochromatic colour schemes were decidedly chosen. It was just that she seemed to detach herself from her reasoning. The detachment made reasoning impersonal and therefore social – a possession of the community, not of its leader. That was interesting. How bodies frame things!

He went to the outer office to say goodnight to the protesters, feeling like a parent quieting down a noisy sleepover:

"Okay, gang. Last chance to use the executive washroom. Then, no more flutes and drums."

The protesters were each cocooned in their sleeping bags. The smell of vegetarian pizza was everywhere.

"Good-night, Mr. Dean," they called back gaily.

"By the way, who's bringing you the pizza?"

The students looked at each other to see who would answer. Then they looked to Ashley Tiffin.

"Robyn Endicott brought it – to demonstrate the Faculty Union's solidarity with the Occupation."

★   ★   ★

Late that night there came a sound at Sheena's office window. *Thump!* Finally asleep on his hard office floor, Galt tried to pull his sleeping bag up over his ears and pretended not to hear it. *Thump!* – the sound came again. A police raid? The sound of a ladder being placed against the window? What if it was the police? What time was it, anyway? Galt rolled over to look at his clock. 3:05 a.m. No – it couldn't be a police raid because Ashley and her group would have been warned by cell phone from the small tent city of supporters camped outside the main door of Sears. *Thump!* Someone was throwing snowballs!

The lights came on in the outer office. The sound had aroused the occupiers.

"Quick! – chain up together," came Ashley's voice.

There was the sound of heavy-link chains being locked around the protesters' bodies.

"*You are my sunshine, my only sunshine. You make my happy when …* "

"Not yet! We agreed to sing when the police actually break in and arrest us."

"Where's the cell?"

"Where's the camcorder?"

"Mr. Dean – something's happening! Are you awake? You're going to be arrested."

Galt struggled out of his sleeping bag and opened his office door. He stood in the outer office in his pajamas. The occupiers were frantically chaining themselves together. Ashley was on the cell phone.

"It's okay," Galt said. "I think someone wants to come up the ladder – that's all."

"Yeah, that's cool," said Ashley into her cell phone. She switched off the phone. "She wants a private meeting with the Dean. Someone unlock the window and throw down the ladder."

"Can't! I'm all chained up."

"Where's the key?"

"We agreed to ditch the key – remember? It's out there in Tent City."

"Shit!"

"I have to pee."

"Mr. Dean," said Ashley, sweetly. "Would you be kind enough to let down the ladder? The person wants to see you."

"Who is it?"

"They wouldn't say over the cell – the police are monitoring our transmissions."

Galt went over to the window, unlocked it, and began feeding the rope ladder down.

"Oh, and tell her to get the key first. I've really got to pee. The Tent City coordinator has it."

"Could you bring up the key to unlock the construction chains?" Galt called down to a figure standing alone in the snow. The figure nodded and went off in the direction of Tent City.

A few minutes later, there was a tugging on the rope ladder and a head concealed in a balaclava appeared at the window. Neatly, the visitor hopped through the open window, removed her disguise and shook out her blond hair.

"Jan!" Galt exclaimed.

"I'm not here – right?" Jan said to the protesters, giving them the key. Then she hauled up the rope ladder and locked the window.

"Right on!" Ashley said, agreeably.

"In your office," Jan ordered with an air of barely contained urgency. "Keep the lights off – I don't want anyone outside to know I've been here."

Galt closed the office door behind them, plunging the room in darkness. He sat near where he had seen Jan sit crosslegged on the floor. She said nothing. He could hear her breathing; after a while, he began to smell the scent of snowflakes on her wool sweater, and a deeper smell of perspiration.

"I figured it out. Are you ready for this?"

"For what?" Galt had no idea what compelled her visit. Evidently, it wasn't just to be with him.

"Actually, I didn't figure it out – it came to me in a dream. But you can't tell anybody. Especially not Mom. Promise me you won't tell anybody."

"I promise."

More silence. She was hesitating, gathering her thoughts, hesitating. Then:

"This Wu dude from Hong Kong. He's not making an endowment."

"I never thought it was that straightforward," Galt broke in.

"Stop! Let me finish. Wu's just a front. He's a front man for Dad. Daddy doesn't do anything personally: he always runs his dealings through a front operation. One he controls."

Galt pondered this cautiously. But his mind kept making sudden little sideways leaps in the darkness. What was she telling him? What was D'Arnay up to? "I had the impression of some sort of partnership. Wasn't Wu going to endow some new Ecology labs in return for space behind the Food Court to build his own science and technology park? Children's educational software – they say he bought some West Coast software firm."

"He didn't buy the firm – Dad did!"

"How do you know this?"

"Because ... because that's the way Dad operates. He silently partners something; then when he's got what he's after, he dissolves the partnership. That's what he did to Mom."

"It produced you, though."

"Oh, right!" Jan said crossly. "Marginalized alpha-flake. Destiny zero. Hardly a growing concern. Wait till you see what he does to Avalon. A national model of the perfect corporate-owned software-producing university – for all of Dad's business friends to admire. I'll bet my knickers Wu won't even be in the picture.

"I shouldn't have told you this," she added. "If Mom ever finds out, she'll kick in Dad's headlights. He's buying Av to screw her."

"Then why's Wu in the picture at all?" Galt asked, keeping the discussion on track.

Galt could sense Jan gazing at him pitifully in the darkness.

"You don't understand corporate power moves, do you? I guess that's why Daddy pushed to have you made Dean."

There was a pause. Then she said: "If you were my age, I'd love you for your innocence."

If I were her age, Galt thought to himself in the gloom. Then he thought of the teleconference call from D'Arnay on the plane while he was flying across the Atlantic. "I've got a corporation to partner with Wu ... can't say right now." And how D'Arnay had backpedalled away from the question put to him today – no yesterday – at Andromeda Place: "Forget Wu – he's not a player in this." Why, then ...

"Wu's the product link to China," Jan explained. "He gets Andromeda into the Asian market. The Chinese can't pirate North-American software anymore. So, Dad produces all the Intellectual Property. Or actually your profs do – for Dad. And other profs, as Andromeda buys up other small universities specializing in whatever."

Galt's mind was still stuck on a question. "Why did Wu tour the Ecology Center?"

"For government funds, dummy! The government's probably going to subsidize part of the construction cost of the Science and Technology Park. They like private partnerships with universities. Besides, Wu helps keep Dad's cloak of invisibility on. Isn't there a conflict of interest if he buys the University while he's the Board Chair?"

Galt looked at the digital clock and sighed. 3:52 a.m. was deleted and replaced with 3:53 a.m. Each minute of time overtook the last, consigning it to oblivion.

"There isn't much time," he said with a heavy heart.

Jan's eager voice was so close to his ear, he could feel her breath. "We'll make history, then – won't we? But I've got a Cult-Studs seminar in a few hours. I'd better go and sleep in one of the tents."

Galt rose and opened his office door. Jan bumped by him in the darkness. In the outer office, the protesters were asleep again. Visible in Ashley's blue childhood nightlight, their bodies seemed thrown every which-way in the unconstrained slumber of the young. Jan opened the window and let the ladder down. Then she turned and faced Galt. She put on her balaclava and tucked her hair in.

"Sweet dreams!" she said, going down the ladder.

★   ★   ★

Professor Lewin's basement office seemed like a paleolithic cave in the Ice Age. Snow was piled halfway up the windows. Crowded together in the yellow lamplight, the students in their winter sweaters, with mitts and boots and toques scattered around the floor, made up a small tribe. Ashley Tiffin's skis leaned precariously against Lewin's bookshelf.

"Common sense," snapped Lewin. "Someone decode 'common sense.' Quick!"

"It is the rhetorical position taken by any group that has reached the top," answered Tiffin. "It means everything is just the way it is – the way you sense it. There is no alternative way."

Lewin relaxed in his armchair. "You're good Cultural Studies majors now. You realize that a culture isn't consistent and uniform. It's made up of subcultures each competing for supremacy. Each struggling for possession of the right to mean. One could say that each culture is striving to make itself identical with reality. Once a group succeeds in making itself identical with reality, it calls that position 'common sense.' All the other subcultures become food for that dominant culture to process."

The students busied themselves in an atmosphere of common purpose. Bosko was no longer in the seminar. He had dropped the course after the Senate meeting last November. Now they could really talk.

"It seems very … well, predatorial, doesn't it?" Ashley said. She had now become the leader of the group. "I mean the metaphor you use: everything feeding on everything else – or trying to. It makes me think of all the different bacteria in the stomach lining."

"Once when I was canoeing," Jan said sleepily, "I saw a rock covered with – there must have been – five or six different kinds of lichen. Each kind of lichen was bumping up against the limits set by each other kind."

"Not quite what I meant," Lewin said. "The dominant culture turns all the others into raw material for its own survival. I don't think your lichen are actually devouring each other."

"Well, they're marginalizing each other anyway," conceded Jan.

"I think we'd better get away from these organic metaphors. It was my fault for introducing them," Lewin said.

"I liked your term 'processed' better," Ashley said. "The victim kind of literally passes through the system of the victor – she has no identity outside the particular version of reality set by the victor. And then the victor who controls the dominant discourse calls that situation 'common sense.' 'Don't think about it: that's just the way things are; you can't do anything about it; it's destiny,' the victor says."

Ashley was irrepressible now.

"That's why Vic Bosko is such a colossal fascist jerk. God, he creeps me out! He wants to stop funding for the Gay and Lesbian Collective because he says the group has an ideology. Groups that have ideologies shouldn't be funded, he says. That goes for Avalon Daycare, World Issues, the Aboriginal Students' Association – every one of them. Yet the Common Sense cowboys are the biggest pack of ideologues you ever met!"

Ashley Tiffin was speaking with the energy of the converted.

"And then he has the nerve to say he has no point of view!"

"Well, he's reached the top. His point of view is just to manage," Jan said. "Which means staying on top."

"Which means making every other group invisible," Ashley replied.

Lewin sat back in his armchair tapping his fingers together under his chin and reflecting. He had seen Ashley Tiffin's other side for the first time. "Or making them visible – but only as scapegoats," he suggested. "You know, when the Nazis occupied Denmark and made the Jews wear the Star of David to single them out, everyone in Copenhagen from the King of Denmark down took to wearing the Star of David too."

There was silence as the seminar group thought about this. Then Ashley spoke up:

"That's a great idea! Let's all be dykes tomorrow. At the All Universities Day of Protest."

Professor Lewin, his teaching done for the day, smiled seraphically to himself.

26

The vast lawns of the Legislature, designed to impress a nineteenth-century citizenry with a vision of settled order, would never have been laid out that way had it been known how well the space lent itself to massive demonstrations against the government. The lawns could hold ten thousand protesters – more, if traffic was diverted from the roads circling the Legislative Assembly, which joined in a four-lane avenue extending past Andromeda Place down to Harbourfront. During the winter of the government cutbacks, the lawns had been filled by welfare moms, childcare workers, transit and construction workers, environmentalists, senior citizens, and fired civil servants. Early in the new year, the lawns became the site for combined demonstrations from what government budget experts called the "M.U.S.H." sector: municipalities, universities, schools and hospitals. Finally, on a blustery February day with the flags on the Legislature lawn flapping madly, it became the turn of the students from all the universities which the Legislature had underfunded. It promised to be the biggest, most peaceful student demonstration ever.

Had Ruairi MacDonald been there at the outset instead of at the very end, he might have mistaken the scene for a gathering of the clans. That effect was underscored by the students from Country Club U., the first to arrive. He would have heard their bagpipes, then seen them marching as if for a football game in their red, blue and yellow tams and scarfs, behind the Golden Gaels University band.

> *Hey, hey*
> *Ho, ho –*
> *Underfunding's*
> *Got to go!*

sang the cheerleaders in their white sweaters and short kilts, doing high kicks. It was a fine day, ideally placed between Christmas and the March Break, to go down to Metro, show some school spirit, then do a little shopping at the Harbourfront Mall. Then came the students from McMonster, led by cheerleaders with maroon and grey pom-poms and a brass band. The music and the chanting echoed off the office towers along the avenue.

> *They say 'cutback' –*
> *We say 'fight back!'*

More buses pulled in with students from the smaller colleges far away to the northwest. Excited and bewildered, the students took the neatly printed signs which the demonstration organizers handed out.

> *Stop the Cuts!*
> *Education is Investment*
> *in the Future.*

The students from the various Metro campuses, a more solemn multitude, walked in twos and threes holding signs they had made in their parents' basements – their only spot of mirth, the Lady Godiva Memorial Band with construction hard-hats on backwards and instruments deliberately out of tune, singing the Engineer's song to the melody of "John Brown's Body" –

> *We are, we are, we are, we are,*
> *We are the Engineers!*
> *We can, we can, we can, we can*
> *Demolish forty beers!*

A row of police officers stood casually in front of a portable waist-high barrier at the bottom of the Legislature steps. Relaxed, they were exchanging banter with the undergraduates, who could be their sons and daughters. The odd snowball was thrown to delighted cheers. Pigeons flew routinely in and out of the Legislature stone-work. Some seagulls, attracted by the crowds, flew up from the harbour, looking for pizza crusts. Altogether, it promised to be a vast, good-natured demonstration.

Then came the students from Avalon and ruined everything. Out of a cavalcade of yellow school buses they poured – an Anarchist army. The whole university had come. And each Avalon student wore the rainbow triangle of the Avalon Gays and Lesbians Collective. Some carried placards saying "Protest the Funding Cut to Avalon Lesbians and Gays." Some carried Anti-Capitalist Convergence signs. Some the red and black flags of the Anarchist Movement. One group carried a cardboard model of the Earth being penetrated by a star-spangled penis. From the first bus in the procession, two Cultural Studies majors were unfurling their gigantic banner with the quotation –

> *"The tradition of the oppressed teaches us that the 'state of emergency' in which we live is not the exception but the rule ... it is our task to bring about a real state of emergency, and this will improve our position in the struggle against Fascism."*
> *Walter Benjamin, 1940*

The banner went before the throng like the quotation-laden banners of a Protestant army. But the students, innocently, had neglected to make holes in the banner to let the wind through. They struggled to keep the message vertical against the stiff gusts that blew from the harbour. There were more busloads of Avalon students banging drums, blowing whistles and shaking tambourines. Many were wearing goggles, gas-masks and vinegar-soaked bandanas against the tear gas. Some sang Bob Marley lyrics. The aboriginal population of Avalon came: they chanted to the beat of tribal drums and raised their Keno-mah-gay-wah-kon Independent College placards.

The Metro Late-Nite Newspulse team saw the new arrivals and

began swinging their cameras around with interest. The protest organizer, a fast-rising preppy politician from the Metro Students' Council, saw the Avalon "Carnival Against Capitalism" sign and behind them another group marching ominously under black flags. He looked worried.

"The Avalon crazies scare the shit out of me. They eat pepper spray for breakfast. Get them out of sight."

But the students from Avalon, educated in street theatre of every kind, had no intention of being marginalized. Automatically, they surged to the front of the demonstration, right beside the Legislature barricades.

"Isn't this just fucking great?" cried Jerry Lewin exultantly. He was wearing his old army surplus forage-coat and Yippie headband from the Sixties.

"Those who do not relive the past are condemned to repeat it," agreed Jake Weisberg paradoxically. The professor readjusted a Maoist cap with its bright red star above the peak. "Revolution now!" he shouted tentatively.

> *Hey, hey,*
> *Ho, ho.*
> *Underfunding's*
> *Got to go!*

The chant rising from the back of the crowd gathered volume, accompanied by the bass drums of the university bands. Now the Country Club cheerleaders were forming a pyramid.

> *Hey, hey,*
> *Ho, ho,*
> *Underfunding's*
> *Got to go!*

The students of Avalon responded with their own chant –

Cut the Bullshit —
Smash the State!

The two chants did an oral tug-of-war in the sub-zero air of Metro. A police captain was talking into a radio. Two mounted officers appeared on horses.

"Don't worry about them. They're doped to the nostrils with downers," Lewin advised.

Jan wasn't so sure. "I saw them on TV prancing their horses sideways into a crowd."

"Yeah, but they're mostly for show. We used to carry ball bearings in our pockets. Threw them on the streets in front of the horses."

There was a hail of snowballs from the front ranks of the demonstration. Then two Avalon students set up a catapult made of wooden planks, and began to lob teddy bears into the police line. The visors came down. Some of the police were fingering their nightsticks nervously. They had retreated quietly behind the barricade.

"This is looking quite interesting," Jerry Lewin said expertly.

"Alright! Nobody rocks the barricade — get it?" The police captain was walking behind the barricade waving the students' hands off it. "Hands off the barricade! We're all going to have a nice peaceful day of protest."

"Motherfucker!" yelled Lewin suddenly. The last time he had yelled that was in 1968 in Chicago.

The police captain eyed Lewin aggressively.

"Yeah? You want to try saying that again?"

Lewin eyed the policeman back.

"The idea hasn't occurred to you — but by pulling your line behind the barricade you've created a conflict situation. And you can't use tear gas in this wind — you'll have to use pepper."

"One more peep from you, squirt, and you're outta' here!"

"You couldn't keep the lid on a demonstration of geriatrics in wheelchairs!" Lewin shot back.

"I say, watch whom you're talking about," said Tony Leland from his motorized wheelchair.

The police captain turned his back on Lewin indifferently.

There was Professor Emeritus Mwangulu (Economics) wearing the pin of the Communist Party of Pan-Africa.

"I didn't know you were a Red!" Lewin exclaimed.

Mwangulu smiled a patronizing Marxist smile.

"*Hands off the barricade!*" The police captain was walking the length of the barrier, skimming a nightstick along the top of it to dislodge the fingers of the Avalon students.

"*Ow!*"

"Should you lay a hand on one of my gerls, I'll have you up before your superiah before you can recite the Riot Act!" came the voice of Faith Rackstraw, piercing the air with four hundred years of combined New World and Old World authority.

"Migod — Faith's here! She'll take the whole line of them out just with that accent alone!" Lewin commented.

Nglesi Mwangulu smiled wryly. "I have faced s.a.s.-trained paratroopers — however, I cringe before the colonial accent of that woman."

The Metro Newspulse TV crew had worked its way around to the police side of the barrier.

"Okay — you got her?" the interviewer called to the cameraman. The camera focussed in on Jilaquns wearing her all-in-one black leather catsuit, an eagle war-feather in her red headband over her goggles. "Okay, roll."

"Can you tell us why you're here today?" the Metro Newspulse reporter asked brightly, her lips pouting and unpouting under fluttering eyelashes.

"Sure can, honey! I'm here to … "

"Cut! Want to take another run at it?" The reporter registered a weary patience.

"You could begin by asking me who I am," Jilaquns suggested. "Before you commodify me."

"Alright – you are?"

"Jilaquns of the Sealion Clan of Qaysun of the Eagle Side of the First Nation of the Haida People."

"Could you tell Newspulse viewers why you're here today?"

"Yes, I'm here to begin the Revolution against white supremacy in this land. Metro Newspulse viewers should ask themselves the following question: why does a mere four hundred years in the New World produce a right to own the land? To anyone from an older culture – mine is thirty centuries old – four hundred years is like last Monday. Recent history."

"Uh – do you want to comment on the student demonstration?"

"Sure. This demonstration is sufficiently air-headed to be safely pushed on the national media, possibly attracting middle-class bores from Washington to London, Mars, Jupiter, and the rings of Saturn. However, this protest, despite its exaggerated postures of superficial bourgeois concern, does in fact bring to the surface the wink-and-nod xenophobia of this parochial Eurotribal government. All parochialism crystallizes into race-purity drives ... "

"Cut. Thank you."

"What d'ya mean 'cut,' you bimbo?"

Jan restrained Jilaquns' arm as it tried to retake the mike. "It's a photo-op, right? We need to exploit the media just as it exploits us."

"The best photo-op that Barbie Doll's going to get today is if she uses her Newspulse mike as a dildo."

Moving away quickly, the news team had picked out Ashley Tiffin wearing her huggy athletic top. She had her arms crossed, so the camera did not catch the double female symbol beneath the lettering – "Avalon Womyn's Rugby Team." However, the reporter noticed the rainbow triangle on Ashley's baseball cap. It looked like a good human-interest angle.

"Could you tell Newspulse viewers why you're wearing this?" The news reporter tried on a voice of affectionate familiarity.

"Oh, that's to show I'm a dyke," Ashley explained earnestly. She unfolded her arms and pointed at the lettering on her bosom. "All lesbians and gays and people of alternative sexuality are working really hard to pay our way through school and we're being given zilch."

"Ashley – a dyke?" Jan asked incredulously.

"Yeah – she's the real thing," Jill replied. "The others are just LUGS."

"Lugs?"

"Lesbians Until Graduation. At least, I hope they are – or alternative sexuality is doomed."

"Sorry, Mom. Sorry, Dad. I hate to bust out of the closet like this – I mean, on the national news and everything. But that's the way it is."

"Good heavens!" said Jan.

"I'm one too – interview me!" called out one of the rugby girls.

"Me too!"

"Is everyone at Avalon … ah, alternatively sexual?" the news reporter asked her mike in astonishment.

"We're all that way!" exuded Ashley. "We're the Gay and Lesbian University of America."

This was a better story. The Newspulse camera did a slow pan of the Avalon students holding their green flags with the Avalon sword and the lettering. "Gay – and Proud of It!" or "Lesbians of Avalon!" One after another, men and women of Avalon gave their statements, coming out of their real or imagined closets on the National Late-Nite News. In the center of the crowd, Victor Bosko, having temporarily abandoned the Common Sense Revolution, stood alone in a Saks-Fifth Avenue belted wool overcoat, holding a small sign that read like a companion wanted advertisement –

> *Straight White Male*
> *and not entirely dissatisfied*

The demonstration organizers were now carrying in a microphone stand to put on risers that had been placed in front of the barricade. Some Metro U. Engineering students were trying to clear a space.

"Okay, move aside. There's going to be speeches." "Could you get your banner out of the way?"

"Get your hands off me, you fucking bourgeois pig!"

"Who's the parade marshal for Avalon? Get your people back!"

"We don't have a parade marshal, dung-brain! We're a spontaneous collective."

"C'mon – clear a space for the mike!" yelled the police captain. He knew that nothing could bring a protest demonstration back into shape faster than an official speech.

The parade organizer tapped the mike. "Testing ... one, two, three. Okay? Let's go.

"Good afternoon. We are here today, in the largest demonstration ever mounted in this place by university students, to protest the government funding cuts to higher education ... "

This brought little response from the crowd, except a salvo of booms on a bass drum and some shrill whistles. The speaker, at a loss, reverted to one of the day's slogans to raise the crowd.

"Education is investment in the future!"

Revolution now!

The chant began just in front of the mike. Quickly, the chant gained power.

Revolution now!
Revolution now!

" ... the cuts to the funding of education will mean rising tuition fees, overcrowded classrooms ... "

Revolution now!
Revolution now!
Revolution now!

Unable to get his voice heard above the chanting, the organizer made a good-natured hopeless gesture. There were scattered boos from the back of the crowd.

"That guy's got the charisma of an empty Nigerian oil barrel," remarked Lewin.

From a new position on the Legislature steps, the Metro News-pulse team had a good over-the-shoulder shot of the speaker facing the crowd. The reporter was talking rapidly into her mike. "We're at the combined universities demonstration at the Legislature in Metro ... "

Suddenly, Jerry Lewin was on the platform in his oversized army forage-jacket and headband.

"You don't know how to do it, kid. Give me the mike."

He grabbed the microphone from the top of the stand, elbowing the organizer aside. There were crazy cheers from the Avalon students. Lewin surveyed the hosts of student faces before him, assembled all the way down to where the avenues surrounding the Legislature joined. He blinked, smiled sweetly to himself. Then:

"Sisters and Brothers of the Revolution!" he bellowed. "Intellectual workers throughout the land ... "

Raucous cheering broke out from the Avalon phalanx surrounding the speaker's platform.

"This government has created a deficit because of years of handouts to the corporate welfare bums. Now they're trying to pay down the deficit on the backs of working students. On *your* backs. Is that fair?"

"*Noooo!*" yelled the crowd.

"This government is putting user fees on learning – making education accessible only to the rich. Is that just?"

"*Noooo!*"

"This government could erase its deficit in a year by ending corporate tax write-offs to its friends in business and industry, including Andromeda Networks over there. But it won't. Is that right?"

"*Noooo!*"

Lewin, feeling the power of the historical moment, let his voice swell in the cadences of a trained actor. His voice boomed back and forth off Andromeda Place and the office buildings all the way to Harbourfront.

"This government, by denying education to everyone but the rich, is out to take away your power to think, your power to criticize, your power to confront, your power to fight back ... "

"Yeah! – power to the people!" yelled Weisberg. "Atta boy, Jerry!"

"So what are you going to do about it?" Lewin cried, flapping the arms of his forage-jacket and seeming to rise above the platform like a bird.

In the confused silence, a single voice called out. It came from the left of the rostrum.

Avalon says Occupy!

The chant was taken up automatically.

Avalon says Occupy!
Avalon says Occupy!
Avalon says Occupy!

Lewin, feeling the crest of a great rolling wave, let the chant be a counterpuntal chorus to his own rising words.

"No, comrades – you don't have to be Augusto Boal to see that this government is based on fear ... "

Avalon says Occupy!

" ... and hate ... "

Avalon says Occupy!

" ... and greed."

Avalon says Occupy!

"But this government cannot silence confrontation. It cannot silence confrontation because we have something of value that even the most heinous dictatorships need, which is criticism. That is the work our education has given us to do."

The students were rocking the barricade back and forth in time to the chant. Then two Avalonians released the little pink robotic tank that charged the police. The police line stiffened. Nightsticks were out. Plexiglass riot shields had been produced from a nearby van.

"Well, hello, dear colleagues," came the voice of Giles Rattenbury, sounding as if he was at a government reception. "And Faith! How are you? You know, I was just thinking – isn't this simply a splendid occasion?" Acting President Rattenbury was wearing a college muffler and carrying an Avalon placard. "Now, where would you think it would be best for me to stand?"

"We appear to be engaged in occupying the Legislature," came Faith's voice.

"How interesting! I've always wanted to do that."

At this moment, there was the roar of twin exhausts of a police motorcycle speeding around the corner of the Legislature. All heads craned to look. But no – it was not a police motorcycle. It was a beaten-up antique Harley-Davidson. The white sword on the green flag of Avalon flew from a single crutch lashed vertically behind the driver. The driver was Professor Ruairi MacDonald, his bandaged forehead visible under his motorcycle helmet, and one leg extended before him in a plaster cast on which the motto of the MacDonald of Clanranald was written with a hospital felt pen: "My Hope is Constant in Thee."

"It's Big Mac! Yay!"

The cheering from the front of the barricade was tumultuous.

"What in heaven's name is he going to do?" Jan asked.

"Mac – over here!"

With slow-moving herculean effort, MacDonald got off his motorcycle. He released his upright crutch. Then, swaying on it drunkedly, he surveyed the scene before him.

"Take number five. We're at the university day of protest at the Metro Legislature." The reporter was speaking quickly and nervously. "Things are getting a little tense here … "

The demonstration organizer, standing behind the speaker's platform, gave a little signal. Suddenly, a group of Engineers rushed the platform. They were jostling Lewin off it.

"*Booo!*"

Jan leaped onto the platform and pulled at one of the Engineers, sending his hard-hat spinning. Then she pushed Lewin off the platform towards the Avalon Womyn's Rugby Team and safety. An Engineer grabbed her from behind and locked his hands under her chest.

"Get your hands off me, meatbreath!"

Jan brought her boot down hard on his instep and simultaneously smashed his nose with her elbow.

Now Jilaquns was on the platform. With a long ululating warcry, she kicked the Engineer in the groin. "*Revolution!*" she screamed into the mike while she pushed another Engineer face-down in the snow.

Then the Avalon students broke the barricade down and stormed through the police line towards the steps of the Legislature.

Avalon says Occupy!

From the back of the charging students came the manic braying howl of an Irish Wolfhound.

Alone on the platform, Jilaquns was screaming, her arm pointed in triumph like a warrior queen. The tribal drums increased in pitch and intensity. Within seconds, the group on the steps of the Legislature had grown. More police appeared from nowhere wearing riot gear and gas masks. Nightsticks were in the air. The crack of the first nightstick went through the crowd like a sickening thud.

More nightsticks were rising and falling. A woman stumbled off the Legislature steps, blood streaming from her mouth.

"*Ambulance!*"

Enraged, the whole mass of the Avalon students charged the steps, pushing the police line backward in the rush. A salvo of placards was flung overhead. The Metro Newspulse crew moved in to get a better view.

"*Love, Freedom, Peace, Joy!*" yelled Jilaquns, still on the platform.

A cannister of tear gas, hurled over the fence, spewed grey smoke. A burning sensation, eyes on fire, a rancid taste in the mouth. More cannisters. On went goggles and vinegar bandanas.

Then the police snatch squad appeared, wearing running shoes and jeans and athletic tops, handcuffs visible on their belts. Swiftly, they rushed the platform and surrounded Jill. Trying to avoid the handcuffs, she was twisting like a harpooned seal.

Now Clio was on the platform, her lips curled back in an ugly dreadful snarl.

"Watch out for the fucking dog!"

"Go limp, Jill!"

The police started to drag her away, still twisting and screaming virulence in their faces.

Clio sunk her teeth into an arm raising a nightstick.

Suddenly, MacDonald was there. With one bloodshot eye he took in the situation. Then, hopping on one leg, he charged with his crutch extended, like a berzerker. The policeman with the handcuffs caught the crutch with its Avalon flag square in the chest and threw up his arms as if he had been speared. The other three dropped Jilaquns; they crouched to take on the giant attacker.

"Ha! Now I've got ye, ye devils!" hollered MacDonald and flung himself at them. In the melee, MacDonald's helmet came off. A nightstick rose and fell repeatedly. One of the policemen was crawling away across the snow. Then another policeman went flying like a bowling pin. With one great arm, MacDonald grabbed Jilaquns around the waist and hauled her up to the platform. With the other arm he was swinging his crutch around his head like a claymore. Then he uttered a Gaelic war-cry.

A policeman, lying in the snow, looked up at MacDonald's blood-shot eye with awe and terror.

"Holy shit!" he said.

A phalanx of Avalon eco-freaks, aborigines, gays, lesbians, anti-globalization activists and anarcho-marxists closed around the plat-form and stood hostile and determined like the remnants of the Republican Guard at Waterloo.

"*We're changing the world!*" screamed Jilaquns, gasping for breath, tears streaming from her eyes.

At that moment, a black limousine with darkened windows was making its way to the front of the Legislature building. It stopped at the foot of the steps. Protesters and police broke off their strug-gles to see what was happening. A chauffeur got out and walked around the car to open the rear door. Slowly, with the unrushed for-mality of a state occasion, a figure emerged wearing a three-piece blue suit.

"It's the Lieutenant-Governor!"

The police captain came up to the limo ready to escort the offi-cial party.

The figure stood, blinking in the sudden daylight and media at-tention, and smiled like a statesman. The chauffeur opened the trunk of the limo, pulled out a small placard sign, and gave it to the dignitary to hold. On the sign in green lettering were the words, "Avalon Forever!" And the university crest in the top corner.

"It's Cameron!" cried Faith Rackstraw.

Mad cheering broke from the ranks of the Avalon students.

"Hello, Faith! What's going on here?"

The Dean and Provost of Avalon smiled a broad smile of pleas-ure and welcome to the cheers.

"Good to see you all. I regret that I was a little bit delayed," he said amiably, hoisting his sign.

"Yay, Cam!"

The Metro Newspulse team immediately closed on the visitor with mikes and cameras.

"Who the fuck is this guy?" The police captain, outnumbered and now out-occasioned, seemed ready to take advice from an expert.

"Right now, he's the most important university head in the country," Lewin replied, firmly pushing Galt towards the speaker's platform. "Make way!"

"No, I have no statement to give at this time," Galt said to the Newspulse reporter, accepting a water bottle from Ashley to wash out his eyes. "Perhaps the university presidents will have something to say later on."

"The university presidents have said dick-all," said Lewin.

"Well, in that case, I do have something to say." Galt took the mike from the reporter's hand. He looked up at the speaker's platform.

On the platform, Ruairi MacDonald stood defiant, with a stain of fresh blood showing on his bandaged head. Jilaquns and now Jan stood beside him. The panoply of an affair of state had produced a lull in the middle of the demonstration, like the eye of a hurricane. At its edges, police were dragging protesters across the snow like toboggans towards the paddy-wagon. Other Avalon students were locked in swaying consoling hugs. A gas cannister, thrown back by the gloved hand of a protester, was spinning on the ground, spraying smoke in a wide circle. The members of the arrest team were conferring together, uncertain of what to do. Clio was watching them tensely, her sad, tired, janitorial eyes suddenly alive with flame and the hackles on her back raised like nightsticks. From her throat came a low blood-curdling growl.

Galt faced the eye of the camera squarely. "This demonstration is happening because the government is destroying your sons' and daughters' futures. Instead of creating an educated workforce, it is letting the nation collapse into a Third World wage economy."

"What does that mean, Mr. President?"

"Actually, I'm Provost. It means that these kids will end up serving hamburgers at the local fast-food outlet. They'll never buy a home; they may never afford to have kids of their own. What the government has done to this generation is a national tragedy."

"How's that?" Galt said to the Newspulse reporter.

"Great!"

"I've got something else to say."

"Okay – roll."

Galt took the mike. "If this Administration privatizes universities, it will make knowledge a private property owned by the corporations. But knowledge is the air we breathe if we are to be free individuals in a free society."

Then the back door of the limousine opened and Jerónimo got out, wearing a beret. He was followed by Jennifer D'Arnay in old faded jeans decorated with a great peace sign and a huge rose extending in crimson thread up the seam.

"Good grief! It's Mom – this is the end!" Jan leaned her head in a gesture of defeat against MacDonald's shoulder.

A large force of police in riot gear began pouring out of a side street. They formed a line on the Legislature steps, waiting for orders. Closer to the speaker's platform, the police captain, like a referee after a bench-clearing hockey brawl, was pointing to Jilaquns and MacDonald, signifying arrests. The arrest team started to approach, loosening the handcuffs dangling from their belts.

Lewin called up to the platform. "Quick – into the limo!"

Immediately, the Avalon student bodyguard channelled Mac, Jill and Jan into the limo. Galt gave a final affectionate wave as the door closed.

"My motorcycle!" bawled MacDonald out the window of the limo as it drove off in a rush, with police and demonstrators hopping out of the way. The police captain found himself cocooned in an affectionate hugging scrum formed by Ashley and the Womyn's Rugby Team.

"Well," declared Jerry Lewin. "That's the best demo' I've ever been in – I mean in terms of getting a complex message across to the media." He took a handkerchief out of his pocket and blew his nose. "We might as well go and have a cappuccino at Harbourfront."

"That's a good idea. There's nothing left for us to do," agreed Jerónimo.

"Nonsense!" Jennifer exclaimed. "I didn't fly all this way for nothing." She tossed her blond hair in the breeze from off the lake.

"Follow me!" she called to the Avalon students, who were standing in angry chattering groups.

"The poor dears are full of anger and they don't know what to do with it. Anger is a weapon. Learn to use it!" she shouted, leading a group of students towards the avenue that ran down to Harbourfront.

The demonstration, having lost its vanguard, lost its power and relapsed into its former holiday mood. The gusts of wind from the harbour blew the tear gas away. Oblivious to the full nature of what had appeared to be skirmishing at the front, the various university bands broke into their football songs. The demonstration organizer resumed his place on the speaker's platform and gazed sadly at the overturned and broken speakers lying on the ground. The Metro Newspulse team gathered its equipment together while seagulls circled overhead and the pigeons flew in and out of the stone-work of the Legislature.

27

Professor Ruairi MacDonald laughed a laugh that was last heard at the victory of Prestonpons in 1745. However, he did not look the least like a Jacobite warlord. With his head re-bandaged so thickly that he seemed to be wearing a turban, and with white hair flowing out to join his beard, and with flowers of every kind heaped about his bed, he looked more like a distinguished swami. The window was open and a warm night breeze rustled the flowers. At the bottom of the bed, Jilaquns held the professor's injured leg in her lap and with surgical magic markers was tracing the formlines of Haida mythcreatures in red and black on his plaster cast.

"I did 305 clicks on a Kawasaki Black Missile once."

"Aye, but you have to keep yer heid down, lassie, or you're sucked right off the damn thing. Even at 280 it's dangerous."

"Still, I'll take a 150-horse ZX-II Ninja over everything. Even at 200 clicks they're just loafing along."

"Give me ma auld Hawg back. I'm too old for this banzai stuff."

"Why does Kawasaki make such fast choppers?"

"Och, it's the horsepower wars. Ever since their 250 C.C. Samurai in 1967, they've always had the fastest bikes."

A glorious bunch of daffodils was carried in by a nurse and arranged with the other flowers.

"'Will ye nae come back again?' with love and respect from Faith Rackstraw," the nurse said, reading the card in a voice of announcement, like a court herald. She was plainly in awe of MacDonald. "You were great on the national news last night."

> *Old MacDonald – he's no good;*
> *Chop him up for kindling wood,*

chanted MacDonald, repeating an old childhood rhyme.

"How are you feeling, really?" Jennifer D'Arnay asked.

MacDonald, looking at Jilaquns and Jan, considered the question with interest.

"I feel pairrfect."

Jerry Lewin was putting the camcorder into its carrying-case.

"Tell them they've got to run the situation back in their reading to the rise of merchant banking in the twelfth century," MacDonald said. "That will put the lecture in perspective. Now, where's that Robyn?"

"I am here," said Robyn Endicott.

"For the Joint Committee meeting, what you've got to do, laddie, is this … "

"I am not a 'laddie.' Please don't call me that."

"Well, whatever ye are — you've got to stuff their unwilling snouts in the 1994 judicial ruling on the ownership of the pension surplus. Tell ' em we'll go to Arbitration before they spend a penny of the surplus on our own retirements."

"Is there anything else?"

"I wish I had a wee dram ta drink."

Jan took the plastic orange juice container from the bedside table and held it out to MacDonald, who scowled at it, then finally took a swallow.

"We have won a great battle," he declared moodily, "in a war that was lost before it was started."

"I don't know about that," Jennifer retorted. "Would you put your money on a place like Avalon if you were an investor? The place is ungovernable. A university full of gays and dykes? I can just see that going down in Hugh's boardroom."

"I don't think it was such a good idea to go down and picket Andromeda Place," Jerónimo said from his chair in the corner of the room. Jerónimo, also hemmed in by flowers, looked like a lesser Jainist sage.

"I had to do it! As soon as I figured out Hugh's shell game, I took the first flight over. Besides, I've wanted to shout 'fuckhead' up at him from his office sidewalk for three years."

Jennifer, sitting on the ledge of the second window, was still dressed in her Sixties jeans and T-shirt, with red, yellow and blue ribbons twined in her hair.

"But what are we going to do now?" asked Jan in her practical daughter taking-care-of-fruitcake-mother persona.

"Naething! Let us savour the victory. That's all we can do."

There was a knock, and the hospital room door swung open to admit Cameron Galt.

"Ah, Cameron! Wasn't that a victory now?"

"Hello, Mac. Hi, everybody. Whatever it was, it sure put Avalon on the national media map."

"Sit ye doun, laddie. I regret I have nothing t' offer ye but orange juice."

Galt took a seat on the other side of the bed behind a pot of azaleas and smiled at Jan briefly. Jan smiled back. Then Galt spoke seriously:

"Mac, I got a teleconference message from Hugh D'Arnay a few moments ago. I've got to tell you that the deal has gone through with Wu."

There was a tremendous groan from the bed. Jan looked out the window at the hospital lawn, feeling the room fill with hopelessness.

"D'Arnay wants me to tell you this myself before you launch another Highland charge. I thought I'd better come up and break the news."

"I'm past leading charges," MacDonald said wearily. "We made some history – and tis over."

"Wu U.," Jerónimo said suddenly, laughing like a child.

"Sanitized corporate education brought to you by the country's fastest-growing invisible software firm," Lewin said.

MacDonald did not join in the laughter.

"I loved the univairsity dairly. Every stone in the place told a story."

"Well, you can't just lie there like a defeated clan chief with your leg in the lap of your royal footholder," Jennifer exclaimed.

"I am *not* a footholder," said Jilaquns. With the red and black felt pens from the nursing station she had transformed the entire plaster cast on MacDonald's left leg into an elaborate totem pole.

"The aboriginal Celts – if I may use that term – derived their kingship from the land," MacDonald explained. "The land gave the chief the right to rule. The relationship was symbolized by the king placing his foot in the lap of a virgin."

Jilaquns put her head back and laughed a loud eagle laugh. "My virginity has grown back mysteriously."

"That's interesting," Jennifer said. "The image survives in the King Arthur stories. The sword of kingship is given to Arthur by the Lady of the Lake. After he dies, Excalibur has to be thrown back into the lake."

"I wonder if Dad is going to change the Avalon symbolism," Jan mused out loud. "Andromeda Toy University."

Nobody laughed. Suddenly, in the silence, from his chair in the corner of the room, Jerónimo said matter-of-factly, "So? Why you don't assert your right to the land?"

"Are you talking to me?" Jilaquns asked.

"You own the land, don't you? Why don't you assert your right?"

"Holy shit!" Jilaquns got up swiftly, letting MacDonald's leg fall to the bed with a thump. "An aboriginal land claim!"

"Sure, why not? You own the land, don't you?"

"Whoopee!" yelled Jenny D'Arnay from her place on the window ledge.

"The McIsaacs Treaty of 1921. The whole Kenomagaywakon Valley was given to the Anishnaabe," Jilaquns said. "The treaty has been violated – although its legal validity is still in question."

"*Dis-pute it!*" roared MacDonald. "Dis-pute it, lassie. That'll tie 'em up in the courts for a century!"

"I think you should call in the American Indian Movement," Jan suggested. "Just to make the point."

"Precisely!" yelled Lewin. "Bring in AIM and start by putting a symbolic ownership perimeter around Teaching Rocks College."

"Set up sweat lodges and the whole bit," said Jennifer with a mad exultancy. "Issue passports."

"We'll want something back for this," Jill observed, looking uneasily at Galt. "Our PH.D. in Aboriginal Metaphysics; a Human Rights policy; maybe rename the university. Oh yeah – and that asshole Bosko has to go."

"I'm not in a position to do any negotiating, you understand. But if demands are made, I'll certainly talk," Galt said slyly.

"Give them everything they ask for," MacDonald said, breaking the first rule of negotiating.

"If the Center for the First Nations helps assert the Anishnaabe land claim, you'll need to get the faculty behind it," Galt said to MacDonald.

"Naw, laddie. Dinni ye see I'm finished? I'm a spent force. All I want to do is destroy myself."

"Nobody else can hold the family together," Lewin pleaded. "C'mon be our Laird again."

"Don't want tae. All that laird stuff is nonsense – and ye know it!" MacDonald laid his head on the pillow and closed his eyes as if to show that no more could be expected of him. "Let Robyn do it – he's a stout laddie. I dinna ken what makes him go, but he has the mark of a leader on him." Then MacDonald laid his great turbaned head on the pillow and began to look out the window. "Tell the nurse when you go out that I need some more Demerol."

★　　★　　★

Later that night, after all the company had departed, MacDonald woke up from his stupor to find that someone had entered the room. The small bedside lamp was on, but it was hardly needed because the room and all its flowers was bathed in the cold spectral light of a full moon. The full moon wasn't needed either because MacDonald, in his delusion, had no desire to distinguish the figure, who was Cameron Galt.

"What is it ye want? Go away. I'm nay ready t'come wi' ye," MacDonald said, as if Galt was a minor functionary sent by the devil to collect his soul. Galt was tiptoeing discreetly toward the window when the phone rang. The huge hand of Ruairi MacDonald fumbled with the receiver. A full five seconds passed before the professor, responding to years of habit, whispered hoarsely into the phone:

"Mac–Don–ald speakin'."

The sweetest voice imaginable was on his phone. "Turn off your light and look out the window," it said. It was the silvery voice of moonlight itself – one of God's angels come to the window to take his soul to heaven.

Gentle Ruairi, heart of gold,
always does what he is told,

MacDonald muttered to himself, repeating another rhyme from his childhood. Could he manage it to the window? *Crash!* He had knocked over something. Flowers. Flowers from the funeral home. There!

MacDonald hung his head out the window under a February moon. There was movement against the snow-white lawn. Girls! Girls they were. And they were dancing in a circle in the moonlight. Fire was coming out of their upstretched hands. "Selkies!" exclaimed MacDonald. "The dance of the fairy folk, to be sure! Och – I niver thocht I had seen it!" The girls danced in a wild circle, naked, their bodies gleaming in the moonlight. They danced in and out of each other's shadows. "Shadows?" thought MacDonald. "Then they canna' be fairies. But they're sure bonny, whitever they are."

MacDonald watched as long as he considered it polite to overlook a sacred dance. Then he hauled himself back to his bed and closed his eyes contentedly.

"The Graces – that's what they are! Ah – Redemption is nigh."

At the other window, Cameron Galt looked down as Jan D'Arnay and Jilaquns, holding sparklers, danced naked on the hospital lawn joined by Ashley Tiffin and the Avalon Women's Rugby Team.

28

"Can I put you on hold?" Sheena was gesturing from the outer office, trying to catch his attention.

"It's CNN requesting an interview by teleconference."

"Switch them over to Rattenbury – he's the President."

"They say they want background story – the issues behind the demonstration. They want to interview you and some of the student leaders."

"I'll call them back."

Click. "Alright – I'm with you, Hugh."

"I need hardly exaggerate the point that the University is a legal entity owned and managed by the Board of Governors," D'Arnay went on. "And the Board Executive wants senior managers to distance the University as fast as possible from that egregious event."

"What event, Hugh?" asked Galt wearily.

"The demonstration violence. Say it was just a minority of shit–disturbers – every university has them. And you've got to say that as Provost and Dean you're holding these individuals accountable for their actions."

"A minority? But, Hugh – the whole University was there. I was there. I can't delegitimate that. Can you?"

"We're losing alumni donations over this. I've had calls already. Would you send your son or daughter to The Queer University?"

Galt gave the idea a second of reflection. He didn't have any children. But what if he did? Well, why not? Avalon had life, energy, difference, affection.

"In any case, I can't do it, Hugh. You know that. As Provost and Dean I'd be betraying the entire community. And I'm spokesman for the community, for heaven's sake. The University isn't the Board, you know. It's students, alumni, faculty, retired faculty, support staff, and just a handful of administrators. Management is just one ingredient in the mix. We're a family here, the Avalon family."

"I'm looking forward to hearing you explain that to the full meeting of the Board. While you're at it, you can explain what you were doing at the demonstration. I hear you gave a statement to the media."

At the hollowness of the threat, Galt knew that D'Arnay was losing his ground. Would he shift it?

"Then there's the little matter of the incident at the hospital last night. Apparently you were there too. There've been complaints of sexual harassment."

"It's hardly sexual harassment, Hugh. A few students decided to take their clothes off and dance on the hospital lawn."

Galt looked up to see Sheena in the outer office draped over her desk in giggles.

"Also there's talk of the University changing its name," D'Arnay persisted. "Some aboriginal name – I can't pronounce it."

"That's because you're not meant to."

"I heard it has something to do with a native land claim – that the University is on Aboriginal land or some damn thing."

"Well, indeed that is a problem. It seems we built a university right smack in the middle of Anishnaabek treaty land."

"I understand the native students are picketing the Mall. Wu's going to turn into a cyborg when he hears this. He's going to be calling asking what in the hell's going on. What do you suggest I tell him?"

"Tell him … oh, tell him the university is unravelling as it should. Tell him other places take a funding cutback like a kick in the groin. They just crumple over and play dead. Avalon's way of handling a crisis is to throw a carnival."

"When Wu calls, you can explain to him all about carnivals."

"I'll be glad to."

"In the meantime, you might prepare yourself for the Board meeting. Bye."

Galt put down the phone and joined Sheena in the laughter. The entire office staff was laughing.

"I think I'd better get out of here. If you need me I'm at the Food Court."

Galt put on his jean jacket with the lamb's-wool collar. Now a member of the Avalon family, he was dressing the part. He walked out the door of Sears and across to the river footbridge.

"Hi, Professor Galt!"

"Hi!"

The students seems to be claiming him as a special member of the community now. The atmosphere of the place had changed since the demonstration. It was freer, more buoyant. And his position in the oral village had shifted. What had MacDonald said? "You're the new laird now." He didn't feel very much like a laird. But he did feel – well, he felt like a Dean. For the first time in his life he actually felt like a Dean. He was the spokesperson for the academic mission of the university and the teachers and students who pursued it. "The wise leader follows the people," he thought.

"Well, hello, dear colleague!"

"Hello, Giles."

The Acting President moved closer to Galt, assuming the affectionate proximity that only diplomats at a cocktail party can gauge perfectly.

"My, now wasn't that a wonderful demonstration yesterday! You know, I was just saying to Faith Rackstraw that we must do that kind of thing more often."

"We're all very glad you were there, Mr. President."

"Well, I must say I enjoyed it thoroughly. I've always wanted to occupy the Legislature. See you anon – if not sooner."

The Acting President moved on with a friendly wave to whatever mysterious destination he was bound, like a ship under sail.

On the footbridge spanning the river, Galt paused to watch a huge ice flow bump lazily against the shore ice, carried downstream on a black current of water. It was a clear February day, with steam rising in straight columns from the laboratory chimneys of the Ecology Center. To his right the Library jutted out into a bend in the river. To his left was the Great Hall of Cabot. He made his way across the bridge and up the path around the Ecology building to the University Heights Mall.

Approaching, he heard the drums and high-pitched singing. Then, at the Mall entrance, he saw the singers wearing shirts displaying the four-coloured direction wheel of aboriginal America – red, black, yellow, white. Other native students were handing out pamphlets. Some carried cell phones. In the field where Wu's factory was to go they had put up a sweat lodge. Over the Mall entrance was a huge sign:

> *You are on First Nations*
> *Ancestral Land.*

Then, in smaller lettering:

> *You may enter by permission*
> *of the Kenomagaywakon Valley Anishnaabe*
> *First Nation and the Center for*
> *the First Nations of*
> *Keno-mah-gay-wah-kon*
> *Independent University*

The natives had cleverly chosen the Mall as their picketing site, and the shoppers were accepting the leaflets – indeed the whole situation – with an easy grace. D'Arnay would not accept the situation with grace, Galt thought. But he had no alternative. If the Board called in the police to force the issue, the students would simply close the Mall. A day's profits lost. Store owners at D'Arnay's throat. The Board had learned something from last week's demonstration.

"You can go in, whitefellah."

It was Jilaquns, laughing. She was wearing the ceremonial black cloak of her people, with the image of an eagle in red, outlined in mother-of-pearl buttons on the back. Her hair fell in long strands from under a wide-brimmed cedar-bark hat.

"Hi, Jilaquns."

She was evidently giving an interview to a reporter from the Severnville newspaper. She broke off the interview and came over to give Galt a hug. The whole university felt like one big hug today.

Flash!

The reporter's camera caught the moment perfectly.

"Whoops!" Jill said gaily.

"It's okay. I couldn't be in deeper shit," said Galt, feeling again his mood of Nietzschean tragic joy.

"See you later."

Inside the Food Court, Waasagunackank was teaching by the fountain. Better not disturb him. A blinding blue pinpoint of light caught his eye. It was Jerónimo at the far wall of the Food Court, wearing a welder's helmet and looking like a demonic dwarf. Jennifer D'Arnay was tip-toeing carefully through an assembly of metal forms laid out in strange black patterns on the Food Court foyer. Apparently, Jerónimo was erecting a metalwork sculpture.

Galt went over to the pastry shop to get a coffee.

A half-familiar, half-forgotten hand on his shoulder. It was Sally.

"Hi!"

"Hi!"

Pause.

She looked like a first-year student – younger, fresher, at ease. The new leather jacket and the earrings made up that look. And also her hair – she had cut her hair close to the scalp. Galt felt like he was meeting a stranger.

"How're you doing?"

"Fine," Galt said noncommittally. Friendly, but noncommittal.

Pause.

"You seem to have become the hero of the University."

Something for his ego. Why does a woman suddenly care for the man she has left? He decided to refuse the compliment.

"It was everybody's doing. We simply became a community, that's all."

"It's going to be a funny place, isn't it?"

"I think it always was a funny place."

Galt realized that he was talking distantly – like a dean to a faculty member. That seemed about right for his feelings.

"After the demonstration, Hannah and I had a great talk about changing the name of the department from Women's Studies to Gender Studies."

"Why not Lesbian Studies? Come out in the open?"

He did not say this bitterly or sardonically. It simply made sense, so he said it.

"I don't think there's as much alternative sexuality around as there pretends to be," Sally said. "It's the flavour of the month."

He didn't say anything to that. Fortunately. Instead, he gazed into Sally's eyes. They no longer had that pleading distant contact-lens look. Over her shoulder, he saw the broad back and tumbling chestnut hair of Hannah waiting at a Food Court table.

"Well, I guess we have to get together sometime."

"Yes, we should," Galt agreed.

"Bye."

"Bye."

No, he had really felt nothing. That was interesting. How could you feel nothing about someone you'd shared your life with? He had read somewhere that the Neoplatonists believed how souls that were meant for each other had already met in a pre-existing heaven. Sometimes the wrong souls got entangled in the lower world in the swirl of time. Avalon, in this case, was a swirl of time, a sort of six-armed Shiva madly throwing souls together in the most unlikely combinations. He and Jan were one such combination. The heaven of the Neoplatonists must be governed by a Human Rights policy, Galt concluded.

Holding his coffee, he politely joined the fringe of Joe's seminar. Joe was sitting on the fountain ledge in his blue cloth pants and zipper jacket. He nodded his head and seemed to raise his voice a little when he saw Galt.

"It comes from the West, from the thunder spirits. Water is the life-gift from the West. You see, each of the four directions is a spirit who gives us things necessary for life: the North, that's the air; East is food; South in the sun – and the West is water. Water is very important to the Anishnaabek. We think of it as the veins that flow through the Earth – through our Mother's body. All the lakes and streams and rivers and ponds are our Mother's body. That's why it is the women who are the caretakers and carriers of water. They look after the water in the ceremonies – they carry it and pray for it. It is women who give birth to human beings – spirit beings – through water."

There were a few aboriginal students, but most of the group were shoppers. Their shopping carts, full of bags of groceries, were parked by the fountain.

"Maybe one of you bought a bottle of water today. Isn't that a funny thing? Maybe you paid $1.39 for it. You paid $1.39 for something that is sacred. Isn't that a funny thing now?"

"I guess that fountain is sort of funny too, Joe," one of the students ventured.

Joe turned to look at the fountain statue of the Lady of the Lake, her arm holding the sword Excalibur high above red basalt rocks.

"Naw – I kinda' like it. Someone is still trying to honour the water spirits. Someone is still trying to remember. You see, power comes out of the water. It goes back into it in the end. Water is sacred to Europeans too. Every spring in the forest is the place of a goddess. Water is sacred everywhere. That's what the fountain means to me."

Joe fell into one of his musing silences, as if waiting to hear what more the water spirit had to say to him.

"Anyways, this fountain is a kind of reference point. It's a reference point for people who come here to trade. And eat burgers."

The listeners laughed at Joe's wit.

"Same with us – the rivers are our reference points. The Creator put us here on Turtle Island, and the rivers are our highways."

Joe looked at his feet for a time, deep in thought. No more teachings were coming. The students and shoppers started to stretch their legs slowly.

"Can I get you a coffee, Joe?"

"Yeah, get me a coffee. That would be very good. Hi, Cameron!"

Galt came over and sat beside Joe on the ledge of the fountain as the students dispersed.

"How are you doing, Joe?"

"Great! I like it here. See? – I'm telling stories in the market-place. Much better than being in a classroom."

Galt laughed amiably. "Keno-mah-gay-wah-kon," he said, gesturing toward the Food Court. "The College of the Teaching Rocks."

"It makes some kinda' sense," Joe said. "The water is gone from under the real Teaching Rocks – up at Stoney. You can't hear the water spirit under the rocks up there no more since the government fiddled the water level on the lakes with all those dams." Joe turned and looked at the fountain again. "Maybe the water spirit has come down here instead."

Joe was silent for a while. Then his eyes sparkled again.

"The University of Turtle Island. Hey – that's much easier to say. Maybe we should call this place the University of Turtle Island. You like that, Cameron?"

Galt didn't know whether he liked it or not. The idea struck from such an odd angle that he didn't know what to make of it. Typically, his response was a managerial reflex.

"We'd have to get the Legislature to change the statute incor-porating the University."

"Sure, get it changed," Joe said, as if altering an act of the Legis-lature was the easiest thing in the world to do. "Thanks," he said to the student who had brought him his coffee. "Cam – whatya' say we go and see what they're making over there?"

On the far wall, Jerónimo had just mounted another piece of

scrap iron and was standing back to survey it. The pieces were discarded parts of electrical machinery – generators and transformers – from the local factory that had once made the equipment for the power dams on the Kenomagaywakon River. Twisted pieces of metal that had hit the assembly-room floor.

Jerónimo lifted his welder's mask. "So? What do you think?"

They looked at a row of huge terrifying humanoid figures of varying sizes fixed to the wall. Round pieces of equipment used for eyes, for genitalia, electrical circuit parts used for brains, arms gesturing crazily. It was as if the spirits of the Industrial Revolution had come unstuck from their original machines and were rising up in the faces of their makers in proletarian revenge. The motif of the proletariat was suggested not so subtly in crossed hammers and sickles which Jerónimo had welded into the hands of several of the figures.

Joe shook his head in mirthful astonishment.

"It looks like a ten-ton charge of Spanish black bulls," Jenny offered.

Jerónimo lifted up the metal plaque on which he had engraved the title of the work. "It's called 'Nightmare of a Capitalist,'" he announced.

"When Giles Rattenbury invited you to do a sculpture for the Food Court, I'm sure he never thought you'd do this," Galt said.

"If the University is sold, we will leave traces of ourselves behind for people to wonder at," Jerónimo said with satisfaction.

Jennifer gestured towards the sculpture. "The last act of the Industrial Revolution occurs in Severnville."

"I better finish this up," Jerónimo said, looking at the remaining forms on the floor.

"We're going to New York. They're doing a retrospective of Jerónimo's work there," Jennifer explained.

"That's wonderful!" Galt said.

Out of the corner of his eye he saw Sheena Meganetty coming into the Food Court.

"Oh, oh!"

Sheena picked her way excitedly through the cafeteria tables.

"Hello, everybody," she said breathlessly. Then she took Galt aside. "You're to call Mr. D'Arnay on the teleconferencer. Right away. I thought I'd better come over and tell you."

Jennifer overheard Sheena's breathless whispering. "Allow me. I'll be glad to take the call for you."

"I'm about to be fired," Galt said buoyantly.

"We all wish to be with you when you're fired," Jennifer declared. "Especially me − I've been fired before by the jerk."

"Is there a teleconference station around here?"

Sheena nodded. "Over there − under the escalators."

Minutes later, Galt and Sheena, Jennifer and Jerónimo, and Joe were crowded around the videophone. "Not one of you says a word, alright? Not even a sigh. And stay out of range of the camera, whatever you do."

"Not if you're going to be sacked, I won't," Jennifer said.

Sheena punched in the return-path code. The great Andromeda Spiral appeared on the screen. Then the image dissolved into a weary-looking Hugh D'Arnay.

"It looks like the face of God," said Jerónimo.

"Sssh!"

"Cameron? I'm recording this because I've got to go to a meeting. I'll make it quick. There's a clause in the contract with Mr. Wu in which we attest that apart from its public ownership, which the government was prepared to sign over, there is no other party having a claim against the university or any ownership interest in it. Standard clause in property transfer situations, right? Now, Wu has got wind of the First Nations land claim, and he's backing out."

The image of Hugh D'Arnay turned severe.

"He also heard about the incident at the Legislature."

D'Arnay held up a piece of paper.

"For your information, his words were 'I didn't know the Cultural Revolution was still going on.' Those were his words … "

"Yippee!" yelled Jennifer.

" … *Call me tonight and we'll try and figure out what to do. The Board meeting is cancelled.*"

The face of Hugh D'Arnay paused for a second, perplexed.

"*God, I hate this University.*"

The image of the Andromeda Spiral came back on, one of its arms appearing to sag. Sheena switched the machine off.

Jenny took Galt's hands and did a little dance. "Ding–dong, the witch is dead!" she sang. Jerónimo gave Galt a great hug and kisses on each cheek. Sheena was jumping up and down with glee. Only Joe kept his composure.

"The University of Turtle Island," he said solemnly.

"The Queer University," Sheena added.

"The nightmare of a capitalist," said Jerónimo.

"Camelot," Jennifer said, starting to sing from the musical.

Epilogue
APRIL

Bud Lassiter closed the window blind to a sharp ray of spring sun-shine that fell across his desk. He buzzed for his assistants. But first, he cleared all the paperwork out of sight – the examination sched-ule, the Spring Convocation list, the summer-course offerings, the two letters received from angry parents about the demonstration. An executive should have no paper material visible on his desk – it set a good example. Besides, a perfectly bare desk was intimidating.

Blake McCabe, dressed in his perpetual jock outfit, came in carrying the updates, followed by Kayte Bubbins with her camp counsellor's clipboard held defensively against her bosom.

"Okay, kiddies. Situation report. What's the damage?"

McCabe reported first while the Registrar typed the figures into the tote program which was copied onto the "plasmavision" wall display.

"On the incoming side, we're down four scholarship prospects since nine a.m. yesterday. Two went to Metro, one to the Country Club, and one went out west."

The figures on the screen changed while Blake spoke.

"Okay. Now transfers – outgoing. What've you got?"

"I lost a couple of bods," Kayte said.

"Anyone give a reason?"

Kayte sighed. "Yeah, the usual: Avalon's wild and hairy; it's stuck in cause heaven; it's full of screaming lesbians."

"Alright – let's hear it for the screaming lesbians. Pluses."

"Twelve since our last situation meeting – and all scholarships," McCabe reported. "Some from the West Coast. Plus nine from the reserves – sorry, I mean the First Nations."

"Doggone!" said the Registrar as the wall display changed.

Kayte could barely contain her excitement. "Wait'll you hear this, chief! I got twenty-three transfers yesterday – most of them schol-arship-level. I mean, they faxed their transcripts from their home universities and everything. Lots of enquiries about global issues, cultural studies, ecology, alternative sexuality, aboriginal learning."

Lassiter considered that Kayte Bubbins had an unusually idiotic brightness as she reported this, as if the influx of scholarship students wanting to switch to Avalon were all her doing. Which could hardly be the case.

"Jeez! – look at all the first-choice switches! That's 547 more first-years than this time last year." Lassiter did some more calculations on the computer. "Plus 332 upper-year transfers. We're back in business, kiddies!"

Blake McCabe and Kayte Bubbins beamed radiance. Lassiter ignored them.

"Whoops! What's this?" Lassiter blinked at the monitor. "What happened to our returning students? Did they forget to pre-register? Are they going to make their minds up in the Fall? Or what?"

Kayte cleared her throat nervously. "What I'm hearing is they're going to study with the retired profs at the Mall. Instead of taking our courses for credit, I mean."

"They are, are they? We'll see about that!" said the Registrar grimly. "In any case, our enrolment's up 26 per cent. Holy horse! It's crashing all across the post-secondary system, and Avalon's up 26 per cent. Are we sitting pretty or what?"

"We don't have room for them all, boss," McCabe pointed out.

"Truer words were never spoken! We're going to have to lighten ship." Lassiter accessed the local Polytechnical Institute records. "Let's see how the poor folks on the other side of the tracks are doing. Hmm! Down 17 per cent and falling. Don't look good, don't look good. I wouldn't want to be in their galoshes."

Lassiter smiled sagely at his assistants. "That's what happens to you if you don't adapt to the changing times."

"Are you going to ditch the Law Enforcement majors, boss?"

Lassiter waved McCabe's question away and typed furiously. For answer, he erased the wall display and flashed his e-mail message on the screen.

As you can see we're swamped with scholarshippers. How about you taking back all the Law Enforcement majors, effective immediately, plus Nurses who haven't declared a parallel major here. Bud-the-Knife.

Lassiter drummed fingers on teak, waiting for the response. Then the pitiful reply came on the projection screen.

Okay.

"Way to go, big guy!"

"That means Vic Bosko's out of here," said Kayte.

"Yep! That dude's goose was cooked the day he came to Av. Sooo, babies – we punch in the anticipated returnees ... "

Tap, tap.

" ... then we subtract the Cops and Nightingales, and ... "

The new enrolment flashed on the screen.

"Gollie!" said Bubbins. "We don't have enough teachers!"

"Don't worry your little socks off, kiddies. We can jack up the college ancillary fees and throw the extra money into part-time sessionals. Plus, we can switch over to a three-term system. Build up the Summer School. Like, pronto."

"I always wanted us to do that," said Kayte. "It's so beautiful here in the summer with the river and everything."

"Hard to crack the books though," McCabe put in.

"'Every little breeze seems to whisper Louise,' eh?"

"What boss?"

"It's an old song."

"Oh!"

"Okay, children. Before you go. What's the little lesson you draw from all of this?"

McCabe went blank. Then he remembered the sign that Lassiter had hung up in the assistants' office.

"Uh – the bee that gets the honey doesn't hang around the hive?"

"No, Blake."

The Registrar's voice had the long-suffering restraint of a primary school teacher.

"The lesson is – generalist adaptability wins out over specialized adaptation every time. The system that doesn't have built-in adaptive potential goes under. And that's why we're surviving while all around us the dinosaurs are falling."

"But Avalon didn't do anything, boss. It's the other universities that all changed," Kayte said.

"Yeah – we clung to our principles," Blake agreed.

"That's what I meant," said Lassiter. "Principles is what counts."

"Right, boss."

"You guys are going to be counselling all sorts of people you never knew existed. Unique and alien life-forms. Better retool your counselling skills. Find out what lesbians eat for breakfast, eh Kates? Try not putting your hair in a ponytail. Get a new set of threads, preferably black, eh Blake? Remember – you're entertainment officers on the cruise ship Avalon on its voyage to strange new worlds."

★   ★   ★

Professor Ruairi MacDonald leaned on his crutch in the warm spring sunshine outside his office. He was wearing his kilt, the better to scratch at the skin under the plaster cast that ran up to his thigh and, in his words, to "perform his ablutions." On the grass of Cabot College, students in denim cut-offs and tank-tops were tossing a frisbee, their flesh released from five months of winter clothing. The sound of a baroque recorder trilled from a residence window. It was exam week, but on an April day like this even exams were a relaxing of the long pressures of winter. A residence cat rolled deliriously on the hot cement path. Armadas of geese trumpeted northward high above the Library. Soon the fish would be swimming upriver to their spawning grounds.

MacDonald, feeling some obscure stirring of ancestral urges deep in his own prehistory, reached out toward his Favourite Student for support.

"'A correct professional relationship is arm's length ... plus an inch,'" Jilaquns quoted.

"Och, lassie – ye'll be the death of me!"

Jilaquns was wearing her skin-tight leather pants, biker boots and a chain-link metal bra. Her lip ornament and medicine pouch proclaimed her membership in a thirty centuries old aristocratic matriarchy. She reached into her medicine pouch and pulled out the draft Avalon Human Rights Policy.

"No!" shuddered MacDonald. "Not that!"

"*Harassment means engaging in a course of vexatious conduct, including verbal conduct, of a serious or overt nature, that is based on a prohibited ground of discrimination which is known or ought reasonably be known to be unwelcome,*" she intoned.

"Not here, Jilly! Not now! There are students watching."

"*Every person has a right to be free from sexual solicitation,*" she went on, "*or advance made by a person in a position to confer, grant or deny a benefit to the person where the person making the solicitation or advance knows or ought reasonably to know that it is unwelcome, or ...* "

Jilaquns took a deep breath and licked her lips.

"Don't leave me hanging, girl – get on with it!"

" *... or a reprisal or a threat of reprisal for the rejection of a sexual solicitation or advance.*"

At the sound of these solemn cadences of negation, four centuries of Puritan denial came to a boil in the complex depths of Ruairi MacDonald. A libido, defined and cross-defined by networks of interlocking vetoes promulgated by endless committees of Presbyters, Dissenters and Covenanters, overwhelmed him.

"Let's do it! Let's do it now!" he said.

"Right now? In the Cabot quad?"

"No lassie. In the Dean's Office."

A smile passed over the face of Jilaquns of Qaysun. It was like the shadow of a raven passing over a Pacific beach.

"Look how this univairrsity has deranged me! It had addled me completely, to be sure. Why – it has driven me to seek my pleasures in their opposites!"

"'The way up and the way down are the same,'" observed Jilaquns, quoting Heraklitos.

"But first, my sporran!" exclaimed MacDonald. "The occasion calls for the dress of ma ancestors."

MacDonald kept the dress sporran next to his PH.D. robes in his office, ready for Convocation. But this was an occasion greater than any Convocation. MacDonald, tempered into the tension of claymore steel by the conflict of duty and desire, knew that he was at the threshold of the most forbidding negation open to an academic. That negation was Freely Chosen Early Retirement – in a word, Resignation.

Alone now in the comforting familiarity of his office, the very thought of it produced a sudden weakening of resolve, a loss of courage. Could he do it this time? Only a salary in excess of one hundred thousand dollars plus untold pension benefits stood in his way. MacDonald examined the hang of his kilt. Then he checked the contents of his sporran. He fitted the *skene dhu* into the stocking of his good leg. The smell of the Pacific against the coast of the Queen Charlotte Islands washed over him. Maybe he would open a hardware store there and banter with the fishermen.

"Goodbye, books," he said wistfully.

The books he had known and loved, lined up like clansmen to say farewell, seemed to salute him. He closed the office door for the last time.

Outside, Jilaquns was waiting by her motorcycle, her knapsack slung over her brown shoulder.

"Dump the crutch – then you won't be tempted to come back. I'll take you over on the bike."

MacDonald threw the crutch into the Kenomagaywakon River. He watched, half-expecting a nymph's arm to reach out of the water, wave, and take it under.

Moments later, Jill's motorcycle blasted down the curving main drive of the university, the professor driving, the princess behind him holding down his kilt.

"I must give the motorcycle a wee workout first," MacDonald declared. "That will help me ta achieve the necessary courage."

★   ★   ★

At Lady Sears College, Galt pushed the last file away and yawned in the April sunlight. In the outer office, Sheena and the secretaries were singing along to Anne Murray's "You Needed Me" on the radio. It had been a good morning. He had cajoled another faculty member into taking Volunteer Early Retirement. The list was practically complete. Among the significant holdouts, Faith Rackstraw remained. She was part of the original architecture of the place; it would take a bulldozer to get her out of here.

A motorcycle blasted by his window.

"It's Jill and Big Mac," Sheena called out. "It looks like he's finally going to do it this time."

"He'll have to get his grades in first," said the Dean.

"They've done this six times before," Sheena added helpfully. "They go up and down the River Road summoning up the nerve. Usually they chicken out and go over to the Food Court Dairy Queen for a Peanut Buster Parfait."

★   ★   ★

"I canna do it!" bawled MacDonald as the towers of Avalon University came back into view. "I dinna hae' the courage of my convictions. This place has besotted me too much!"

He reached into his own medicine pouch – but Jill's hand was there first. She extracted the flask of single malt Highland whiskey made at the distillery where the ferry leaves for Skye.

"You shouldn't drink this stuff," she said, tipping her head back and draining the entire contents of the bottle. She flung the empty bottle in a graceful curving arc into the Kenomagaywakon River. "You people can't handle it."

"He'll put me on the Shuttle-bus and Parking Lots Committee."

Automatically, Jilaquns reached into her medicine pouch. "I am you. That also is you." She seemed to be referring to clause 12(c) of the Human Rights Policy, which she proceeded to whisper into the professor's ear: "*The decision shall be implemented by the Provost and Dean, or other appropriate university official, through administrative procedures or disciplinary action ... *"

"Lower down ... No, you fool ... lower down on the page!"

" *... Possible sanctions include verbal or written apology, written reprimand, barring from the campus, transfer, demotion ... *"

"Och, I love it!" MacDonald screamed. From out of his childhood memory came Question Eighteen of the Presbyterian Shorter Catechism, which he proceeded to recite in the words of the first (1647) edition: "'*Question:* Wherein consists the sinfulness of that estate whereinto man fell? *Answer:* The sinfulness of that estate whereinto man fell, consists in the guilt of Adam's first sin, the want of original righteousness, and the corruption of his whole nature, which is commonly called Original Sin; together with all actual transgressions which proceed from it.'"

" *... suspension, mandatory training / education ... *"

"How d'ye have such power over me?"

" *... dismissal or expulsion.*"

"Wonderful!" said the professor. "But ... that's draft four you're reading. Draft three works better for me."

The motorcycle came to a squealing stop in the parking lot beneath Galt's window.

"I wouldn't have believed it – but the stars never lie. Jupiter is leaving the house of plenty," Sheena commented.

Seconds later, MacDonald was standing in the Dean's Office, saying the words he thought he'd never say:

"I'm workin' in a salt mine … and there's nae more salt!"

"Are you sure you want to do it this way, Mac? If you took the buyout, you'd leave with a lot more."

"You've accumulated eight Earned Years of Service," Sheena added.

"Gie' them to some puir beggar that needs them. This is the only honourable road. I dinna want t'end up rotting in the Food Court trying to remember the clauses on Sexual Harassment."

"You've been our Laird of Avalon always," Sheena began sentimentally … "

"Aye. And now I must go. Goodbye, Cam. Ye're a guid mon."

MacDonald extended a mighty handshake, which became a hug. Jilaquns joined the hug. Sheena too, her eyes streaming with tears.

"Avalon will never be the same," cried Sheena, beginning a moist Irish lament. "It is the end of our time, to be sure."

"Stop yer greitin, woman. 'Tis a better place to where I'm going."

Galt and Sheena escorted the couple to the door.

"Farewell, Cameron of Locheil. And please – please don't let them emeritize me."

★   ★   ★

The motorcycle sped west over the rolling hills of Cavan and Bethany, Jilaquns driving, her favourite professor's kilt tucked under her bum and his cast sticking out at a crazy angle. MacDonald felt the warm wind blowing on his good leg.

"Now this is Academic Freedom!"

"We'll be at the mouth of the Skeena in four days," Jilaquns said. "And then, Haida Gwaay."

"They're trying to make us talk like computer terminals in a pairfectly rational world," MacDonald said. "They've taken away God's greatest gifts to man – Sin in this world … and Redemption in the next."

"You Christians are so exotic."

"Nobody is going to erase my personality!" MacDonald yelled.

"The old people called them *Xhaaidlagha Gwaayaay*. The Islands at the Boundary of the World."

"Aye – the Outer Isles." MacDonald began to sing the first bars of 'The Road to the Isles.' I'll build us a castle there."

Jilaquns of the Sealion clan of Qaysun laughed unending peels of Eagle laughter. She reached into her medicine pouch for the Avalon Human Rights Policy and flung it over her shoulder.

"We won't need that anymore," she said.

The document lay by the roadside, its pages inspected random-ly by the wind.

★   ★   ★

At the Virtual Café the umbrella tables were set out on the patio on this first spring day. Jerry Lewin sat at one of them, gazing through sun-glasses at students who had looked so different only a month before. The transition from winter to spring evoked a change in style and personality. As if emerging from a cocoon of heavy-mindedness, the students were now all body, wearing shorts and tank-tops. To Lewin, they looked like so many shoots of plants springing out under the sun. Thinking reeds. Jan herself, across the table from him, seemed especially reed-like with her bare legs draped over the arm of her chair, swinging lazily.

"It's sad you're retiring. You're a wonderful teacher, you know."

"No, my dear. I'm not. However, it's kind of you to say so in any case."

"But you are, really."

Lewin raised his sun-glasses and looked at Jan sternly. "Young lady, you fail to discern the obvious: I have nothing to teach."

"C'mon, Jerry. Look what you did for Ashley. She's flying from strength to strength. Next year she's running the Student Union."

Lewin pretended to shudder. "In Ashley Tiffin, I fear I have cre-ated a monster."

"Well, you taught me a lot."

"I have taught you nothing. Don't you see? I am a radical deconstructionist. *Ergo*, I have nothing to say. Moreover, I have no grounds on which to say the nothing which I have to say. *Point final!*"

"Socrates was a deconstructionist."

"The comparison is grotesque, my dear. Socrates, at least, had the grace to swallow hemlock just when he was beginning to articulate sclerotic republics. How's that for class? One could say his voluntary early retirement had a certain measure of class."

Lewin twisted and untwisted his serviette frenetically.

"I suspect he saw the degree to which his reading of Pythagoras corrupted him, and therefore he deconstructed himself."

"Pythagoras?"

"And Parmenides too! Disembodied cosmonauts, both of them. Utterly senile. It is terrifying when the student, pushing middle age, nesciently joins his senility to that of his masters. Students should never resemble their teachers."

Lewin gestured toward the patio of the Virt. Groups of students were talking excitedly at the tables as if with the coming of spring they were meeting each other for the first time.

"Rather, the obverse is true: teachers should resemble their students."

"Maybe you're having a mid-life crisis."

Lewin pondered the thought briefly.

"Perhaps. Nonetheless, I am on top of the condition, intellectually. I no longer resemble any of my students – with the possible exception of your esteemed self. I have become unredemptively senile. Power, when it becomes unredemptively senile, tries to configure the cosmos in terms of the one reality that mocks any dream of a managed cosmos – namely, the body. The body and its genealogy, by which I mean time, growth, history, decay. Power tries to close the gap between cosmos and body. And lo! – the ideal state as a human body. The self trying to make itself identical with reality until there's nowhere to shit anymore."

Jan nodded, trying to visualize the metaphor.

Lewin continued, his fingers playing excitedly as if his thoughts were a concert piece being played on an invisible piano.

"So the shit has nowhere to go in the air-tight system. It just thins out and thins out like a membrane between the body and reality. Shit to aerie thinness beat. There's nowhere to put the waste, so it hardens in the categories of the system like cholesterol, causing transient ischemic attacks. Our demonstration last February was one such transient ischemic attack. For a moment, the state forgot where it was."

Apparently satisfied with the perception, Lewin took a sip of his lemonade.

"My mother wanted me to be a neurosurgeon," he confessed.

Jan gazed at Lewin's ever-moving fingers. "You certainly have the nervous energy."

Lewin continued as if he hadn't heard the compliment. "However, there's no stopping that senility. When the body gets old and frail, it tries to monumentalize itself in cosmic harmonies. It seeks to make itself at one with the stars in permanent regions of praise. That, my dear woman, is the modern corporate empire – from Plato's *Republic* to your distinguished father trying to make himself identical with the Andromeda galaxy."

"Now *your* comparison is grotesque. You're not the least bit like my father."

"I am teaching knee-jerk scepticism to an already radically sceptical generation. In doing do, I am merely handing them off to the nihilism of the postmodern corporate world. Besides it's inelegant. Do you see this white hair? I do not wish to be an aging deconstructionist. It is the most graceless thing in the world to be – an aging deconstructionist. Therefore, like Prospero, I intend to drown my books before I do any more damage."

Lewin paused on that note of finality. Perhaps he had been talking too much about himself again.

"What are you going to do?" he asked Jan.

"Oh, I don't know. Save a rainforest or something. I'm not coming back to Avalon."

"You'll come back. They all come back," Lewin said firmly.

"What about you?"

"Ah-ha! I haven't told you. That's because I haven't told anybody. I shall whisper it in your ear."

Jan brought her legs down from the chair-arm and leaned forward like a conspirator.

"I am going to open a theatre in Metro."

"Wow!"

Lewin shot up from the table and became grandiose.

"Yes, boys and girls. The Magic Carnival Theatre is opening in Metro with Yours Truly as artistic manager and director. I intend to direct the wildest and most outrageous theatre the world has ever seen. A theatre dedicated to a single proposition. And what is that proposition, you ask? It is simply this: *Being trumps everything!*"

The students on the patio listened with amusement, then resumed their conversations. Lewin sat down again, regaining his air of seriousness.

"We're going to open with *Hamlet Turning*. But you, young lady, have given me an idea. I shall rewrite the play from Ophelia's point of view."

"Oh! By Being, you mean body."

"Precisely! But I should not wonder at your prescience. As I say, you, after all, provided the idea. Ophelia's was the body that got squeezed out. It got squeezed out in the corporate revenge tragedy."

"Can I play Ophelia? I'll bring my trapeze."

"What a powerful idea! Of course. Ophelia narrates the play from a trapeze at stage left. In stream of consciousness. And stream of gesture. Certainly, my dear colleague. You shall play Ophelia. Ophelia on a trapeze. Hey, that's what we'll call it — *Ophelia on a Trapeze*."

"Cheesy, I think," said Jan.

"Maybe so," agreed Lewin, smiling wickedly. "You must protect me from the excesses of my enthusiasm."

"Or your despondency."

"Indeed. That too."

Jeremy Lewin, ex-professor, and Jan D'Arnay, ex-student, stayed and talked about theatre until the afternoon sun made long shadows across the patio.

★ ★ ★

"Alright – that's the list of next year's sessional positions," Galt said. "Lots of work for the sages in the Food Court. We can get them back into formal teaching where they belong. They're total teaching animals. If that's okay with you, we can sign it off."

Robyn Endicott took the list which Galt extended across her desk. He had called for the meeting in the Dean's Office, but she had suggested they meet here, in her tiny office at the top of the Library.

Galt examined the office while Endicott examined the list. Offices are the bodies of their inhabitants, Galt concluded. In which case, this office had the chaste compactness of Robyn Endicott. No books, no clutter, not even a filing cabinet – just the computer and white walls. And a print of Matisse's dancers that matched her blue eyes. And a small vase in the classical Chinese style holding slender sticks of perfectly arranged pussy willows. It was late in the day, but a setting April sun filled the office with light. The light came from a picture window that looked out over the river turbulent with the spring run-off.

Then Cameron examined Robyn Endicott. She was to be his future bargaining opposite at meetings between the Board and the Faculty Union. She was wearing the black wool sweater and black corduroy pants which seemed a kind of uniform, a collar of a white blouse peeking out above the pullover. The black hair. She seemed trim and asexual, with the strong upper body strength of many of her generation. Perhaps she lifted weights. In truth, Ms. Endicott struck Galt as a complete mystery.

Robyn was looking across at him with her vivid level eyes.

"It's okay, but we can't sign it off. I'm not empowered to do side-table bargaining. It can probably be signed off at the next Joint Committee."

"Oh, 'sign off' was just a metaphor. It wasn't meant to imply a formality."

"A metaphor – I see. Well, this outcome is provisionally acceptable to the Union. You haven't got the average teaching ratio here – but I'd put it at ... let's see ... "

Robyn Endicott did some calculations in her head.

" ... ninety-six students per Full-Time Equivalent faculty. Is that what you've got?"

Galt didn't know whether Robyn had worked out the calculation on the spot, or whether she'd half-prepared it beforehand, or whether it was a probing shot in the dark. In any case, it was an impressive bit of theatrics. She was going to be tough to bargain with.

"Yes, ninety-six. A bit low on the Humanities side, because of the small-group teaching."

Cameron glanced up to see if Robyn agreed with the imbalance. If she did, she wasn't showing it.

" ... high on the Science side because their teaching is done in big lecture courses."

"Sooner rather than later, the Science sector is going to get tired of paying for small-group teaching in the Liberal Arts," Robyn said.

She suddenly stretched her arms and yawned in the sunlight.

"Sorry. In any case, I'm glad we saved the Humanities and Social Sciences."

"I am too. We saved everything – even the Native Studies PH.D. But it's going to be a different sort of university."

Robyn picked up the Voluntary Early Retirement list and surveyed it for a last time.

"Yes, Big Mac, Jerry Lewin, possibly Faith Rackstraw – all

gone. Though it wouldn't surprise me if they came back. They all do, you know."

"They are like gods and heroes," Galt mused. "The age of the gods and heroes is over."

"The age of the ordinary human beings is about to dawn," replied Robyn.

They looked out of the picture window onto the river, and, across the river to the Ecology Center and the illuminated sign of the University Heights Mall. The native land-claim blockade had ended, the issue having disappeared into the courts for half a lifetime. The university was left without a president and with a Chairman of the Board who had suddenly found other interests.

"The University of Turtle Island," Robyn said.

Galt permitted himself another moment of self-congratulation. "We appear to have saved it."

"For a year," Robyn replied carefully. "For a tradition to survive it must be reinvented daily." But then she changed her mood. "Perhaps we can reinvent it so well that one day we will be its gods and heroes."

Galt laughed. "This ordinary human being is hungry. Would you like a bite at the Food Court?"

"That is subject to negotiation," Robyn said, suddenly smiling. "If you'd like to come to my place, we can put together something better."

"No side-table bargaining." Galt joked.

"I don't have a side-table," Robyn Endicott said seriously. "We'll have to eat on the floor."

★   ★   ★

This is almost the end of my story. But I want to take you back once more to the Mall because that is where the story began. It is evening now, and the retired professors are getting ready to start their new Summer-session night classes. Jake Weisberg and Tony

Leland and Joe Waasagunackank are sitting at their Food Court table – the one they usually sit at, by the fig tree. The eternal trickle of water plays off the statue of the Lady of the Lake, more soothing than any piped-in music. Faith Rackstraw is there, and Clio who is rooting for french fries and muffin crumbs.

"I don't know," Jake said. "Teaching was more fun when we didn't get paid. Now I have to order textbooks and educational software and all sorts of crap." He gestured toward a pile of Politics 100 textbooks piled near the computer terminal.

"My educational software is up here," Joe said, tapping his skull.

"My software is becoming rather soft," muttered Tony. "In any case, those books are just for show. Jake says whatever comes into his head anyway." Leland evidently had no texts available for his course in Philosophical Logic.

Faith Rackstraw had textbooks available, however. Editions of Sophocles and Homer and Sappho filled a row of shopping carts lined up beneath the fig tree. "Nevertheless, one must put forth a credible ... er ... *display* of knowledge if the Dean – bless his heart! – is going to allow us to continue teaching in this fashion, out here in public view."

"The Dean had no choice in the matter," Weisberg responded gruffly. "The upper-year students want to take our courses instead of the University's. Avalon was losing income. That's why Galt had to put us on salary."

Leland grinned broadly, showing his new dentures. "And that means we at last have a Dental Plan."

"I guess we gotta' have nice-lookin' teeth for our students," Joe said. "I'm going to the dentist tomorrow."

"Me too. I've got years of dental work saved up." Jake rubbed his jaw doubtfully. "And my wife does as well."

Faith glanced over at Clio. The wolfhound, having checked the garbage bins, was now standing on her hind legs with her paws on the pastry shop counter, where the Avalon student with the crazy eyes was feeding her sausage rolls. "I daresay Clio's teeth require work too. My goodness, she lost three of her teeth at the Demon-stration."

"C'mon," Jake said. "You can't have your dog's teeth fixed on the Dental Plan."

Faith Rackstraw drew herself up stiffly. "I simply don't see why not! The Plan covers same-sex partnerships."

Jake Weisberg laughed heartily. "She may be the same sex, Faith – but she's a goddam dawg."

"I see nothing in Robyn's wording of the Dental Plan that re-stricts ... er ... *spousal* relationships to human beings. Indeed, the words 'human being' do not appear in the language of the Plan at all."

Now Joe and Tony joined in the laughter.

"Just have her teeth fixed and send the bill to Dean Galt."

"Get her fitted with a set of dentures."

"Grieve it, Faith!"

"Why, I believe I shall! It would be the occasion of a perfectly good grievance. Everybody knows that Clio, far from being a 'god-dam dawg,' has been a loyal servant of the University since the day she led the first Convocation."

"We'd better stop this – here come our students," Joe whispered.

The Summer evening course students were beginning to arrive. Some were examining the textbooks which the professors had ar-ranged for sale.

"Heigh-ho!" sang Professor Leland elegiacally. He gathered his Oxford teaching gown around him so it wouldn't run under the wheels of his motorized wheelchair. Then he propelled the chair toward his allocated teaching space near the computer terminal where a sign said: "Philosophy 105: Symbolic Logic."

"No textbooks!" Faith said reprovingly. "You forgot to order them. My, my!"

"Do you know something, Tony?" Weisberg called out impious-ly. "You're going to have a stroke right here in the Food Court of the University Heights Mall, giving your last lecture from memory on Symbolic Logic."

"Not at all!" said Leland blissfully. "Come and see."

The professors went over to where Tony was facing the Avalon computer terminal. Tony punched in an individual access code number. Suddenly the monitor flashed to life, displaying the words:

Alice in Logicland ©

and an image of the White Rabbit anxiously consulting his pocket-watch and beckoning the viewer to follow.

Leland grinned like a maniac. "Just follow the White Rabbit" — he keyed in a command — "down the rabbit hole."

Now the viewers seemed to be falling down a long shaft. But the shaft resembled an underground library, because shelves of books flashed by, their titles indicating classics of Western civilization. Then *thump*!

"Now you're in Logicland," declared Leland as a huge idiotic egg filled the screen.

"State your name and business!"

Humpty Dumpty commanded abruptly.

"He means sign into the course," Leland explained, entering Jake Weisberg's name.

"It's a stupid name!"

Humpty Dumpty interrupted.

"What does it mean? A name must mean something."

"Well, I'll be damned!" said Jake Weisberg.

"I've mapped the Symbolic Logic course onto *Alice's Adventures in Wonderland*," Leland said proudly. "Robyn helped me do it. Do you want to go through the looking glass?"

The professor touched the keyboard. At once, Humpty Dumpty's face dissolved into a chessboard stretching away as far as the eye could see. There was the White Rabbit again, indicating the square from which the player had to begin.

"You proceed through the labyrinth, learning Symbolic Logic interactively from the various teachers, then applying it correctly in looking-glass situations to reach your next square," Leland explained with glee. "Do you wish to meet a teacher?"

Leland tapped a key. Now the monitor was occupied by an immense caterpillar sitting on a mushroom and donishly smoking a pipe.

"What are you called?"

demanded the Caterpillar.

"My name is Jacob D. Weisberg," Leland entered.

"But what are you CALLED?"

repeated the Caterpillar imperiously. Its voice was dry, flat, nasal and urgent, like an Edwardian philosopher.

> *"I already know what your nem is, old boy. You told my deah colleague Humpty Dumpty that your nem is Jacob Weisberg. What I wish to know is — what are you called?"*

"I guess I'm called Jake," Weisberg answered feebly.

Evidently, the machine picked up Weisberg's voice, for the Caterpillar blinked its eyes serenely, and said:

> *"You say you are called 'Jake.' Very good! But that's just what you are called, isn't it? You see, there is your nem, and there is what you are called — that's quite another thing. Indeed, our*

exchange leads me to wonder – do you, in fact, know who you are?"

Jacob D. Weisberg glared blankly at the screen, feeling rising anger. The Caterpillar spoke again:

"Who ARE you?"

At this, it blew a cloud of simulated smoke at Weisberg's face.

"Ectually, old chap, if you don't know who you are, you should really visit the Forest of No Names – shouldn't you? That's the Eighth Square. Simply follow the White Wabbit."

Leland looked up from the console at the others. "This session goes on to teach Russell's Theory of Logical Types. You know – the class cannot be a member of itself, nor can the member of the class be the class itself."

But the others were not listening to him. They were riveted to the face of the Caterpillar. The face of the Caterpillar was growing larger and larger, more and more severe.

"Why, that's *your* face!" exclaimed Rackstraw, for the face on the Caterpillar was now plainly that of Tony Leland.

"And that kinda' sounds like your voice," added Joe.

"You old death-cheater! You've immortalized yourself in cyber-space," remarked Jake Weisberg, feeling betrayed.

"Yes," said Tony Leland joyfully. "I shall go on teaching forever."

Silence fell upon the group. The sound of water splashing in the fountain was mixed with the murmuring of students. Faith Rack-straw was filled with a new awe. "How does the game end, Tony?"

"Oh, the player advances from square to square as a white pawn out-arguing illogical adversaries who are red chessman. Or should one say 'chesspersons'? Then she reaches the far end of the board and becomes a Queen."

"Then checkmate!" Joe said.

"Oh, no − not at all! Ectually, she gets to *choose* her mate. After graduation, then partnership − isn't that the custom?" Leland summoned up a menu of potential future mates, all kings, all experts in respective branches of logic. "Then you start a new adventure in Logicland − but with an intelligent interactive partner instead of the White Rabbit. If you want to do modal and three-valued logics, you choose him. Or formal semantics − you choose him."

"But the program is dreadfully ... er ... heterosexual," interrupted Rackstraw. "What if you want a same-sex partner?"

"Then you simply confide your desired sexual inclination to Humpty Dumpty when you sign in. The audio changes too. The game is keyed to five gender differences."

The students had gathered in nervous expectant groups now. It was time to teach again − a new term had begun. The professors took their places near the fig tree beside the fountain, under the green banners of Avalon.

★ ★ ★

Here is the end of this oral history. It is the end of a story about a community of scholars, and how that community − students and teachers together − found its best self during a year when governments and corporations gobbled up the places of higher learning one by one. And this is now one of the stories of Avalon, and it's true too. It's all true just as I have told it. I know because I was there and I saw it happen, and if you don't believe me you can read about it in one of Hugh D'Arnay's newspapers. The newspapers never lie.

Or you can come up here and visit the place and see for yourself.

Avalon is only an hour and a half from the metropolis, though it seems like a lifetime away. People say the place has changed but, you know, communities don't really change all that much − not if you've lived in one as long as I have. When you arrive, you'll smell the clear air of the north blowing through forests of pine, making the great Avalon flag with the sword on it flap at the top of the Library. The students still dress in all the styles of an indigenous, human world — woolen gloves from Tibet, sweaters from Peru, necklaces from the First Nations of America. There will always be that carnival of styles. There is something about the place that beckons a freedom, even an elegance of spirit. You see, it is the talk that matters — not so much what people say as the feeling that they are free enough to say it, so that ways of seeing and ways of being are nourished constantly by the habit of conversation. They are still talking here. On the shuttlebus to the campus, on a winter evening with snow in the air, the bus simply rocks with noise. There isn't that spirit of talk in the metropolis. There is only work and daily-ness, then watching videos in the evenings. There are no stories.

Avalon University is only an hour and a half away, but there is the distance — the distance in time, not space — in a world made out of change. But how vivid it all is! Sometimes, in the little out-of-the-way silences in the roar of the metropolis you hear it — and then the stories come, and it is all here, the person you were, the company you knew, in that little university chattering away end-lessly, high against the wilderness at the top of the world.

ABOUT THE AUTHOR

Sean Kane teaches and writes at Trent University in the Kawartha Lakes region northeast of Toronto, Canada. He is the author of *Wisdom of the Mythtellers*, an exploration of the oral conditions and ecological basis of myth. Besides oral literature and philosophy, he also teaches creative writing at Trent, and was the inaugural Stephen Leacock writer in residence at the Leacock Humour Festival. He lives in Peterborough with Kelly Liberty and son, Owen.